CASCADIA FALLEN

SPIRITUS AMERICAE

AUSTIN CHAMBERS

Copyright © Austin Chambers, 2020

All rights reserved.

This is a work of fiction. Any resemblance to actual events or persons, living or dead, is purely coincidental. Everything is the product of the author's imagination and is not to be construed as real. No part of this book may be reproduced in any form or by electronic or mechanical means without written permission from the author, except for brief quotations in a book review.

<u>CREDITS</u>

EDITOR – Emily Rollen

FINAL PROOFERS – WMH Cheryl & Barbara Butterton

COVER BY – Fusion Creative Works, Poulsbo, WA

ISBN Paperback: 978-1-7339593-9-1

ISBN Hardcover: 978-1-966164-92-0

Published by Crossed Cannons Publishing, LLC
P.O. Box 334
Seabeck, WA 98380-0334
pkodell.com

Cascadia Fallen
Spiritus Americae

PROLOGUE

On A Wing and a Prayer.

About Fifteen Years Before Tahoma's Hammer

"How's Tucker taking it?" thirty-nine-year-old John Cronin asked his wife, Maria, from his intensive care hospital bed. The Seattle police officer had just endured an entire night of emergency spinal and pelvic surgery, the result of an off duty paramotor crash.

It had been a cool and breezy September evening, nearing the end of the Pacific Northwest's short parasports season. Like most powered-parachute pilots, John had made a beeline straight up to his normal flying spot after his shift was over. For the Army truck-driver turned police officer, the freeing feeling of flying in the open wind had become the drug that helped him decompress from his job. Taking up paramotor six years earlier had taken a serious investment in both the gear and the training. Strapping a motor on one's back and flying around like a seated Superman wasn't something people should just go and do.

The small local Arlington Airport north of Marysville, Washington, was friendly to the alternative flying sports. John had noticed only one other para-pilot that early evening, a guy named Travis that he knew to be a newer but 'coming-along' pilot. They had discussed a plan to film each other from behind to get some footage. Before take-off, John had made a mental note of the graying system building to the north. *We should be on the ground long before that gets near.*

The pair were both wearing action cameras on their helmets but were trying to shoot with handheld, higher-resolution cameras for the trailing footage of each other.

It all happened in a split-second. Turbulence. John re-grabbed his brake handles and applied a slight pressure to the trailing edge of his wing, ensuring the front edge would keep a high angle-of-attack through the rough patch of wind. He was flying about fifty feet below and behind Travis.

"Brakes!" John yelled at the younger pilot as he noticed the telltale signs of a wing-collapse forming.

Travis' wing started to surge forward from the buffeting winds. His failure to recognize that crucial one or two seconds of warning sign was the deciding factor in the coming catastrophe. As the wing moved forward in relation to his body position, the winds started hitting the top, closing off the foils.

John screamed at the top of his lungs once more as he saw Travis' wing start to collapse. "Brakes!"

By the time Travis yanked on the brake cables, the wing had folded over on itself, causing him to drop suddenly and violently—right into John, who was desperately trying to veer to his left. It was too late, as Travis' motor and body, cords, and collapsed airfoil caught the edge of John's wing with enough force to yank him down and follow them in a tangled, straight-down descent.

As John was reaching the red pull handle on his reserve chute, a packed black pouch in his lap, he hit the kill switch in the throttle control tethered to his left hand. He was starting to spin upside down and clockwise, part of the mess of paracord and fabric trailing Travis. His flying partner was on his own—sheer adrenaline was forcing John to worry about himself. They were maybe six hundred feet above ground level. Time was critical.

John's right hand found the big, red loop and yanked. The reserve was now out of its container, retaining the pack-shape that it had ever since John did his annual practice throw and re-pack back in March. He cocked his right arm into his chest until he felt the chute hit him and then flung it straight out to his right as hard as he could.

The reserve chute did its job—mostly. John's next action was to try to pull on his brakes all the way and finish collapsing his own wing. The tangled mess of loose cords and cables, combined with the spinning of being entangled with Travis' kite, made it so that John couldn't find his brakes. It was a bittersweet result—the extra drag was helping catch some speed, but not nearly as well as the reserve would have done on its own. Travis failed to get his chute deployed until they were a mere eighty feet up, which was at least a hundred feet too late.

The pair landed in a field just off the greenbelt of trees behind a country home in a sparsely populated area.

Fourteen hours and a helicopter ride later, John was in ICU at Harborview Trauma Center on the hill overlooking Seattle. A few moments earlier, John had learned that Travis had perished. His concern, now, was for his own ten-year-old son. His other children were in his thoughts, too, but they were only three and four years old. He knew they wouldn't retain the long-term memory of almost losing their father like Tucker would.

"He's taking it okay," Maria said. "He can't wait to see you."

Maria wore a concerned look on her face but was hesitant to mention what was on her mind. Like most husbands, John could read his wife's face and knew something was wrong.

"What is it?" he asked. "I can tell something's bothering you."

Her face cracked a small smile as she tried to hide her emotion. "Don't worry about it, babe," she said. "There's always time to worry about things later."

John closed his eyes, less as an escape from the conversation and more as a way of trying to control pain. The post-surgical meds were obviously good, but being restricted from movement was starting to make his skin itch. He opened his eyes again, looking around the ICU room, taking in the array of instruments and hoses managing his vital signs for the nurses.

"It's the job, isn't it?" he asked his wife. "You're wondering how I'm going to be able to work like this…"

Maria looked down at her folded hands in her lap and then slowly looked back up at her husband with a slight tear in her eye. "Yes," she admitted with needless shame. "I'm sorry, honey, but it does worry me now that I know you're going to be okay."

John turned his head to look at his wife, eyes flushed with emotion. "I'm so sorry, sweetness," he pleaded with his wife, choking ever so slightly with sorrow. "I was in denial that this could ever happen, and now I've jeopardized everything!" He was burying the desire to tear up, which caused his face to flush in the losing fight.

Maria edged her seat closer to his bed and took his hand into hers. "We will get through this, babe," she said. "We always do." She rose from her chair to grab a tissue so she could wipe his eyes for him.

John turned his head once more, letting his gaze drift to the grey clouds over Seattle, staring at the buildings next to the hospital, wondering when his life would be somewhat normal again. "Never again," he mumbled under his breath.

"Come again?" Maria queried.

The thought had ingrained itself in John's mind in the time since he had come out of surgery. He looked back at his wife. "Never again," he said with newfound resolution, despite the pain medication. "I'm going to fix that thing and sell it. I will never put you through this again."

Maria sat silently, wishing there was a way she could tell her husband that he will one day regret not getting back on the horse. "Babe," she finally said, "you can't make a decision like that just for me."

"It's not," he reassured her. "I'm done. Done. I will *never* fly a paramotor again."

1

The Face of Evil.

TAHOMA'S HAMMER PLUS 32 DAYS.

THE CARTEL MOTORCADE pulled into the parking area of Seattle Volunteer Park Conservatory with a roaring thunder. Not only were they using their technicals—trucks that had machine guns and grenade launchers mounted on them—but they were now using captured police and National Guard vehicles, too. In the middle of the motorcade was an armored truck, the type that would have been used to escort cash and other valuables in the days before Tahoma's hammer. On this great day, it was filled with prisoners—captured police and guard members who were being brought to the park to send a message.

Most days, the park was filled with people using the pond in the south end to gather their drinking water. Residents from Capitol

Hill, Stevens, and even as far away as Miller Park made the daily trek to get water from the pond. Reynaldo Hernandez knew this would be the perfect place to find an audience for relaying a message—a message to the rest of Seattle and the Pacific Northwest.

The motorcade navigated the round circular drive around the park's statue of William Henry Seward to turn around and reposition themselves for a quick exit. The statue—of the man who was Secretary of State under Abraham Lincoln—seemed to Reynaldo like a fitting place to send a message of liberation and hope. *I'm surprised this statue still stands,* Reynaldo thought, half-surprised that the stone monolith withstood Seattle's dabble in anarchy in recent years.

He hopped out of the passenger seat in the second vehicle with a powered megaphone in his hand and immediately started giving orders to his cartel soldiers. There were seven vehicles in all, which seemed like a safe minimum number to Rey. While not a full-sized army, the cartel had done a good job of invading and taking over entire sectors of the city. This was a direct result of Reynaldo's two-pronged invasion strategy. Part One had been to liberate the mostly ethnic-minority prisoners from the Monroe Correctional Facility and unify them under one leadership. Part Two had been his various plants into all of the local gangs, who used a variety of tactics from subterfuge to sniper attacks to infiltrate the gangs and assassinate their leadership. The police and National Guard staffing levels had fallen to less than thirty percent at this point in the crisis. They just could not maintain control of Seattle. After Rey's hostile takeover of all the rival gangs, taking over an entire neighborhood in Seattle seemed like a walk in the park—now, quite literally.

"Jefe," one foot-soldier said as he approached Rey, "where do you want us to line them up?"

"I think Bruce Lee's grave site might be a good location," Reynaldo decided. He scanned the park to the south. There were just too many pop-up markets being used for trade and barter in the way there. He watched most of his soldiers take quick control of the park. The people would follow them out of curiosity, he realized. "Yes," he decided aloud. "That is where you should take them."

The cartel soldier acknowledged the order and retreated to go follow it through. Reynaldo continued to stroll along the vehicles, looking at the crowd before him. Almost everyone was looking at him, not quite understanding if they should be afraid or not. *Don't be afraid*, he thought to himself. *I'm here to save you, not hurt you. But you will see that soon enough.*

"Hector," he called over to one of his lieutenants. "After this business is finished, I want to add this location as one of our welfare distribution sites," Rey said. "Get it on the list as soon as we get back. I want these people fed by tonight."

"Si, Jefe." He caught himself. "Oh, sorry boss," the man said, reverting to English. "I am try remember use English a-as my first language, now." The Spanish pigeon dialect was slowly improving for Hector and most of the men.

"It's okay, Hector," Reynaldo said. "Go on, my friend, I know you're trying."

Reynaldo turned to the crowd that had slowly returned to their bartering despite the interruption by the cartel convoy. He looked through the light drizzle under the gray skies and pulled the megaphone up to his mouth.

"Excuse me," he said with a pleasant but authoritative voice through the electronic speaker. A few people turned to look, but business carried on. "Excuse me, please," Rey said again, this time a little louder. More people turned to face him. He used his other arm to start waving them toward himself. "It is okay, I'm not going to bite! We are here to help."

Once Rey saw that some of the crowd was starting to wander toward him, he himself started walking through the gap between two trucks, northward toward the Bruce Lee Memorial. As he meandered the approximate hundred yards toward the gravesite, he occasionally glanced backwards to make sure the crowd was continuing to follow him.

A small squad of his cartel soldiers was escorting the National Guard and police members, bound in handcuffs and shackles. This definitely had the crowd's attention. The procession was slowly marching up the road just to the west of Bruce and Brandon Lee's graves. Rey's soldiers started corralling the crowd toward the Lee graves, forcing the Guardsmen and police to their knees on the little road.

Reynaldo stood on the bench near the graves so he could stand over the crowd and address them.

"My friends," he said into the megaphone once again. "Your so-called protectors have been a blight on your city for far too long. We are here to bring a new order, to protect you from the protectors, so to speak." He paused to see if he had their attention. He did. "They did nothing but attack you, dividing you by race and social-class… demeaning your existence. You tried to defund them, yet the billionaires who live here and call themselves Champions of Social Justice did everything in their power to keep you under this public army's thumb!"

This began to get a few of the onlookers yelling out slogans like 'Fry 'em!' and 'All cops are bullies!"

"Friends, you have nothing to fear from us," Rey continued. "We will be back tonight with food. Go…go and tell your friends what you see here today. Spread the word. Mar de Paz Services is the peaceful sea that will calm this storm for you. What you're about to see" –Rey was really pouring on the daytime-soap-drama— "will not be pretty." He paused, listening to the agitation of the crowd start to grow. "But it will be…*Freeing!*" With that, Reynaldo nodded his head toward one of the soldiers.

Two of the police officers tried to make a break for it, but the guards behind each one were ready to pounce. These cartel soldiers had years of experience sending messages just like this to the families of their rivals. They shoved them back down and cracked them in the back of their heads to stun them. Some of the other police and Guard members were crying, and one was begging for his life.

A few in the crowd could be heard wailing, their emotion overcoming them as they were about to witness their first murders. The majority were cheering, though, whether from actual hatred for the police or just plain supporting the cartel out of strong survival instincts.

The third cop down the line wanted to die on his feet, and in a lack of that, decided on the next best thing. "Yessssss, Jesus loves me!" He sang the old Sunday School song learned by millions of Americans. "Yesssss, Jesus loves me!"

Pop! The first officer was shot in the head, causing all of the rest to flinch and try to stand again. More guards moved in to help suppress them and hold them on their knees.

"Yessssss—" Pop! They weren't waiting for him to finish his song. Down went number two. "Jesus lov—" Pop! The rest started screaming, but the guards continued to kill their victims over the next few seconds.

Good, Reynaldo thought. *It has truly begun now,* he said to himself. *The winning of hearts and minds is key to our success. Here's to hoping that today's mission is a success. We need to stop the civilian forces from banding together before they figure out how to resist.*

THE SMELL OF SALT, engine oil, and old fish was the thing that finally woke Tyler from the trauma induced slumber. His head pounded as the fog lifted, and he started to realize that what he had experienced was, indeed, real. His eyes flitted around a little bit as he experienced a mild nausea from letting the light in. He tried to move his hands to his head to assess the damage, but he couldn't. He slowly realized his hands had been bound behind his back.

Despite the headache, he started to look around the small hold of the boat, hoping to find something that would provide an answer or at least a glimmer of hope that he could escape. As his eyes adjusted to the darkness, he slowly made out the shape of Gene lying next to him. The pair of Slaughter Peninsula Posse members had been thrown onto a pile of nets and life preservers.

Tyler could hear the steady rumble of a marine engine, coupled with the mild rocking of the boat. He assumed they were being taken east to Seattle or some other location on that side of Puget Sound. He continued to do a slow assessment of his body. He moved his legs and figured out that his feet were not restrained. He could only see one way out of the hold, and he knew there was no escape—that he would have to go past whoever had abducted him. He used his right foot to try nudging Gene, hoping he wasn't dead.

After a few tries, Gene started to moan and grumble. The veil of darkness was slowly lifting off of his head as well.

"Gene!" Tyler hissed. "Gene! Wake up!" Tyler said as loud as he dared, which was barely a grunt above a whisper. Gene's grumbling was eventually accompanied by the body shudders and movements that Tyler had just gone through.

"Uuunnnnnggg," Gene groaned.

"Gene! Wake up," Tyler whispered again.

"Wh-where are we?" Gene asked, letting Tyler know that he was alive by doing so. "Wh-what happened?"

"We were ambushed," Tyler responded. "And now we're in the hold of a boat. Try not to move."

"What?" Gene replied, his mind still not quite accepting the reality of the events that had unfolded less than an hour earlier. The men had been stripped of all their gear. "What do you think they want?" Gene asked in a very concerned voice.

"I'm not sure," Tyler admitted, "but it can't be good. Do you remember anything?"

"Uhhhh… an explosion, maybe?" Gene responded, still trying to shake the cobwebs.

"To say the least," Tyler replied. "As we were approaching the truck, they pulled up in a van and killed Julia and Kendell with an RPG." Tyler couldn't believe the words that had just come out of his mouth. It was like something from a B-movie or a nightmare.

"They're—they're dead?" Gene asked incredulously. He still was a little foggy on everything that happened.

Tyler glanced at Gene to see if his eyes had adjusted to the dark yet. "Nobody could have survived it," he said with a hint of desperation. The pair of men sat silently for a couple more minutes before Tyler spoke again. "Do you still have your posse patch on you?" he asked in a concerned voice.

"Y- yes," Gene said. "Or at least I think I do. I keep it in my front left pants-pocket. W-why?"

"Because we need to get rid of those," Tyler explained, thinking back to his training as an Air Force officer over fifteen years earlier. "You need to understand something," he continued. "As soon as these guys don't need us, we are dead. Got it?"

"Y-yes," Gene replied in a horrified tone. "But what about the patch?" he asked, not quite understanding what Tyler was getting at.

"That patch ties us to our group, our families," Tyler explained. "If they find out about it, they will use that against us. Understand?"

"Y-Yeah," Gene acknowledged. "I understand. What about yours?"

As if on cue, Tyler started digging at his right rear pocket. The restraints made it difficult but not impossible. "I'm going to bury it under this pile of rope and life preservers and hope they never find it," he explained.

"Wouldn't it be better to drop it in the water when they're taking us off the boat?" Gene asked.

"Can't take that chance," Tyler explained. "There may be too many of them. One of them is bound to see."

"O-Okay," Gene said. "But I can't reach. You're going to have to get it for me."

He started scooching his body toward Tyler's. Tyler started rolling over on his left while Gene scooted over from what used to be Tyler's right. Gene did his best to get his front pocket right up into Tyler's hands. In a less dire circumstance, Gene would have never allowed another man to put his hands that close to his crotch. But propriety was the farthest thing from his mind at that moment.

It took a few moments of struggling and creative movement before Tyler could finally feel the patch at the tips of his fingers. He pinched with his forefinger and middle finger, and said, "You're going to have to scoot down and try to wiggle the pocket hem past the patch as I hold it. I can't go any further with my arms being restrained."

Gene complied, and eventually Tyler was able to get the patch past the hem of the pocket. Like he did with his own, he shoved that patch as far down the pile of materials as he could.

About that time, they could tell the engine was throttling down.

"I have no idea how long I was knocked out," Tyler said. "We could be in Seattle already."

The men could hear voices starting to trickle down into the hold, now that the engine was quiet. Tyler thought he caught some Spanish words. Both prisoners went instinctively quiet.

After listening for about thirty seconds, Tyler finally whispered, "I think we pulled up to another boat."

His theory was confirmed as a different engine started to throttle back up. The men could tell that a second boat was slowly pulling away. Just then the entire hold erupted in the noise of gunfire. The sounds of at least four rifles echoed throughout the hold, hurting their already damaged and bleeding ears. The pair of posse members scrunched as low as humanly possible, expecting bullets to start riddling through the hull of the boat. But no bullet holes ever arrived. Eventually the noise died down, and the gunshots ended completely.

The arrival of one of the cartel soldiers was preceded by the sounds of his footsteps tromping down the boat's ladderway. There was still smoke seeping out of the rifle slung across his chest. The two men looked at the soldier in horror, Gene wondering if they were about to die. Tyler knew better. He understood that they wouldn't have gone through all that effort to capture them just to kill them in this boat. The soldier looked at them, scanned the space to make sure they weren't up to something, and then went back up the ladder.

Something tells me that we are in for a lot of pain, Tyler thought.

PHIL WALKER, Lonnie Everly, and Buddy Chadwell had been up in the north end of Slaughter County, beginning to train the new branch of Slaughter Peninsula Posse. They had been joined by Deputy Sergeant Charlie Reeves. Together they had formed a training coalition under Sheriff Raymond's authority. The remaining peace officers in Slaughter County knew it was a matter of time before the vast majority of peacekeeping was performed by community members. Sheriff Raymond knew that the National Guard would soon disband altogether. He also knew that the cartel problems in Seattle would eventually find their way to the Slaughter Peninsula. It was all part of the peacemaking process from the recent standoff between the authorities and the gun club. The sheriff had allowed Phil and Charlie to be the head liaisons for forming new branches of the posse.

In the early afternoon, Charlie received radio chatter over the official security nets about a loud explosion in the western part of the county, somewhere southwest of the Bogdon submarine base. With all the earthquake damage, traveling was a long and arduous process that involved zigging and zagging through multiple neighborhoods and roads to find a path north to south. They weren't just dodging downed overpasses—there were landslides, sinkholes, toppled billboards and the like. It was easily a two-hour venture. The 'toll stations' were continuing to pop up on the routes most heavily travelled, though they usually pulled a Houdini when a police or Guard vehicle was approaching. Charlie had updated Phil about what he knew, which wasn't much. Collectively they made a decision to suspend the training and return together, since they had all travelled in Charlie's patrol rig.

On the trip south, Charlie had agreed to drop Phil off first before he headed down to the Emergency Operation Center in Bartlett. When the patrol rig finally showed up at the gun range, they snaked their way through the vehicle trap and into the main parking lot. It became immediately obvious that something was up.

"What's going on?" Phil asked Don Kwiatkowsky as he got out of the green SUV. The sight of several men and women gearing up in full tactical kit planted the seed of concern in his belly.

"Tyler's patrol never returned," Don explained. "And there was a huge explosion somewhere north of here." Don's face showed the same concern as all of the other faces that Phil scanned.

"Hmmmm," he said in his usual groan. "We need to slow down just a bit and think."

By then, Charlie and the others had gotten out of the patrol rig and approached Phil and Don. It suddenly occurred to Don that Charlie probably knew something the rest of them didn't. He looked directly at the deputy sergeant and asked, "So what was it?"

"I don't know," Charlie explained. "The EOC sent a Guard patrol out to investigate, but they haven't found anything yet."

"Where's the gator?" Phil asked, scanning the parking lot for the range's small utility vehicle.

"Down by the common," Don replied, referring to the new structure the club had built out of logs. "Why?"

Phil ignored the question, looking at Charlie instead. "Let's ride up to our command post and take a look at Tyler's patrol plan. That should give us a good idea of where to start."

Phil had really hoped that things would start to smooth out now that the issue with the county had been pacified. *Obviously, I was hoping for too much*, he thought cynically to himself. *So much for getting off the prosthetic and onto the crutches.*

The pair of men wandered down the main stairs from the parking lot to the rifle line on the right and climbed into the gator. Phil fired up the little green machine and took the range's south road up to the south end of the field where the command post had been built. They were there in under three minutes. They climbed out of the gator and walked into the main command post tent, where they found Jerry and a few others scanning maps.

Without any greetings or pleasantries, Phil looked directly at Jerry and asked, "You got Tyler's patrol plan handy?"

"Right here," Jerry explained. "I figured you would be wanting to look at it as soon as you got back."

Phil looked over the small dry-erase board they used for their daily patrol plans. "Alright," he said. "This gives us a starting point. When was the last time they checked in and from where?" Phil queried.

"About 12:45," Jerry said. "They were working this road here." He pointed to the paper map.

Phil's eyes darted across the dry-erase board one last time, and then he looked at Charlie and said, "May I suggest that we relay this information to the Guard unit and head that way ourselves?"

The big Native American deputy concurred. "Yes," he said. "But I think it should just be us and not a whole squad of upset people looking for their loved ones."

"I agree," Phil said. "I'll smooth that over." He handed the board back to Jerry, and the two men headed outside.

They scrambled into the gator and proceeded back up to the main parking area. He looked at the group of eight men and women who were geared up and impatiently waiting to leave, figuring that Tim Webster was probably the guy in charge of the pending reaction-force.

"Tim," he called out, waving him over to talk to him and Charlie privately.

"Lemme, guess," Tim started. "You guys think we're overreacting." His face was already showing a bit of irritation at what he figured was coming.

"No, not at all," Charlie explained. "But I also have a Guard unit out there already. Let us do our investigation. If we need backup, we'll call you guys first. Deal?"

Tim knew it really wasn't a question. "Sure, but just remember that these are our family members." He wasn't happy about the polite command.

Phil put a hand on Tim's shoulder. "I'll be going. This is my family too. Okay?"

That seemed to satisfy Tim just a little bit. Without a reply, he wandered back across the dirt parking lot to the small group to update them on the plan.

Just a pair of minutes later, Charlie and Phil were driving north along Canal Vista Highway. Charlie called in the updated information to the EOC, who relayed it to the Guard unit that was out looking for the source of the explosion. Although trees had been largely cleared from the roadways since the hammer flipped life upside down, mudslides and sinkholes still made travel a tedious process through this rural and less populated area.

Over the course of weeks, the mudslides had been slowly shrinking from a combination of wind, rain, and people with tractors. It took Phil and Charlie nearly twenty minutes to arrive at the road where they needed to start looking. The Guard unit was already there waiting for Charlie to show up.

Charlie got out of the rig and had a quick conference with the sergeant in charge of the unit. He then got back in and told Phil, "They're going to take point."

The two rigs started to slowly travel south along the cracked rural road, easing their way under the canopy of fir branches that had managed to resist the massive earthquake. There was an obvious smell and smoke in the air, which could be detected even in the overcast gray sky. After a few minutes, the National Guard Humvee hit the brakes, calling to Charlie on the radio.

"Burning tire on the right side. In the brush," Phil and Charlie heard the man say over the air.

The men started scanning to see if they could see it. It wasn't until the procession started traveling southerly again that they could. The Humvee was about fifty meters ahead of the deputy's rig. As it rounded another slight curve, it hit the brakes again.

"Contact!" they heard the excited sergeant say into the radio.

Charlie hit the brakes. He and Phil couldn't see what was happening, but they both associated that word with an impending ambush that never happened. They observed the guard unit get out of their vehicle and start hastily establishing a perimeter. The sergeant was walking back to Charlie's rig. Phil and Charlie got out.

"What'cha got?" Charlie asked.

"Looks like the remnants of an old white pickup. Like something blew it up." The man wore a concerned look on his face.

Phil and Charlie exchanged concerned glances. Phil started craning his neck to look through the brush and fir trees to see if he could see any other wreckage. They joined the sergeant on the walk south and eventually passed the Humvee.

Phil knew immediately it was one of the vehicles the range was using to send patrols out. His pulse quickened as he realized that something horrible had happened to his posse members. He felt his intact right-leg buckle at the knee just a little bit.

"Brother, you all right?" Charlie asked.

"I have to be," Phil said looking at Charlie. "The only other reaction I could have right now would not be good."

The three men joined the rest of the Guard members on a slow procession south to the burning wreckage. The explosion had flipped the truck over-end onto its roof. Most of the bed was gone, as was the axle and driveshaft. The transmission had managed to stay underneath the main body of the vehicle. What was left was blackened with char and still had small spot fires burning on it. The sergeant ordered his team to start canvassing the homes in the area, trying to find out if they knew anything.

Phil and Charlie slowly proceeded around the wreckage. Phil caught sight of something that he wasn't ready to see. At first, his mind told him it must be something else. The smell of burning flesh hit his nostrils and caused a wave of vomit to start running up his throat. He had seen and smelled this once before in his life, during the Gulf War in 1991. It was that memory and experience that had allowed him to keep his lunch in. He suppressed the urge to puke and looked over at Charlie, seeing that he had managed to do so also.

Before them was a charred torso laying in the brush like a piece of discarded burnt BBQ.

Kendell, Phil thought, suddenly overcome with a wave of both sadness and intense rage. *My God. Who could have done this?*

The two men continued to scan the forest, brush, and farther down the road. They were met with more pieces of the bloody puzzle, realizing that Tyler's Patrol had been ambushed by an evil worse than either of them had prepared themselves for.

"I...I can't believe what I'm seeing!" Phil exclaimed. "What animals could do this? What horrendous monsters are we dealing with, here, Charlie?"

Charlie didn't answer. There was no answer for that question. After several more minutes of looking around, the Guard sergeant approached Phil and Charlie with an update.

"We made contact with two houses that have people present," he said. "Nobody is talking."

"Show me where," the fiery ginger demanded. "I'll get them to talk!" he said angrily. He started to march off in the direction the sergeant had come from.

"Phil!" Charlie called out to him. He started jogging to catch up to his closest friend. "C'mon, brother, just hold up a second. Let me get some more resources out here. It's getting dark. And you have a heavy job to do back at the range. We'll get some lights and more people out here and launch a full investigation."

Phil knew Charlie was right. He stopped, looking at the man who once saved his life, not knowing exactly what to say. Neither man did. But the looks on their faces spoke volumes.

2

On a Mission.

Tahoma's Hammer Plus 21 Days.

There was a light drizzle coating Sequim, Washington, as Nick Williams walked into town. He had the rain hood on his bluish-gray Columbia raincoat pulled up and cinched tightly around his jawline. In the pre-dawn hours of 'non-sleep' sleep in his hammock in Sequim Bay State Park, Nick had decided that he would don his one set of civilian clothes for the trip into town. He didn't want to draw any undue attention to himself. *Better to look like Joe Trail-Mix,* he thought to himself, *than to tip off everyone that I'm a professional soldier.*

His rain pants made a swoosh-swoosh noise as he walked along Highway 101, taking the few miles to think about his course of action. Plan A was to find some phonebooks to check. He knew that might not be as easy as it sounded—real phone booths were a thing of the past, and most stores were probably shut down. He decided it would be easy enough to break into one if he had to.

He did not have such a great feeling about Plan B. Sequim was a relatively small town, and he had a face nobody would recognize. *Surely by this point these people know better than to trust a stranger,* he thought. The only thing he could think of was to try to sweet-talk someone at City Hall, if it was even still up and running. *Slim chance of that. I'm most likely going to have to go talk to the cops,* he thought. *If there are any left…*

Nick did his best to look like the rest of the travelers as he was walking up the highway. He kept a close eye in all directions—*head on a swivel, as they taught us in basic*— but he did it as cautiously as he could. He didn't want to draw attention to himself just by how he was keeping an eye on his own back. He noticed that most people travelled in packs and had some sort of system of pull-carts or wagons. Vehicle traffic still existed, but it was much rarer to see.

Nick noticed the roads up here still had the same cracks and crevices as the rest of the areas he had been since the hammer fell, though less of them. The key difference along the southern edge of the Strait of Juan de Fuca was the amount of coastal wave damage. *Can't even begin to imagine how it looks on Whidbey Island,* he thought, thinking about the piece of Washington state that took the brunt of the wave's force. *Or the coast.*

Nick cruised westward under the gray sky and drizzle between a lower forest of trees and occasional lavender fields to his north and a thick forest that ran like a carpet up the foothills and presented itself as a green, fir mountain. After two hours, he came up on a checkpoint that spanned the entire westbound lanes of the highway. It was staffed mostly by armed civilians, though there were two police officers as well. They were corralling everyone into a choke point and forcing people to provide identification before they could continue West or down the off-ramp into town. When he reached the guards, Nick handed them his Army retirement identification.

One of the volunteers wrote his name down and then started

flipping through some papers to see if he could find Nick's name on any of the log sheets. After several seconds of flipping through a couple of different papers, he finally looked up and said, "We don't have your name as having checked-in at one of the checkpoints further east on the highway."

Nick just stood there and stared back at the volunteer for a few seconds, contemplating what to say. He wanted to let the captain-obvious moment hang in the air just for a second or two. Finally, he said, "Huh, that's kind of weird." He was going for sincere with his tone, but his one raised eyebrow was full of sarcasm.

While the volunteers were staring at each other and trying to decide if they should let Nick pass, he heard some other names being broadcast on the radios set up near a police vehicle. *Must be relaying the names of pedestrians up and down the highway,* he thought.

"Where you headed?" a different volunteer finally asked.

"Right here into Sequim," Nick replied truthfully. "Checking on my aunt and uncle." The first volunteer wrote his destination down on the clipboard.

"Their names and address?" the second volunteer asked.

Nick wasn't expecting that question. He knew their last name was probably Schwartz. "The Schwartz's," he said. "Don't remember the name of the road. I'll know it when I see it."

After another minute, the building crowd of pedestrians behind Nick started to get a little testy. The volunteers finally decided to let Nick pass. He started up the final stretch of road into the actual town. He guessed that about fifty or sixty percent of the nomads were continuing west on the highway. The rest were heading into Sequim with him. *I wonder if it's because people have family here, or that they heard about some sort of food or shelter that's available.*

He paused when he saw an abandoned Black Bear Diner on the left side of the road. *Wonder if I can find a phone book in there.* He did a loop around the diner and the hotel next to it, looking for threats. Both buildings had been boarded up, and both buildings showed signs of forced entry. *People obviously don't care about other peoples' property anymore,* he thought. *Not when they're wet or hungry.* He decided not to draw attention to himself by trying to find a phone book here. He joined the herd rambling westward into Sequim once again.

Within another twenty or twenty-five minutes, Nick had started to pass more hotels and a QFC shopping mart. There were tents in the QFC parking lot that caused him to stop and look. He meandered through the wide array of tents and canopies, observing what was going on. *Seems like trading posts and bartering stations are the new normal.* He continued on to the QFC, which appeared to be open but under the protection of some sort of the armed security. There was a line of people waiting to get in. *Don't know if I want to waste my time standing in that line just to find a phone book,* he thought. *May be tougher than I thought.*

Nick wandered down the road just a little farther, trying a few different stores and having no luck. He finally managed to find a phone book at a little RV park on the left side of the road. He noticed that the RV park was full, a bright orange 'No Vacancy' sign painted on a full sheet of plywood right at the entrance to the park.

"No vacancy," the manager said unexcitedly, not even looking up at Nick.

Yeah, he thought. *I can read.* Nick left the snarkiness in his head, as he said, "Actually I'm just looking for a phone book. Trying to find my uncle, but I haven't been here in many, many years, and I don't remember where he lives."

The man looked up and gave Nick a cautious glance. After several seconds, he reached below the counter. Grabbing the phone book, he plopped it onto the counter-top with a hard thud.

"Thanks," Nick mumbled. *I guess people are finally starting to realize they shouldn't just trust anyone anymore.* He thumbed through the pages, going right to the S section. There was one Schwartz residence in the small town's phonebook. *I'm still not sure how I'm going to know if it's the right house. Tons of people stay unlisted now. Here's to hoping somebody's home.*

"Gotta pen and paper?" Nick asked.

"Nope," the man said flatly.

Nick ripped the page right out of the phone book and turned to leave.

"Hey!" The man started to protest at Nick's back, but Nick Williams was already out of the building before the sounds even hit the wall.

It took Nick another two hours of trying to find the location of the residence. He had stopped and asked a few different people for directions. As unfriendly as people were before the hammer fell, they really didn't like talking to strangers afterwards. When he finally found the house, he introduced himself to the person who answered the door. It turned out to be a family of people who had no knowledge of Dr. Stuart Schwartz. *Well....that sucks,* Nick thought.

He headed out of the small neighborhood and back out onto the main drag.

It didn't take long to find the local Emergency Operation Center. Nick assumed that any police officers that would help him track down the Schwartz residence would be there anyhow.

Just like everywhere else, there was a line, and this time Nick had no choice but to stand in it. He noticed that people had to present ID just to be able to talk to the authorities. *Guess I can't pretend to be Stuart,* he thought. This felt like an 'honesty is the best policy' situation to Nick, so he decided to pull out his military retirement card once more.

The line eventually took Nick into a giant canvas tent in the parking lot of the police station. The person staffing the table wasn't a police officer, but a CERT volunteer. As soon as Nick presented his military ID, though, he attracted the attention of the nearest officer.

"Who are you looking for?" the volunteer asked.

"It might be easier if you bear with me for a small story," Nick said. "I've been tracking a sexual predator, and I believe he's on the way to set up an ambush here in this town on a very specific person."

The police officer raised one eyebrow with a suspicious look. "What makes you believe that?" he asked, not quite ready to take Nick at face value.

"Because I was tracking him, and on the night he killed several people, I found evidence that he's tracking the son of an out-of-stater who lives in this town."

"Why were you tracking him?" the cop asked, more interested in that than in helping Nick.

"Does that matter?" Nick countered.

The police officer studied Nick's glare for several seconds and finally decided it might be better if he didn't know the answer.

Nick continued. "The last name of the people is Schwartz, but I've already checked the only Schwartz in the phone book, and they claim they're not related to one from out of state."

"Well, I guess your out of luck then," the cop said somewhat plainly. "What do you think we can do for you?"

"I'm hoping you have some database, such as the ability to look at tax records… Maybe help me identify where these people live…for their own safety," Nick said, having a hard time believing he had to paint the picture for Barney Fife.

"Mr. Williams," the cop began, "Do you really think I'm going to tell you where these people live? What if you're the sexual predator?" A sudden look of concern crossed the cop's face. "Where are you staying while you're here in Sequim, Mr. Williams?" He passively put his hand near his holster, which tripped like a big red flare to Nick.

"You serious?" Nick asked incredulously, looking down at the cop's gun hand.

"As a heart attack," the cop replied in a concerned tone.

"I'm camping at the state park east of here," Nick said, trying to cooperate, and trying even harder to keep his cool.

"Susan," the cop said to the CERT volunteer, "when Lieutenant Reynolds gets back, would you tell him I'm escorting Mr. Williams back to the state park?"

Nick let out an audible sigh, but he didn't say anything. He knew there was no point in arguing and putting himself more on these people's radar than he already had.

"Sure thing," Susan told Officer Beller.

Nick had an icy stare, but he was trying not to give the cop too hard of a look. "Have you ever seen the movie 'First Blood'?" he asked the officer.

Officer Beller ignored Nick, instead motioning for him to follow him out to his patrol rig. Without so much as a word, he ordered Nick to get in with the wave of his hand. Nick complied, and a short minute later found himself being driven back to the state park that he'd walked out of her earlier that day. *At least I get a ride*, he thought angrily.

When they pulled into the park, the cop asked, "Where's your car?"

"I came by boat," Nick explained to the skeptical police officer. "I'm telling you the truth. I've been tracking this guy since McNeil Island. He's the worst of the worst, and you people are in for some trouble if you don't help me out."

Officer Beller just looked at Nick for a few moments. "Look," he said, "I'm going to level with you. I believe you. But that doesn't matter. Our town has established policies and procedures, and I'm not going to break them just for you. I wish you the best of luck on your journey. Now get out."

He had stopped where Nick indicated, and he actually parked and got out. He watched Nick walk down through the bushes to the boat tied up to the broken tree. *Thankfully I hid my supplies,* Nick thought. As he untied his boat and fired it up, he looked at Officer Beller one last time. *I'll be back. Whether you know it or not, whether you like it or not, whether you believe me or not, I'll be here to protect your butt.*

TAHOMA'S HAMMER Plus 25 Days.

. . .

"Football One-Oh, your presence is requested at the main gate," John Cronin heard in his radio. He recognized the voice as Jeremy —also known as Soccer Three—one of the adult children of one of the property owners out here on the north side of the river near North Bend, Washington. "Priority two," the medically retired Seattle police officer heard Jeremy add.

"Copy, Soccer Three," John said. "I'll be there as quickly as I can get there."

The titanium in John's back—courtesy of a sudden stop after a rapid experiment with gravity—usually required that he go out and walk every hour or so. But since this was priority two, he decided he would actually take the pickup truck. He set down his book—*Back to Basics*—and turned the gas down on the old school Lantern. He'd been catching up on old school homesteading techniques while listening to the shortwave radio. He was making it a point to listen to the radio more often, as he was growing concerned with the increasing levels of violence just to their west in Seattle. *So glad we stocked up on those rechargeable batteries.*

He got up out of the easy chair and meandered through the main living area of the fishing cabin, spotting his youngest son, Evan.

"Ahh, that's right—your brother and sister are both out at perimeter posts—you seen your mama?"

"I think she's still next door helping patch that hole in the Cortez's chicken pen," replied the seventeen-year-old. He was in the middle of darning socks—something that his parents insisted he and his siblings learn. John had made it perfectly clear to everyone that they needed to make their clothing last as long as humanly possible.

"All right," John said. "I'm heading up to the main gate. Let Mom know if she gets back before I do."

He headed out and jumped into the 2007 forest-green Ford F-150. One minute later he was slowly pulling up to the gate. He got out of his truck and stretched to make sure his back was limber after sitting and reading for the last hour. Dusk was in the process of turning into night, and the temperature had dropped the normal fifteen degrees in the last two hours, the standard for western Washington in November. The chill and light drizzle made his bones ache.

John could see a couple of the guys from the south side of the river standing at the gate. Over the prior two weeks, they'd developed a working relationship and a stable level of trust. The tightknit community on this side of the river had formed a well-trained group called Phalanx. The other side was well-meaning but much less capable and prepared. As the hand-picked head of security for Phalanx, John was the default guy to call for unplanned events that didn't necessarily warrant a full security alert. Though John hadn't been an active police officer for over fifteen years, he still had by far the most experience in handling criminals and other security issues.

"Let 'em in!" he told Jeremy, almost in a scolding manner.

At this point, he assumed all of his normal gate guards had learned who the key players from the other side of the river were. *Gonna have to create some sort of access list,* he thought. *That way I don't get called for stuff that I don't need to anymore.*

"What's up?" he said to Earl and Conner as they approached him near the small guard shack after being let through the gate. They both wore concerned looks on their face, and that instantly put one on John's face as well. "Fellas…something I should be worried about?"

"No—well, not yet," Earl replied worriedly. "This is something more of a personal matter."

John led the pair of men into the little eight-foot by twelve-foot shack and motioned for them to have a seat. They declined. "What's going on?" The looks on their faces had managed to make John's heart beat just a little bit faster.

"As you know," Earl started, "Conner and I are the only real fighting experience over on the south side of the river."

John nodded.

Earl continued. "Tonight, my teenage nephews showed up

without the rest of the family. They—" Earl got a lump in his throat and almost began to choke on his words.

After several deployments to Iraq and Afghanistan with Earl, Conner knew when he could speak for his best friend. "Earl's family was ambushed on the way here," he said bluntly. "We're going out to see if we can find them. Looks pretty grim, so we're taking two others with us, which will leave our side of the river a little thin." He glanced at Earl, who nodded and was ready to resume.

"On top of that," Earl continued, "it would be nice if we could extend the training you guys have so graciously given us—just a little bit. I'm hoping we can rotate some of our watch standers over here, and you have some of yours cover our gate. A little cross training, so to speak."

John nodded. "My first hunch is to say no problem," he stated. "But let me run it by a couple others just in case. As far as the family thing goes, you have my sympathy, and of course we'll help however we can." *Somehow that just doesn't feel like enough,* John thought to himself. "Do you need us to help you on this mission? I don't really want to go to the others with this request, but it's the right thing to do." *These neighbors are our allies now. Time to put our money where our mouth is.*

"No," Earl stated. "Not that I don't appreciate it, but I want a small half-squad of four people, max. Light and fast. Conner and I were in the Rangers," Earl reminded him. "Too many troops, and we're just trading our surprise advantage."

"Gotcha," John said. "When you guys heading out? Tonight?"

"Before dawn," Earl said. "They were coming from the I-90 pass. My nephew said there was snow up there. Weather...darkness...too many things out of our control to be trying to leave right this moment."

"One last question," John said. "Do you guys have any smoke or frags?"

Earl and Conner felt like bad preppers, but they had to answer honestly. "No," Earl admitted. "You offering?" He was half joking.

"I bet we can scrounge up a couple of loaners," John joked. "But we'll want 'em back," he said tongue-in-cheek. "All right," he continued, "I and a few others will go over at 0800 tomorrow morning and personally handle the details on the cross training." He thought for another moment before he continued. "Might I suggest that you guys leave as many details as you can about what your plans are...just in case we need to come after you next." He realized how that might have sounded. "Uhhh...no offense. I just think it would be prudent."

"None taken," Earl said. "Mission planning was kind of my thing in the Army. I'll jot down as much as I can think of. And thanks again, John. I can speak for the whole southside neighborhood when I say we appreciate all your help."

With that, the three men shook hands and headed outside. John offered one more round of best wishes as Earl and Conner made their way back to the gate and across the bridge to the south side of the river. *I hope you guys complete your mission and get back soon.* His mind drifted back to the radio reports from just a few minutes earlier. *I got a feeling in the pit of my stomach that we're all going to be fighting a much bigger battle soon.*

Tahoma's Hammer Plus 27 Days.

Conner came slogging back down the snowy hillside and walked right past Jack and Larry to where Earl was playing rear-guard for their little formation. The former Ranger-turned-equipment operator had convinced his former battle buddy to let him take point. *He's right,* Earl had told himself when Conner had proposed the idea at the beginning of the mission. *Jack's a software guy, and Larry, well shoot... I really don't even know what he does.* Earl had reluctantly agreed to let Conner take point under the excuse that he was more expendable than himself since it was Earl's sister they were going after.

Earl hadn't even spoken to Natalie in several months, the way adult siblings tend to drift apart when they get to middle age and start living their own lives. It had been three years since they'd seen each other, the last time being when Natalie's family came out to the cabin for a week of fishing, horseshoes, and bad childhood stories. But it was those childhood stories that made her his sister all the more. She was the one bright spot in his memories, and he would rescue her or die trying.

The four men took Earl's pair of quads and made their way east along the I-90 corridor, departing the town of North Bend the morning before. They took trails that Earl knew about because of the trail maps he'd collected over the years. The going was slow because they were being cautious about being ambushed themselves. They would 'Crazy Ivan' on an unscheduled basis, shutting down the quads and performing SLLS—Stop. Look. Listen. Smell — for up to ten minutes at a time. Just a month earlier, Earl would have never believed they would have to do this. But the experience of him and Conner killing three scumbags who were trying to rape and murder his daughter had convinced him there was no such thing as being too cautious. As badly as he wanted to get to his sister, a life of Army experience had taught him to be patient and not make a bad judgement by rushing.

Earl could smell the cold, crisp air of the light-gray system over their heads—more snow was on the way.

"I think I found the ambush site just over the crest," Conner informed. "We lucked out—the snow is old and crunchy. Left some tracks. If there had been fresh snow, I may not have seen the signs."

"What did you see?" Earl asked.

"Utility vehicle tracks that suddenly stopped and changed direction. Lots and lots of footprints of different types and sizes. Some game tracks, too." He frowned, not enjoying the thought of trekking up the mountain in the hard snow. "It's been a long time since I studied game tracks, but I think there might be a cougar out here. There was some disruption down in the bushes off the side of the power line run, too. We might find some more clues if we give the whole site a more thorough look."

"Roger that," Earl said. "Do you think we should abandon the quads here?"

"At least until we get up there and figure out where they went," Conner concurred. "The vehicle tracks head south, up the slope. We can make the new guys come back and fetch the quads once we've secured the scene."

Conner informed Jack and Larry of the plan, and the four men began a staggered-column patrol formation, heading back up the slope that he'd come down just a few moments earlier. Conner called for a halt as soon as he got near the crest of the hill. He waved for Earl to come up to the lead of the column. As soon as he heard Earl take a knee next to him, he murmured, "See that?" He was pointing to a bunch of deformations in the snow about a hundred meters down the hill.

Not only was Earl scanning that, but he saw that Conner's tracks from earlier ended there. He turned around, motioning to Jack and Larry to keep an eye on their flanks. "Cover me," he whispered to Conner as he started down the slope, hugging the tree line as best he could without getting into the deep snow. He cringed as every step announced his presence to the forest with a nerve-grating crunch.

Slowly, cautiously, Earl progressed down the slope, keeping close to the tall, green firs and trying not to expose his profile lest he be targeted by the same adversaries that killed his brother-in-law and kidnapped his sister and niece. He took a knee when he was about ten meters away from the messed-up snow, taking one last opportunity to look, listen, and smell.

After three excruciating minutes, he waved Conner to join him. In turn, Conner waved up the other two to the crest to cover them. About two minutes later he joined Earl and the two proceeded to cautiously start scouting the site.

"See how all this snow looks piled up like it was shoveled?" he mentioned to Conner. "Like they were trying to cover something…"

"I have an e-tool back on the quad," Conner mentioned, referring to a folding shovel in Army lingo.

Earl looked at his buddy and thought for a moment. He looked down at the ground and used the butt stock of his rifle to cautiously probe the biggest lump of snow. The snow was a lot deeper down the small side slope towards the trees than the twenty or so inches they were standing in. He was able to push his rifle down so that almost all of it was in the snow. *Whew! Thought Roy's body might be under there.* He pulled his rifle back out and decided to try to use it as a makeshift shovel, shoving some of the snow off the pile. When he did, the unnatural sight of crimson revealed itself. *Oh, hell!* he thought. He scooped more of the snow off the pile, revealing more dark red blood.

He shot Conner a concerned look, and the two began to hurriedly repeat the process. It became obvious that there was a track leading down toward the tree line. Almost instinctively, Earl re-slung his rifle and aimed it at the trees as he went down the thick drift to investigate. When he got down there, Conner could see his brother's air deflate just a little bit as Earl's shoulders slumped. He turned to look back up toward Conner.

"Found Roy," he said with a sudden gloominess that matched the gray sky. He scrambled back out of the tree line and up the slight slope of the power line run where his buddy was standing.

Conner was already studying the tracks that ran up the slope to their south. They seemed to disappear into some sort of trail that cut through the forest. "That's bigger than a game trail," he said to his buddy.

"Yup," Earl agreed. "And what do you want to bet that we find a cabin somewhere up that slope?"

"Whether it's on that slope or the next, we'd better get moving," Conner said. "With as long as it took your nephews to get to the cabin, they could be long gone by now." He hated stating the obvious to Earl, but sometimes people under duress needed to be reminded of harsh truths, and that's what best friends were for.

"I know," Earl said just a little bit testily. He looked at his Army buddy and then apologized without words just by softening is tone. "Would you go get the other two and the quads? We obviously don't have the time to bury Roy, but I can at least try to set up a marker for later."

Earl watched his best friend head back to the crest of the slope they were on. He started playing out the scenarios in his head. *Gonna have to hide the quads soon. Those can be heard from a long way off if there's no other noise around. I'm banking on the fact that most criminals are at least a little stupid. And the fact that there are very few cabins up here in the state forest.*

3

"I've always found, give me a pack of cigarettes and a couple of beers, and I do better with that than I do with torture."
General James Mattis

THIRTY-TWO DAYS AFTER TAHOMA KNOCKED THE PACIFIC Northwest back to the 18th century and caused a massive infrastructural and economic catastrophe that spread around the globe, the rhetoric between China and Russia finally reached the ocean's surface. The Silent War had already been waging between the two countries' submarine fleets for a few weeks, starting when the Russian submarine Kazan (K-561) detected flanking maneuvers by three Chinese diesel submarines. She sank two of those submarines in the successful evasion, though China claimed that all three were destroyed in the battle.

On the evening before day thirty-three, China sealed off the border with Russia indefinitely with surgical missile strikes. Of the twenty-six crossings on the 2,600-mile-long border, all four railroad crossings and seventeen of the twenty-two bridges were completely destroyed.

Simultaneously, a People's Liberation Army Navy Submarine Type 093 class submarine launched one of their top-secret, gas-cloud, YU-12 torpedoes, capable of reaching a submerged speed of 400 knots at the Russian Heavy Cruiser *Yuri Andropov*. It took twelve seconds for the torpedo to travel 6000 meters and sink the ship, killing all 893 men on board. It took parliament in Moscow less than four hours to vote on and declare war with China.

Both countries had already been building up their forces along the border for the month prior, but now Russia started moving some of its western forces east. The Russian Prime Minister ordered the fleet at Vladivostok to prepare for a major engagement.

China's Central and Northern fleets were itching to get into the action themselves. Beijing was using their Southern Fleet to finally take full control of the sea lanes between the Pacific and Indian oceans, under the assumption that the United States Navy was in no position to stop them. Both countries had been preparing for this eventuality in the month since Tahoma woke up.

On the home front, the United States wasn't faring much better. What had started as civil unrest as a result of power disruptions had turned into a straight-up fight to keep any western city safe. After the cartel had presented itself in Seattle, it had become apparent that they were now making power plays in San Diego, Los Angeles, San Francisco, Sacramento, and Denver.

President Jeremiah Allen—the first member of the Libertarian Party to be elected president of the United States—was reluctant, but he used a little-known clause of the National Defense Authorization Act to enact a midnight to six AM curfew for all states west of the Mississippi River. Meanwhile, roughly seventy percent of America's ground and air forces were being staged in the western third of the country. Approximately twenty percent of America's East Coast Navy was in the process of transitioning to the West

Coast. The president began to give nightly briefs from the Oval Office in an attempt to keep the country together.

In Washington, the state-level Emergency Operation Center had been moved to Vancouver, near the border with Oregon. Camp Murray, near Joint Base Lewis-McChord, had been completely wiped out by the mud from Tahoma's lahars. It was from that location that Governor Marsha Saylor—upon learning of just how badly the police and National Guard were being beaten by the cartel in Seattle—declared in her weekly radio address that "we might have to find a way to work with them and build some bridges." The collective gasp by radio listeners all across the United States could have collapsed a hot air balloon when they heard that. The future was shaky and uncertain, save for one solid fact—ever since Tahoma blew her top and wiped out key portions of the internet, subversive agents across the globe, government or otherwise, were moving to secure their futures.

Tahoma's Hammer Plus 33 Days.

Reynaldo walked into the little two-story concrete structure through the barn-style shop doors on the east side of the building. The first floor of the building was a shop and the second floor an office, designed to support the operations of the nearby Seattle grain elevator. The facility—normally used to load cargo ships specifically designed to carry grain to Asia and South America—was relatively intact. Rey's men discovered that the pier hadn't suffered any significant damage, as there was no ship tied to it during the earthquake and volcano. Most of the multiple rail lines near the giant green silos were completely destroyed, covered in broken grain cars and other box cars, as if a giant child had a tantrum. The silos themselves were intact, though they showed serious cracking. The small concrete structure that his crew had commandeered for their boat operations was still standing and somewhat resistant to the cold and rain.

One of his special operation teams had just returned from abducting two people from the civilian militia over on the west side of Puget Sound. Reynaldo had been monitoring the activities of the police forces and National Guard all over the Western portion of the state. He had been disappointedly shocked to learn that a large civilian force stood up to and then aligned with their local police and guard units. It took some convincing, but he was able to assure his bosses that they needed to gather some intelligence on what had happened.

As a former member of the FES—the Fuerzas Especiales in the Mexican Navy—Reynaldo understood a few things. Winning the hearts and minds of the local populace was one of the most important things they could do in this mission. If certain elements of the local populace started to figure out that they could provide their own food and protection, they wouldn't need him or Mar de Paz Services anymore.

His team spent one full day and one night observing the activities of that militia, based out of a private shooting club in the western part of Slaughter County. They were well-trained and well-armed. In a stolen van, his team radioed for guidance on what their orders were. Reynaldo wanted to send a message.

"How many of them are there?" he asked.

"Four," the soldier in charge of the unit told him via radio.

"We only need two," Ray told him. "Send the rest out in style. We know the civilian police and army forces are fully aware of our presence now. We may as well let them know that our reach is any where we want it to be."

That morning, his Special Operations team packed up their camp and followed a patrol to an isolated neighborhood, waiting for the right moment to strike. They grabbed two of the militia members and made their way back to the hidden boat they had come over on. A few more hours had passed, and Reynaldo was staring at one of the men, bound to a chair with multiple wraps of duct tape. The man with short, dark, curly hair—*in his late thirties by my best guess,* Reynaldo thought—had a terrified look in his eyes and was breathing heavily through the gag taped to his head.

"Where is the other one?" Rey asked one of the soldiers in rapid Spanish, hoping their prisoner didn't speak it.

"In the boiler room," came the reply. "Do you want us to keep them separated?" the man asked his boss.

"No," Rey said. "If anything, hide some cameras in that room. Let them talk. Let them think we can't hear." The man nodded in understanding.

Switching to English as he walked over to within a few feet of the man, Reynaldo decided that he would try to simply ask first. More than once, just asking had worked. *Some people just can't stomach the thought of torture.* Rey nodded to the soldier guarding the man, who ripped the gag and duct tape off of his lower face.

"Hello," Reynaldo Hernandez greeted." My name is Rey. What is yours?"

The man was scanning the room, eyes flailing wildly. He was choking and gagging a bit, recovering from having the gag in his mouth. After a few seconds, he looked at Reynaldo but didn't say anything. Reynaldo chuckled and walked to his right slowly, retrieving a heavy wrench off a workbench.

Tyler could hear the grime and gravel on the shop's floor make a slight crunch sound underneath Rey's custom leather boots as he turned back and slowly began to walk toward the captive.

"I don't much care for doing the dirty work, myself," Reynaldo explained to Tyler. He chuckled a bit as he said, "Not that I haven't. I just don't prefer it. No...you don't get to my spot in any cartel without knowing how to extract information. So, my friend, all I ask for is your name." Reynaldo went silent.

Tyler scanned the room and noticed there were at least a half-dozen guards scattered around. He was terrified, and the thought of escape seemed as far away as the moon at that moment.

"T-Tyler," he stammered, wondering in his own mind what information he could possibly have that these guys wanted.

"Tyler!" Reynaldo said slowly and with gusto. "Such a good, American name, mijo," he commented, absentmindedly slipping into Spanish. Rey let the big wrench slowly glide down and hang by his leg. "What is it you think we want to know, Tyler?" the cartel boss asked.

"I-I really don't know," Tyler replied with as much honesty and sincerity as he could muster. "W-we don't have any money to offer—"

Rey's laughter cut Tyler off before he could say anymore. He was still grinning as he asked, "Do we really look like we need your money?" He paused for a quick moment. "Try again," he ordered a little more sternly.

"I think we both know," Tyler said, grunting from the pain of the restraints on his chest, "that it doesn't matter what I tell you—you're going to torture us anyhow. I've read about what you cartels do to each other. I know what's in store for us," he said, putting forth as much forced bravado as he could. "What's my motivation to actually tell you anything that would help you?"

Ohhhhhh, Rey thought to himself, letting his eyes drift off Tyler to stare into nowhere for a moment. *We have a smart guy, here. Huhhh...* He looked down at the wrench hanging by his side and then looked back at Tyler. "I don't know why, but I like you. It's probably because you cut to the chase. So I'm going to be honest with you. You're in for a long night. But it doesn't have to be. And remember, if you resist too much, we'll just talk to your friend. Pass your torture on to him, so to speak."

Tyler said nothing with his words, but his scared and angry glare spoke volumes. Reynaldo dropped the wrench, turned, and gave some final instructions to his men in Spanish before leaving.

The soldier came over to Tyler with a grin that revealed crooked yellow teeth and a stench that smelled like ten-day-old sweaty-butt. He had an M tattooed on one cheek and a 13 on the other.

"So," the man began slowly, "which do you want first? The beating? Or the waterboarding?"

BEFORE THE DUSK could giving away to another gray November day, Charlie had already come back out to the range to pick up Phil. They were headed to the scene to continue the investigation into the atrocity.

"What do you think these guys wanted?" Charlie asked.

"That question has kept me up all night!" Phil replied angrily. He was staring at the trees that had fallen in the forest along the Canal Vista Highway. Whereas all of the trees that had crossed roads had been cleared, nobody had yet made their way into the woods to salvage the usable lumber. *I guess not everyone is as lucky as we are at the range to have horses to help with that kind of stuff.* He turned his head toward his partner. "I got no idea, bud. I mean why on Earth would anyone use an RPG on a pickup truck?"

"That's what bothers me," Charlie admitted. "There's no reason to do that whatsoever."

After another silent minute of driving, Phil said, "Well…there's one reason."

"What's that?" Charlie asked, slightly perplexed.

"Because they can," Charlie's face was still unsure of what he meant. "It was a message," Phil explained. "'We can do whatever we want.'"

On the rest of the short drive, Charlie briefed Phil that a squad of National Guard preserved the scene all night, scouting for clues or anybody that would talk to them. On the last leg of the trip, they were waved through the checkpoint staffed with two Guardsmen. Charlie pulled over behind another deputy's rig and parked. The two men proceeded to go talk to the 1st Lieutenant who was in charge of the scene.

After Charlie introduced the officer and Phil to each other, he asked, "So what's the latest update on what you guys found overnight?"

"Well, first off, we think the bodies..." The man paused, trying to find a way to talk about the delicate topic in front of Phil without being offensive.

"Go on, LT," Phil urged. "I've seen a thing or two in my day."

"Sorry," mumbled the young man who, for some odd reason, reminded Phil of his son Crane. "We picked up in excess of thirty body parts. None of us have any forensic training, but they appear to be from two people based on shape, skin tone, and remnants of clothing."

"Two?" Phil asked with sudden surprise. "Are you sure?"

"Not one-hundred percent certain," the lieutenant replied, "but reasonably sure, yes."

Phil and Charlie exchanged concern glances. "How big of an area did you canvas, Lieutenant?" Charlie asked.

"We're on our third pass," he explained. "We push the circumference of the blast zone about fifty meters each time, which means we're now searching out up to 150 meters."

"Have your people found any signs?" Phil asked, being somewhat short as he did. "Blood trails? Tracks?"

"Nothing, Mr. Walker," the young man said. "Sorry."

"That means the others may have been kidnapped!" Phil exclaimed in an angry, loud tone to Charlie.

After Charlie gave Phil a few minutes to blow off his understandable anger, they spent the better part of the next ninety minutes sifting through the piles of wreckage and discussing another plan to try to get information from anyone left living along the sparsely populated road.

The arrival of another military vehicle caught everyone by surprise, even the National Guard members.

Phil and Charlie started to walk to the checkpoint, as did the lieutenant in charge. When they arrived, the distinct camouflage pattern of the US Marine Corps Marpat could be easily distinguished on the uniforms of the men standing in front of them.

"What ya' got?" Charlie asked the guards at the checkpoint.

"They're from the submarine base at Bogdon," the soldier told his lieutenant, ignoring Charlie.

Charlie led Phil through the checkpoint so that they could talk to the Marines without disrupting the Guard members. It hadn't occurred to Phil until that moment that Charlie retained his lieutenant promotion, despite the best efforts of former Director of Slaughter County Emergency Management Sandy McAllister. She had attempted to demote him several days earlier.

"I'm Lieutenant Reeves of the Slaughter County Sheriff's Office," Charlie told the Marines. "What brings you fine men this way this morning?"

"Mornin', Lieutenant," the marine in charge said. Phil recognized the man's rank insignia as being a Gunnery Sergeant. "I'm Gunny Twogood. We're from the security forces at the submarine base. We heard reports of a rocket propelled grenade, and in the interest of preserving national security, we decided we had better come check it out."

"Sadly, Gunny," Charlie replied, "you know just about as much as we do at this point." He nodded toward Phil as he continued to speak. "This is one of our community leaders. A team of his people were ambushed by an unknown foe yesterday."

"With a rocket-propelled grenade?" the gunny asked incredulously.

"That's....kinda what we were wondering about, too," Charlie mumbled.

"You're not part of Bogdon's normal security forces, are you?" Phil asked pointedly. He was still trying to cope with what had happened to his people and was in no mood for games. *Why aren't you Marines out here finding and killing the cartel*, he thought to himself.

The corners of the gunnery sergeant's mouth gave the ever-so-slight hint of a smile. "What makes you say that, sir?"

"The blue diamond," Phil said flatly. "When I was part of Marine Corps Security Forces, we weren't part of First Division."

The ever-so-slight grin on the gunny sergeant's face turned into it an obvious smile. He turned and looked at his Marines. "Which one of you dipwads forgot to take his unit patch off?" he said with the stern tone of a dad who'd just busted his kids stealing cookies before dinner.

The sergeant was still looking back and forth at his Marines when Phil nodded toward the unit designator plate mounted to the front bumper of their Humvee.

The gunny's face crinkled with frustration, and he decided to change the subject. "When were you at MCSF?" he asked, knowing better than to call Phil sir again.

"Two tours," Phil explained. "One on each side of Desert Storm." He stuck his hand out and introduced himself. The gunny took it and shook it firmly.

After a couple more seconds of awkward silence, the gunny said, "Alright...I guess I'll level with you guys. The regiment is here to protect certain items until those items no longer need to be protected at this location." Both Phil and Charlie understood what the Gunny was hinting at. The Marine NCO continued. "Our orders are very clear—we are not to engage in civilian law enforcement matters. But..." he drifted off, looking for words.

"But...when a cartel from a foreign country launches a rocket attack, the waters get a little bit muddied, don't they?" Phil asked rhetorically.

"Exactly," the gunny concurred. "If this—" he used a nod to motion toward the destruction before them—"is tied to cartel activity, that's something we want to keep a very close eye on."

Charlie took over. "I was under the impression that you all have a liaison down at the Slaughter County Emergency Operations Center."

"We do," he agreed. "But sometimes a little HUMINT can clear up a fuzzy picture," the marine said, referring to human intelligence. "Savage! Najera!" the gunny called out. Two Marines quick-timed it up to him.

"Yes, Gunny," Najera said smartly.

"Get regiment up on the battle net," he ordered. The two disappeared for a bit while Charlie, Phil, and the gunny made small talk. Less than three minutes later, the two marines were back and holding a battle grid laptop computer up for the gunny. Gunny Sergeant Twogood made a request for whoever he was talking with to go get Sergeant Major Piercy onto the call.

While they continued small talk in the wait for the Sergeant Major to appear on the screen, Phil was silently impressed. The Marines had some sort of communication system that was completely independent of using any of the civilian cell towers. *But of course, idiot. These are front-line Marines, able to operate in any third world warzone. Which I guess we are one now...*

Interrupting his thoughts, the senior noncommissioned officer could be seen donning a headset and settling himself in front of the screen on the laptop that was now resting on the hood of the Humvee.

"What's going on, Gunny?" Sgt. Major Piercy asked. He wasn't irritated, but he also didn't believe in micromanaging a simple recon patrol.

"Sergeant Major, I thought you should meet the civilians who have been investigating this rocket attack. This is Lieutenant Reeves from the Sheriff's department and Phil, from…"

It took a second for Phil to get the hint. "Oh—Phil Walker, one of the leaders of the Slaughter Peninsula Posse. A team of my people were attacked on patrol yesterday, for no known reason."

The Sergeant Major's face drifted off, his eyes revealing that he was trying to capture an old memory. "Walker…Walker…Seems like I once knew a Phil Walker right here at Bogdon, or at least knew of him. Was that you?"

"Sure was," Phil answered, somewhat shocked. "I'm sorry, Sergeant Major, but you aren't ringing a bell for me, here." He chuckled with slight embarrassment. "My red hair's been turning gray for quite a while…"

The sergeant major laughed a little bit. "No, no, it's okay, Walker. But it does make sense as to why Gunny had someone come and grab me for this call."

"That's right, Sergeant Major," the gunny clarified. He looked at Phil and Charlie. "You see, I knew he was at MCSF early on in his career. I thought maybe you two knew each other."

The ranking NCO on the tablet screen replied, "No, I believe Mr. Walker left as a result of a severe injury a month or two before I showed up here. Back then, we used the LAV-25 for cruising around the base. We call those things the Rolling Thunder—loud and dangerous, with a high center-of-gravity."

"All true, Sergeant Major," Phil verified. "I had a career-ending back injury as a result of that wreck."

"So…it definitely was a rocket attack, huh?" the Sergeant Major asked, moving the conversation along. Phil could sense a bit of concern in his voice.

"Definitely," Charlie replied. "If you all have any intel that the Slaughter County EOC can use, it would be much appreciated."

"We'll keep that in mind, Lieutenant," the Sergeant Major replied. "But as I'm sure Gunny told you, our primary mission lies inside the base."

"Understood," Charlie acknowledged, while Phil also nodded.

The conversation wrapped up, and the Marines packed up and left, leaving Charlie and Phil with a feeling that things may be worse than they realized.

Tyler was woozily entering and exiting consciousness as two cartel soldiers dragged him by the armpits toward the boiler room. They had, indeed, both beaten him *and* used waterboarding. *You*

never even bothered asking me any questions, he kept repeating in his own head.

Just as they approached the doorway and stairs leading down to the boiler room, it opened and two other soldiers were prodding Gene to enter the main shop. For a split moment, the two posse members locked eyes and exchanged looks of terror, Gene because he had no idea what was about to happen, and Tyler because he did.

Tyler's voice was raspy and his teeth were wobbly and bloody, but he had the presence of mind to try to pick his woozy head up and warn his partner. "Don't say anything," he mumbled through loose teeth. "We're dead as soon as we talk!" He screamed the warning as the two men passed each other. The man holding him on his right armpit used his free hand to smash Tyler in the side of the head as hard as he could, ending Tyler's attempt to warn his partner.

They dragged him through the door and down the stairs, rounding the turn in the stairway and down the other half of stairs into the main boiler room. Once they reached a large steam manifold, they bound his hands and installed a set of shackles. They then tethered the shackles to some chain that was wrapped around a manifold, leaving him in a bloody lump and exiting the cold, dark space.

I'm praying for you, Gene. Praying that it ends quickly for you.

4

Long shot.

TAHOMA'S HAMMER PLUS 22 DAYS.

THE EVENING BEFORE, Nick used the cover of darkness to slowly creep back to the state park he'd been escorted out of just a few hours earlier. He tied up farther down the shoreline, just in case the cop was parked and waiting for him. *Wish I had my night vision with me*, he thought. Like the rest of his supplies and gear, he'd hidden it in the bushes.

There was too much wave and mudslide damage for Nick to walk the shoreline back to where he had originally parked his boat and goods. He hiked up into the more open area of the park and took a knee, spending several minutes watching and listening for anything that might be a problem. He finally skirted the tree line and found the spot where he'd originally exited the woods when he went to town the morning before. From there he backtracked to his cache of supplies.

Ever since "Officer Fife" escorted him politely out of town, he'd been trying to think of what he should do next. The only thing he knew was that they were passing names of people traveling on foot via radio. Except for some wild-card factor that he couldn't predict, he knew Sticky would have to come up that highway if he wanted to find the Schwartz family. He arrived at his gear and decided to change back into his multicam battle uniform.

After he changed clothes and boots and handled a few other matters, like getting his battle rifle ready, he decided he needed to consult a map. Like he had done on Fox Island a couple of weeks earlier, Nick draped a heavy poncho over himself and his map and used a flashlight under the protective concealment of the garment. He studied the map of the Olympic Peninsula North Shore and decided there were probably a couple of major junctions and intersections that would have other checkpoints. *Discovery Bay. That's where I'll go.*

Nick set up his hammock and tarp and grabbed a few hours of shuteye.

The sound of brush moving woke him with a start at some point after that. His instincts told him to jump out of his hammock, but his training kicked in. Out in the woods, motion was usually what gave the prey away to the predator—especially at night. He remained in his hammock and very slowly moved his head to a position to see a raccoon wandering around within a few feet, checking out his stuff. *Ugghh...*

Nick slipped out of the hammock, causing the raccoon to go on alert. When he stood, he looked around and finally decided it was just better to leave. Nick drank the rest of last night's water ration and secured the rest of his equipment.

He repeated the slow, long process of making his way back to his boat in reverse of what he had done the night before. He was more exposed in the morning dawn, but it was also easier to see that there was no apparent police presence. He did notice other campers in the park, though, and that gave him concern.

Well, that settles that question. Nick knew then that he was going to need to move all of the supplies back to his boat. He saw other campers and realized that his supply cache would not be safe for a prolonged absence. *Maybe out in the deep forest,* he thought, *but definitely not here in a state park. Apparently everyone with no plan just thought they would come live in the park.*

He fired up his boat and drove it the short way back to the original fallen log he'd tied up to two evenings earlier. He went through the process of moving all his equipment back to his boat. *Lessons learned,* he said to himself. *Will need to hide my stuff in a much denser set of woods…around a lot less people. And not go to the cops for help anymore.*

After forty-five minutes, Nick was finally able to make the slow navigation over to Discovery Inlet and down to Discovery Bay. It took quite a few hours, because he was going barely faster than a troll. He stayed close to shore, travelling down the west side of Discovery Bay. He noticed quite a few homes on the water side of Highway 101. A few of the homes had private docks, but very few of those were intact. Even the secondary and tertiary effects of the tsunami wiped out almost everything.

One thing that did catch Nick's eye, though, was that most of the homes look boarded up and vacated. By the time he got close to the south end of the bay, the day was several hours old. He tied up to a piling that used to be part of a private pier. He chose that spot because one home was within sight, and it appeared to be vacant.

He cautiously climbed out of the boat and approached the home with his hands high in the air. *Don't want to get shot.* He stopped and studied the structure and eventually decided to just go knock on the door. When nobody answered, he performed a cursory walk around the entire property, deciding that the place had been abandoned…or the people were dead. *Not sure I want to stay here, but this will give me a place to think.*

Nick went back to his boat, grabbed his rucksack and a few

other pieces of gear and set them on the shore. He retrieved his machete and whacked several branches off the nearest trees to cover his boat. *That'll have to do for now.* He grabbed his gear and headed back up to the house to settle in for a bit. He scanned around for a few seconds and then used a rock to smash through a bathroom window on the side of the house. After crawling in, he cautiously took fifteen minutes to clear the house before heading back to the back patio. He busted out his camp stove and a little bit of food, using the opportunity to refuel and think. After he ate, he decided to walk down to the shoreline with binoculars and see if he could look at the south end of the bay.

Nick could see the checkpoint down at the junction of Highway 20 and Highway 101, but he was much too far away for this to be a useful intelligence gathering spot. He sat down, making himself comfortable and continued to eyeball the checkpoint as dusk approached. He thought about his encounter at the checkpoint in Sequim the day before, looking at his multicam uniform. *I just had an idea...*

Tahoma's Hammer Plus 27 Days.

Two evenings after Sticky Wood first introduced himself to the pirate called Shotgun, he found himself in the town of Sequim, Washington. The morning before, he and Shotgun took their time recovering from a hard night of drinking whiskey and smoking bowls of meth.

Shotgun and his crew of sometimes-fishermen were part of the Risen Dead Motorcycle Club's unofficial meth distribution network. They had their fingers in every criminal pie on the north end of the Olympic Peninsula. Shotgun had assured Sticky that he had contacts in Sequim that would help him find the house of Stuart Schwartz's family.

By the time they were feeling well enough to go do anything, Shotgun convinced Sticky that it would be better to start the next day. Rather than take the road and risk providing names at the checkpoints, Shotgun and a few of his "employees" gave Sticky a ride down to Sequim via boat, where they had contacts waiting to pick them up.

"So, what's the plan again?" Sticky asked.

"One of my long-term customers in this town works for City Hall," Shotgun clarified. "We're gonna go pay her a little visit."

Shotgun's contact drove the little red and black Chevy Blazer around the outskirts of Sequim and across Highway 101 up into the foothills of the Olympic Mountains. They took several small back roads, passing nice homes at first, that gave way to older, single-wide trailers. The road changed from paved to gravel—not that it mattered since everything was cracked and bumpy from the earthquakes. But Sticky realized they had entered the realm of his most common customer—poor, white trash.

The Blazer pulled into a driveway and was greeted by several people drinking beer around a fire. There were three dogs running around acting quite aggressively. Trash was strewn everywhere. One of the people around the fire was a woman who looked to be in her mid-fifties. As soon as she saw the red and black Blazer, she started beating feet to get into the house.

"Hey, Linda," Shotgun yelled at her before she could get inside the structure. "How ya doin'?"

"Hey, Shotgun," a less than enthused Linda replied. "Good to see you," she lied.

When Shotgun, Sticky, and the driver approached the fire, not one of the men stood up. They knew who they were talking to with Shotgun, and even though they didn't know Sticky, they recognized the look of a senior predator in his eyes.

"C'mon back over by the fire, Linda," Shotgun said. He sounded sociable, but it wasn't a request, and Linda knew it. She slowly crept to the fire, trying to stay on the opposite side from the fisherman-meth distributor. "Nawww...no, no Linda—over here by me!" Shotgun ordered, once again sounding much friendlier than he was being.

"H-hey, Shotgun," Linda said once more. "Listen—we ain't got no—"

"Whoa, whoa, Linda—slow down! I'm not here to collect. I'm here to give you a chance to get that monkey off your back."

"Sure, Shotgun," Linda said apprehensively. She knew there was no such thing as a free ride. "What do you need?"

"We need an address," Sticky replied for his friend.

Linda look at Sticky and then at Shotgun. "I wish I could help you, Shotgun. Really! But the computers are down." A slight look of relief crossed Linda's face, and she thought she had successfully evaded the request.

"Now, Linda...we both know there are paper records for backup. Right?"

Linda could see she wasn't going to get off quite so easily. "Uh, yeah, but...you know, those are in archives. Everyone'll know I'm diggin' through them…"

"Ohhh, mannnn," Shotgun grunted. "That sucks." He wasn't even trying to hide the sarcasm. "Sounds like a problem you need to solve, Linda."

"Look, Shotgun, they're gonna know somethin's up. I ain't even been to work in two weeks."

"Yeah, c'mon, Shotgun," one of the skinny tweakers by the fire said. "If she starts trying to dig through the archives after being gone so long, they'll know something's up."

Shotgun and Sticky both glared at the man, who wisely decided he'd better shut up. Shotgun returned his gaze to Linda. "Make somethin' up," he said forcefully. "I don't give two cents what you say, but we want those addresses by this time tomorrow."

"W-what's the name?" Linda asked in a nervous tone.

"I want the address of every property in this area owned by someone named Schwartz," Sticky said coldly and directly.

Sticky started fingering the large fixed-blade knife hanging on the side of his right hip, stepping a little closer to the fire and eyeballing each and every man there. He was practically daring them to start a fight, but not one of them felt like dying that day.

NATALIE WALKED out of the root cellar and through the defunct greenhouse out into the snow. She was getting used to the daily ritual. For the first several days, one of the men would come grab her and drag her to the house. More recently, it had been one of the other women. Natalie had been conditioned at this point to not even try to escape. She knew the elements in the mountains would be against her anyhow.

The green house had broken panes of glass and various pieces of discarded furniture and household goods. If it had ever been used to grow vegetables, it showed no signs of it anymore.

Natalie trudged through the snow on her usual morning routine, looking to gather a bucket of frozen water from the rain barrel on the corner of the mountain cabin.

"Not yet," the other woman scolded. "House," she commanded.

Natalie did as she was instructed, bypassing the rain barrel and continuing up the path around to the front of the cabin. She could smell the smoke of the cabin's lone fireplace, burning wood that was too green to burn cleanly yet. There was a rich, moist smoke that hung in the air. She walked up the three creaky steps under the covered porch, opened the door, and entered. When she did, one of the four kids—a boy about five years old—screamed at her while wiggling his hands at the side of his head.

"Wench!" he yelled at the top of his lungs.

"Hey!" They all heard one of the men yell from a different room. "You little turd! I told you to stop yelling that!"

Natalie had learned to ignore all the kids. None of them had any manners, and she almost felt sorry for them. There wasn't much sympathy left in her heart for anyone else. She just wished she could die. Her husband had been murdered, and she hadn't seen her own children since *that day*. Just looking at these people caused an intense rage in her to build, but she dared not do anything to upset them because beatings and rapes were much more likely to happen, she'd learned.

"Get in here, girl!"

My name is Natalie, you human filth!

They'd never even bothered asking her name. As far as they were concerned, she didn't have one. The word "girl" had inadvertently become her name. Natalie was nudged into the cabin's kitchen area by the woman who had entered behind her. When she got in there, she saw that all eleven of the adults were waiting for her.

"We got a special treat for you!" the leader snarled.

Natalie had figured out he was probably the father of at least two of the other men. She pegged him to be in his mid-to-late-sixties. She wasn't sure what all the family dynamics were, but she knew the four women belonged to four of the men. That left her to "entertain" the other three men—when she wasn't doing chores.

"Hey, you," the old man said, viciously laughing. "Today you get to find out who your new husband is!"

Natalie stared in disbelief, trying not to let her anger come out on her face and cause yet another brutality. She sat there quietly, knowing she was in trouble either way. If she talked out of turn, they beat her for speaking without permission. If she didn't speak when they wanted her to, they beat her for being insubordinate. It was a no-win situation. In the end, the beatings were coming either way, so she decided to just never talk to them again.

"Still giving us the silent treatment, huh?" the old man said. "Suit yourself!"

"And don't look so dejected," the meanest of the three single men said. "You got yerself a chance at a real life, here," he said, almost disbelieving that she couldn't recognize what an opportunity it was.

Natalie just cast her eyes down at her feet, waiting to hear whatever new creative punishment they had come up with. She didn't care what they called it—she was a slave, and she knew it.

The younger man continued. "Ya see—Dustin had himself a brainstorm. We're all tired of having sloppy seconds. Decided we should compete to see who gets you as his wife."

This got Natalie to look up. For a moment, the group of kidnappers all thought they had finally found the thing to make her talk again. But she didn't.

The man continued. "We're gonna flip a coin for you. Odd man out wins. Whatcha think?"

Once again, Natalie didn't respond. She casually glanced around the kitchen, looking for a knife or anything that she could use to end herself. As usual, they'd left nothing out that she might use against them.

Wham! The old man had slammed his fist down on the table. "Yore part of this family now, and yore gonna speak if it's the last thing you do!" The old man had grown tired of the silent treatment, and he'd thought of one last way to get Natalie to speak. "Don't you want to know what happened to yer daughter?"

Tears welled up in Natalie's eyes instantly. In a matter of two seconds they started streaming down her filthy face. She looked up, looking at the other women who were all looking away. She started to openly sob. Finally, "Y-Yes!"

"Then this silent treatment crap stops now!" the patriarch yelled, his voice echoing off the logs. The room went quiet once again. "Ask nicely," the old man commanded.

Natalie was stammering, but the words finally started to slip past her salty lips. "P-please tell me what happened to my daughter," she slowly begged.

"She don't exist no more," the old man said coldly. "You might as well ferget she ever existed," he said with pure evil in his toothy grin. "The sooner the idea of her living is gone, the sooner you can go on to having yer own life again."

"That's no answer damn it! You tell me what happened to my daughter right now! I swear..."

This caused most of the men in the room to start laughing, even the old man.

"Yore in no position to swear by anythin'," he said. "But I'll tell you, anyways. We fetched 'nuff gasoline to run the generator all winter." He stood up. Despite his age, a lifetime of hard work had made him a hard, old man, and he was still powerful looking, even under a whiskey gut. "Now, you think about that girl this one last time. We got heat and electricity 'cuz of her. You get her out of your system, and you ferget she ever existed."

The old man pointed at the front door with his eyes, silently instructing one of the women to start escorting Natalie on her morning chores. As she was exiting the cabin she heard the old man say, "By the time you get back in here with water, you'll find out who your husband is."

5

Dark Days.

Tahoma's Hammer Plus 33 Days.

Between Puget Sound and one of Seattle's more prominent northern neighborhoods—Queen Anne—sat a vast array of rail-lines and a giant, concrete grain elevator. Built in 1970, the Pier 86 grain elevator was, in the eyes of many, an ugly eyesore in what had otherwise become a quaint, hipster metropolis. Nestled between the railroad tracks and the shoreline, the bulk of the complex was a 500-foot-long, eighty-foot-tall array of concrete silos. At the south end, there was a nine-story access and machinery building. A large conveyor ran off of that end, southwest toward the water, where it crossed over the Elliott Bay Trail and ran above a pier that banked sharply south.

The 500-foot-long pier had small supporting piers on both the south and north ends. It was designed to tie up large grain-hauling cargo ships. The conveyor was supported by five large, metal-frame towers that carried the grain to four telescoping-boom hoses. It was those hoses that could fill a cargo ship in just a few hours.

Reynaldo Hernandez stood on the end of the pier, wondering if the recent and sudden stop of grain flowing to China was something he needed to be worried about.

At that moment, though, Reynaldo was ecstatic. He was watching the youngest ship in his three-ship flotilla—La Nina—slowly breast over to the pier under the aid of a captured tugboat. With its bow pointed north, the forty-year-old cruise ship looked more like an old hospital ship than the giant monoliths of entertainment that had taken over the cruise industry in more recent times.

The dated 584-foot ship, longer than the pier it was headed for, had old, dirty white paint and orange rust stains running down the hull at its various drain outlets. It had the familiar ports on three levels of passenger cabins. The proud ship had been recovered by Rey from a recycling center in India. Reynaldo's cartel paid to have it towed to Indonesia, where it went through an overhaul process, converting many of the dining rooms into hospitals and berthing compartments and the various other entertainment areas into storage.

The mission for Reynaldo's Fleet for many years had been simple—take food, medicine, and doctors to the coastal villages along Central and South America. Providing critical services and nutrition to children, Rey had discovered, was always the fastest way to gain loyalty from a local populace. It wasn't until the very first time that Rey's ship was down for many months of maintenance did his cartel leaders finally realize the true value of the ship.

When this ship had been out making port calls and delivering goods to dozens of villages, the intelligence provided by those villages kept their rivals at arm's length. For several months, they never lost a single shipment and survived four different ambushes unscathed. Over the dozen years that Rey had been building and running Mar de Paz Services, he had learned that it really took three ships to guarantee they would always have at least one operating.

These entitlements are key to keeping the locals from turning against us, Rey thought as he watched. *Something most governments learn—and most citizens don't.* He knew full-well that the unique isolation of the Seattle area and the magnitude of the disasters were a once-in-a-millennia opportunity. *The municipalities have failed to provide. Enter…me…*

After La Nina had arrived and unloaded at their captured pier near Blaine, Washington, Reynaldo decided she didn't need to join the other two ships on a second trip of bringing supplies, soldiers, drugs, and trafficked humans. Always a forward thinker, Reynaldo knew that he needed a back-up plan—an escape route—just in case things in Seattle didn't go the way he thought they would. While he fully intended to set up his operations in the city, having one of his ships on standby to leave at a moment's notice was simply a wise move. There was absolutely no way the ship could be approached without his army knowing about it.

Reynaldo and his men had been on the ground in the Pacific Northwest for two full weeks. *There is something oddly comforting about seeing your ship tied up to the grain elevator pier,* Rey thought. It was like seeing an old, long lost friend one could rely on.

La Nina carried her own crew of about 280 people. Over two hundred of those were dedicated to the operations of the ship, from staffing the bridge to manning the engine room. The rest were dedicated to security and other tasks, as designated by Rey. They had used one of their four gunboats to run some of the ship's crew over to the pier to act as line handlers. They were also manning the stolen tugboat.

Rey knew that the vast majority of these people's dedication to the cartel was based on one of the oldest instincts known to man—*please don't hurt my family.* Still, they were handsomely paid to ensure that the temptation to take bribes from rival cartels was not worth risking one's life for. Rey was impressed as he watched their professionalism in action—successfully tying the ship to the pier and moving a gangway over at a location they'd never been to.

Rey walked north along the pier, moving right past the newly installed gangway that reached through the side hatch of his command ship. His crew was also in the process of mooring his gunboats, the stolen tugboat, and a few other ships they had procured over the last several days. This included the fishing boat his team of operators had used to retrieve the two militia members from the west side of Puget Sound the day before.

As a former member of the Mexican Special Forces, Reynaldo had undergone SERE training. Anyone trained in resisting and escaping capture would have known to hide anything of value before the captors could find it. He climbed onto the fishing boat and went down into the hold where the captives had been bound and gagged. Rey squatted—looking and thinking. He moved a few ropes and life preservers around, not knowing exactly what he was looking for—*but I'll know it if I see it,* he thought.

"Jefe," he heard from behind. He stood up, recognizing the voice of one of his most trusted lieutenants.

"Gilberto, what can I do for you, my friend?"

"La Nina is secure and accessible. Did you have any specific orders for offloading supplies, product, or women or children?"

Deep in his psyche, it bothered Reynaldo that they trafficked anything...or anyone...that another person wanted. *But without a demand, there would be no supply,* he reminded himself in an attempt to quiet the conscience on his shoulder. "No," Rey said, thinking for a moment. "We will continue with the original plan and handle all of those tasks first thing tomorrow morning."

"Si, Jefe." Looking around the hold of the small fishing boat, the lieutenant asked, "Is there anything you need me to handle here?"

"No, no," Reynaldo said, barely stifling a small chuckle. "I don't even know what I was doing in here. It must have something to do with my next appointment."

Rey passed the lieutenant, who then followed him up the small ladder out of the hold and off the fishing vessel. Neither man had seen the small, tattered, brown patch that had stumbled its way out from under the very last life preserver Rey had moved. It was stitched with a circle, and inside that circle was a set of crosshairs, a small volcano shape in one quadrant, and the letters SPP in the other three quadrants.

GENE GROANED and grunted in pain, wondering if it was pure chance or a planned and intentional design for him to stare at the welding machine. He couldn't feel his arms anymore, and the heavy rope wrapped several times around his wrists had rubbed the skin raw. He had a pain shooting through both elbows that was nearly unbearable. He'd been standing in the shop, on his tippy toes for so long that he no longer remembered what the forklift looked like. He knew he was hanging from the raised forks of a forklift, and they had set the height so that he was barely able to use the balls of his feet to hold some of his body weight.

Gene's body was in shock. The building was cold, and he was stripped naked. The intense fight or flight reflex had kept his blood pumping and adrenaline flowing for so long that he was now exhausted and covered in sweat, as if he had just run a race. Back in his mid-twenties, Gene had taken a bad spill while rock climbing. Up until that day, he always thought he knew the fear of knowing you were about to die slowly and painfully. But on this day, Gene realized he'd been mistaken all those years.

The salty perspiration had slowly started to evaporate off him. His body temperature was starting to drop, and his muscles we're cramping all over his body. He barely had the presence of mind to register the arrival of the nicely dressed, good looking man who he presumed to be the leader. In the stupor of what he thought was a dream state, he heard someone say *wake him up*. The vile splash of cold urine hitting him in the face with a surprising force, startled Gene.

In front of him was the guard who had been watching him for the last three and a half hours, holding an upside-down Gatorade bottle. Behind him and to the man's right, standing next to a shop workbench, was the man who had ordered him to be woken up.

"P-please!" Gene began to beg. "Please don't hurt me!"

"Ahhh, yes, well, we are long past that," Rey answered honestly. "I mean—I have members of my team that thrive on such things. You wouldn't want me to disappoint them, would you?"

Gene didn't answer. He had no training nor expectations of what was about to happen. As a man who read the news and watched TV shows, Gene knew that it didn't matter. Besides... he'd caught a glimpse of Tyler—he knew beatings were coming next. *Maybe you should just beg for death.* Though Gene's heart was full of fear, his mind kept reminding him that the very worst thing that could happen was that he finally got his salvation through Christ.

The pudgy, balding Navy retiree and IT specialist hadn't always been a man of faith. He found it about fifteen years earlier, and he'd tried his best to study the scripture and live a Christian life ever since. And ever since they had been captured, the scripture of Psalms 53:5 had repeated itself in Gene's mind, like the persistent drip of moisture from an air conditioner on a hot July day.

There were they in great fear, where no fear was: for God hath scattered the bones of him that encampeth against thee. Thou hast to put them to shame, because God hath despised them.

Gene's only hope was that they would hurry up and get it over with.

"Your friend showed uncharacteristic resolve," Rey told Gene. "But he talked... eventually. As will you..."

"W-what is it that you think we know?" Gene pled.

"Anything," Rey stated matter-of-factly. "If you want to make it easy on yourself, just look into your mind and ask yourself, what is that one thing I shouldn't tell him. And then do."

Gene's mind immediately flashed back to the patches that Tyler had hidden in the boat the day before. *Did he tell him about the patch? Did he tell him about our security procedures at the range?*

"I don't know—"

"Wrong!" Reynaldo yelled. "I don't have time for games." He nodded at one of his henchmen.

The older cartel soldier had green tattoos that had long turned gray on his leathery skin, reflection of a life of violence and harsh living. The balding man donned a set of electrician's gloves and moved a couple of switches and a dial on a large, specially modified welding machine. The pair of leads running off of the welder each ended at a large alligator clamp. The man grabbed a pair of sponges with the clamps and dunked them in a bucket of cold, Puget Sound salt water. With no delay, hesitation, or remorse in his eyes, the man applied both dripping wet sponges to the sides of Gene's scrotum, sending 440 volts through his testicles.

"Aarrgghhhhh! My God!" Gene screamed at the top of his lungs. "Please just kill me!"

"Far from it, my friend," Rey said pleasantly. "But I've already told you how to make this easy on yourself—just give me something —*anything*. And take pleasure in knowing that your friend will not have to endure any more of this himself."

Gene refused and endured three more rounds, which only brought more and more enjoyment to the cartel members. He'd always heard there were few humans born that could withstand torture. And he thought he had read once in a *National Geographic* magazine that most people crack in just a few hours. *I don't think I can make it a few hours. What can they do with that patch?* he reasoned with himself, the way that people do when they are put in unreasonable situations.

"There's a patch!" he screamed, feeling both relief and regret. At this point it wasn't that he was afraid to die and meet his maker

—it was that he was afraid to live with himself if something he did got Tyler tortured. He understood the logic of what Tyler had said—that as soon as the cartel thought they were useless they would kill them. But logic had no place in the mind of a tortured man. Gene was reacting on instinct—the need for security at the foundation of Maslow's Hierarchy.

Reynaldo walked over slowly and nodded to a different soldier. The man pushed forward on the forklift lever, causing the mast to lower and allowing Gene's bodyweight to crumple under him. Gene lay on the shop floor, shivering in the fetal position, wondering if this was the end.

"You've done well, my friend," Reynaldo said in as soothing of a voice as he could. "Now...tell me more about this patch."

IN THE WEEKS following the devastation of Tahoma's hammer, an international effort had been put forth by several nations to send supplies via sea. While the highways, airports, and seaports had all been damaged beyond recognition, one thing that ships could do was anchor and send supplies via small boat. That is, if they could navigate past all of the hazards.

Over the course of time, the trees, wrecked boats, and other flotsam and jetsam that resulted from numerous landslides around Puget Sound had all made their way to the shorelines. The sea-lanes were slowly opening. In short order, armed gangs on boats had begun to raid some of the relief ships before they could make it all the way down to Seattle. As a result, the international effort began to make its way around the north end of Vancouver Island, bypassing most of the Strait of Juan de Fuca in the process.

Reynaldo Hernandez had anticipated the eventuality of international relief supplies coming in by ship. What he had not anticipated were the pirates.

We need more gun boats, he thought to himself. *I need to make sure those are priority when the rest of my flotilla shows up for round two.*

He was watching the second ship in two days weigh anchor just off downtown Seattle. He didn't mind the friendly competition when it came to providing for the people. *But no way will I let the American Federales get credit for this.*

In the void of authority which grew each day—a result of most of the police and National Guard members abandoning their jobs once it became apparent that the federal government wasn't going to be able to provide assistance—grew more opportunity for Mar de Paz Services to root themselves permanently.

"I have a new project for you, Miguel. I need you to run the welcoming committee for these ships," Reynaldo explained.

"Whatever you say, Jefe," his most trusted captain replied. "But I thought in the grand plan, we weren't going to assume any civic leadership roles. Wouldn't a welcoming committee fall out of line with that objective?"

"The situation is...flexible," Reynaldo explained.

Rey had no problem with Miguel asking for clarification. This deep into the cartel, a leader could only trust a small handful of people. Ironically, those were the people who were around him the least. That level of trust meant being able to rely on that person to do the right thing without an ulterior motive. Miguel was one of only a few people that Reynaldo could set loose on a task and not need to keep a tab on for several days.

"You are correct. The last thing we want is to try to replicate government. But we won't be doing this for the benefit of the city of Seattle," he explained. "If anything, we'll be showing the world that Mar de Paz Services is who they should be sending those supplies to in the first place."

"Ahhhh," said the taller and younger assistant. "We'll need some boats. Not all of those supplies are making it down here—a problem we need to handle in a way that deters future piracy."

"Already communicated to headquarters," Reynaldo said. "In

the meantime, we will continue to procure any boats that seem to work and outfit them with our armament."

"And where should we be staging all of these supplies for distribution? I don't think our new headquarters will be large enough…"

"I agree," Reynaldo said quietly. "I just don't know if this idea is going to spread us too thin. I'm trying not to bite off more than we can chew," he explained. "But our new subservient gangs are going to have to earn their keep. Even with the levels of death and devastation that this area has seen this month, there are a lot of people to take care of. Most of them have flocked to a few key, large environments, like those sports arenas. Unfortunately, those same areas are where the last strongholds of civil authority are camping out."

The two cartel leaders, binoculars to their eyes, continued to watch the big vessel set its twelve-ton anchor not too far from Seattle's destroyed Pier 69. They were perched on top of one of the taller apartment buildings between Seattle's recently renovated basketball and hockey arena and the waterfront.

Reynaldo's Army had taken the sports arena as the west end of their base camp, and the Bill and Melinda Gates Foundation Building as its eastern perimeter. In between was the Memorial Stadium football field and the International Fountain portions of the Seattle Center. These fields provided plenty of area for Rey's Army to have a central base camp. They were slowly pushing their perimeter out via patrols and establishing posts at major intersections.

Next to Rey and Miguel, three men were establishing a machine gun nest, complete with sandbags, both for protecting the base camp and to observe the activities along the Seattle waterfront.

"Other than this new assignment," Rey continued, "your other top priority will be to continue to establish our network for secure communications. I'm going to take your other assignments off your plate and give them to some of these new members to test their capabilities. Regarding where to have those ships offload their supplies, let me know when you have their full understanding of who they'll be dealing with. By then, I'll have your answer." Rey's eyes darted around the cityscape as he decided to shift topics. "There's just so much destruction downtown…I think we're going to need to route all of that stuff up here near us. There's a few other parks east of the interstate highway that we'll have to secure for our own use."

Rey started walking back toward the damaged building's fire escape, indicating to Miguel that it was time to get going on this new task. *Now it is time to go check on these new patches. No time to waste on this new mission.*

6

Alternate Plans.

Tahoma's Hammer Plus 23 Days.

"What'd you say your name was?" the scraggly looking man asked Nick.

"Nick Williams," the retired Army sniper replied coolly.

"And you live where?" the man asked skeptically.

"I'm from the Olympia area," Nick answered honestly.

He was at the checkpoint where Highway 101 and Highway 20 intersected at the bottom of Discovery Bay. It was one of two larger checkpoints amongst the series of smaller ones spanning from the Hood Canal Bridge to the city of Port Angeles. Nick knew that the area was just too dense with brush and undergrowth for people to make any decent time trying to get around checkpoints. But since they were all checking IDs, he figured that probably would be what

Sticky does. This was Nick's back-up plan, put in motion by the Sequim Police Department.

If Stuart Schwartz passed through here, this would be the best place to find him.

"I recently retired from the Army and was up visiting a few different family members when the quake hit. I was at my Uncle Jake's, not too far from here. He wasn't in the best of health anyhow. He finally died of natural causes a few days ago." Nick was trying to put on his best Oscar winning performance.

There were a total of six men and women staffing the checkpoint. *This older scraggly one thinks he's in charge,* Nick thought.

"Sorry to hear that," one of the younger men said. "What was your uncle's last name?"

"Schwartz," Nick said, knowing the question would play right into his lie. The other four people at the checkpoint were in the process of pushing foot traffic along their way in both directions. Like the other checkpoint Nick had been at, they were collecting names, looking at identification, and noting these things for radio traffic that seemed to happen on a scheduled basis.

"Never heard of him," the younger man said, looking at his partner.

"Me neither," the older man said, still scrutinizing Nick's retired-military identification. "But...you seem to be who you say you are. So, what are you doing here?"

"Well," Nick said trying to act sheepish. "I have another uncle that lives in Sequim. I'd like to check on him, but I don't recall where he lives exactly. I'm hoping to catch my cousin, who I know to be traveling on foot. I figured I would volunteer my services here at the checkpoint in the hopes that I can find him." He acted like he just suddenly had an idea. "Say... would you guys be able to tell me if he's already passed through here?"

The two men just looked at each other, both wearing expressions that said *I'll take a hard pass on that...*

"Everyone's been throwing the papers in that box inside the

tent," the grumpy old man said. "You're welcome to go look through there, but I ain't gonna...." The old man turned away from Nick and the younger sentry continued to scan the lines of people waiting to go in each direction.

The younger man just raised his hands as if to say *don't ask me.* Just like that, Nick Williams was now a volunteer at the Discovery Bay checkpoint. He walked over to the tent as if he owned the place and went inside. He commenced looking for the box of papers.

I'm wondering if you're ever going to find the needle in the Proverbial haystack. This had better work, he thought glumly to himself.

TAHOMA'S HAMMER plus 27 Days.

THE TSUNAMI that ran west to east in the Strait of Juan de Fuca had done serious damage along the north shore of the Olympic Peninsula, but not nearly as devastating as the areas impacted head-on by the wave, such as Washington State's western coast and the western shore of Whidbey Island. Many of the private and charter fishing vessels in the city of Port Angeles had been damaged but not completely destroyed.

In the days that followed, a few groups of boat owners, most of whom specialized in running charter fishing operations, had slowly started to realize how important their operational boats had just become. As others made repairs, the local fleet started to grow, though not nearly as large as the few hundred boats and small ships that pre-dated that fateful day.

While a few of them were tied to Shotgun's smuggling network, most weren't. However, they all knew that Shotgun wasn't someone to be messed with. Fuel was becoming much too scarce to waste on daily fishing trips. As the days grew into weeks, Shotgun and his small fleet of criminals were becoming bolder. Charter boat owners were being forced to consider the potential of being robbed when they went out for food. It was a matter of time before someone resisted and wound up dead.

"I just don't see the point, Sweet Pea," Jennifer Smith's father told her. "It's a matter of time before those guys outright kill someone and take their boat. I don't mind fighting for what's mine, but I ain't risking your or Andy's lives just to prove a point."

The pretty, long-haired brunette couldn't believe what she was hearing from her own father. "We have to stand up to them, Dad!" she said in an exasperated tone. "Seriously! They're just going to continue to run all over everyone if we don't do something!"

"I get that, Jennifer," her father said, tired of arguing with her on what was becoming a daily battle. "But we are one boat with three people! You'll understand when you have your own kids, someday…"

Jennifer looked at her younger brother Andy for some support. The normally quiet Andy predictably let her down, keeping his opinion to himself. "Big help you are!" she complained at her brother, never afraid to tell him her thoughts. She looked back at her father. "Then we need to get with the others…talk them into forming some sort of pact. If we all went out and fished as a group, there would be safety in numbers. Especially if we're armed."

"Even if we did that, Sweet Pea, there's still the fuel issue. Where do you propose we get hundreds of gallons of diesel? They have control of every fuel station on the coast!"

"Then let's get creative," she said in her normally insistent tone. "I know it's a lot of work, but we could siphon from the school district's bus barn or make a trade with some of the farmers. There's like four or five private airports. They're all going to want to eat fish, just like the rest of us!"

Jennifer's father grew quiet, staring at the fire-pit while mulling over the points she was arguing.

She got out of her lawn chair and headed back to their house. She and Andy had both grown up in the charter fishing business.

Never married, the thirty-three-year old looker had moved back in with her family a year earlier, after the end of her longest relationship—two years. Jennifer's mother was hand-washing dishes on the front wrap-around porch of the one-hundred-year-old, two-story farmhouse. She let out a deep breath.

"Sometimes I don't know how you were able to stick it out, Mom," Jennifer said. "Talking to him is like yelling at a brick wall."

"Well, you two are a lot alike," her mother retorted with a small chuckle. "Both of you get stuck on an idea and hate listening to reason."

Jennifer knew her mother was right. "That may be true, but since I'm usually right, it seems dumb when he's being hardheaded." She knew that sounded arrogant. *But it's so true!*

"So, what is it?" her mother asked. "What's the bright idea that he's not listening to?"

"I'm worried about those thugs at the marina pirating all the relief supplies, and"—she put major emphasis on the word and—"keeping the rest of us from fishing at the same time!"

"Well, honey, those guys are the dirtiest crooks in town, and everyone knows it. People are going to have to get really desperate to want to fight them."

"That may be true, Mama, but you don't wait 'til that moment to learn how to fight…"

"Thanks for the morning prayer, Erin, as usual" Vince Cortez said.

Every morning the leaders and family heads of the Phalanx group on the north side of the Snoqualmie River's North Fork gathered for a daily briefing. After the families had settled into their routines after the initial earthquake and eruption, the briefings had started to become more efficient and speedier. That all changed five days earlier, when Marshall Oakley, the main HAM radio operator for the group, reported that a large gang had attacked the Monroe Correctional Facility. The meetings had suddenly become much more focused on threats in other parts of King and Snohomish Counties. The group didn't force any particular religious views on anyone else, but they did open their meetings with a quick invocation, usually led by Air Force veteran Erin Harmon.

"Lord knows our state and country need it, right now," was all Erin replied as gleefully as she could manage.

"Marshall? Any new intel on this cartel stuff from the various preparedness nets?" Vince asked the group's primary HAM radio operator.

Though several of the group had lower and mid-level HAM licenses and a variety of equipment and experience, Marshall was by far the right man for the job. The borderline genius could make a listener's head explode just with the words of describing signal modulation, power supply, or the virtues of a di-pole antenna.

"From the sound of things, the National Guard and police in Seattle have taken a defensive posture at the sports arenas. Their manpower is negligible. The people who were sheltered in the arenas have been rioting almost non-stop. I hate to say it, but anarchy is about to reign in King County, and this gang that *miracled* itself out of nowhere is the only authority poised to do anything about it."

The look on John Cronin's face was worried and wrinkled, like an old leather tool pouch. "Have you heard anything actionable?" he asked Marshall. "Locations of troops and movements? Numbers? Actual activities they're performing?" The former Seattle cop was also a truck driver in the Army many moons earlier. While not infantry, he had the basic knowledge of what he should be asking.

"It sounds like they're setting up food and medical centers," came the answer John was dreading.

"What!" gasped a few of the others.

Vince didn't say anything to quiet them, but as the meeting's chair tasked with keeping it on schedule, he gave them all his hush-up expression.

"Locations?" John asked Marshall.

"A few parks, mostly inside the city limits, I guess…Why?"

Ignoring the question, John said, "I need you to reach out to all of the other groups. We have to figure this out. Use these questions to guide you. Where are all the other gangs? Why aren't they attacking this large army? Where are they providing services? This will help us, if we want to sneak in and learn something. It will also tell us where to avoid large crowds of angry, hungry people. And most importantly, where is their CP?"

"What are they doing here?" wondered Lawrence Teall, one of the family heads.

"Nothing good," came John's curt reply, which caught the group off-guard a bit. "Sorry," he mumbled toward Larry's direction, though his mind was obviously moving a hundred miles per hour.

"John, should we be worried?" Erin asked. "Even way up here in the isolated foothills?"

You all have been preppers for years! John thought. *Why is everyone suddenly so naïve? They're all living in denial…*

"Yes," John said, looking around the shop near Vince's cabin that they used for the meetings. "In fact, when the guys across the river get back from their rescue mission, we need to check in with the various militias' and groups' leaders to discuss a battle plan."

The order of the meeting broke down after those words, causing Vince to find a piece of firewood to bang as a gavel. He called the meeting adjourned, to be reconvened that evening, which would give Marshall some time to reach out to the network for more information. As people started to filter out into the cold rain, he called after the head of security. "John. Can you hang? I want to show you something…"

John nodded and continued to listen to the sidebar conversations as people left. Once the shop was clear, he asked, "Something sensitive?"

"Maybe…" was the mysterious answer. "I want you to talk to my grandson. He's in the cabin." Without even waiting for an answer, the retired helicopter mechanic started leading his neighbor into his mountain homestead.

As they trudged through slushy, low-level snow that was washing away in the day's forty-degree rain, John asked, "Is this the family member that just showed up a couple of days ago?"

"Yup," Vince answered, stopping to do a quick check of his chicken-run's fence for signs of rat or raccoon invasions. "He worked in electronics before all this. No practical life-skills, that one," he said somewhat disappointedly. "But smart as they come. Made parts for a Boeing sub-contractor."

The rustic lodge was warm from the large fireplace. The pair of men could smell chili cooking when they walked inside. "Alex!" Vince called when they had shut the door.

"On the way, 'buelo." Within a few seconds, a young man came down from the loft, and then wore a surprised look when he saw John.

Looks to be maybe twenty-five, John thought. *Vince must be volunteering him for guard duty.* "Hi. I'm John," he said, sticking his hand out to the new resident.

"Alex," the young man said politely. He then looked expectantly at his grandfather.

"You see—Alex and I were talking aviation," Vince explained. "What with his job, and my career in helicopters." John's face morphed with confusion as his assumption was proven wrong. Vince went on. "This led to a conversation about drones, air superiority, and such. I mean—" Vince practically chuckled "—we all know this gang or cartel will be using them, right?"

"Yeah, yeah…" John's face changed to one of piqued curiosity. Without even asking, he slid over to the cabin's couch and plopped down. "What's this about, Vince? You guys got a super-slick drone, or something?"

Vince and Alex exchanged glances as they each plopped into an easy chair in front of the fireplace. "Hey, 'buelo, that was all theory, you know…I've never actually done it myself…"

Now John was actually curious. "Done what?" he asked, looking at the two.

"Junior here knows how to build an infrared detector circuit card!" the old man said proudly.

It was lost on the security chief. "Uhhh…okaaayyyy…."

"Really?" Vince asked incredulously. "I thought you'd get it immediately!"

"Uhhhh…."

"For tracking," Alex explained. "I saved a YouTube video on my iPad and showed my Grandpa how easy it is to make a home-made IR-tracking missile."

This totally caught John off-guard. "A what?" He waited to see if he was being 'punked.' "No way," he said out loud.

"Not like a real missile," Alex explained hurriedly. "It was a compressed-water powered motor on a hobby-sized glider. It flew maybe fifty yards…Maybe. It was a video from some dude in India…"

"But it tracked?" John asked. "As in… course adjustments?"

"Yes," Alex confirmed, not believing that these old farts couldn't believe it.

"And you could build one of these circuit card-sensor things?" John double-checked

"Easy. With the right parts, probably less than an hour."

John and Vince were finally on the same wavelength. He could see Vince smirking at him. "Air superiority," Vince said with a cat-ate-the-canary grin. "We could deliver a guided bomb!"

If we can figure out how to fly it there, John thought.

Tahoma's Hammer Plus 28 Days.

. . .

THE STENCH almost made the old killer and rapist gag. *Ohhhh myyy Gaawwwdddd,* the ex-con thought ironically. He had just entered the home of Stuart Schwartz's parents on a lightly developed road in the foothills between Sequim, Washington, and the Olympic Mountains.

I'll hand it to Shotgun, Sticky thought earlier that morning. *He commands the fear of that tweaker chick.*

In order to get into City Hall, Linda had to eat some crow for abandoning her job. Fortunately for her, though—when the apology was falling on deaf ears, she reminded the current city manager about their romp in the back of his truck every 4th of July back at the beginning of their careers. *How you gonna explain to your wife how I can describe that tattoo next to your little ding-ding?* she threatened. By midday, she was handing off the information to Shotgun and Sticky.

Shotgun had provided Sticky an option to outsource this job to his local trustees, but Sticky was having none of it. *This one is personal,* he explained. Linda had acquired the actual purchase and sale deeds on file with City Hall for every family named Schwartz—nine in total. It was the name and address of the purchaser of a specific property that had told Sticky which home to go to—the one purchased by Dr. Asher Schwartz of California.

Doctor. Why do these greedy Jewish doctors still call themselves doctor after they're retired?

Sticky knew instantly that at least one of them had died in the house. *A couple of weeks ago, I'm thinkin'...* He pushed the door closed behind him. The homes in this area were situated on parcels that were big enough to be fairly private but still close enough to be considered a neighborhood. Most of them looked abandoned, but he wasn't going to let fate have some concerned neighbor walk by and see the door open.

The home was large and spacious and had a commanding view of both Sequim and the bay a few miles north of it. Some of the windows were broken. Furniture was strewn. *Just like almost every house,* Sticky thought. He dodged kicking things as he slowly made his way through it.

When he got to the kitchen, he could tell that a lack of food and water had quickly become the Schwartz's biggest issue. *Why didn't they go to a FEMA camp or somethin'?* he wondered for a brief second.

He checked the entire house, not finding anyone, but also not finding the source of the stench. *Dog died under a porch, maybe? Naw, too strong. Gotta be human…*

As Sticky opened the door to the attached garage, he was rushed by flies and an odor that would have knocked a buzzard off a medieval plague-wagon at a hundred paces.

Christopher "Sticky" Wood vomited instinctively and violently, much in the way many of his rape victims probably had in the past. His vomit was light on food and heavy on whiskey, which didn't help matters. He ran outside for some fresh air. *No way am I going through that door.*

He looked around the property, keeping an eye out for other people as he used a small rain puddle to wash out his mouth. He spotted a constructed outbuilding, which he figured to be a gardening shed. Inside there, he found a shovel, which he hauled back around to the closed garage door.

Forcing the blade under the door, he pushed down on the shovel, which pushed the door up just a bit. The garage door creaked as opener-tracks and locks were fighting each other from the unplanned incursion. Sticky took a couple of cottage stones from a defunct flower bed and stacked them behind the fulcrum of his shovel. This gave him extra leverage, and—SNAP!— this time the fiberglass handled tool was able to force the garage door open despite its parts fighting him. He grabbed it and pulled it up so that it was now about half-open. The surge of stench and flies wasn't as bad once he was expecting it. He saw a Mercedes with a garden hose stuck in the tail pipe. *Well, well….Now what?*

7

"If pleasure was not followed by pain, who would forbear it?"
—Samuel Johnson

THE WORLD WAS PRACTICALLY ON FIRE AT FIVE WEEKS INTO THE events. China and Russia had started surgical strikes and limited engagements, both at sea and on their shared border, and those had continued daily with lower-intensity conflicts. America's fiscal, power, and internet problems had far-reaching and world-wide impacts. The rerouting of trucks and ships to the West Coast's southern ports had slowed the shipment of grain to China considerably. The dollar had been weakened as the world's reserve and petro-currency for well over a dozen years prior, but America's shaky e-commerce had been the nail that sealed its coffin.

The Hammer's trickle-down effects were growing worse by the day, and sometimes by the hour. The power outages and rolling blackouts west of the Mississippi River had started to become a common occurrence, sometimes lasting days, except for Texas, which had its own independent power grid. Riots were not just limited to the major cities any longer. Even smaller towns were starting to see crowds by the hundreds protesting the lack of electricity and internet and the sky-rocketing prices of food and goods.

As word slipped out of the RIZ—the Rainier Impact Zone—of the cartel setting up shop and starting to provide food and medical for the populace, people in other states began to lose their faith in the nanny state. In Los Angeles and Denver, people began incorporating a plea for the cartels to help them with their "protests," something the cartels were only too happy to do.

The President of the United States and his staff just couldn't keep their eyes on all of the moving parts. While trying to beef up his foreign policy and move the military to the south-western states to face the pending Euro-Asian aggression, at home he was dealing with attacks on his lack of response to the disasters more directly. Every day, the press briefing was a virtual blood bath for his press secretary. *Katrina looked like a day at the picnic*, and other such comparisons were being made to the president's lack of action for the RIZ. Jeremiah Allen, America's first Libertarian President, had made no friends with the media as it were, but with the power outages, collapsing economy, and cartelification of the western states, he was the laughing stock and target of every media outlet on the planet.

TAHOMA'S HAMMER Plus 34 Days.

THE FOUR-FOOT by four-foot dog cage was bittersweet. The cartel guards had provided one each for Gene and Tyler, not for their comfort, but to eliminate the hassle of messing with chains and bindings. Each of the Posse prisoners had his own cage in the cold, semi-dark, and damp boiler room, and they were kept covered with cheap, wool moving blankets. *For the psychological effect,* Tyler knew. *Need us to feel isolated.* The two men were not gagged, however, and Tyler figured it was probably because the room was bugged. *I want to tell Gene that I cracked! We need to find out what the other confessed.* Tyler knew from his old Air Force SERE training that they shouldn't talk openly about anything of intel value. *I only wish we had made time to train the whole Posse on some code phrases for this situation. The thought of being kidnapped seemed too impossible. God, we were fools…*

"Tyler…" he heard Gene mumble weakly. "I…I—"

"Don't worry about it," Tyler cut him off. "Gene, do not say anything about whatever you told them." He heard Gene start sobbing, both from pain and guilt.

"I-I know," Gene said compliantly through his tears and hiccups. "Are y-you okay?"

"I'll live," Tyler mumbled, wincing through the broken ribs, missing teeth, and probable concussion as he comforted his partner.

The two men talked of missing their loved ones and wondered when the torture would start again as a way to pass a few moments. When Gene had calmed down for several minutes, Tyler knew it was time to propose his plan. "Listen. I want you to promise me something."

Gene was quiet…thinking for a moment. "Don't think like that! God has a plan for us, Tyler—"

Tyler cut him off again. "Gene. Stop. Listen! If either one of us is let go or escapes, we need to keep going."

"H-huh?" Gene asked, not sure if he was understanding. "Abandon each other?"

"Gene! Promise," Tyler instructed. "If you make it out, don't turn back. And neither will I."

"I-I…can't promise that, Tyler!"

"Look—"

This time it was Gene's turn to be direct. "No, Tyler! We're stronger together! Don't make me promise that!"

Tyler let the air grow quiet for a bit before pressing his point. "I appreciate that, friend. But one of us making it back is more important than both of us dying. I don't like it, either. But it's the way it is. Now promise me..."

After a long, quiet minute, Gene finally agreed. "Okay...I promise..."

Both men sat quietly after that, not wanting to upset the other with their sobbing.

ELI FOUND Phil on the rifle line, shoving his plate carrier and patrol pack into a large surplus parachute bag he'd purchased years earlier specifically for his Posse Kit. "Don said you wanted to see me?"

"Oh, hey...yeah. Lonnie and I are taking Fred's truck down to the Bartlett EOC." Just the mention of his recently killed longtime friend made Phil sad again. Fred had been the gun range's very first casualty in this new, harsh world a few weeks earlier. "They radioed for a meeting. I have a job I need you to start handling. Find some hard workers, but they need to keep their mouths shut. This little project could cause some squawking and drama..."

"Well, don't stop there," Eli insisted. "What's the big secret?"

Phil spent several minutes quietly going over a project for Eli out on their eastern perimeter. When he was all done, he asked him for any last questions.

"No, not really...it's just a bit of a mind-screw to think that this is where we're at..."

"Hmmmm...you're telling me..." Phil said, thinking back to the events that had transpired in the recent days—Savannah's abduction...the deaths of several friends, including his own son's heroic death down in the shipyard...being abducted and almost killed because of his own stupid decision making...the gun range residents getting into a small-scale shootout with the National Guard...*It's enough to make you lose faith in humanity,* Phil often thought.

While only five or so miles down the hill to the Slaughter County EOC in Bartlett, the trip took a near full hour for Phil and Lonnie. Ever since Tyler and Gene's abduction, the exit protocols for leaving the property had grown longer. All three manned fighting positions on the club's western border had to report no contact. They were still staffing the hidden observation post in the woods to the west, as well. Once everyone was reasonably sure the path was clear, the vehicle snaked its way out of the sandbag trap near the front gate.

They travelled much more slowly than they had grown accustomed to over the previous five weeks, stopping often to scout slowly around curves and good ambush points. Once in Bartlett, Phil could tell things were at a critical point. Any people who hadn't made their way to the FEMA camp attached to the EOC were fully aware of the new rules. Possession was now ten-tenths of the law, as it were—and whoever possessed guns and friends with guns was probably going to eat and live another night. People were learning to bunch together into defendable houses. They were learning to crowd those structures to capacity—there was a balance between having the right amount of real estate for your supplies and food, and the right amount of people to defend it. They were learning to keep fires hidden and windows blackened with plastic and blankets. The outside fire barrels were buried, with large holes punched into the side and multiple grates or metal screens laid over them to block as much light as possible.

*The rain…*Phil thought. *What a curse and a blessing at the same time.* The usual heavy drizzle and sometimes rain was miserable and downright deadly if one didn't have the correct gear. It was a natural deterrent for some of the two-legged predators. It made sneaking through the woods and underbrush much quieter, which was good if you were the one doing the sneaking. Otherwise, it made it harder to detect intruders on your own perimeter. *But at least we'll have plenty of drinking water.* Phil once again prayed a small thanks that so many people had purchased water filters back when 'prepping' had been trendy.

Lonnie made the last right turn and slowly approached the gate at the National Guard Armory. "We're a little early," he told Phil as he looked at his wristwatch.

"That's alright. The last of these troops all know me as a regular, now."

While being covered by several others on watch, a lone soldier approached Lonnie's rolled-down window and looked inside. He seemed to recognize Phil. "Password?"

As part of the Sheriff's official County Posse, Phil had been privy to a constantly changing list of verification words. He had to memorize a new list each week, as the only copy was kept in the EOC. "Toledo…no—wait. Hard to tell what day it is anymore." He closed his eyes so he could count days and events in his head. "Cookies," he announced with confidence.

"It's Toledo," the corporal said, smirking just a bit. "Captain Reeves just came by ten minutes ago, so I know you're not on the naughty list." He turned away from the window and nodded to the others to start the process for manually opening the gate.

I coulda sworn today was cookies, Phil mused to himself. *Whatever today is…Seems like the names of days quit mattering once weekends didn't exist anymore…* After the hammer, every day was a workday.

Lonnie took the truck to the central dispatch building, and the pair of men slowly strolled inside. Civilians with rifles slung on their backs would have been a major security threat six weeks earlier. Now, it was the *new normal…*

Charlie greeted them at the lobby of the dark, stuffy building. "They called up to say you were here," he explained.

Lonnie and Phil shook off their hooded raincoats and draped them over their arms as they followed Charlie farther into the building. They entered a room that had diesel-generated electricity powering the lights, a few fans, and computers. It wasn't the main EOC dispatch, but a small room down the hall that the officers-in-charge of the deployable forces used for their daily planning and intelligence gathering.

"Captain Reeves, huh?" Phil quipped. "Brother, you're collecting promotions and demotions faster than I can keep up with."

"Phil. How are ya?" Phil heard Sheriff Raymond say from behind him. He turned to see that he'd just entered the room himself.

"Sheriff," Phil said in a cordial greeting. "Right as rain," he said. *Hmmmm, rain….*

The sheriff looked at a guard member to his left, who was sitting at a computer. "Corporal, could you get the big screen fired up?" he asked, nodding toward the big monitor hanging near a large, plastic conference table.

"Yes sir," she barely mumbled as she went to power it up. Once she did, she returned to her computer and pulled up some stuff to place on the screen.

Hmmmm, Phil thought. *Must be something important if we're getting a briefing.* As the monitor and computer finally settled into talking to each other, Phil could see a satellite photo of Seattle on the left side of the screen. The right side was filled with a smaller map of the same area in one corner and a spreadsheet in the other. He took a closer look at the satellite photo and realized it was fresh. He could clearly see several buildings toppled, including the famed Space Needle.

"That's somewhat sad and scary," was all he could say. Lonnie was moving in for a closer look, too.

"Have a seat, guys," Charlie said. Once they'd all settled at the conference table, he continued. "This cartel thing has our full attention."

Phil and Lonnie were still marveling at the photo. "Where'd the picture come from?" Lonnie finally dared to ask. "That's too high up for a drone shot," he said, clearly thinking in terms of civilian drones.

"Our military liaisons," the sheriff answered plainly. "They're trying their level-best to stay out of civilian governing affairs. Doesn't mean they don't want to help, though."

"Correct," Charlie continued. "When it comes right down to it, the cartel will eventually be their problem, too."

"Right," Phil said, looking at the sheriff and Charlie both. "Exactly. They could solve this problem in a day or two." He was a bit confused by their stoic silence. "So why aren't they?" he asked bluntly.

"Not their mission, Phil," the sheriff said. "They're protecting those things that don't exist. You, of all people, should know that." The sheriff wasn't trying to be snarky, but he was fully aware of Phil's resume.

Phil let it slide, recognizing that it wasn't meant to be a slight. "So…what's so important about these photos?"

Charlie and the sheriff glanced at each other, and Charlie caught the slight go-ahead nod from the sheriff. "The National Guard and cops in Seattle are getting their butts handed to them. On a platter." As Charlie continued, Phil turned back to the screen. He stood up and slowly walked over to the big picture. "If you look in the Seattle Center, you can clearly see trucks, tents, even a couple that look like captured Guard vehicles. We think that's where their CP is."

"What about down here at the arenas?" Phil asked, pointing at the south end of the picture.

"That's the FEMA camps and what remains of the civilian government," Charlie answered.

"For the whole city?" Lonnie asked in disbelief. Charlie just nodded.

"There's more, Phil," the sheriff said glumly. "There's…nothing we can do about it, but…there's problems abroad, too, both domestically and internationally. There has been severe power and internet problems throughout the west, here in America. And…it sounds like China and Russia have started some sort of shooting war."

Phil cast glances amongst the three men. *Sure. Why not? Might as well have World War III while we're at it...* It then dawned on Phil that their own National Guard commander was absent. "Where's Adam?"

"Major Matsumoto is at a meeting with the security forces at Bogdon," the sheriff answered, referring to the submarine base. "Trying to *strike an agreement,* if you know what I mean…"

Phil turned back to the picture. "Any idea where my Posse members are?" He wasn't hopeful.

"No idea, at all, brother," Charlie answered. "But see that ship at the pier? North end of the bay, by Queen Anne Hill?"

"Yeah," Phil said curiously.

"That wasn't there two days ago…"

REYNALDO HERNANDEZ STOOD at the picnic table under the tent, fondling the patch once more. *Not bad,* he thought. After learning of it in the torture session, he sent men over to inspect the small boat a little more closely. They returned with two of them. He'd just sent one out with some troops to find a seamstress to hire. *Hire…*he thought. Rey was a true believer, but he was no fool. He knew that most of the locals would perform work and tasks out of fear. *At first,* he continued in his own mind. *But they'll come to see El Mundo Nuevo soon enough. Once people learn that they have nothing to fear in exchange for full compliance…*

He was watching a few of his troops finish having a bite to eat. *Another special operation,* he thought. *My teams are the best. They took down the local gangs from the inside. They'll take out this…posse…too. The gringos have been unexpectedly weak. Even as fat as they are, I thought they would be more challenging than this.*

He'd received word from Mexico that other branches of his

cartel, as well as other familias, were starting to take the first steps in exerting dominance in other American cities. He looked at the patch rolling around in his fingers, almost letting his daydreams and the rain on the tent lull him to a peaceful sleep where he stood. *Posse*, he said in his mind once more, this time laughing at how ridiculous the word was. *I wonder if these fat militias will be the same everywhere…*

8

Go Time.

TAHOMA'S HAMMER PLUS 28 DAYS.

EARL KNELT NEXT TO CONNER, who was staring at a run-down homestead from the tree-line. "Well?" he asked his fellow Ranger-vet and best friend, who had halted the small patrol as they made their way steadily up a snow-covered game-trail.

"Very dark. We're gonna need to scout this thing for a while. If they have an OP, I haven't found it yet," he said, referring to a possible observation post for the property. "With the clouds and little moon, I might've missed this place, had it not been for all the junk scattered around the yard."

As the point-man, Conner was wearing the one pair of night-vision possessed by the group. He handed Earl's combat helmet back to him so he could take a look.

"Roger," Earl acknowledged. "Where do you figure the main access is?" he asked as he donned the helmet and lowered the optic.

"On the left, maybe…Kind of looks like we're on the right end of the house. Looks like a shed or greenhouse out back, to the west."

"Uh-huh," Earl agreed. He mulled things over for a quick moment. "Copy. I think the snow's too crunchy. This approach is going to suck whether we do it at night or in daylight." He scanned his Luminox watch, which glowed for years on end without needing to be recharged. "0330," he mumbled to himself. "Hunker down," he told Conner. "I'll move Jack and Larry up and we'll spread out in this tree line."

"Roger," Conner said nonchalantly, keeping his eyes on the dark field and homestead to his south.

After he stood up, Earl took one last look at the property, trying to find his sister's gas-powered Cub utility vehicle. *Stables, greenhouse, carport…I guess it could be in there. But how do I check without being seen?*

Earl's small fire-team planted themselves downhill and in a tree-line at least sixty meters from the cabin. The drizzly, gray November day didn't yield any daylight until well into the seven o'clock hour. They could hear the occasional chicken, but the light mountain breeze rustling through the tall fir branches made it difficult to hear much else. Each teammate had taken a turn maintaining a watchful eye on the property while the others rested. Earl felt Conner's hand shaking his shoulder.

"Huh…Wha-" Earl said with a jolt, his mind coming back to the daylight that didn't exist when he'd closed his eyes. A career of Army training had taught him to react with as little motion as possible. He shook his head just a bit and blinked his cob-web eyes a few times, finally settling them on Conner, laying in the snow next to him.

"We have activity," he said. "Greenhouse."

Earl slowly rolled off the lined poncho he'd been sitting on, getting prone and following Conner on his elbows back up to the edge of the tree line. He took the binoculars from his buddy and scanned the back of the property. After another thirty seconds, he saw two figures come out of the rundown greenhouse.

"Only one went in," Conner said.

This made Earl pull his eyes of the binoculars and look at his friend. "Did I hear that right? One?" He was still groggy.

"Affirmative."

Earl went back to studying the two figures, each wrapped up in a hodge-podge collection of blankets. "Possible females…" Try as he did, Earl just couldn't distinguish if one of them was Natalie. "It would seem fitting that one going in and two coming out indicates a captive…" He was trying his best to keep his cool, but the desire to run in guns blazing was strong. "Do me a favor, Con-Man. Get good and clear, find some decent branches, and get started making an improvised stretcher."

"Huh?" came the confused reply.

"I have an idea to try to get closer," Earl said.

"J*ENNIFER*!" her brother hissed as loudly as he dared.

"Why are you whispering?" she shot back from behind the binoculars. "It ain't like they can hear us!"

"He's right, Sweet Pea," her father yelled out from behind the helm in the cabin. "Quit staring! If they think you're snooping, they'll hunt us down!"

The Smith family was making their usual venture out to fish, headed west on the strait, something they were doing only every few days to save fuel. The twin-engine forty-foot Rampage was easily seen, displacing over twelve tons of water and hosting both an enclosed cabin and a "flying-bridge" on top. The family had several poles and outriggers established, trying to catch enough not just to eat, but to barter, too. *Limits and seasons are a thing of the past*, Jennifer recalled her father saying. The big vessel was just a bit older than her, but they had taken great care of it.

"The way I see it, they'll leave us alone 'cuz they figure the more people we feed, the less troubles they'll be dealing with at their black market," she reasoned.

"Or…the more often they see the rest of us, the more they'll think we're competing," Andy countered. Her younger brother was quiet, but when he spoke, it usually counted for something.

Jennifer pulled the big, waterproof binoculars off her face and looked at him. "Just you shut up," she said, which was her usual order to him when he made a valid counterpoint. She turned her gaze forward under her thick, orange rain hood and called to her father through the open cabin hatch. "It's pretty obvious they're robbin' that ship! Maybe we should call it in or somethin'?" It was a half-suggestion.

"Are you out of your damned mind, Jennifer? To who? We haven't seen any authority since *the wave*," he reminded her somewhat sternly.

"Well, it looks like he's grown. That dirtbag has like five boats working for him, now," she replied, glassing four miles to the northeast. She could plainly see the small fleet of fishing vessels harassing some sort of larger ship that had a red cross painted on the side. She couldn't tell the name or registered country. "I don't think they're trying to commandeer the ship, just board it and rob what they can off-load by hand…"

I don't care if you're scared, old man, she thought. *We need to get all the others in alignment, and soon…*

CHRISTOPHER "STICKY" Wood was settling into his new sniper roost, a lesson he took from being hunted recently himself. He had wandered up the hill through the spacious, hilly neighborhood. The homes and properties were built with high-end retirees in mind, earning the original developer his profits not by squeezing every home he could into the space, but by providing plenty of space between homes for a higher paying clientele. Unlike most of the greenbelts and small woods between streets and neighborhoods in Washington State, this particular one had open fields of lavender with the occasional lilac. The home Sticky was occupying was near the highest, southern end of this Olympic Mountain foothill. The normal woods and brush occupied the land farther to his south, but he had a fairly clear observation downhill and to his north.

There was a large wooden deck with a decent view of several homes on the road below, including the Schwartz's. He had reclosed the garage door, hoping that the odor would stay contained. He wasn't extremely worried about authorities anyhow. *Seems like this Mayberry town is only worried about the folks down on the north side of the highway,* he concluded.

Sticky took control of the home cautiously, finding it vacated. *Still, someone could decide to come home at any time.* He set up an old school trip alarm using tin cans leftover from whatever the occupants had eaten after the start of the disaster.

Shotgun had outfitted Sticky with a rifle and some food for several days. He wasn't opposed to procuring some more from what was seemingly a mostly abandoned neighborhood, but he was trying his best to keep a low profile. He established his sniping roost on the deck under a dark quilt he found in the house. The upscale home's roof extended over the deck, offering him good rain protection from anything that wasn't being blown in from due north. He wondered, once more, who his adversary had been, fairly certain it was an Army-vet relative of the rape victim who had killed herself. *In another life, I might buy you a beer,* he thought.

His mind turned back to his prey. His primary plan wasn't to snipe Dr. Stuart Schwartz, but he knew he might have to once the good doctor found his parents in their present state. *No telling what you'll do after that. But you made my brothers bleed to death. And for that, you will pay…*

"Please don't shoot!" Earl yelled. "Help! Help!" He was panting heavily, his breath blowing out of his lungs like a flameless dragon as he dragged Jack on the makeshift branch-and-poncho litter up what used to be the cabin's driveway. He was trudging through the snow, glancing in every direction while trying not to look like he was scouting. "Please help!"

"Stop right there!" He heard the voice of an older man command him from inside the structure.

Dang! he thought. *I need about twenty more feet to see into that carport!*

"Alright!" he yelled back. "Don't shoot! My buddy is hurt! We need help!" he slowly set the litter down and raised his hands. "He fell down a ravine! We need help!" Earl could see a few flashes of movement as blinds and covers over windows moved in three different spots and on both levels. He had no doubt about barrels pointing at him that moment.

"Drag him back to town!" the voice commanded from the slightly ajar front door. "Mister, we ain't playin'! You need to be goin'!"

"Please!" Earl tried one more time. He was stalling, waiting to hear from Conner on the small radio. He had an earbud under his knit beanie, tucked under his collar and plugged into the small radio under his coat. The big Ranger took a step as he pled his case. "Look, we took a buck this morning. I'll tell you where to find it if you just help me with my friend! He needs to warm up!"

"I'm at the back," he heard Conner say into the earbud. "It could be her, but whoever she is, she's definitely a hostage. Wait! They're taking her and a bunch of them are going up to the second floor. Including kids. I got several hostiles on both floors, unknown how many. Most of them armed with long guns."

"Please, mister!" Earl pled once more. "I'll trade you our deer!"

The front door slowly pulled open, and two people in tattered clothes slowly came out—one man and one woman. The man had a hunting rifle trained on Earl, and the woman was holding a 12-gauge shotgun. "Bring him closer," the man commanded from the covered porch.

Definitely not the same voice, Earl thought. He reached down for the two branches, feeling the hard, old snow crunch under his glove as he scooped and lifted. He began to drag the device once more. As if on cue, Jack started wailing from the new motion. *Don't oversell it!* Earl thought. As he trudged over the icy snow closer to the cabin, he kept his head low, feigning more exhaustion than he truly had. As he took a quick glance left towards the carport, he could see an old pickup truck. He still needed a few more feet to be able to see past it. He was commanded to halt once more. *Damn!*

"Go check it out," the man gruffly told the woman. She walked down the creaky steps, slowly and suspiciously eyeballing Earl as she made a wide arc toward him and the stretcher.

Earl set the branches down once more, using his feigned exhaustion to stumble the last two or three steps with raised hands. He stumbled and glanced past the truck, seeing the bright yellow utility quad in the wide open next to an old rusty engine still hanging from an engine hoist. *Bingo,* he thought coldly. *You're all dead men...*

He picked himself back up off the ice and snow and heavily trod the four feet back to the stretcher, fully aware the nervous lady was bound to fill him with buckshot. Jack was laying there, bundled up in a mylar blanket so well that his face couldn't really be seen.

"I think his ribs are broken," Earl said, giving Jack the correct phrase for *crap's about to go down.*

"Lemme see!" the rough-looking woman said from under winter wrappings. She had wandered to within four feet of the homemade stretcher. Earl bent down and pulled the mylar blanket up on the side of Jack closer to himself. He purposefully held it high so that the lady lost sight of all but his head.

"Oh, hell!" Earl yelled. "He's bleeding!" He picked his AR-15 up off of Jack's chest, dragging the mylar off toward himself to keep it covered. As the lady bent to get a better look, she saw the muzzle of Jack's shotgun raise up from his chest, his hands on the weapon's stock down near his crotch.

Frozen in a slow motion fear, as if watching a cartoon coyote walk in the air before he realizes he has run off the cliff, the lady said nothing. The look on her face said it all, as her eyes grew as wide as saucers and her mouth opened in a gap that made no screaming noise.

Earl was already leveling his rifle up to the top of his shoulder, flipping the safety off like he'd done ten thousand times before. He knew his first two shots would be all the signal Conner would need. Larry was in the woods behind the dilapidated cottage. The experienced elk hunter was covering that whole side with his Weatherby.

POP! POP! Earl's rifle screamed, almost instantaneously with the thunderous BOOM! of Jack's shotgun. As the man on the porch developed two sudden leaks in his forehead and throat, the woman experienced the wrath of a slug perforating her cervical spine. Jack's shotgun muzzle was a mere three feet from her. Between the slug and the blast, it almost appeared as if her head had come off, though it didn't.

"Mooooovvveeee!" Earl yelled at Jack, who was already scrambling off the fake gurney. The pair started running for the front of the cabin as blankets and shades were being ripped off of windows. As they got onto the porch, they could hear glass being broken from the front windows. The men slammed themselves up against the logs on each side of the front door.

At the back of the cabin, the door flew open and an armed man started to run out, not anticipating that the enemy would be standing right there. Conner pulled his trigger, and from the distance of five inches, the 62-grain steel-core bullet ripped through the man's sinus cavity and brain pan at three thousand feet per second. He was dead before he could feel the burn of the muzzle flash on his face. His body fell in a slump, and Conner had to backpeddle a couple of steps to make sure he didn't get knocked over. The old wood deck croaked as he leapt over the pile of meat and began to sweep the death funnel he was about to enter. He swept both sides of the door as he entered what was essentially a mud room. It led straight into the pantry with a wide doorway. Conner entered the pantry and cautiously approached the other entrance into it, along its left side.

Back at the front door, the cabin's residents started to realize that their foes were at the front door. As two men pulled their rifles from the upstairs windows and started to cover the stairway, the two at the windows on either side of the front door pulled into the room and started shooting at the doorway. Earl had taken a kneeling position and was eyeballing the wide-open door, which was hinged on Jack's side. As soon as he saw a muzzle start to sweep around the door, he began to fire, connecting with the middle-aged redneck several times. He saw wood fragments splintering off the logs near Jack, who was anxiously scooting himself down the wall, trying his level best to become one with the floor. The incoming rounds were mostly being stopped by the open grain of the big fir logs that created the opening for the door.

Earl stayed against the wall as best as he could as he stepped out and turned his body left, making his way for the window that the adversary had abandoned. He did an effortless shoulder change with his AR, switching his hands in their positions on the rifle seamlessly. He was able to "slice the pie" on the edge of the broken window frame. Switching to his left shoulder had allowed him to keep his body behind logs and let his rifle be the first thing into the window frame.

Earl pivoted his barrel on the frame, his eye looking through the electronic sight. He made visual contact with the man five feet away, who was oblivious to his presence and still pumping rounds into the door frame. Earl shot him twice in the head, once again yelling for Jack to move. "Take that other window!" he commanded.

In the pantry, Conner exercised discipline with his trigger when the doorway he was approaching suddenly started filling with bodies trying to flee the carnage. His main focus wasn't on the size or gender of the bodies, but on the hands. The first two pair he saw were empty, but the third person in was sporting a pistol. Conner dropped the person as soon as he saw a head and torso. The pistol clattered to the floor as the man's body filled the pantry doorway. The other two people—one man and one woman—were taken aback by Conner's presence and the sudden gunshots. They fell to the floor and began to beg.

"P-please!" the man yelled. "Don't!"

Conner unslung his rifle and butt-stroked the man square in the chin, hitting the 'button' and knocking him out cold. The woman was screaming hysterically. After re-slinging his rifle, he grabbed her with both hands and shoved her back into the kitchen. He couldn't afford to stop, and he sure wasn't about to take the time to frisk and tie her up properly. He swept in all directions as best that he could as he entered the kitchen. He put his foot right in the middle of the woman's back, planting himself in a semi-crouch as he tried to assess what was happening. Compared to the dawn daylight outside, the cabin was dark, and all he could see were shadows and shapes.

Back up front, Earl hissed at Jack. "Cover those stairs!"

After switching shoulders on his rifle again, he made his way to the front door and began to slice off his small chunks of the pie as he cleared to enter. He paused for a second, reaching up to his radio toggle that was just a few inches downstream from his earbud.

"Entering the front," he said to Conner.

"Move," he heard his friend reply.

He came into the room, stepping over one of the bodies and scanning for threats. He could hear foot traffic on the creaking and rickety floor that separated the main cabin room from the upstairs area. He contemplated calling out for a surrender. He had no idea how many more enemy they had to fight. He had no idea if there were non-combatants. He was in the middle of the main room, staring at an open, cottage stairway on the right side, a back room with what appeared to be some form of kitchen in-between, and a small hall to the left.

Keeping his rifle shouldered with just his shooting hand, he reached up and toggled the earbud once more. "Where ya at?" he asked Conner.

"In the back door to the kitchen."

"Clear the back," Earl ordered. "We're covering the front."

Without speaking, Conner gave the silent and trembling woman under his foot a shush sign with his finger to his lips. There was a countertop between the kitchen and the back room that he knew someone could be hiding behind. He slowly walked to the end of the counter, but before he broached the end of it, he just knocked an empty fruit basket off the counter and onto anyone hiding there. He heard it hit the floor and nothing else. He immediately covered the corner and rounded it, finding nobody. He swung his rifle back around and cleared the rest of the space.

"Clear," he said loudly enough that he didn't bother with the radio. "Moving."

"Move," Earl replied.

Conner came out of the space next to the kitchen's other counter. Earl headed for the small hallway while Conner covered his back. He cleared a small bathroom and closet and returned to the main room.

"How many more shooters you got up there?" he yelled at the stairs.

"'Nuff that you're all dead when ya try to come up!"

What I wouldn't give for a flashbang right now! Earl thought.

Bubby? Is that you? Am I delirious?! Natalie wasn't quite sure what was real anymore.

The patriarch held the captured .357 revolver squarely on the top of the stairs, careful not to get too close to them. The old man's survival instincts were strong—he was avoiding broadcasting himself near any of the upper story's windows, too.

"You all might as well just accept it!" he yelled with the rage of knowing he'd lost members of his clan. "You're all dead! Git it?! D-E-D! Dead! You can't come up – and as soon as you try an' leave, we're gonna kill ya'!"

"I got two of yours still alive down here," Earl yelled.

Bubby! Natalie screamed in her head, not quite comprehending that the moment was real. She was lying in a pile of broken window glass, being guarded in one of the front corners by the two women. The children were all hunkered down, whimpering and scared to death. Two of them were actually holding onto Natalie. Her mind pushed through the fog of war, the countless days of torture, rape and abuse that had strung itself along into one long nightmare, quickly dissolving into understood reality.

"Buuubbbbyyyyyyyy!" She screamed as loud as her terrified and hoarse voice would allow her.

The three remaining men weren't expecting that. One of the women started to slide on her knees along the floor, about to pound Natalie in the head with the butt of a Ruger 10/22. Within two seconds, the patriarch started to scream an order to kill her when one of the rear windows of the house exploded in fury with the sound of glass turning into a thousand shards and the roaring boom of Larry's hunting rifle echoing outside the cabin.

The log cabin's open floor plan was simple: a set of stairs entered a hole in the floor on the north end of the structure, several feet off the wall. That end of the upper floor was wide open, with lumber and plywood constructing a pair of bedrooms out of the south end. The patriarch had kept everyone in the main room so that he knew exactly where every moving piece was on the life-and-death chessboard.

As Conner's head began to break through the plane of the upper floor, his body driving up the steep wood stairs as quickly as his legs could pump through a fresh surge of adrenaline, the three men were still reacting to the temporary distraction. Both of the other men were on the front half of the house, covering the blind-side of the stairs. The man on the left caught the motion of the foreign invader first. He leveled his AK-47 to his shoulder.

Natalie had shaken the little fingers clutching onto her arms off and was lunging at the woman who had been scooting toward her. She got her hands on the woman's throat before her captor was able to get the Ruger's barrel pointed at her. A .22-caliber bullet exploded out of the rifle, impacting one of the logs Natalie had just been leaning against a mere four inches above the kids. Natalie squeezed as hard as she could. She could feel cartilage cracking under her palms. *I'll die before I let go of you—you murderous witch!* she screamed in her head. On the outside it was the war-cry of a woman possessed.

Dynamic room clearing was an infantry soldier's most dangerous assignment in urban fighting, something that both Conner and Earl had done in real combat in Iraq. The former Ranger was following his training, clearing the path of least resistance. As he crested the top of the stairs, he was clearly seeing the old man, who was spinning back around from looking at the exploding window behind him.

POP! POP! POP! Conner's AR-15 screamed as he pumped three rounds into the old man's head and chest from a distance of six feet. The patriarch crumpled, still holding the revolver. Conner was fully off the stairs and starting to spin to his right. Earl was about halfway out of the stair hole himself.

KA-BOOM! The upper floor exploded in a much different and larger sound, as the AK sent a round through the top of Conner's left shoulder, exploding into his muscle and clavicle with extreme prejudice. He screamed in agony as the shockwave of energy sent a surge of pain like he'd never experienced before. Instinct caused him to drop to his knees and let go off his rifle to grab the spot. Training took back over when he saw the other man, the one who hadn't fired yet. He was sneering at Conner through the open sights on his AR-15, enjoying the look of terror and pain on the invader's face for a moment.

Two more shots rang out. POP! POP! Earl's AR sent a round into the throat of the man who'd shot Conner at the exact same instant that the little Ruger elsewhere had cooked off again. The small semi-auto had chambered another round as Natalie was squeezing the life out of the woman. She had relaxed her grip in the moment of the fight just long enough for the trigger and bolt on the gun to reset. This second unplanned shot found its mark, but it wasn't the children. Her rifle's muzzle was swinging wildly in the fight to breathe, and she was pointing it directly at her husband. She shot him in the leg just as he was getting ready to kill Conner. The sudden pain caused him to flinch and react just long enough for Earl to get around the stair protrusion in the middle of the floor and finish the man off with a three-round burst. Conner fell face first to the floor in writhing pain, grunting loudly to avoid screaming.

9

Tricks Up the Sleeve.

Tahoma's Hammer Plus 34 Days.

Rey stood staring at the open-ended buildings with a large, metal net suspended between them, thinking about the extravagance of it all. These buildings resembled many of the actual quake-damaged structures that were not much more than barren steel skeletons after the disasters shook the glass and contents right out of them. Many of the older buildings did actually snap somewhere mid-structure and collapse or start leaning against a different building. *Like a giant building made out of dominos and one got knocked over too early,* he thought. But not these. These were made to look unfinished on the ends on purpose. *What kind of maniac has the wealth and extravagance to make a state-of-the-art structure look unfinished on purpose?*

The Bill and Melinda Gates Foundation was more than a set of buildings—it was an empire built specifically to influence the world. To some it represented great hope, and to others, great influence and control ripe with abuse.

Everyone was worried about the conspiratorial New World Order, Rey thought amusedly. He began to walk west, his protection detail turning to follow him about five paces behind. As he walked west, he looked straight up at the giant net, formerly a one-of-a-kind, light-up piece of symbolic art. *All that any of this symbolizes to me is hypocrisy*, Rey thought. *This foundation should have spent a little less time and money trying to vaccinate highly survivable illnesses and a little more trying to stop...well...us.* That thought made Rey actually laugh out loud, not caring what his men thought. *But these structures are new and were built well!* Rey also knew that the benefactors had probably not been impacted too badly by the disasters. *I'm sure they took a helicopter to their estate in Montana, and a plane from there to New Zealand to live a long and prosperous life...*

On the campus' southwest corner was an intact parking structure. "Have the rolling command rig we captured established up there," he told a lieutenant travelling with him, nodding towards the top with his eyes. "The antennas can use the extra height." He wondered how badly the radio signals would be affected by the damaged or collapsed skyscrapers to the south. He glanced back at the foundation's two primary buildings. "Those will become our dorms eventually. Until we're certain we have control of the city, everyone is staying in their tents."

"Si, Jefe," his soldier replied, making a few notes on a paper pad.

The troupe continued across a parking lot and into a small football arena with partially covered bleachers on both sides. There were multiple military-style tents and vehicles occupying the facility. Rey glanced at his watch and headed for the tent that housed his special operators. *Almost time.*

Several minutes later he was meeting with about twenty men, most of whom who had participated in the gang-infiltration mission. Most of them were Mexican, but there were men from other countries and ethnicities—special forces men that Rey had personally recruited, including four Americans. All of his special forces were multi-lingual and highly trained in combat tactics.

He spent forty-five minutes reviewing a new mission. He admitted there was a lot he didn't know, reminding them that the initial objective was observation, not direct-action contact. A messenger came in with a bag, and Rey broke into a big smile when he saw him.

"Ah, yes! These are the patches we modeled off of what you men helped uncover by bringing the two prisoners back." He pulled a handful of them out of the pouch and passed them around. Some of them men chuckled when they saw them, wondering what good they were. Rey appreciated the skepticism—it meant his men trusted him when they felt they could question something openly.

"They had a code word that went with it. I'm sure at this point the patch and the code word have been declared compromised. It matters not. This is the lead we have, and if you absolutely have to use it as part of your cover, then do so."

There's a reason you get paid well and your families live comfortably. Don't forget that.

"Mama, when's dinner gonna be ready?!" Phil heard his granddaughter ask with a fairly whiny tone as he walked into the large log-structure they had recently built smack dab in the middle of the rifle line. They'd installed a river-rock fireplace at each end. On the eastern end they also installed an industrial woodstove with an oven-box, large cooking stove, and even a coiled pipe that ran through the firebox to heat water that was plumbed through it. The well house for the property wasn't too far away. The well-head had a back-up hand pump on it, but one of the range members had recently wired up a battery bank, inverter, and solar panel to the pump and pressure tank. There was a one-and-one-quarter inch hose that ran around a berm and connected the well to the deep sink that was in the log structure's kitchen end.

Phil was very proud of *the Common*—the club members had worked hard to build it out of fallen trees. He was even more proud of his daughter, who came up with the idea. She and Big Tony, the gun club's former bottled water delivery driver, were the key custodians of the Common. It provided a much more viable option for the roughly two-hundred people to prepare shared meals much more efficiently than people cooking on small propane stoves in their tents and trailers. The food went much further, too.

Lack of food is still poised to be our biggest enemy, Phil thought, *aside from dying horrible deaths at the hands of a drug cartel.* Tahoma had enacted her wrath during the second week of October. *It'll be months before anything of real volume takes off in the high-tunnel greenhouses.*

The Common was slowly filling with tables and chairs—plastic, scrap wood, fallen timber, even a few recliners trucked in on trailers. Savannah was using crayons to do her homework at the table closest to the kitchen area. Payton was next to her, rehydrating veggies and sausage from her father's freeze-dried supply.

"About a half-hour, honey," Payton told her daughter.

Most families had adopted their share of the work in an organized fashion. It was usually the same people from the various family or friend units that were working on a communal dinner each afternoon.

"Hey," she said to her father, as Phil walked up and threw his full leg over a wooden bench to straddle across the table from them.

Savannah sighed her discontentment with her mother. "You always say that..." Then, "Hi, Grandpa."

Phil noticed that she was returning more to her old self the farther she was removed from the abduction and rescue. He also noticed the enthusiasm for 'camping' and 'going to school in a conex box' was quickly evaporating.

"Hey, Peaches," he said, smiling softly and using her nickname. Phil had a thing for nicknames for his girls. "Olive," he said, looking at Payton Olivia Walker, "how you feeling? Getting enough food and rest?"

"Daadddd," she grumbled. "Don't start…"

"Dr. Schwartz made it clear that you should take it easy," Phil argued.

"What'd they want?" Payton asked, changing the subject. She was outgrowing the desire to argue with her father over everything.

Phil accepted her dodge, as he was outgrowing the need to be right all the time, too. "Talk about the cartel thing," he said while picking up one of Savannah's crayons.

Payton looked up. "Oh?" Her face was her mood ring—she showed her worry instantly.

"Nothing imminent, honey," Phil said reassuringly. He looked into the kitchen area, scanning for Teddy. "Have you checked on Teddy today?"

Payton nodded. "He's still understandably depressed." Teddy was Tyler's husband. While Phil was still a bit old-fashioned and reserved on the gay marriage topic, he was sympathetic to anyone who lost a loved one, particularly after his own wife had passed away from cancer several years earlier. "You should check on him," she suggested.

He picked up her meaning. "If I had something to say besides I'm sorry, I would. I'm pretty sure he blames me for the whole thing. And let's not forget that they're most likely abducted, not dead." Phil reached over the table and started coloring on Savannah's geography project, which his granddaughter completely ignored.

"It would mean more than you realize if you just go talk to him," Payton said as she pulled the crayon from Phil's hand and shoved his hand back onto his side of the table. It was all done on autopilot, with neither of them acknowledging it had even happened.

Phil looked down at the wood bench between his straddled legs. "In a bit, honey. I want to get off the leg for a while." He switched to crutches whenever he could to keep the skin conditions on his amputation at bay.

Payton stood up to take the mixing bowl of hydrated items over to the big pot sitting on the wood stove. "I forgot to tell you," she said. "The older Horn kid came by looking for you. Something about some scrap metal?"

"Oh! Good!" Phil said. "Working on something to replace the SPP patches."

"Hmmm," Payton said as she walked away.

Phil leaned over the table and picked a different crayon up. "Do you think your mama is mocking me when she says 'Hmmm' like that, Peaches?" He started rubbing the black crayon over the dark orange he'd colored earlier.

"Nawww. She always says that, Grandpa. Just like you!" she squealed when she realized it.

"Huhhh," Phil said, purposefully choosing a different sound effect. "Watch this, Peaches!" he said with mock enthusiasm. He pulled his pocketknife out of his pants pocket and started scraping on the black crayon he had drawn, revealing the orange underneath it.

"That's kinda neato," she said…impressed, but not really.

"It is kinda neato, isn't it?" Phil said, more to himself than his granddaughter. An idea had just been born. "I'll be back by dinner," he said as he walked east and then north to go find the Horn family's camping spot.

As he walked north on the cross-range road, he passed the spot near the other firepit where the Slaughter Peninsula Posse had been born, not long after Crane had passed away. He caught himself daydreaming about that night and suddenly realized he'd walked a hundred feet without realizing it, almost passing the Horn's tent. He stopped by the small group of tents pitched in the northernmost action bay and learned from Thad Werner, the Horn's neighbor and the club's dedicated chiropractor, that John Horn and his sons were up at the field helping Eli with a project.

Perfect, Phil thought. *I can get updated on two projects at the same time.* He was far enough along to just continue the whole trek on foot, despite wanting to use the Gator.

Ten minutes later, Phil was crossing the field where the Command Post and largest gardens and greenhouses were. He was nearly there when he found the Horns, Eli, and a few others walking out of the trail that Josh and his team had cut east off the range's property before the big fight with the National Guard. They were all carrying a variety of tools and looked dirty and tired.

"Phil!" Eli said, pleasantly surprised. "It's getting dark…we're wet and tired. Just headin' down for supper."

"Don't let me stop you, brother. I'll check on the project when I catch up to you. I'm actually here to talk to Horn about a different task." John Horn was one of four John's at the range, and everybody had taken to calling them all by their last names.

Phil joined the group as they headed back across the field and down the hill he'd just come up. "I found some tin, and I found some sheet metal. I think the sheet metal would be a longer lasting product to make some tags," Horn said. Phil had decided that they needed to replace the patches, as painful as that was going to be.

"Agreed," Phil admitted. "I have an idea for fool proofing it. But we're going to need some disappearing paint and UV lights."

Tahoma's Hammer Plus 35 Days.

Rey was watching the daily chaos at the "Clink"—Century Link Field—and T-Mobile Park on a set of screens. In this case, he was in his new command vehicle, which his troops had captured relatively intact, except for some bullet holes, after an engagement with the local authorities. The big diesel rig was a rolling communication platform on a giant F-650 chassis. It was the pride and joy of the Seattle Police Department's Incident Management team—or it used to be. Rey's technicians removed the equipment that had been on the near side of the freshly installed bullet holes to make room for some of his own gear. The vehicle was nestled safely in the center of Memorial Stadium, about as close to the center of his claimed territory as he could get it.

The camera angles he was watching from were from two different towers on the south end of downtown, including near the top of the Columbia Center Tower. *One of the perks of being the boss,* Rey admitted to himself. *I can make other people climb seventy-something stories with gear so that I don't have to.* In addition to setting up food and medical distribution centers and machine gun nests, Rey's men were now setting up observation posts all over town, especially up in abandoned skyscrapers. This task fell on his newest, indentured prisoners and American gang members.

The process wasn't without its hazards. There had been a few attacks on some of his men as they ascended the towers. Those buildings that hadn't lost all of their glass and still seemed somewhat structurally sound had started to become the impromptu collection points for the worst dregs of society. *Other than us,* Rey thought amusedly. *But this is why we use the expendable soldiers, isn't it?*

People that were off their mood-altering meds for too long were being expelled from the FEMA camps. If they didn't die of dehydration or starvation, they had to wind up somewhere. The dark, cold towers had become mini cities in and of themselves...trading camps for food, water, and anything else a person desired. The people in them were filthy and unkempt, and certain areas on every floor reeked of human waste. Rey's army had learned to never go into one with less than a full squad. Once the "residents" figured out the cartel were the drug distributors, they became welcomed guests.

The exception to that was the Wells Fargo building, which for some reason, was where everyone who just vanished seemed to wind up. Rumor was that the people who had taken up that facility were prone to cannibalism.

On this day, Reynaldo Hernandez's observation teams had been built with several extra people to carry out an operation. Rey's men had carried with them up the two towers a total of ten six-bladed drones, each capable of carrying a payload of up to eight pounds. They were able to add a little additional weight by removing the drones' skin, lights, and cameras. As entertaining as Rey would have found it to watch the action from the delivery vehicle, they didn't actually need the cameras. These drones had been programmed just a few hours earlier in the same command vehicle Rey was sitting in. They had been given an independent GPS point to fly to and ignite an electric squib when they were about twenty feet off the ground.

The view from the tower cameras will have to suffice, he told his command team. *Be safe, amigos,* he told the departing field team.

At five minutes after three in the afternoon, all ten of his pre-programmed drones took off from the two derelict skyscrapers and started flying south, almost immediately descending to an altitude of four hundred feet. *Let's toy with them a bit,* he'd told the programmers that morning.

Rey watched in amusement as the drones began to buzz over the heads of various security points belonging to the Washington National Guard and last remnants of the various police agencies. The loud, buzzing, man-made insects were following pre-selected routes and turning at their waypoints to change directions and altitudes suddenly. Care had been used to select altitudes and durations to ensure that the drones missed each other.

The programmers couldn't account for variables, however. As the buzzers started the final descent, one Guardswoman made a lucky shot with a specially modified shotgun that had launched a drone-capturing net, dragging the device down before it reached its final destination. Another drone flew straight into a flag mast hanging off the side of a building, something Rey's programmers couldn't see on their satellite photos. But ultimately the mission was a success, as eight drones, each laden with eight pounds of C-4 plastic explosive, caused several seconds of chaos and confusion before hovering over several security checkpoints around the FEMA camps and detonating themselves.

10

Critical Decisions.

Tahoma's hammer Plus 28 Days.

Throughout the intense fight, Natalie continued to squeeze the woman's throat. The other woman had watched everything unfold and had dropped her gun to scoop up her own child.

"Get in here, Larry!" Earl yelled into the little mic and earbud. "When he gets there, come up, Jack!" he ordered.

He scanned all of the room again, keeping his rifle up. He knew Conner was down, but that wasn't the moment to help him. He wanted to throw a second round into the man he'd shot in the throat, but he didn't trust that he wouldn't shoot right through the floor. He squatted just a bit, and with the looseness of his sling, had the capacity to send his rifle straight down muzzle first with a hard-striking blow to the gurgling and grasping man's forehead.

Insurance, he called it. *At least he gets to die asleep, now.*

Earl could hear his sister wildly screaming as she continued to choke a dead woman. *Clear the other rooms,* he commanded himself. He managed to verify the two rooms were vacant about the time that Jack had finally arrived up the stairs.

"Help Conner!" he yelled. He walked over to his sister slowly, eyeing the last woman and children who were all scared, sniveling and shaking with fear. "Don't move!" he commanded them with an angry, pointed finger. At 6' 2" tall, Earl Garren could be quite intimidating when angry. He took a knee next to his sister. "Nat."

She was sobbing, flushed in the face with rage. *She's gonna make herself pass out if she keeps it up,* Earl realized.

"Nat. It's over. She's dead."

As he put his hand on her shoulder, two of the quivering children began to cry for their mother, screaming and bawling. *Awwww, hell!* Earl thought as he looked at them. *This is a real goat-screw if I ever saw one...* Earl slowly slid his gloved hand down Natalie's arm and placed it on her hand, coaxing her to let go.

"Nat. It's me."

His sobbing, enslaved sister was now forced to accept that the ordeal was real and hope hadn't died after all. She relaxed her grip, looking up at Earl. That's when the real emotion showed up. "B-Bu-B-B –" She couldn't even call out for Bubby, as the weeks of fear and rage overtook her. She fell into her big brother's arms, bawling in a combined state of stress and relief that only people freed from human trafficking could ever truly understand.

Earl held his sister while glancing over at Jack and Conner. Jack had Conner lying on his back while he used a knife to try and cut enough of his coat away to expose the wound. Because Conner had made his way directly to Earl's after the disasters, he was only outfitted with Earl's spare gear. He had a backpack out in the snow that he'd ditched as part of this battle plan. Earl yanked his own first-aid gear, called an IFAK, out of a pouch on his plate carrier. He threw it at Jack. "What do you see?"

"Just an ass-ton of blood," Jack said. The software developer had never dealt with this kind of thing before.

"Take a dressing out of that pouch and apply pressure. Fast!" Earl commanded. "Listen to that wound! Do you hear air?"

After Jack fumbled with a vacuum-sealed pouch and pulled out a thick dressing, he pushed it onto the wound. He bent and slowly lifted it, though his ears were still ringing from the gunfight. "I-I don't think I hear air!"

"Good," Earl said, trying to calm down a bit. "That dressing unravels like a Z. Start packing it into the wound." He swiveled his head toward the stair-hole. "Larry, you okay down there?" Earl yelled, ignoring the radio.

"All good! Got these two tied up!" he heard back.

"Nat. I need to check on my friend." He held onto his sister, forcing her to stand up as he stood. She slowly composed herself, showing signs that she would be able to walk on her own. "C'mon," Earl nudged as he tried to hold her around the shoulders with one arm and move toward his buddy at the same time.

Natalie nodded that she understood, not quite ready to try using words yet.

Earl moved to Conner and Jack gladly slid over. He bent close, putting his eyes and ears into play, trying to lift the dressing Jack had stuffed into the hole just enough to see where the wound was.

"I think it missed the lung," Conner said in a slightly shocked tone. "Did we get her?"

Earl looked up with moist eyes. "We got her, brother. We saved her." He kept pressure on the bandage with one hand and put the other one around his buddy's neck, cupping the side of his head. "You saved her."

Just then Earl felt a nudging. It was Natalie – the former triage nurse was kneeling next to her brother, gently bumping him as a way of saying move. Earl gave her a surprised look. "Move over," she softly commanded. "Let me look." With a hard-to-hide look of surprise, Earl scooted away, clearing the room for his sister. "What's your name, soldier?" Natalie asked.

"Conner," he grunted through the pain.

"Conner?" she repeated. "As in, *The Conner*? The one who was such an idiot in all of my brother's war stories?"

Conner would've laughed if he wasn't in such immense pain. "The same. Owwww!" he yelled when Natalie started feeling around both sides of the shoulder.

She was looking down the chest as best as she could with all of the clothing still there. "Cut a little more there," she instructed Jack, who had moved to Conner's other side. She continued to look, listen, and feel. "I agree. I'm not seeing or hearing any air or frothy blood. Looks like it destroyed your clavicle, though."

"Well that sucks," Conner said.

Earl laughed a bit. "That's your takeaway, brother?"

"Just trying not to cuss in front of the lady," Conner joked with a wince. "But I sure could go for some mother-lovin' morphine."

Earl, Jack, and even Conner all chuckled a bit. Natalie was still way too emotional. If not for an intrinsic need to treat her would-be savior, she would still be a wreck.

"W-what are you gonna do with us?" stammered one of the remaining female prisoners. All of them were down in the dining area on the first floor, though Earl had left the one tending the children unrestrained.

He looked at his sister. "Your call. Either of these women show you any mercy?"

Natalie had been sitting in one of the old worn out dining chairs, thinking about what she wanted for several minutes. She had been staring down at her father's .357 revolver, taken from the still-warm, dead hand of the old patriarch. She finally stood up. With cold, hard eyes, she looked at Earl and said, "I don't care what you do with them. But I want my goats back!"

Earl wasn't worried about that. He'd ensure that all of Natalie's stuff was reclaimed before they left. She stormed out of the cabin to check on Jack and Larry. They were reinforcing the now-real stretcher that Conner had made and tethering it to the yellow Cub. Conner was laying on the front porch, wrapped in the decoy mylar blanket and a pair of crocheted afghans they'd taken from the cabin.

In the cabin, Earl looked at his seven captives—three adults and four children. "Look, I don't want to kill ya…but I will. But since you two were running, and you dropped her weapon and tended to the kids, I think I'll let you live." An open sigh of relief crossed their faces as they all started to bark their thanks.

Earl held a powerful hand up. "Just…just stop. Save it. Here's how this is going to work." He looked at the kids and addressed the oldest looking one. "How old are you, kid?"

"Eig-eight," the scared boy answered.

"That'll do. Name?"

"B-Billy!" The kid started to cry.

"Billy, calm down. You're going to be fine. You're just going to walk with me for a bit, so that you can bring one of the hunting rifles back to your tribe when we're on our way. Get it?"

"C-Can't ya' just leave one?" the scared boy asked earnestly.

Earl laughed. "Uh—no. That's not how it works, Billy."

The woman from the pantry chimed in. "Billy…sweetie. If he wanted to hurt us, he'd already gone an' done it. Just do what he says, an' come back," she ordered.

Earl's reasoning had been to let the kid bring back one hunting rifle for the starving family. He would set the scope's sights off as far as he could, just in case the lone male got a wild hair to come after them. His real reasoning, though, was a bit more nefarious. He knew they'd all be freed within a couple of minute of leaving. He wanted one kid with him as leverage. *You follow us, the kid gets it.* His face made that perfectly clear to the adults.

"I'm afraid to ask," Natalie said, eyes swelling with tears once more, "but…my boys?"

"They're fine, Earl said, which made his sister start crying with joy. They had tracked back down to the spot where they'd hidden the quads, probably a full two miles from the cabin. They'd just let the boy take the rifle with him to start heading back.

Natalie was overjoyed to hear that, but her face creased with worry once more. "They took my baby, Earl!" She only used her brother's real name when she was desperate.

"What do you know? What'd they tell you?"

"Nothing!" she exclaimed. "The day they took us, the day they shot Roy—" She stopped, flooded with emotion.

"Anything, Nat. Any tidbit. Did they trade her? Did they—"

"Trade!" she exclaimed. "Yes!" her eyes darted back and forth, searching the foggy memory of the nightmare. "F-fuel! Something about having fuel for winter!"

Earl's face was stoic. He looked at the makeshift gurney behind the Cub, then at the others and the quads, deep in thought. He stayed silent.

"What?" Natalie demanded.

He looked in her eyes, still thinking. Finally, "Alright. But what I say, goes. Got it?"

"Whatever! What are you thinking?"

"Not whatever, Nat. Say it. Say 'deal'," he said, taking her back to their childhood.

"Fine. Deal. Whatever! Now—what are you thinking?!"

"Feel how the temp has dropped?" he said, looking up. "Snow's comin'. These vehicles have only been working because this snow is packed and frozen. We need to get as much traveling done as we can while we can use them. Larry and I are heading down to Snoqualmie Pass on one quad. You and Jack will take the Cub and one quad back to my cabin."

"No! Earl! If my daughter is—"

"You said deal, Natalie. You're in no shape to go on a snipe hunt. She might not even be there. And Conner needs to get back down there. There's a team of people down by the river that'll be able to pull those bone fragments out." Earl was in NCO mode.

Natalie had tears flowing, but she knew her brother was right. The small rescue team disbanded, with the rescuee now in charge of getting the wounded Conner home before they froze in the mountains.

Tahoma's Hammer plus 29 Days.

Josh, Jeff, and Stu didn't have too much difficulty getting a ride across Hood Canal. During the disasters a month earlier, the structure that had been the fourth longest floating bridge in the world broke loose when the residual effect of the massive Strait of Juan de Fuca tsunami shot south-southwest and smashed into it. The two fixed ends hadn't fared much better, one of them barely standing and the other crumpled over into the tidal zone. It hadn't taken long for people whose boats had been up on trailers to be put into the water for providing rides. After a couple of days, fuel had become an obvious concern. As they'd heard what had happened down in Bartlett, people were required to provide fuel as *part of* their payment for one-way transport.

Charlie had long ago learned about the bartering system from the north end deputies and had pre-warned the three gun-club residents to bring some, along with some sort of food to barter with. Payton had provided some of the apples from Phil's tree, as they were starting to go mushy. The three travelers had barely made it the three miles up the long, steep hill in Jefferson County when they ran into their first checkpoint.

"Hold up," Josh ordered the trio as he pulled his small monocular neck-strap, retrieving it from his coat's interior.

"Fine…"—huff-huff—"by me!" said a panting Stu, who put his hands on his knees. Jeff just turned away and rolled his eyes.

Josh scanned the checkpoint. "They've already seen us, so it's a moot point to try and dodge them." He stared through the one-sided optic for a few more seconds. "Seems legit." He tucked the device back into the front of his coat and started walking again.

All three of them had rifles slung on their backs, a posture Josh had ordered to keep a nervous Nelly from shooting first and asking questions later. There was a slight uphill, and it took another ten minutes to cover the five hundred meters. They were all travelling at Stu's pace.

At a month into the disaster, anybody alive had either been through checkpoints or knew somebody who had. They took their place in line. Josh surveyed what he was seeing from the east-bound pedestrians. People were bundled, dirty, and keeping their distance from each other. *Like pack animals afraid to make eye contact*, Josh realized. He knew there was a delicate balance in the art of eye-contact—too much would get you attacked…but so would too little.

They went through the process of providing their names and destination for the first of several times. It gave Josh an uneasy feeling. *Like we're being tracked.* But his experience in Iraq had prepared him for this. He understood exactly why these points existed. He guided his nephew and precious cargo in the form of a doctor through their first checkpoint experience.

As they continued west on Highway 101, he said, "We need to get off-road by two hours before dusk. I want to get at least a full klick off this road to whichever side is the high ground."

"The high ground…" Stu repeated. "Just like in the movies. What is it about the high ground? What makes it so darn special?" Stu was trying to be funny, not fully comprehending Josh's experience with loss in Iraq and the demons he'd fought over it in the years since.

"Words won't do it," he said coldly. "Let's see if you still need to ask that after the first time you're ambushed."

JOHN CRONIN WAS at the main gate, taking his turn on watch and deep in thought. Something had been nagging in the back of his mind for the entire two days since his conversation with Vince and Alex. The idea had warranted enough merit that John solicited some volunteers to escort the pair of men on a mission for parts. The team, four men and two women, had gone with Vince and his grandson back into Redmond, risking exposure to the threats to fulfill two equally important shopping lists. Every mission carried risks at a minimum, and 'travel tolls' were guaranteed.

One half of the mission had been to take Alex to the site of his former employer, which was a multifaceted electronics firm. Alex's department modified circuit cards for aircraft communication and navigation systems for Boeing. They had a large warehouse of the parts and tools needed for a variety of tasks. Getting in had been a challenge, though it was one that the team had been ready for. Vince had grilled his grandson about the facility, and the team brought a variety of abnormal tools with them for forced entry. They wound up using a sledgehammer, a Haligan pry-bar, and a pneumatic driver operated by a scuba tank, to blow through heavy locks and doors. The vacant building's shipping roll-up doors had been forced open by starving people, but the heavier and more secure personnel doors leading into the test bench area had required the specialty tools.

Once inside, Alex had procured several electronic parts, servos, batteries, wire, solder, tools, and the most important pieces—IR sensors. He filled his grandfather's old duffel bag so they would have more than they could ever think they would need.

The other half of the mission had been to a black market that had been set up in Kent, near the largest Amazon warehouse in the region. At almost one million square-feet, it had been ransacked less than two weeks after the disasters, as people were quickly overtaken by a desire to 'get theirs' before everyone else had stolen the good stuff. By this point in the disaster, the place had been stripped clean, and a series of markets had sprung up all over the city. They were looking for Infrared markers—battery operated beacons that were invisible to the human eye but would scream like a spotlight to anyone wearing night-vision devices.

Fortunately, they would seem broken to the vast majority of people who possessed them. On the flip side, who would want a broken flashlight? That would let the savvy know that they're worth something.

To barter for them, they had pre-packaged several zip-lock bags with the apocalypse's favorite currency—.22LR ammo. John had advised them to use that as their fallback plan, first offering a handful of other items they considered spare. Most of the members of Phalanx had been preparing for years. They found spare water filters, stainless water bottles, and expired MREs that people in the group had been holding onto for years for just such a bartering emergency. Disposable lighters were now worth their weight in silver —literally. Preppers who didn't have several dozen packs of dollar-store lighters stored just for bartering were kicking themselves. They also explained the mission to the residents on the south side of the river, who had responded with more bartering donations.

"You've been awfully quiet tonight, boss," said Renee Sherman, one of the two people on front gate duty with him. They were parked in the little wood yard-shed while Erin's daughter, Lacey, took her turn out near the gate, scanning for potential threats with the night-vision binoculars.

"Oh, sorry," John said, knowing he really wasn't. "Thinking about the haul the team came back with today."

"So, what was that all about?" Renee asked. "Everyone seems pretty hush-hush about it."

John turned to look at the young woman. "Well, we have a chance to try and make a…let's just call it a special tool. There's some trouble brewing with the gangs. We may need all the *special tools* we can get."

"Okay," Renee replied, somewhat disheartened she couldn't be trusted with the plan. "I get it."

"Look, kid, don't take it personally. We just need to compartmentalize everything. The more one person knows, the more they can spill if one of the bangers get them."

"Well, did you all get everything you need?"

"Hopefully. Apparently, we need to go raid a hobby store or two next. One thing at a time, I guess."

Renee could tell John was just appeasing her, so she quieted. John went back to thinking about payload delivery. This whole idea had too much complexity, which made the chances of failure high in John's mind. The former cop was a firm believer in the KISS method—keep it simple, stupid—when it came to warding off Murphy. He knew at least four of the Phalanx team members that had managed to procure everything from grenades to construction grade plastic explosives over the years. Making their airborne weapon go boom wasn't his concern—getting it over the cartel intact…that was what worried him.

They had learned on the radio that not only did they shoot down the National Guard helicopters early on in the engagement, they had actually captured one. The cartel owned the skies. Nobody in their right mind would try to fly a small plane near downtown Seattle. *Not that we have an aircraft or pilot anyhow,* John thought. *At least…not a fixed-wing pilot.*

11

Mind Over Matter.

ABOUT FIVE WEEKS AFTER THE DISASTERS, A DYNAMIC IN THE paradigm shifted in the Western cities in America. The years earlier had been strife with polarizing politics, giving rise to organizations on both ends of the political spectrum that had been preparing for all-out conflict. But something unheard of had happened just one federal election cycle prior, when a third-party candidate had taken the presidency by taking the majority of the electoral votes. Things had remained tense, but the rhetoric had ratcheted down just a bit, as had the violence that had been plaguing the cities.

But as the on-going economic, electric, and internet crises continued to take their toll, a power vacuum developed in cities like Denver, San Diego, Sacramento, and Portland. The gangs had already established a firm foothold in Los Angeles and San Francisco many years earlier, but now they were actually impacting almost every city in the West. Taking a cue from the success of the

Mendoza cartel's powerplay, all of the sub-branches that collectively were called MS-13 by the American media had begun to take a more direct control over their cities, one neighborhood at a time. The American president had been too distracted by the increasingly violent skirmish between China and Russia and too trusting that the governors would be able to handle the problems in their states.

Some of the governors and mayors had been trying to stay ahead of the gangs' influence by calling National Guard units and placing their police on overtime. All that did was reactivate the Marx-based organizations that had fought so hard to enact socialist ideologies disguised as a fight for rights and liberty. The protests started and evolved into riots as the police state grew. All the gangs really had to do was sit back and watch, ready to pick up the pieces when the vacuum had taken full hold.

Tahoma's Hammer Plus 36 Days.

"Gene! You doing okay?" Tyler asked his partner, unsure how many hours had passed since the last time they'd spoken. He was guessing it had been two days since they'd even been out in the main shop, getting tortured. He was in immense pain, both from physical damage and from a splitting headache. Sleeping, or more likely just laying still, was the only way to find relief. There was only so long one could lay in the fetal position before even that started to hurt, though.

The guards brought them water and dog food twice per day, allowing them out to use a bucket. *Must be that sadistic leader's way of feeling humanitarian*, Tyler thought. *Or he just doesn't want to step in our waste the next time he tortures us...*

They'd even been given some rags from the shop. Tyler instructed Gene in stuffing those into his armpits and crotch. "Keep the skin warm in places where the blood is close to the surface," he explained.

Gene began to rustle a bit. "Uuugghh...yeah, but I think my balls may be...be..."

The Navy veteran was a computer jockey—he'd never been trained in how to handle this. He started to weep because he couldn't openly admit he thought his testicles would be damaged beyond repair if he survived this. After he got his tears under control, he decided to check on his comrade. "What about you?"

"Stiff...sore...cold. Even if they opened the cage door, I don't think I could move. I j-just can't seem to warm up!" He gave that a moment to sit there, and then asked Gene, "How long you figure we've been holed up down here?"

"Feels like a few days...but I have no way of knowing for certain. My injuries are making it difficult to think about anything else." He thought for a moment longer. "And like you, I don't think I'll be able to run."

The pair went quiet for a good ten minutes, but Tyler wanted to keep Gene talking to keep his mind off his electrocuted nuts. "Gotta ask you a serious question, Gene."

"O-okay," he said weakly.

"Why do born-again Christians target gays so much?"

Gene had been expecting the conversation before they were tortured, but at this point it caught him completely off-guard. "I—I d-don't understand..."

That caught Tyler off-guard. "Whaddya mean you don't understand?" *How can he NOT understand the Christian history of forcing their belief systems on anyone who believes in gay rights...abortion...* "I mean, how can you not see how you changed when you found out Teddy and I are married?!" Gene shuffled around a bit. Tyler could hear him groaning in pain. "What...what are you doing?"

"I'm sitting up. You and I are about to have a serious conversation. I don't care how much pain I'm in. I want to be lucid and understand everything clearly."

"I'm not trying to start a debate, Gene," Tyler said. "I was just hoping that we could be honest with each other after all of this…"

"There is no debate, Tyler. You and I are just two people with our beliefs." He gave a strategic pause. "But the truth doesn't care what you or I believe, it's just the truth."

"Well, that didn't take long," Tyler said in a frustrated tone. "That's exactly my point! You guys always think you're right!"

"So do you!" Gene countered.

The pair were quiet while they each thought about their next points. Tyler finally said, "Look—I'm not going to argue. We need each other, and I think you and I can at least agree on that. But I do want you to know that it became glaringly obvious by how you treated us that you weren't pleased to find out we're gay."

Just then, the door from the shop flew open and a cartel soldier holding a lantern came pounding down the concrete steps with two dog food bowls and a jug of water.

"I am truly sorry if I treated you and Teddy badly," Gene said. "Truly. And I want to pick this back up when we can."

"Hey, Phil!" he heard Horn say as he stepped off the office's front patio. There was a hard November rain pounding from the southwest. He had pulled up the rain hood on his camo coat and was about to climb into the Gator. "I don't know how you managed to do it, but thanks for procuring that special paint. I gave a sample tag a good coat and tested it inside one of the conex boxes with a UV light. Glows like a champ. Once it hardens, I'll see if some clear coat will protect it."

"Ah, good. Finally, something's going right. And good thinking on the clear coat."

Phil wanted to know if this idea would work, but he was in a hurry to get in the gator and go check on two of his other pet projects. Savannah's coloring project had given Phil the idea to paint a secret phrase on the new metal tags that would replace the now-compromised SPP patches. They could spray paint over it and put some sort of phrase or sticker over the spray-paint as a decoy. If a patrol ever doubted the validity of the tag some other Posse group presented, they could scrape the paint off and check with a UV flashlight.

Several years earlier at the annual banquet, Phil had given all thirty range officers a little flashlight with a UV bulb and glow-in-the-dark body as a thank you gift for their hard work that year. While not all of them had made it out to the club after the disaster, he had the surplus—the club had purchased a bulk of fifty.

As Phil turned to climb into the Gator, Horn continued. "Say—what did you want the control word to say?"

Phil finished climbing behind the small scooter's wheel and just stared at Horn. "Uhh…I hadn't even thought about that. Gimme a little bit, and I'll get back to you before you mass produce."

"Right on," Horn acknowledged.

Phil started the Gator and headed for the road that diverges from the main gate and head's up range. He crossed over the range and stopped off by a conex near the southern perimeter. He hopped out and hobbled over to the door and gave it a little rap with his knuckles. He saw a pile of cardboard tubes laying on the ground outside.

"Come in!" he heard through a mostly closed steel door.

Phil entered and saw two dim lanterns providing light to the father and son duo of Theron and Stephan Middenberg. "How'z it goin'?" he asked. The box was strong with the scent of saltpeter and sulfur.

Stephan pointed in the corner. "If the old man would just let me lead, there'd be twice as much by now." He was pointing at a tightly sealed tub of powder from the self-contained fireworks. While the big show quality mortars had proven useful, and probably would again, all the smaller stuff they had procured from the local crime family weren't much use just as a firework. The Middenbergs were disassembling them for parts.

"Maybe you should just have a nice, tall glass of 'kiss my butt'," said the plump father to his lanky son.

Phil laughed. "I think maybe you guys should prop the door open just a bit!"

Though he knew Phil was joking, Theron explained, "Can't. We're already trying to dehumidify in here." He pointed to three of the plastic-bucket, desiccant dehumidifiers that people had provided from their RVs.

"Hmmmm," Phil said. "Yeah, moist potassium nitrate isn't much good, is it? Just thought I'd check on you guys. Just…be careful, okay?"

"Stuff's pretty stable," Theron commented. "We might've made a few 'Dupont spinners' for fishin' over the years." He was smiling sheepishly as he said it.

"Was there anything left to eat?" Phil asked, laughing. "I thought grenade fishing was a joke."

"Yeah," dead-panned Theron. "It's a joke. We'll just go with that."

"Alright, fellas. I'll get out of your hair." He went back to the Gator and took the southern perimeter road to the field up on the hill. Phil parked the Gator next to the Command Post trailer and tent at the south end of the field. *Sloppy, sloppy mud,* he thought looking around at the mess. *Gonna need to get some pallets out here… maybe build a deck.* He remembered the back deck had collapsed on his split-level home just two miles north. *Maybe some of the lumber will be usable.*

"Hey, everyone" he said as he ducked into the walk-in carport style canopy.

The club's lead HAM radio operator, Jerry Horst, was in the middle of teaching a few others the fine art of calculating how long to make an antenna that would be resonant on several of the HF frequencies. They had been using a long pair of wires called a dipole, but now he wanted to use a loop hanging from the trees.

"Howdy, Phil. Everything alright?" Phil only showed up to the CP when there was something specific to discuss.

"How's your local AmRRON net been holding up? You all still passing local intel up and down the peninsula?"

"Three to four times per day, like clockwork. Plus there's still some traffic on the local emergency management nets to monitor. Why?"

"As much as I don't want to, I think we need to get our scouting and salvage patrols going again. Just wanting to get a bead on any security issues you might be hearing about."

"Ohhh," Jerry said. "Just the usual stuff. Murders. More and more people being found dead from starvation or just plain old suicide. There was a big fight at the FEMA camp in Bartlett this morning."

"That's what I was afraid you'd say," Phil said with a dark tone. *I need to tell Charlie to get his family back out here,* he thought. *Enough's enough.*

"So, what's the issue?" Jerry asked.

"Food," Phil mumbled as he opened the zipper flap and exited. "Always food."

He found himself wondering if the rain had driven the team who was working on his special project to the east side of the range to seek shelter. *I should go check on Eli and the guys.* He passed the two, large 'poor-man's' greenhouses made out of PVC pipe and plastic, realizing they were going to need to do something better if they wanted those things to last through winter. *Of course, they'll be working still. That's what these people do—just keep plugging. I can't recall a time I've seen a better example of the American Spirit,* he thought. *It will help us get through winter, and just maybe save our Washington…*

As he got to the mid-field trail that led east to their eastern perimeter, his eyes caught a motion in the exposed garden to the north. There was a small doe, about eighty meters away, grazing on grass. Phil took his slung rifle off his back. He flipped his magnifier in front of his red-dot sight to expand the view several times. *Scrawny.* The temptation to shoot was strong. *Fudge-cycles. She wouldn't even dress out to be sixty pounds, I bet.* Phil didn't want to hunt a deer with a caliber like 5.56 mm anyhow, but when people weren't getting enough food, some things became ethically fuzzy. The doe looked up at Phil, and her nose twitched the air just a bit. He re-slung the battle rifle onto his back and started limping east again, wondering what the next big crisis would wind up being.

12

Tough Choices.

Tahoma's Hammer Plus 29 Days.

The night before had gone somewhat smoothly for Josh, Stu, and Jeff. They had pitched themselves a low-angled and low-height lean-to style tarp that was big enough for two of them at a time. They piled up debris on the low side gap to keep wind and rain from being pushed under. One guarded while the others slept.

If someone had told Josh a month earlier that he would be camping with his nephew and a Jewish plastic surgeon, he'd have slapped them. As it were, the training that he and Phil had rushed Stu through was evident. He had been keenly aware of his muzzle and finger anytime he was handling the rifle that Phil had lent him.

Each of them chowed on a can of tuna for breakfast. They broke camp and hiked back out through the underbrush and low-hanging cedar and fir branches back out to the highway. It started to rain.

As they progressed west, they occasionally moved off to the side of the road to give plenty of clearance to a much larger eastbound group. About once or twice an hour a vehicle would stop by, sometimes with groups of people fleeing to higher hopes, sometimes with groups that resembled a civil patrol of some sort. It was during one of these occasions that Stu ventured too close to the shoulder, slipping down a particularly muddy and steep slope. He slid down the wash for a good twenty feet, slamming into the base of a tree where it leveled out.

It happened so fast, Jeff and Josh couldn't do anything but watch.

"Hoooo-llyyy crrraaapppp!" Stu yelled as he slid. THUD! "Son of a...!" he screamed in pain.

Jeff scrambled down the muddy slope, slipping and landing on his butt once but regaining his traction. The ordeal delayed them only a bit, but Stu was fairly certain he had a good ankle sprain. This had slowed their pace considerably, and by the late afternoon they had only progressed to the intersection of Highway 104 and Center Road. It was only one-third of the roughly forty miles they needed to travel to the Schwartz house.

They came to a junction of that intersection, running into another large checkpoint. There was no line, and they were able to stroll right up to four armed men who were guarding the one vehicle sized gap in an offset row of jersey barriers.

"What's with the limp?" the tallest one asked Stu. He was direct, but not overly aggressive.

Stu looked up into the man's magazine carrier. He then looked up some more. And then some more. Finally, he saw a smiling man in his early to mid-thirties looking down at him from behind a bushy, reddish-brown beard.

"Well, I'd tell ya, but I'd have to kill ya," quipped the short, balding physician, referencing a movie line that had been born about the same time as this giant. Stu's ankle hurt, he was desperate to get to his folks' house, and he was hungry. And there was a natural smart-alec in him that still lurked deep under the reformation he'd gone through over the prior month.

Jeff guffawed and Josh just smirked, wanting to see if the good doctor could back-peddle with a sprained ankle.

The other guards all made a few small sound effects and smirks, as if openly thinking, 'you gonna let this twerp get away with that?' But the young farm-boy showed great poise, to Josh's delight. *I don't really feel like apologizing for Stu with these boys…* Aside from that, he could see a vehicle rolling up from the west, and four new men and women showed up. This had caused no concern to the checkpoint staff, which told Josh it might be a shift-change.

The tall redneck broke out in laughter, which broke the ice for all of them. "I'm pretty sure you can't reach the ejection seat either, little Goose!" he said, causing everyone to laugh, even the ailing Stu.

"Let's just say my two-sizes-too-big hiking boots didn't handle a slippery slope too well," Stu explained. "I'll live."

"You should get that thing elevated," the man explained.

Josh winced, not wanting the doctor to make another smart crack. *It might not go over so well, this time,* he thought.

"I appreciate that, friend," Stu said politely. He pulled his California driver's license out, expecting they would need that. This prompted Jeff and Josh to cough up some IDs, too. One of the other men scanned the names against the list and verified they had passed through the checkpoint near the bridge a day earlier.

"California!" exclaimed the tall one. "What're ya doing up here in the north country?"

"Trying to see if my parents are still alive," Stu said honestly and earnestly, almost wanting to see the man eat some humble pie.

"Awww, dude…well. That's understandable." The other guard handed them all their stuff back.

They were waved through the gate and started limping along past the men, who were now busy trying to conduct a shift change with the new arrivals. The trio continued down along the hilly highway and decided to abandon the day's trek in search of a camping spot so Stu could get his foot up. Josh found what seemed to be a grassy field and led them into it, figuring there would be a game trail on the far side of it. *Might get lucky and find something to shoot for supper...*

They heard a vehicle pull up and stop—it had come from uphill and east, the direction of the last checkpoint. It caught the small team's attention when it stopped on the road where they had just left a minute earlier. They all turned to look.

An old brown Chevy Tahoe with the rear passenger side window down revealed the tall checkpoint guard. "You guys got a hotel for the night?"

Jeff and Stu started the whole *look around at each other* process, but Josh pushed right through them and started making his way to the vehicle. The other two stared at each other for a second before Jeff took off after his uncle. Stu hobbled after them.

"You don't gotta ask me twice," Josh said as he approached the vehicle. He could see all four of them in it, so he headed for the double doors on the back. "I was in the Army. You'd shudder to know some of the places I've slept."

He and the others stuffed themselves into the back of the laden SUV and felt it lurch as the men started driving.

"I figure you guys can crash in my barn for the night," their new friend said. "Name's Chad," he said sticking his hand over the back of the bench to Josh for a shake. "Chad Dutchman. But my friends call me Tiny."

On the trip, the travelers learned that Tiny and his buddies—Jeromy, David, and Brad—all manned the checkpoint in the afternoons. This allowed them to work their homesteads in the morning and evening. They were all neighbors who lived within a few miles of the checkpoint. Within five minutes, Jeromy had pulled the rig over and was dropping Tiny and his new houseguests off at his small farm.

Stu hobbled and limped as he climbed out of the cramped back of the SUV. "I do appreciate this, Chad," he winced in pain. "Are you sure your wife will be okay with this?"

"Really, dude? I tell you my friends call me Tiny, and you still call me by my real name?" Chad was doing his best to act mad.

"Well, then what should we call me?" asked Stu. "Gigantor?"

Tiny laughed, always appreciative when someone could throw a crack right back at him. "Here she comes now. Why don't you ask her yourself?"

A petite, pretty brunette about Chad's age walked out of a chicken house and introduced herself as Shelby. She was holding a toddler and a basket of eggs. "I hope you boys aren't expecting supper!"

"Naw," her husband said, "they weren't promised no supper!" He winked at Stu. "Just a bed in the barn."

Who'd a thought... Josh mused to himself as the bantering continued. They were making their way to the barn to ditch their gear... *that we'd find such compassionate folks this far into the disaster.* He could tell that the Dutchmans weren't fools—just good judges of character. *Maybe there's hope for humanity, yet.*

JENNIFER HAD SPENT the day driving around the outskirts of Port Angeles while her brother and dad scanned for threats. Between the three of them, they had a 1911 pistol, a hunting rifle, and two shotguns choked for bird hunting. Under her father's instruction from the rear seat in the quad cab pickup, she had travelled around to as many of the fishers' houses that her father could think of. They'd started with the ones he knew and liked the best, but by the end of the afternoon, they'd killed the remainder of the old Ford's gas tank visiting several others. Along the way, they'd received a few *you know who you should invite*s from some of them. Most of the people invited had agreed that this was needed and overdue.

"Go ahead, Sweet Pea," her father nudged. "This whole thing was your idea."

Sitting under a collection of canopies and tarps around the Smith's firepit was close to sixty folks. Some of the boat owners' crafts had not survived the wave, but there were a total of fourteen operating vessels of various sizes being represented by the crowd. Most people had come with their fishing crew, who was normally a family member or two. As the day had progressed, the invitees began to include various members of the community who were known for their love of guns and country as well as known military experience. The evening rain had tapered to just an annoying drizzle that drummed lightly on the coverings.

"So, I don't really know how to start, y'all," Jennifer yelled so all could hear. "Least, not with anything different than what we said earlier today. Oh!" A sudden and vicious thought had just occurred to her. "Dang! I think I need to say right up front—if this discussion gets out, my family and I could be in real, actual danger. Please, please, PUH-leeazzeee don't blab about this with people!" She could see heads nodding. "The pirates are real, you all know that. Everyone knows who they are and what they're capable of."

"So, cut to the chase, Jenn," yelled Darby Dodds. "Do you expect us to go in, guns blazing to fight these guys?" This brought with it some murmuring and head nodding.

Grrrr...my name's Jennifer, you donkey. "I don't—"

"I hope not, 'cause look around. We'd look like McHale's Navy!" Darby was screwing with her, and the older men in the crowd were eating it up. Several people started to openly laugh.

Is this because I dated your worthless son, Darby? Jennifer asked herself. "We have things we c—"

"And just how do you—"

"Darby Dodds!" Jennifer screamed, taking back control of her meeting. "Are you and that lazy son of yours going to help? If not, just get the hell out right now!"

This caused several of the women and a few men to cheer, while the men who'd been laughing with Darby all started catcalling, making *she told you* remarks and other demeaning comments.

Darby busted up laughing. "I'm just yankin' yer chain, honey!"

While the crowd was still recoiling a bit, one of the other women stood up. She was the grandmother of Thomas Sults, one of the most well-liked and respected fishers in the Port Angeles fleet. Once enough people saw her standing, they all started quieting down.

"Most of you know my family," she said quietly, but as loud as her little voice could carry. "I was born in 1947." Though not purposefully, the frail woman was turning on the old-lady charm. "I was one of the lucky ones. See...what you don't know is that our family name used to be Schultz." This got a few surprised looks. "I recall the stories my father told me of how he had to flee Germany as a teenager, before they could conscript him into the army." The crowd had grown so quiet that the fire's crackling was competing with the rain on the tarps as the predominant background noise. "As a girl, I was captivated by his stories. As a young woman, I studied history in college. And now...as an old lady...well...I guess I don't really know what to say, except...I'm scared."

There! Jerks! Jennifer thought angrily. *Eat a big-honkin' piece of humble pie!*

The little old lady finished what she wanted to say. "It is only because our family has been canning and raising chickens and rabbits that I'm still alive! I can feel it in my bones! What happens when those men want what's mine?" The guilt-trip had worked—the men were all respectfully quiet. "I'd like to hear what she has to say."

After a few seconds of crackling fire, Jennifer continued. "Thank you, Mrs. Sults." She looked to the crowd. "I have an idea. And, yes, Darby isn't far off. We will be patrolling the Strait. We need some help, though. And this will be dangerous. But we have numbers—for now. We have to stick together! Now...who owns the cool guns?"

The small town of Snoqualmie Pass wasn't really a town, per se. It was a village of small rental homes that served to house employees at the ski lodges and resorts. There was a small gas station, a couple of restaurants, a few boutiques and shops—all serving the guests and employees of the summer and winter tourist industries on *The Pass* on Interstate 90. The only other major facility was a Washington State Department of Transportation unit geared up for plowing the highway and dealing with traffic accidents.

The seasonal employees had already started moving into the rentals and lodges when the disasters had struck. Many had stayed, still stuck in normalcy bias about the state of things. By the time they'd realized how bad it was, the snows had started to clog up the broken highways and steep hiking trails. In all, there was a population of almost four hundred, many of them meeting at the one strip mall of shops and boutiques every night to make a community stew.

Earl and Larry had to abandon the quad not too long after the snow started. Earl decided to park it in a spot that wouldn't be too steep to try to dig it back out, if he had a chance. They hiked the same powerline trail into the small town that Natalie and her unfortunate family had used a few weeks earlier. There were plenty of tracks chewing up the snowpack, and the fresh stuff was light—*maybe two inches per hour,* Earl calculated. For a bit, tracks were still visible—human, horse, off-road vehicle, wagon, and some game like bobcat, bear, and cougar. The lack of deer and elk tracks was obvious to Earl. *I'm regretting never buying snowshoes,* Earl thought as they broke through the gap that could be considered the edge of town.

It was late afternoon, and they gravitated toward the small strip mall with the crowd, keeping hoods up over beanies, trying to remain as *gray* as possible. As they walked past the last pair of rental homes, Earl saw the gas station on the left, figuring it to be the one that Natalie said had practically robbed them of their chickens.

There was a small contingent of men bundled up and standing around a trash barrel fire. *Must be the local gang*, the bearded Ranger thought, unimpressed. He and Larry had opted to keep their rifles slung on their fronts but were trying to keep them pointed down to reduce their threat posture.

"Seems like more and more people are carrying rifles," he mumbled to Larry as they turned right into the strip mall parking lot.

There was a pair of armed guards who cut them off and stopped the men from walking straight to the community stew hub. "Just hold up," one of them said gruffly. "This is for residents and guests. You're neither." He was a bigger man, like Earl, and had the tone of someone not afraid to fight.

"We're stranded up on the pass. My mom is ill…We're just looking to see if someone with a snowplow or horses can come up and give us a hand." *Everyone has or had a mom*, Earl said to himself, hoping.

"You two ain't getting anywhere near that food," the big one rebuked sternly. "And why can't you wanderers ever come up with something new. 'Stuck at the pass,' my butt!"

Earl instinctively tightened the grip on his rifle, which the two men caught.

"Look," said the shorter one, trying to defuse the tension. "Nothing happens without Tank's permission." He pointed at the gas station behind Earl and Larry. Larry had turned back to look, but Earl and the big guard had remained eyes-locked.

"Tank," Earl repeated. "Got it. He must be big, then." Earl caught the bully's grimace as he and Larry turned to head in that direction. When they were about halfway across the slushy road, he stopped Larry and spun him for a quick, whispered conversation. "This Tank is who we're looking for. Sounds like a real Boss Hogg wannabe. The plan is to stay humble, let them run us out of town…"

"What if they follow us?" Larry asked, a little confused about the wisdom of drawing a pack of hunters.

"Oh—they will," Earl clarified. "Not sure of their approach… could be a group…could just be one or two, which is what I'm hoping."

Larry scanned both ways to ensure they were still alone in the street between the two groups. "What'll that get us?"

"The bottom line is that we'll need to get this Tank character alone. To do that, I need to know where he lives…"

Larry understood. "Alright, Earl. I may not have your combat experience, and I may be sixty-five, but I ain't afraid to help you get that little girl back. You lead…I'll follow."

13

Luck o' the Irish.

Tahoma's Hammer Plus 30 Days.

"Geez, this thing is huge!" John exclaimed.

Alex and a small team had rapidly begun to work on the delivery vehicle as soon as all of the custom parts had arrived. They were working practically around the clock. It had started with making the molds and shapes they needed for the fuselage and wing. John's scout party had managed to find everything on the shopping list at three different former hobby stores, all of which had been boarded up, and one of which had been picked almost clean. They had brought back a variety of rigid cardboard, Styrofoam, carbon fiber, epoxy, and a few other pieces.

"Your guys surprised me," said Dexter Armstrong, one of the others working on the model. "They brought back some good stuff.

If the payload isn't too big, we may be able to slap together two models."

"Good to know," John said, eyeballing the custom-shaped Styrofoam wing. "This thing is a good five feet long. Are you sure it's big enough?" He and Vince had stopped into the garage at one of the other Phalanx homes to check on the project.

"That's only half of it," Alex explained. "There'll be two of those we bond together and lay into a custom notch on the fuselage." He and the lead HAM operator, Marshall, were busy soldering electronics and trying to figure out how they were going to mount the IR sensors in the nose of the forming craft.

"So, help an old cop out," John inquired. "Why can't we just fly this thing? Bomb them like on 9/11?"

"Couple of reasons, really," Dexter started.

Vince jumped in. "Radio control range, right?"

"That's part of it," Dexter said as he took the wing out of John's hands and laid it on the left half of the notch on the fuselage. "See it now?" he asked John.

"Certainly. And I'm sure this thing doesn't get a lot of range. I've watched a few model airplanes on YouTube. Seemed like a money-sucking hobby."

"It is," Dexter agreed. "Or…was." His mood turned serious. "I'm not sure what you know about aviation," he continued.

This made John almost laugh out loud. He didn't talk about the paramotor accident that almost ended his life and gave him a permanent back injury. *If you only knew…* And what really bothered him most was how his own son Tucker had taken up the sport when he turned eighteen. After several years he'd gotten used to it, but the fear of losing his son in the same type of accident that had killed his acquaintance was almost too much to bear. The fact that Tucker had become so good at it that he was a full-time instructor before the disasters had made John secretly proud. He was just constantly disappointed in himself that he'd never gone back and mastered his fear of something that, at one time, had offered him so much enjoyment.

"Like my son does now, I used to paramotor. I understand the thrust to weight and gravity issue just a bit."

"Oh, so you get it, then," Dexter said, completely missing any small clue John may have left there. "If you want to add any real volume of explosives to this thing, we have to limit it to just the electronics, servos, and a battery. No fuel or motors. No receiver for taking in control signals. We might be able to get twenty ounces per square foot of wing. That's why it is also thick, not just long. We need to have a wing shape that really provides lift so it'll glide a long way. Which leads me to ask…"

"Where are we launching from?" John guessed.

"That's the million-dollar question…" Vince sighed.

"Exactly," said Dexter. "If you try to smuggle this thing down to a skyscraper, it's going to be difficult to hide—even if you leave it in pieces, which I don't recommend. We're going to need to augment these securing straps with some dowels and glue."

I just knew you were going to say that, John thought pessimistically.

"I'm working on a plan," he said as politely as he could muster. "Could this thing be towed?"

Dexter looked at the others. "Towing? A tow point would have to go right into the nose…"

"That ain't gonna work," Marshall said. "We need all four of these IR sensors up there."

"Well, hold on…" Alex put in. "The dude in the video from India made a smaller model with all four sensors built right into the circuit card. That doesn't mean we have to do it exactly the same." Josh could see the young man's eyes getting a glaze as he was thinking in his head. "They all need to be up front, but putting them in a grid design is really just easier on our minds to comprehend. As long as they're all up front getting signal, the way we have them send data to the control surfaces is all in the programming, right?"

Marshall looked at the plane, but he was seeing math and a computer in his mind's eye. "Yeah, I suppose…."

"It would take a little work to calibrate," Alex continued to Marshall, still talking him into it. "But I think it would be doable." He looked at Dexter. "Yes, I think we could mount these sensors around a tow point and make it work. But you're still faced with the same questions with your tow vehicle."

John gave Vince a nod, telling him it was time to go discuss stuff. *Not really*, he thought somewhat tensely. *There's only one right answer to that question.*

He brought Vince up to speed on his idea as they headed to one of the fighting positions along the river. He knew Tucker was on watch.

"Hey," his son said when his dad and Vince showed up unexpectedly. The two men slid down into the timber reinforced foxhole to get under the limb roof with his son. "What's up?" He could tell by his dad's face it was important, but not life threatening.

"Man, it gets kind of snug in here when two old geezers squeeze themselves in," Vince joked.

"Yup," said Tucker, who still had two more cold hours to sit there. "It does. So, what's up?" he repeated with a slight annoyance.

His dad paused for a minute, hesitating and searching for the right words. Finally, John just blurted it out. "Where's your paramotor?"

"Locked up in the canopy of my truck," his son said. "That thing is my bread and butter." As his love and expertise in the sport grew, so did his cost for having the best gear he could afford. The wing, motor, blade, reserve chute, floatation device, protective gear and other odds and ends represented close to fifteen-thousand dollars in goods. "Why?" he asked suspiciously, eye-balling the two old-timers who wore suspicious looks on their faces.

No. Freaking. Way! I think that's him! Nick Williams was trying to pull the little photo that the man on Fox Island had printed for him that night. *I can't believe this worked!*

He was looking at Stuart Schwartz in the flesh. Or at least he thought he was. He was digging through his right cargo pocket, feeling for the small sandwich baggie. *I'll give it to that little Fox Island group—they were blindly naïve about how close to death they were, but they were organized doing it...*

Nick started to slide a little closer to the gap in the concrete barriers. At that moment he'd been taking a turn scanning the overall crowd, trying to teach this little security checkpoint about monitoring body language and other unspoken cues. He began to eavesdrop on the checkpoint as they processed the doctor. *Now, how to tell this guy I know what he did without scaring him off...* But Nick quickly realized that wasn't his only problem. It became obvious as the doctor passed through the process that he was with one other— nope...looks like two—men. *And even though the one looks like a fresh boot, they don't look weak.* Nick realized that was a good sign after thinking about it. *The doctor's will to live is strong, I'll give him that...* Nick still recalled the blood spray the doctor and his scalpel and bear trap had drawn out of the two bikers.

The trio started to move up the hill on their next leg, and Nick followed. They'd made it about a hundred meters when Nick heard "Williams!"

Don't look back, Nick commanded himself. *You have half an MRE back there. Just leave it.*

"Williams!" Nick heard again. This time it was so loud that he saw the head of the tall guy next to Schwartz cock just a little bit. He also saw the man's lower arms disappear to his front.

"Yo! Nick! Where you headed?"

Nick just kept walking. Another ninety seconds passed.

Suddenly Josh turned around, startling Stuart and Jeff. He had his AR-15 at a low-ready position, ready to flip the safety if he thought he needed to shoulder the rifle. "You got a problem, dude?" he asked with a serious tone.

Nick's hands shot up to near his shoulders. His rifle was on his back. Even though he had a pistol on him, he had no intention of making the men he'd been waiting for nervous. "No. Actually…I'm here to help you solve a problem. Are you Schwartz?" he asked looking directly at Stu as he slowly kept walking to the stopped group. "Doctor Stuart Schwartz? From Los Angeles?"

Josh drew on Nick, flipping the safety off as he shouldered the weapon. "Stop!" he yelled.

Nick stopped immediately. "Whoaaaa…easssyyy…."

"Interlock those cookie grabbers, scumbag! Put 'em on the back of your head!" Josh was all business. He scanned past his quarry and saw that the checkpoint had gone back to business and was completely ignorant of what was happening two hundred meters uphill. "You guys scan around to make sure we're not being ambushed," he commanded Jeff and Stu.

"You're not being ambushed," Nick said as calmly as he could. "Do me a solid and lower that." He could see the wheels spinning behind Josh's eyes. "Please? One Joe to another?"

Josh flipped the safety and very slowly lowered his rifle to a medium-ready position. "That obvious?" he asked un-amusedly.

"You got 11-Bravo written all over you," Nick replied with the kind of respect that only vets understood when one met another.

Josh sighed a bit, and then looked behind him, and around, scanning. "Old habits," he said. He had lowered the rifle back to full rest but kept his hands in their positions on it.

Stu had decided he'd watched the macho guys long enough. "Mind explaining how you know me?" he asked. "And keep in mind that I realize you could've gotten what you told us off that clipboard over there."

"Trust me." Nick said calmly as he lowered his hands. "I've been gambling a lot to find you. And your life depends on hearing what I have to say."

"It's getting too deep!" Jack yelled back to Natalie from about eighty feet ahead. His quad was spinning tires and digging itself down. They had tried laying branches in front of it, hoping that momentum would keep the vehicle on top of the packed ice. The fresh stuff was just falling too fast.

Natalie's heavier, six-wheeled utility rig was sinking too much, too. "I think we need to find somewhere to camp!" she yelled up to him. "Until this blows over!"

Jack waved to signal he heard her. He hopped off the quad and hoisted the big backpack off the back-rack, donning it. He grabbed his shotgun and walked eastward up the trail towards the others. "I really don't feel like going backwards," he told them. "I'm going west to find a good spot to try and throw up some tarps." It was his hope that as they decreased elevation, the snow would be more manageable or even non-existent.

The heavy plastic leaf-bag hanging off the back of Natalie's vehicle flipped open on its right side. Grimacing from his homemade limb-and-poncho gurney, Conner told him, "Nothing extravagant. The snow will be falling off branches in volumes that can hurt. Throw something up between some heavy bushes that aren't directly under branches, if you can find it."

"Makes sense," said the software engineer. "I'll keep my travel down to ten minutes…Figure I'll be back within…forty?" he quizzed Natalie.

"Sounds good." *Not that I have a watch*, she thought as she watched Jack disappear around a small curve in the trail. She looked toward Conner, who was trying to reconfigure the leaf-bag as a snow cover with his good hand. *I bet that shattered bone hurts like a SOB*, she thought. "Stop fussing," she scolded as she tried to do it.

Conner was in too much pain to argue. "Thank you. You should go get out of the wind until he gets back," he suggested from under the plastic, mylar, and blankets. "And drink some water," he suggested, echoing those medics in the Army that used to annoy him so much.

Natalie was still in physical pain from her variety of injuries, and she didn't even dare try to think of her emotional mindset at that moment. Having Conner to look after had been an unfortunate blessing…a needed distraction. "You're in shock. And I told you to quit fussing," she said, with just a small hint of nurse's charm, not flirtatious…more…motherly.

You've done plenty, she thought, almost choking up—the elation of being rescued was perpetually pushing itself to the front of her mind. Conner had ended the old man—the lead demon in her nightmares. And that was something she'd not soon forget.

14

Tough Breaks.

Tahoma's Hammer Plus 30 Days.

"It don't matter what you do!" the tied up man told Earl defiantly. "They're gonna track ya! It's what they do! It's what they been doin' ever since Tank took over!"

"You're awfully mouthy, considering you're hanging over a ravine," Earl said calmly. He was rummaging through the pack of a man he and Larry got the drop on. Just as he predicted—*man, these third-world warlords all think the same, don't they? Even the American ones—* someone had followed them out of the small town. *It's hard to fathom that within a week of the fall of law and order, Conner and I had to kill three criminals, and within a month, a tourist town now has a warlord.*

Only Earl and Larry weren't a caravanning family. They had set up a simple ambush. Earl had been pleasantly surprised to find it was just one man. "Why'd they send just you?" he asked his prey, just an average looking man in his mid to late thirties.

"Not gonna tell you anything else! Just gonna wait 'til they show up!"

"Heh!" Earl said, raising his eyebrows. *They won't get the chance.* He looked at his partner. "You may not want to watch. Why don't you go downhill a bit and keep an eye out?"

Larry nodded without word and disappeared. At first, they'd just tied the man's hands up and made him sit in the snow. As Earl snooped through the tracker's gear, he found a piece of rope and had an idea. After a few minutes, the two had managed to suspend their foe from a fir branch. He was over a small ravine, just a couple of feet out from Earl, where the ground sloped off steeply.

Earl looked down. "Won't kill ya, what with the snow and brush, but daaaannnggg!" He looked up and smiled at the man. "It sure is gonna hurt like the dickens when you break both your legs!" Earl looked again. "On second thought, maybe it *will* kill ya..."

"You sick son-of-a-!" the man screamed. "Let me go!" he howled.

"You're pretty thin," Earl said. "I bet you could stand to be hanging from your arms like that for several minutes." He was being calm and nonchalant about the whole thing. "Whereas that fatty down there guarding the food..."

"Let me down!" the man commanded.

"I need to know where to find Tank," Earl said. "After that... maybe."

"Tank would kill me! No way!"

Earl pulled a knife out of its scabbard on his hip. He looked over the edge as he spoke. "You see...that rope you brought isn't true kern mantle. If it were, I could cut through like half of it and it would still hold you." He looked up at the man. "They design it to keep climbers alive even if it gets worn out on a rock, you see..."

He was calmly instructing the man as if it were a ropes and knots course. "But that cheap crap you got there?" Earl chuckled. "Lemme guess—Lowe's? Home Depot? That's just a three-eighths utility rope." He put the blade to the rope where it angled down to the bottom of the tree.

"Wait!" the man yelled.

Earl stopped. "Go on," he calmly commanded.

"Please!" The man was starting the bartering process all over again.

Earl put the edge back on the rope and pulled it toward him, nicking the outer fabric.

"Alright! Alright! Stop!" the man screamed. "The ski lodge! Not the little one! The fancy one!"

"Who all is there?" Earl demanded. He'd grown tired and had shifted his tone to all serious. He put the edge back on the rope.

The man was huffing and puffing, eyes wide as he watched Earl's knife. "All his gang! Like thirty of us!"

Damn! Earl thought.

"B-but he stays in the private residence behind the lodge!" the man screamed in a panic. "Just him and whatever floozy he takes home that night!"

"Just him?" Earl demanded. "No guards?" Just a small nick with the blade.

"O-one! We take turns! E-everyone just sleeps on the porch when we're on watch!"

"One last question, and you're free," Earl promised. "Who's buying the kids?"

"I don't know, man! I swear! Yes! I seen 'em moving kids! But I got no knowledge of the business, man! I just work to eat and stay alive!"

Earl had no intention of letting this snake go warn anyone. "Thanks," he said calmly as he made good on his promise. He freed the man with the assistance of gravity, giving the rope the final cut it needed to release tension. The man let out a scream as he fell, momentarily disappearing into a steep snow drift, the reappearing as he smashed into the rocks thirty feet below and rolled downhill. Earl watched him bounce off a tree before stopping against another one below that. He wasn't moving. *I'd rather starve than help traffic kids, you piece-o'-dung...*

"I THINK WE SHOULD TRUST HIM," Jeff said. "He probably coulda picked us off while we're over here gabbing."

Not likely, Josh thought. He'd kept a close eye on their new friend, even though they had all let their guard down a bit and followed him to his hideout near the water. The would-be high-school senior had already proven himself to be quite capable in a fight, having been involved in everything thrown at the gun range members thus far, including the early rescue of Savannah. But Josh had always had a fondness for his favorite nephew. He'd not grown nearly as close to Eli's other two kids—twenty-year-old Shay and thirteen-year-old James.

"Alright..." Josh conceded a bit. "If Stu wants to, we'll at least hear him out."

"My curiosity is definitely piqued. I'm strongly considering that he may be telling the truth. I mean, 'your life depends on it' has a somewhat ominous tone," he said, actually chuckling just a bit.

"I guess that's it, then." Josh led his group back up the lawn. Nick had advised that they follow him to the house he was holed up at—there was a fairly well concealed firepit, he explained, and he had rice and beans to share. They kept quiet on the walk up the hill, which pleased everyone just fine. Stu had tried to prod Nick a few times, and he kept putting him off. Neither Nick nor Josh wanted to be distracted while they were walking.

The trio had been standing near the saltwater inlet, Josh keeping his back to it while he watched Nick build the fire in the backyard firepit of what was probably someone's expensive retirement home at one point.

"So, just what—" Stu started to ask but was cut off by Josh, who shot him a look.

"So, the multicam could have been bought online. What unit were you with?"

"Been retired for over five years, now," Nick explained. He figured he might have to swap stories with Josh to earn some trust. "Did a full career, retired Master Sergeant…was a light infantry sniper for most of it. But didn't get to do as much fun stuff as a senior NCO." He scanned Josh's face in the gray afternoon light to gauge his believability. "Retired out of 25th ID," he said, referring to the Infantry Division out of Hawaii. "And you?"

Quid pro quo, huh? Josh thought. *I guess trust is a two-way street.* "I was in for five years, 3rd Cav. Did my tours on both sides of the build-up in '07."

"Mosul…" Nick said, impressed. "I heard that was some tough dirt…I was with 10th Mountain back then. We'd just gotten back from Afghanistan at that point." And like that the two men had broken through ninety percent of their trust issues.

Josh looked at Stu as if to say, *Go ahead. What're you waiting for?*

Stu brushed it off. "Nary a soul in this state, except for my parents and one sailor in Bartlett, would know to be looking for me. This ought to be a good story. Why don't you just tell it, and I'll interject if I have a question." Stu settled into a lawn chair and propped his swollen foot up on the stone firepit.

"I'm hunting a man. No—a predator, really." Nick was watching Stu's reactions closely. "He escaped from a facility for his kind on McNeil Island." This had meant nothing to Stu. "…and landed on Fox Island."

Stu shot up, pulling the swollen ankle and foot back to the ground as he leaned forward. "You have my full attention."

"He discovered his motorcycle club brethren had been killed in a particularly gruesome fashion." Nick looked around. Jeff was thoroughly confused, and Josh's lightbulb was just starting to come on. His head snapped in Stu's direction.

"Go on," Stu tried to say, but his throat had dried up suddenly and the words barely escaped.

Nick was secretly pleased that Dr. Schwartz was rapidly becoming scared shirtless. "He found a business card and…let's call it a 'signed confession'—left by you—and he's been coming after you ever since." Mic drop. The fire popped as a small moisture pocket in a piece of firewood exploded.

The silence grew just a bit awkward, as Josh was wondering just what Stu had done, Jeff was finally catching up, and Stu was wondering if the man before him was actually the predator chasing him. His hands were shaking in his lap, as he contemplated how to get to the rifle he'd leaned against the back of his chair. The .22 Carmen had given him was in his backpack up on the patio. He decided to be blunt. As he stood up, he asked, "Are you him?"

Josh kicked himself for not thinking of that and whipped his head. He and Nick were five feet away from each other. He shifted his weight as he planted his feet after spinning toward Nick. "Well?" he demanded.

"Easy!" Nick said, putting his hands out, fighting the instinct to draw in his own defense. "My retirement ID will tell you who I am! And the perp is a low-life rapist dirtbag named Sticky Wood. He raped a lot of women, including my sister." He left out the part where she killed herself a few years later.

There was a heavy tension that only came to a conclusion when Stu exhaled and began to hyperventilate. He'd forgotten to breathe when the shock that the man might be the killer had hit him. "Whewwww! Alright, alright…At ease, Josh…I believe him."

Josh kept his hand postured to his right hip. "Get out that ID," he said. "Slowly," he reminded Nick.

Nick slowly pulled it out of his front pant-pocket and handed it to Josh. He scrutinized it thoroughly, finally relaxing and handing it back.

"Sorry, Nick. We just can't be too careful."

"I get it," Nick said scanning all three of them. "I've been trying to figure out how to tell you without getting shot for days!"

The men all looked around at each other, slowly chuckling and shaking their heads, wondering how poorly the almost-Mexican standoff could have gone.

Stu had started to put the pieces together. "I'm assuming he found out about my parents?" He was confused. "How…"

"I tracked him to Fox Island the night after you… Anyhow, he tortured the neighbor who had taken you off island." This caused Stu's face to pale as he sat back down in the lawn chair. "Badly, before he finally killed him," Nick added.

"I take it you just couldn't get a shot on him?" Josh asked.

"He's wily. I was tired, I made a mistake. Truthfully…I'm lucky. It was dark. He escaped by boat, and I'm plain lucky to be alive."

"Then what's the plan?" Jeff chimed in. "Is there a way we can help? I mean—he doesn't know about me and Josh."

"Yeah," Nick agreed. "I was pondering that, too, on the walk up the hill just now. I've been waiting for him to come through a checkpoint, but I doubt he will. He's part of the largest meth-cooking gang in the Northwest. Which means connections." He moved around to stretch a little, picking up the pot he'd brought out of the house for the rice and beans. "We have to assume he's up here, and probably already waiting for the Doc to show up."

Great, Josh thought. "Which means we need to take our time and do a good counter surveillance without being seen," he said.

"Exactly," Nick acknowledged.

"But first—Stu…since my nephew's life is on the line, here, I think you owe it to us to tell us just exactly what you did to these bikers."

"I THINK SOMETHING'S OUT THERE!" Natalie said from the mouth of their small, manmade cave. They were bunched up around Conner's stretcher, which was up against a giant, old fallen cedar. The log was almost five feet thick at the root-ball. Cedars were usually more resilient to the Pacific Northwest winds, but even trees that had stood for three hundred years hadn't been impervious to Tahoma's hammer. Jack and Natalie had taken fallen limbs and made a hasty debris hut by leaning them on the log. Conner talked them through the act of fire making with wet tinder, something neither one knew how to do. They had warmed up some rocks in the fire, and Jack had used a gloved hand to spread them around their little shelter.

"Everyone quiet!" Conner hissed, trying to listen. They could hear fresh snow packing every once in a while, but it was very stealthy. Mostly all they heard was the odd quiet of falling snow drowning out the wind.

"I need to check it out," Jack said.

"No...Jack, just sit here a bit," Natalie argued.

"He's right," Conner said. "Sorry, buddy. It's all on you. Remember, don't get tunnel vision." He resisted the urge to throw out a worn-out cliché about swivels.

Jack slipped out of the hut, pulling his shotgun with him. He crouched next to the root ball for a bit, scanning. He then moved around it and out of Natalie's sight.

Conner could see Natalie was about to call out to Jack. "Tssttt," he quietly noised at her.

Did he just shoosh me? she asked herself with a small tad of Karen attitude. He was shaking his head no when she looked at him. Natalie gave him a stern look, but she complied, trusting his security experience. They continued to look at each other, when the quiet suddenly exploded!

"Aaarrggghhhh!"

They heard Jack scream as one round fired out of his shotgun.

Natalie and Conner heard the sound of a life and death fight being drowned out by Jack's screams.

Without hesitation, Natalie grabbed the .357 laying on top of her pack and slipped out of the covering. *I'm gonna kill you, you son of a—*

As Natalie whipped herself around the far side of the fallen root-ball, she expected to find a man—any man—fighting Jack. Instead it was a two-hundred-pound cougar that had his throat in its mouth. It spun on its feet, pulling Jack with him in a powerful stroke. The growling was unmistakable—*you're next*, it was saying to Natalie. The cougar was sensing this new threat as a competitor for its fresh kill.

Until that moment, the most nervous Natalie had ever been was the first time she was allowed to use a scalpel while assisting in surgery. That paled compared to the shakes she had as she tried to cock the revolver. *Damned gloves!* she screamed in her head as the adrenaline coursed through her veins.

The cougar let go of its bleeding and moaning victim, baring its bloody teeth at Natalie. It stepped over Jack and did a semi-charge before stopping in a low crouch. It let out a loud roar. Natalie was trying to strip the gloves off her shaking hands. The two foes were about eight feet apart—well within the leaping range of the hunter.

You've been through so much! Just calm down and make it count! Natalie wasn't sure if it was her own voice or that of God, but her hands stopped trembling. She cocked the revolver, as the very few times she'd ever shot a revolver, that was the only way she'd ever done it. She looked down the barrel and squeezed. BLAM!

The hollow-point impacted the cougar's shoulder and it let out a loud whelp as it hobbled off through the brush. Natalie cocked the gun once more, and the shakes returned. Her senses were on full alert and she heard something behind her. She spun around!

"Me!" Conner screamed, laying at the bottom of the root-ball. "It's me!"

"Dang it, Conner!" she screamed at him, spinning back around.

She held the revolver up as she trudged through the bloody snow and brush to try to get to Jack.

"Jack!" she screamed as she knelt next to him. His eyes were twitching but they weren't looking at her. Over half of his throat was gone, the shotgun lying next to him. The cougar had gotten his carotid arteries—both of them. He had but a few moments left before the lights would go out completely.

15

Crucial Conversations.

Tahoma's Hammer Plus 36 Days.

"Tyler," Gene whispered after the guard had left. "Can we continue our discussion?"

"I suppose, Gene," Tyler said. "But I'm not debating. And I'm not letting you tell me what a sinner I am. I'm in too much pain to deal with it."

"Nothing like that," Gene promised. "We have two different beliefs, and I don't see that being an issue in our predicament…and I'd like to think it wouldn't have to be an issue in the unlikely future if we survived all of this…"

"Let me ask you a point-blank question, then," Tyler said. "What gives straights the right to get married, but not me? I am who I am, Gene. Despite what a man-tainted Bible says."

"Fair enough," Gene mumbled. "Not that it'll help, but I don't think the government should be telling anyone who can or can't get married, straight or otherwise…"

"So, you're for gay marriage?" Tyler asked point blank, knowing the answer was no.

"I'm for letting people live their lives and then deal with the repercussions they've created," Gene said.

"That's dodging the question," Tyler said straightforward. "Answer it, Gene! Try being honest."

"Honesty gets people with my beliefs verbally attacked," Gene countered. "But the answer is no. No, I'm not. But my dodgy answer merely meant that I feel that marriage should be between a straight couple and God—and the ordained minister. But your question perfectly exemplifies a point I wanted to make in bringing this conversation back up."

"What's that?" Tyler said, a little testily.

"I understand—completely—that there are hypocritical Christians. To me, the question should be about sin, not specifically homosexuality. But every Christian, not just the hypocrites, constantly has to defend his or her beliefs on the gay topic. The media, social media, even you guys—everyone assumes they know me and my thoughts without even asking."

"I told you the conversation was done when you called me a sinner," Tyler said.

"Typical," Gene countered. "Why is it your side of the debate always gets to accuse my side of hate but never lets us finish speaking?"

Tyler huffed in exasperation. "Just make your point and be done, already!" He was tired of hearing it and shifted his injured body around in the cramped cage. He had bumped the door with his foot and thought he heard a clunk.

"I'll cut to the chase on all points, then," Gene said. "I think if God loves us and created everything, then He was able to inspire men to write his instruction manual—the Bible—and protect His intent when future men screwed with it. I believe in its definitions of sin…all sin. But I also see so many supposed Christians violating the definition of sin themselves—whether in pre-marital sex or lying or what have you. I see and acknowledge the hypocrisy. And I can't tell you how to feel or what to believe, but like all humans, I have some sinful temptations that are hard to resist. Beyond hard, even. No matter how much I try, I will always fail at controlling them. All I wanted you to know is that I understand and acknowledge all of that. And if I've treated you differently, I'm sorry. This has been a learning experience for me. You may not believe it, but I care for you, particularly after all we've gone through."

While Gene had been trying to summarize his thoughts, Tyler had started feeling the cage door, investigating the source of the noise. "Gene—"

"Anyhow," Gene continued. "I'm hoping you'll—"

"Gene! Shush!"

"—consider my points and trust that I want to be frien—"

"Gene! Quiet!" Tyler finally blurted as loud as he dared. "I'm trying to tell you that my cage's lock is open!"

CARTEL LEADER REYNALDO HERNANDEZ stood at the table at the end of the tent, looking over his teams of operators. He had briefed them on their game plan. They would spend the rest of the evening prepping their equipment, stocking supplies, and loading the two boats. There were sixteen of them going on this assignment—four teams of four men. In the wee hours the next day, the boats would take two teams each and drop them off at various parts of the Slaughter Peninsula. It was on those teams to procure a vehicle and make their way to the west part of the county.

Rey had printed a large satellite photo, complete with an outline of the gun club's property lines. He had reached back to Mexico, where the parent organization had a team of hackers who were able to do a few tasks. They reached into the cloud and pulled up the West Sound Sportmen's Club parcel information from county accounts. They retrieved every bit of data on its members that they could—discovering that the leader, one Phillip Edward Walker, had killed three members of a local drug ring while trying to save a policeman—and lost part of his leg in the process. They had a real-time satellite photo of the large wood structure smack-dab in the middle of the club's rifle line. They could tell where the gardens were and where all the trailers were. They even had the probable fighting positions marked. The cartel had sent all of this to Rey via digital HAM radio.

Reynaldo and his teams worked through a plan, picking primary and backup positions to rendezvous once on the other side of the water. The teams were to remain under the radar, checking in with updates and for new orders at midnight each night. They were to look like they were on a civic patrol, only showing the patches and mentioning the Posse if absolutely necessary. Reynaldo had expected to take up to three days gathering intel.

"Jefe, there are bound to be citizen militias forming over here, and in greater numbers," one of his men asked in concern. "Wouldn't we be better served ensuring our new recruits are battle ready?"

"You are correct in your assessment, Orlando. Our radio operators are keeping a close ear on the airwaves, fixing positions. There are, indeed, a number of them. The important thing to remember about gnats," he said looking at all of them, "is that even when there are a thousand of them, they're still just gnats!" This caused a few courtesy chuckles, but his men respected him too much to pander with butt kissing. "I feel that the air-strike on the arenas has had the desired impact, demoralizing any such cowboy-mentality in the gringos. But—this mission is about just that concern, my friend," he said looking back at Orlando. "This particular group has proven crafty and resourceful, not only winning a stand-off against their own policia, but convincing them to join forces in the process.

This is the core of your mission. Find those with this mindset…and when the moment is right…destroy them loudly and violently."

Tahoma's Hammer Plus 37 Days.

The door to the boiler room slowly pushed open. Tyler realized that being stuck down in the dark space with only his thoughts and Gene had helped his eyes adjust very well. The nighttime light coming in from the high windows had illuminated the dark shop quite well. *I guess the guards decided locking this boiler room door was too much work or not needed.* He decided that the shop must be guard free, but he wasn't about to risk his life on a whim. He slowly pushed the door open just enough to get his head out and listen. After a few more seconds of waiting to get clubbed to death violently, he pushed the door open a few more inches and stepped out.

There were big swinging doors on both sides of the building—the kind that full-sized vehicles could drive through. He walked over to the side on the grain elevator pier side of the building, hearing generators running. Tyler cautiously stooped below the chest high windows in the large swinging doors and slowly slid up for a peek—*something's going on. Lots of commotion loading a couple of boats.* That's when he saw the ship. *Whoa! Where'd that come from?*

Tyler realized that he must be in Seattle or elsewhere on the east side of Puget Sound. The temptation to flee inland was his first impulse…*except, if the cartel controls this pier, then what else do they control? And when they discover I'm gone, what'll happen to Gene?* Despite his philosophical differences with the man, he harbored no ill feelings toward him. *Then they'll canvas the area until they find me…*

Tyler stepped away from the window and knew exactly what he had to do. He slowly crept back toward a workbench, careful not to knock anything over—*this is when the hero kicks something in the movies,* he thought. He knew exactly what he was looking for—a pair of adjustable crescent wrenches. He rummaged through the tools by feel. When he thought he found one, he'd walk closer to the light coming from a window. About three minutes later he'd finally found what he was looking for. Tyler made his way back to the boiler room where he found Gene praying for Tyler's safety.

"Tyler!" Gene said when he realized his partner was back. "What're you doing? We made a pact!"

"I'm getting you out of here," Tyler said as he felt his way to Gene's cage and tossed the blanket off of it. He began to feel for the door and lock.

"No! Tyler! You'll make too much noise busting the lock! Just go! Get help!"

"Give me a minute," Tyler said. "I need to at least try this idea."

"What idea?" Gene insisted.

Tyler explained what he was doing as he did it. "See…I recognized the feel of the standard brass combo lock like we used when I was in the Air Force. I remember learning this trick in SERE training."

He went quiet to concentrate on what he was doing. He opened the jaws on one of the wrenches and placed it through the lock's shank so that it was sort of grabbing the brass body. He did the same thing with the other wrench on the far end of the shank, which placed the curved backs of the two wrenches against each other with the handles at about ninety degrees. He pushed the handles toward each other, which turned the wrenches heads and jaws into a couple of big cams. This applied pressure to the shank, and it popped out of the lock. Both pieces of the now broken lock clattered to the cold, concrete floor.

He slid the galvanized slider of the dog cage's door and opened it.

"Holy cow!" Gene said. He started to crawl out of the cage, but as he stood up a searing pain shot through his groin. "Unngghhh!" he moaned, trying desperately to be quiet.

"Your nuts?" Tyler asked.

"Uh-huh!" Gene grunted his reply. "They're bad, Ty…I mean real bad. I don't know if I can walk!"

"Well, I'd check, but I know how that'd go over in your church," Tyler quipped.

Gene laughed. "Don't, man! It hurts to laugh. What're we gonna do?" Tyler was under Gene's left arm, holding him up.

"Well, they just fed us an hour ago, so we know they won't be back until morning. I saw them loading some boats. The shop is dark—nobody in it. I say we sit tight in the shadows and try to get on one of the boats."

"Why not slip out and off the pier and just disappear?" Gene grimaced.

Tyler was starting to lead him up the stairs. "You can hardly move. If we can stowaway, then we're on the move, they don't know where we went, and you're able to sit still. And we'll be on the west side of the water…maybe…"

Gene blew out a big breath at the top of the stairs. "Okay. You're right. I couldn't even breathe as we walked up here." Tyler did another quick check of the shop and re-opened the door to lead Gene out to it. "And Tyler—I'm really, really glad you came back!"

16

The Mission Must Continue.

TAHOMA'S HAMMER PLUS 31 DAYS.

"LARRY, you know how to operate that AK?" Earl whispered. "Things could get dicey pretty fast."

"I've shot a few of them," Larry acknowledged from behind his tree. They had taken the rifle off of the man that had tried to tail them.

"Alright. Even with my suppressor, we can't afford to lose the element of surprise," Earl said, bringing him up on the game plan. "I'm going in alone. I just need you to cover me and call out 'Fallujah' on the radio if you see anyone comin'."

Larry nodded. "Good luck, Earl. If trouble starts, I'll take out as many as I can," Larry promised. "Just remember I can't see every approach from these woods."

Earl slipped the night vision device down and started creeping through the forest to the back side of the cabin. The thought to pretend to be part of the gang and approach the front had occurred to him, but it seemed too risky. *These guys have a routine, by now,* he told himself. *Been together long enough to know each other's clothes…even the way each other walks.* He knew his activities in the house would bring a certain level of noise—he had no choice but to take out the front guard—silently.

The smell of seasoned fir emanated from the fireplace as he slowly crept around the large fancy cabin behind the ski lodge. Earl stayed in the dark as much as possible. He had to travel halfway down the structure's front to get to the covered porch that was partially recessed by the shape of the building. He paused on the corner and crouched a couple of feet, slowly peaking around the wall. *Sleeping sure enough,* he thought. *Just like dead piece-of-crap said…*

Earl watched the guard for a couple of minutes. He was wrapped up in a quilted blanket, and sitting on a front porch rocker, rifle leaning against the doorframe five feet away. *Time to commit.* He slipped around the corner and onto a shoveled sidewalk. He could feel and hear the sand crunching under his feet. *Shoot!* He opted to speed his walk up, pulling his rifle and sling up momentarily. He ducked his head out from under the sling as he stepped up onto the porch, careful not to catch it on his helmet and NODs. With his rifle free, he shot its butt directly into the sleeping man's chin, hitting 'the button' and knocking him out. Earl pulled two zip ties he'd transferred from his pack to his cargo pockets out and secured the man's hands to the rocker. He used his knife to cut up the blanket, stuffing a piece in the man's mouth and using a long strip around the man's head to hold it in place.

He tried the handle, and the door opened. Earl slipped in and closed the door. He saw the flickering of the fireplace dancing on the walls of the entryway and dining room. The cozy cabin had been set in a mountain décor, with no expense spared. The handrails on the stairs were a highly varnished oak, and there was a chandelier made out of antlers over the dining table. Earl cautiously walked, placing heels down first to keep his rifle's muzzle from bouncing.

As he made his way past the dining and kitchen area, he walked under a six-foot wide archway into the main living area. He raised his NODS—the fireplace was emitting plenty of light. He could see the back of a man sleeping in a large, high-back reading chair, two mostly empty rum bottles on the floor next to him. Earl kept his rifle on the man as he slowly approached from behind and to the man's right.

The large throw rug on the lavish wood floor helped silence his boots for the last dozen feet of travel. Passed out in the chair was a man, easily 6' 4" and about four-hundred pounds. *Tank...*

Earl looked around to ensure they were alone. A bear skin rug complete with head between the reading chair and the fireplace was the nearest company. *I think this room and my suppressor would be soundproof enough.* He pulled a pair of older backup tourniquets out of his left cargo pocket and threw them on the man's lap.

"Wake up!" he yelled, jamming his suppressor into the man's sternum forcefully.

"Uggh! Hey!" the big man yelled, not fully awake, and definitely not sober. He shoved at whatever was touching him, but Earl yanked the muzzle up as he took a pace back. The man started to open his eyes. "What the—"

"Wake up, dick-lips," Earl said calmly.

Tank started to get up despite clearly recognizing the receiving end of a bullet dispenser. "You're gonna—"

WHAM! Earl center-punched him with his barrel, right in the solar plexus. The man's inebriation had made it all too easy, though he was quickly gaining his wits.

"You're a dead man!" he yelled. "Dead!"

"So, I've heard," said Earl. "Put those on," he ordered, casting a quick glance at the tourniquets Tank hadn't even seen yet.

Tank glanced down at his lap and shot his look back up. "What?! No—"

POP! His resistance was futile, as Earl provided the proper reason for Tank to put on a tourniquet by shooting him in his left knee.

"Arrrrgggghhhh!" Tank screamed in agony. His eyes widened, and the face behind the dirty blonde and graying beard started to lose color. He started to hyperventilate.

"I ain't doing it for you," Earl explained.

Tank began to scramble to get the thing over his foot, but his large size made it difficult…almost comical. He finally figured out to take the strap completely out of its buckle and shove it under the wounded limb.

"Yep," Earl instructed. "Now cinch it. That's right. There. Now start turning that windlass until that strap hurts worse than your knee."

Tank was still grunting loudly as he was finishing the process. "Just who the fu—"

"Other one!" Earl yelled over him.

This time Tank didn't hesitate. He started putting the tourniquet on his uninjured right leg. "I don't know you, mister, but you're a fool! You don't save the life of a man who will kill you for shooting him!"

"Ha!" Earl laughed. "I'm not saving your life, you idiot! I'm just making the pain last longer!"

POP! Tank's right knee exploded in fury, and the screaming and writhing in agony process started all over. Once he'd secured the second tourniquet, Earl could see the man's will to resist had been badly damaged. He was sweating profusely and looked like a ghost. His fat legs made it hard for him to get good constriction with the tourniquets. "Wh…what d'ya want, mister?" he asked between pants of breath.

"Blonde girl. Sold to you by some scum up from Wolf Mountain almost two weeks ago. She'd be four. Her name's Katherine. Say it!"

"K-Katherine…" Tank was becoming submissive in a hurry. "L-look, man…"

"Spit it out, Tank! This can go on all night!"

"Th-that's what I'm tryin' to say! She's not here!"

"Bull!" Earl yelled as he bashed one of the wounded knees with the business end of the rifle, causing another yell in pain.

"No! Serious, man! There's a huge market for kids, but not here in Snoqualmie Pass!" He said it as if he couldn't believe he had to explain it.

Earl thought for a moment because the low, tourist-related population probably wouldn't actually have a high demand for trafficked children. His expression revealed his rage, as he yelled at the top of his lungs. "Where? Who?"

"It was Cartel, man! I-I'm sure of it!" Tank pleaded. He knew he was in over his head with Earl.

"Seattle?" Earl demanded.

"Wha—? No, man! They were Russian or Ukrainian or somethin'! They went east!"

"East! You'd better not be lying to me, Tank!" Earl said as he shoved the barrel within six inches of the man's face. He knew better, but he could also tell Tank was bleeding out and in no shape to fight.

"I swear! H-his name was…" Tank was trying to jar through the pain. "Max something!"

"Liar!" Earl yelled, resisting the urge to end it. He had the man talking. "What was a Russian trafficker doing here?!"

"Travelling east, man! Stuck in Seattle after the quake, just like everyone else! He had guns, we had girls. It was an even trade! Dude's name was Volkov, or somethin'…Goes by Pozhar! He's missing his right ear!"

It was all sounding true to Earl. Tortured amateurs didn't make up stories about Russian mafia and think of names on the fly. "How many kids? Where was he taking them?"

"Three men…taking six kids…please mister…"

"Where?" Earl yelled as he pressed the muzzle closer.

"New York…"

Earl screamed in his head, afraid to believe what he was being told, yet somehow it all made sense. He pressed the suppressor into Tank's mouth and squeezed the trigger. He pulled his rifle out of the corpse's face and marched to the front door, not realizing just how much time had gone by. He opened the door, stepped onto the porch and saw an empty rocking chair.

"Fallujah!" he heard Larry scream into his earbud.

"So, what're you thinking?" Josh asked Nick as he stretched.

Nick was stretching and yawning, too. *Probably let my guard down a bit too much, but that sleep felt goooooood,* he thought. *And it is nice having someone to watch my back for a spell.* "For the next few moments, some instant coffee," he said as he got up and knocked on the glass door to call Jeff in from his small watch station in the woods next to the house. He started looking for his boots. Nature was calling. "Let's round up the Doc. Everyone grab a bite and a sip, then we'll figure it out."

While the small team took a few minutes to get the sleep out of their system, Nick took care of coffee and making room for it, then pulled out one of his Sequim maps. About fifteen minutes later, all four of them were sitting in the commandeered living room, staring at it.

"It beats nothing, but I do wish we had a topo right now," Nick said, referring to a topographic map. "It's safe to assume elevation increases with southerly travel, right?" They all nodded, acknowledging the fact that they were travelling east-to-west, situated northeast of the Olympic Mountains. Nick knew he was mostly explaining this to Stu and Jeff. "So, to a sniper high ground is gold. Stu, why don't you start with telling me about where your folks live."

Stuart looked over the map and got his bearing on where the

only highway came into town. He mumbled a few things to himself, as he used his finger to take the exit and head south of the highway. A few lefts and rights, he finally said, "Right about here, I think. Address is 14355."

Nick reached up with a sharpie and dotted it, allowing Stu to pull his finger back. He spent the next half-hour peppering Stu with anything he could remember. What did the house look like? What were the distinguishing features? Cars? Flowerbeds? Deck? Which side is uphill? Where are the closest neighbors? How many? Who are they? What about the next street over? Up? Below? Stu was apologetic and frustrated because he knew so little.

Nick pulled back and looked at the map as a whole. He noticed a forestry service road that headed south about a mile east of Stu's parents' neighborhood. *There...*

"Alright, fellas," he announced. "Here's what I propose. Stu, you and Jeff stay here and keep a low-profile. Josh and I will take my boat a little closer to town and then hike this forestry road. We'll find a trail somewhere to cut west and try to get some eyes on this neighborhood."

"What will that do?" Jeff asked.

"Maybe not much. But if we can get a clear look, I'll be able to see where I would set up an ambush. And more importantly...a counter ambush..."

IT WAS GROWING dark with evening as Natalie tightened the improvised sling and swath holding Conner's arm to his chest. "I told you to stop fidgeting," she scolded. "All you're doing is making your fever worse."

"I gotta admit," Con-Man said, laying down on a set of garbage bags stuffed with maple leaves next to the fire, "I feel like freshly microwaved dog-turd..."

Me too, Natalie thought as she worked on her patient. She had been forced to bury her trauma, focused on getting to her sons. She knew that when she did, the full impact of everything would finally hit her. "At least we made it below the main snowfall today." She was soaked and shivering.

Conner said, "Get under this mylar with me." Natalie looked horrified. "Seriously. If you trust your brother, then you can trust me. Even though these blankets are soaked, the mylar is keeping the heat in." Conner was laying on his good, right shoulder, facing the fire. Natalie picked up the mylar and scooted next to him, pulling the foil blanket and wet layers above it back over herself.

That morning, back at the big cedar, she had announced she was going to bury Jack, but Conner talked her out of it. "Earl'll find him when they come by," he advised. "Neither of us is in the condition to put our remaining energy into that. The shovel is on the quad they took. Ground is frozen. The best we can do is cover him with enough branches that keeps animals from reaching him too easily."

"That seems…so…disrespectful." Natalie started to weep slowly, thinking about how the man had lost his life saving her. *None of them would be here if we'd just stayed home. Roy would be alive. My babies!* She started to cry heavily, sobbing.

"I'm sorry, Natalie. It's the reality of things. We can build a cairn of rocks on this tree. Earl will find it. He'll find Jack. He'll have a look around when he finds the vehicles. I promise."

They covered Jack and broke their camp, and Conner committed to walking. Natalie fashioned a good walking stick for him from a branch. His legs weren't injured, but the stick would still help with balance when trudging downhill along the snow-covered powerline run.

Conner could no longer wear a backpack, so they used cordage to attach his gurney to his hips with a makeshift belt outside his coat. He dragged as much gear behind him as he could manage. Over the course of the day, Conner tried to keep a pace count, though his fever was making him ill and he wasn't very lucid at some moments. He estimated they'd only travelled four or five miles, but they'd decreased elevation by at least a thousand feet, probably more.

They found a pair of fallen trees in which one had crossed another at angle. The little space was roomier, and the branches had made for a decent roof. After they'd gotten a fire going, Natalie collected some water from a nearby stream and helped Conner settle into his spot.

Thinking back to the morning's sorrow about Jack, Natalie said, "You awake?" She was the front spoon facing the fire, trying to not lean too far back into his wounded limb.

"Who could sleep?" Conner joked through the pain.

"I realize I forgot to tell you thanks. I'm sorry…"

Conner could tell she was going to start weeping again. "Did I ever tell you about how I met your brother?"

Is he delirious? He knows we've never met! "Uh—obviously not," Natalie said with just a small hint of sass. "Let me guess," she said as she wiped at the eyes that had started to moisten a moment earlier. "In the Army."

Ignoring her joke, "We went through Ranger school together. I'd only been in for like thirteen months, hadn't even deployed yet. Earl was already an infantry sergeant with combat experience. There's this first phase for like three weeks where they wash out the ones that won't hack the rest of it. I know this may be surprising to you, but I was the class clown…"

"Shocking," she said sarcastically.

"No, it's true," Conner said, missing the tone as he was half-asleep with fever. "That's where he started calling me Con-Man…" Conner was trying his best to finish the story to cheer her up before he passed out from exhaustion. He shook his face. "Anyway, the physical part of it was easy for me. The discipline…not so much…" He paused, thinking.

After a long silence, Natalie said, "And…?"

"Earl took me under his wing. Made me realize that being Han

Solo in a team environment doesn't work. Earning my tab was the best thing I ever did. Aside from my kids, I mean." He paused for a moment. "Next to them, there's nobody on this planet I love more than my best friend."

The fire snapped in the silence. "Where are your kids? I take it they're safe in another state somewhere?" Natalie asked, receiving only light snoring in reply.

17

Skin of Our Teeth.

Tahoma's Hammer Plus 31 Days.

"I'm going out the back!" Earl yelled into the radio as he slammed the heavy wood door. A round went through the door a few inches above Earl's head.

"Got the back covered!" Larry said.

Though Earl couldn't hear it, Larry had already taken out two pursuers with his hunting rifle. It was still the wee hours of the morning and too dark to see much.

Earl ran back through the large living room and karate kicked the glass French doors leading to the impressive wood deck. They splintered the center post out, losing half their glass in the process, as the 6' 2" combat vet knew better than to stop for anything.

He pushed through the pieces of door and ran for the stairs that led from the deck to the snowy yard between the cabin and the woods to the west. He didn't have the time to find the little earbud button to key up his mic. He just sprinted for the woods, flipping his NODs down, which turned the snow into a bright green reflector. He knew about where he'd left Larry.

As soon as he saw his partner take another shot, he yelled, "Larry! Coming from your south, and I ain't stopping!" Larry's muzzle flash had been a huge beacon to the incoming horde—the snow and trees around the two men began to take fire.

"Switch guns!" Earl yelled as he passed Larry. Earl wasn't in the best of shape and they were running uphill in the snow—and now he was towing a sixty-five-year-old man. "There's a small crest for a little dell just up here a bit! We have to make it there!" Earl yelled at Larry as the two tried to sprint in almost eighteen inches of fresh powder.

They could hear probably six to eight people behind them. As Earl reached and jumped over the small crest, he pivoted and dropped to his knees. Larry was huffing and puffing, with about twenty meters to go. Earl saw the beams of flashlights cutting through the dark around the fir trees.

Pop! A shot flew over both their heads, as Larry finally crested and plopped down low next to Earl. "You ever see *Butch and Sundance?*" Larry cracked.

Earl ignored the old man. "Reach into the rear, lowest pocket on the back of my pack," he ordered.

Larry did as ordered and shoved his hand into the pouch. "Is that—?"

"Yes. The round ones, not the cylinders! Grab them!" He was starting to throw bullets down at the group.

"They're going to know where we are!" Larry protested.

"Correction!" Earl yelled as he passed the man, grabbing the two fragmentation grenades from his hands. He started running south below the crest in the dell, where they couldn't be seen. "Where we *were*!"

Larry dragged himself back up to a low squat and tried to keep up. They ran another hundred meters. Earl was looking up. They were in a large grove of trees with heavily laden branches of snow.

"Hand me that AK," he ordered. "Keep running south! Count two hundred paces and find a good hiding spot! Go!"

The old man took off, and Earl let the AK fall in the middle of their tracks, as if someone had dropped it. He then got to one knee and laid the round fragmentation grenade under the rifle.

This is some real 'Red Dawn' magic, here. Let's hope this works…

He set the handle directly under the rifle and slowly pulled the pin, carefully making sure the handle stayed squeezed. Once the grenade started cooking, there was nothing to do but pray. Earl was too old and tired to run at least five meters in the snow in five seconds. He carefully backed away. He could see the lights approaching the crest, so he took off for the south in a sprint to catch Larry.

A few minutes later, he was behind another snowbank with Larry, waiting…hoping to hear an explosion that never came. The pack of men caught up and were slowly spread out along the trail. The snow was too fresh and deep to run in and it gave them away anytime they stopped and made a plan.

"The snow, Larry," Earl whispered. "They know we're here."

Larry squeezed his hunting rifle, kissing it on the stock. "I'm ready, young fella."

Earl popped the pins on the two smoke grenades Larry had dug out on their small respite, throwing one to the east and one to the west. The men could hear them, but the woods, pre-dusk light, and snow made them hard to see.

Earl could tell there was a commotion ten to fifteen meters north of his snowbank, as he heard men arguing about what to do. He yanked the pin out of the second frag grenade and gave it a good toss over the bank. Five seconds later…

KA-BOOM! He heard at least three sets of screams. He and

Larry sat up and looked to acquire targets. He was able to pick out at least two, which he dispatched with several shots.

"Cover me!" he hissed to Larry. He got out and could see bodies through some of the smoke. The screaming helped him home in on the carnage. *He shoots, he scores!* he said to himself, realizing he'd gotten at least four of them with the grenade toss. He heard the report of another dispatched by Larry's hunting rifle. Earl started to walk north again, seeing a wounded man running away.

He began to sprint after the man. *Need to make sure none of these guys makes it back to town.* He started following a blood trail. Earl was most of the way back to the booby trap that had never been sprung when he saw the escapee crawling in the snow.

"You'll never reach it in time," Earl said.

"You!" the man said as he turned and looked at Earl. It was the big one with the attitude who had tried to keep Earl from reaching the stew pot about twelve hours earlier.

"Awww, what the hell—go ahead," Earl egged the man on. He sped up the pace of his crawl toward the rifle, thinking that he and Earl were in some sort of quick draw competition. *All's fair in love and war,* Earl thought. *Although, I always heard that if you fight fair then your tactics suck.*

Just then, the bully reached the AK he thought was his reprieve of safety and spent the last five seconds of his life wondering just who Earl Garren was.

Tahoma's Hammer Plus 32 Days.

The forest service road had shown signs of people using it, with trash strewn everywhere. Nick and Josh had passed more than one burn mark indicating places where people had lit small fires. They were keeping a five meter distance between themselves, Nick leading and on the left side of the road, Josh on the right. The men were carrying their rifles up front, not sure exactly who they would run into. The road crossed over into the next valley after they crested.

"I sure wish we had the right kind of map," Nick said. He had even used the little GPS device on his boat to take a look for some better guidance but to no avail.

"I have a Gazetteer back home in Shelton that would have all this on it," Josh said regrettably.

Nick looked back in surprise. "You're from Shelton? How'd you wind up in Slaughter County?"

"Tagged along with my brother's family to his in-laws." He thought about the accuracy of that. "Well…to his in-law's bugout location…"

"And that's where you came to guard Stu?"

"Pretty much. Stu's a doctor in a world that suddenly found itself two hundred years back in time. And this place we're staying is about sixty percent geriatric." He left off the part about his biggest concern—that Payton was entering month seven of pregnancy. "Knowing his folks are probably…" He stopped scanning long enough to look at Nick, who was looking back at him. "…you know. We figured he'd need a place to stay when he figured it out, so Jeff and I are here to bring him back safe and sound."

Interesting, Nick thought as he turned his head back to scanning. He stopped and stared west at a small path. "Let's try this game trail. Hand me that machete, will ya?"

Josh took the blade off the side of the man's pack and handed it to him. The pair started west on a game trail. There were still occasional pieces of trash. *Everyone has hunted this land to extinction*, Nick thought. *Jerks can't even pack their trash out.* They ducked under branches and stepped over logs, only using the machete where the trail grew over with huckleberry and salal.

"So, this location…" Nick said about fifteen minutes later. Josh looked puzzled. "Where you're staying…"

"Ohhh. It's a gun club. The main guy is an ex-Marine."

"Don't let him hear you say it like that!" Nick kidded.

"Yeah, yeah. I wouldn't much care, except—" Josh stopped short.

Nick stopped and turned out of curiosity. "What?"

Josh started smirking, sheepishly. "Nawww. Never mind." He looked forward, trying to get Nick moving again.

"What? Is the dude you're daddy or something?" He studied Josh's smirk.

"Would you get moving, already?" Josh insisted.

"A girl," Nick concluded. He turned and started hiking. "There's a girl. Lemme guess—he's her daddy?"

"Dude, shut up!" Josh said as they continued to hike west. "How on Earth could you tell that by looking at my face?"

Nick started laughing more than he wanted to on a patrol. But he did miss the camaraderie of giving another soldier a hard time. "Easily," he said. "Gettin' laid is about the only reason an 11-Bravo would care what a Marine thinks!" They both had a good laugh.

"It's not just the girl," he admitted. "This place has become family. We've already gone through a world of crap. I...I feel fortunate to have met these people. And—we're starting to protect the community...patrols and such. Formed up a posse endorsed by the sheriff." Josh didn't feel like telling the whole story. "What about you?" he asked, changing the topic. "What are you doing after the hunt is over?"

"Well," Nick said as they were about to crest the hill, "turns out I have a lady friend, too. Not too far from here, actually." It had just dawned on him that he'd done nearly a full circle since the beginning. He held up an upright hand, telling Josh that party time was over. They slowly crested the trail at the top of the hill and stopped. Nothing but a valley and another hill. Nick pulled the map out as Josh caught up to him. "See that creek on the map?"

Josh knew that creeks on maps were always in the valleys. "Probably just past that next hilltop, then."

Counting a small break, the pair spent three more hours crossing over the next peak and finding a clearing below the crest.

Nick doffed his pack and opened it, pulling out a hard, plastic watertight case. He retrieved a mil-spec M-151 spotting scope. It would provide forty-times magnification.

Josh gave a low whistle. "Man, I bet that cost a pretty penny!"

Nick just looked with a slight grin but didn't say anything. He left it in the case while he took an all-black tripod off the side of his pack. He set his poncho on the ground and started adjusting the tripod, which would enable him to stay seated. After he'd assembled the whole unit, he started scanning the roads below him. He pulled the map out of his coat pocket and referenced it a few times. He finally looked at Josh.

"You might as well get comfortable. Just keep an ear out for trouble. I think I know which one is Stu's house—and I see exactly where I would be surveilling it from."

18

New Alliances.

THERE WAS ONLY SO MUCH PRESIDENT JEREMIAH ALLEN COULD DO. The United States Military was making every possible move it could to the American West Coast. Not only was part of the Atlantic Fleet being pushed through the Panama Canal to change homeports to San Diego and Pearl Harbor, the American President had worked out an emergency revision to the protection agreement with Japan —the aircraft carrier U.S.S. Halsey was destined to pick up her airwings in California and change homeports to Yokosuka. The Washington State Naval Shipyard was trying desperately to have her seaworthy after narrowly getting the vessel out of a destroyed drydock without flooding the ship. The president had been promised that the ship would be on the way to San Diego within a week.

Across train tracks and highways in the southern half of the US, Army and Marine units were in transit, leaving a bare-bones force on the East Coast. The president had been forced to activate the Eastern states' National Guard and Reserve units, as the Western states' units were tied up with riot control. In the gulf city of Pascagoula, Mississippi, decommissioned naval ships—particularly those meant to haul aircraft, tanks, and troops—were being put through emergency overhauls. The Navy had been trying for many years to correct an error of too much force reduction from the 1990s, but there just hadn't been time. The ships were being made habitable and provided with new electronics for their Combat Information Centers. The engine rooms and other systems were just too time-consuming to upgrade in a state of national emergency. Another world war had been brewing for close to two decades, and the release of Tahoma's hammer had been the kettle's call.

TAHOMA'S HAMMER Plus 37 Days.

"How ya doin', James?" Phil asked his radio operator.

James Bryant, though only thirteen years old, had trained and learned enough from Jerry that he was now standing Command Post duty as a lead operator. Jerry had personally grilled the young man enough to know that had they still been in a time of law, young James would be able to pass the technician's test and operate without walking on other people's signals. That was good enough for him. After watching Jerry for a few weeks, he was finally able to give Jerry a chance to go move around a bit. He'd been mentored in all facets of running the Command Post—keeping the log, marking activities on the map, and taking reports from the salvage and intel patrols.

"Pretty good, Mr. Walker."

This made Phil grin. "James, I've told you to call me Phil."

"I know, but my dad says to call you Mr. Walker. I don't wanna get in trouble."

"Ahh," Phil understood. "Jerry must have a lot of faith in you to leave the CP."

"I guess. This stuff is fun—at least, when I actually understand what they're saying. The HAMs use lots of letters and numbers as code to keep things short. That's why we have these posters," he said, pointing around.

"Gotcha…well, good job, young man. I never had the interest to learn all this…kind of wish I had, now…"

"It's not too late, Mr. W!"

If only that were true, Phil thought. *Just too stinkin' busy all the time.* "I suppose not. Now, did Jerry remind you to text me on the mesh network if anything urgent comes up?"

"Yes sir. Say, I've been meaning to ask you—any idea when my brother and uncle will be back?" The teen showed a bit of concern on his face.

"Sorry, bud…no. But they know how to take care of themselves. I wouldn't sweat it until there's a real reason to." Phil put on a confident face, but inside he was growing a bit concerned, too. "You have anything to report?"

"There is traffic from the north end that I put on this message form here. I was going to let Jerry look at all of this when he got back…"

"No, no…it's alright, James. I don't need to be called for every detail. There's an art to sensing when something is unique or urgent. It's the kind of sense you get when you turn into an old fart like me or Jerry."

Phil scanned the traffic log while James laughed. *Interesting…a civil navy of sorts up in the Strait, keeping the piracy at bay. Unknown number of boats…estimates as high as twenty…maybe more…* "James, is there a way to get ahold of these boats if we need to?"

"I'm not sure…sorry…"

"Relax, my friend. Just do me a favor and ask Jerry when he gets back on duty. Okay? Now…the real reason I'm here is to have you make a contact for me. You up to that?"

"Yeah! I mean yes, sir!"

"At the next scheduled time, I need you to arrange a meet up of Posse leaders. Tell them…" Phil picked up the current roster of code words that had been pre-arranged to give location, time, and priority. "…Sandpiper. Tell them Sandpiper. Ya got that?" James was jotting it in the logbook.

"Yes sir!"

"Thank you, son. Keep up the good work," he said as he exited the canopy. *Son…* And like that Phil once again thought of Crane, though each time he was just a tad less sad. *I miss you, boy…*

He walked back down the hill. The rain wasn't horrible, though he did miss the days of pulling up a weather radar on his phone. He stopped in his tent to get off the prosthetic when his phone buzzed. He checked the mesh-text and saw that he had an unexpected but welcome guest up at the office.

Phil kept on the fake leg for a bit longer and wandered up the path to find Charlie and his family in the small trailer. "Hey!" he said as he gave Mel a hug and high-fived Charlie's kids.

"Will work for lodging!" Melinda Reeves said a little nervously. Though initially resistant to move out to the gun range earlier, once at the range she didn't want to leave. It was only after her husband and Phil had a temporary falling out that she and the kids had braved the FEMA camp in Bartlett.

"You know you don't have to beg, Melinda," Phil said as endearingly as possible. He could see her eyes tearing up, though she was trying not to cry in front of her kids. "Why don't you all go set up your gear? I think your old camping spot is still open," Phil told her and the kids. "Deputy Dog will be along in a couple of minutes." They watched Melinda drag her kids out to Charlie's patrol rig to grab their stuff.

Charlie went first. "I…I guess—"

"Save it, brother. Buried hatchets, as your heritage goes, and all that. Is it getting bad down there?"

"I don't know what we're going to do, man!" Charlie was in a place where he could vent and speak freely. "The sheriff and Adam mean well, but there's just too many people. The good news is that any Guard and police left are staying for good. The bad news is that it's like watching a reality show—people always sneaking off for sidebar conversations, backstabbing… The way everything is crumbling is like watching a grape turn into a raisin at a hundred miles-per-hour."

"Yes, I even get a sense of that out here," Phil admitted quietly. "There's always going to be people who push their own agenda, no matter how upright they seem on the surface…"

Charlie decided to change the subject. "Got anything else brewing? Anything to report, I mean?"

"Nothing you guys don't already know."

Phil led Charlie back out of the office. He watched his friend help his family start retrieving their stuff and headed back for his tent. When he got there, he ditched his pants and prosthetic to try and grab a nap before manning a fighting position for watch that night. *This cartel thing…I don't know if I'll ever actually sleep until we figure this crap out once and for all…*

TAHOMA'S HAMMER Plus 38 Days.

LATE THE EVENING BEFORE, Tyler and Gene watched the cartel finish loading their stuff onto the two boats. Several trucks of men disappeared through the rubble of train cars and broken pieces of road, made drivable by American construction workers and heavy equipment operators who didn't feel like watching their families die painful and slow deaths. There were but two cartel soldiers guarding the pier.

"We're going to have to find a moment of opportunity," Tyler said. "Surely those two won't stay planted in one spot all night."

"What if they come in here?" Gene asked, concerned.

"That's what this is for." Tyler was holding a four-foot long piece of pipe he'd found in the shop. "The other thing we need to remember is that there's probably crew on that ship. Anyone could come out for a cigarette at the exact wrong moment."

Their opportunity finally came when one guard went onto the ship—*probably to poop*, Gene thought—and the other roved slowly down to the end of the pier. They snuck out as quickly as Gene could travel, and under the cover of night snuck right back onto the boat that had brought them there. All of the miscellaneous life preservers had been shoved into the front of the hold to make room for boxes and bags of equipment and supplies.

"This is comms gear, I'm sure of it," Gene said as the two painfully pushed their way past it to bury themselves in stinky old Mae West style floatation devices and fishing buoys.

"Maybe some of it," Tyler said. "How can you be so sure?"

"Those NSN numbers. It's military, American. I was in information security when I was in the Navy. Learned a few things about the gear."

"Huh," Tyler grunted. "From the looks of things, these guys are operators," he said as he peeked into a zipped gear bag. He looked at Gene. "We need to be as quiet as church mice when they get to wherever they're going!"

Less than three hours later, the soldiers had returned and departed on a pre-dawn trip northwest across Puget Sound. An hour later some of the cargo disappeared from the hold and some of the men departed. The small vessel headed south for thirty minutes before stopping again. The process repeated itself.

"Dang!" Gene scream-whispered at Tyler as the now empty vessel fired back up to leave—presumably east. "Some of them didn't leave!"

"I know! We need to run up and just fly off the back of this boat as fast as we can."

"No!" Gene was terrified. "I can't move that fast!"

"We got no choice, Gene. We're dead men if we go back to

Seattle on this boat!" Gene didn't say anything, but Tyler had the impression he was going to freeze up from fear. "Look! We have to go! Push through the pain. I'll head up the stairs first. Every second counts! We're getting farther away from shore!"

With that, Tyler led the way—he wasn't going to stay, and he knew leaving was the only way to spur Gene into moving. He pushed his way out of the fishing gear and life preservers and headed aft. He stood aside from the stairs when he got to them and could hear Gene trying to move through the mess, too. When he sensed his partner behind him, he moved up the ladder and cautiously tried to sneak a look. He waved Gene up.

As low as he could whisper, he cupped Gene's ear and said, "The aft deck is clear. You make a break for it, and I'll stop and shove anyone who comes after us into the water."

Gene's teeth were shaking as he looked at Tyler. "G-good luck!" And with that, Gene started running up and aft as fast as his tortured body and fiery balls would let him.

Tyler had no intention of stopping. He lied through his teeth to get Gene the confidence he needed. He got right on Gene's back and started shoving him in the middle of it as hard as he could. The two men jumped off the stern of the vessel and plummeted four feet into the water. Razors of icy pain shot through Gene's broken body as the men hit the fifty-four-degree water. Gene made a bubbling sound as he screamed while submerged. He started to shoot his way up and Tyler grabbed him and held him down, half expecting to see Hollywood style bullet trails coming after them. Gene started to panic and eight seconds later broke free of Tyler's grasp, shooting through the surface. Tyler followed.

"What the Hell?" Gene yelled through coughs, while Tyler was shushing him to be quiet. He spun around to get his bearings.

"We need to swim that way." He pointed. There was a broken piling and pier farther north along the shore from where the cartel soldiers were still handling their gear. "Quietly!" he whispered.

There was a medium density rain that helped mask the sound of their strokes, which gave Tyler the confidence to try regular swimming versus dog paddling. He knew they only had moments before their bodies would freeze up and they'd drown. The two made their way past the pilings, grabbing onto the broken pier deck. They were surrounded by sunken boats, and the shore less than two hundred feet away was littered with trash and pieces of boat above the tideline.

"C'mon, Gene! We can rest when we get there!" Tyler urged.

The two battered, frozen men slowly made it to land and pulled themselves up onto the gravelly bank. *Th-tha-than-thankk-y-youuu, L-Lo-Lor-Lorddd,* Gene thought. He was so cold even his mind was shivering.

TYLER CAME to in the back of a truck bed. An old canopy was keeping the rain off him and Gene. It smelled of fish and bait, though there wasn't any in there at that moment. Gene was curled up next to him, covered in what looked like a horse blanket. He looked at his own, naked lap and realized he had one, too. He scanned around and could see the back of a man's legs.

Odd…this truck is surging and driving slower than my grandma… He decided it must be a weird dream. There was an old milk jug sitting between them, about half full of sloshing water. He took a long pull on the jug and laid back down, falling back asleep instantly.

A while later, he woke with a start as he heard voices. *The cartel!* He shot up and hit his head on the truck canopy, instantly crashing back down next to Gene. "Oowwwww!"

"Don't do that," he heard a grandfatherly voice calmly say.

Tyler repeated the cry, as it were just one more in a long list of pains he had accumulated. He looked down to see two men of Native American heritage staring at him.

"Whatchu got there, Floyd?" he heard the taller one say. He couldn't see his face.

"A couple of naked white boys…"

"Yeah, I can see that. I mean, what're two naked white boys doing in your trailer?"

"Yes, but that's not what you asked," the older one said as he and the other walked out of sight around toward the front.

"H-He—" Tyler's voice cracked as he tried to call out. He slowly sat up and stooped his head. After taking another drink of the lukewarm water, he called out, "Heeellloooo?" He could hear multiple muffled voices approaching, getting louder as they spoke.

"…sounds like one of your white boys is up." Just then the men returned with two more.

"Hey, there!" the oldest one said.

"H-Hey…" Tyler said. "I guess I'm not dreaming, then."

"Heh—no…no… Let me help," the old man said, reaching in.

Tyler leaned forward and took the old, leathery hand, trying to keep the horse blanket in front of him. It was still wet and cold outside. As he slid out onto the open tail gate, one of the younger ones, probably an older teen, was there to offer a full blanket, which he did without saying anything. Tyler took it as he was reaching for the gravelly ground with his feet.

"Thank you," he said to the young man, who was already walking back around the truck bed. "Wh-where am I?" he asked the old man who was looking at him inquisitively.

The middle age taller one said, "Where do you want to be?" in as mysterious of a voice as he could. He started laughing loudly, drawing a rebuking look from the other.

"Must you always do that?" the shorter, older one scolded.

"Ha ha! You act like we get naked white boys here all the time! Can't a guy have a little fun?"

The older one looked at Tyler. "I'm Floyd," he said sticking his hand out to shake Tyler's. "You're at my place. I found you washed up on the shore."

Tyler looked around and saw split-wood fencing all over. *Must be a small horse ranch…* "Please tell me this is Slaughter County," he said hopefully.

"It is," Floyd said. "You're on the Suquamish Reservation. Got any idea how you wound up on our shore?" He watched as the two younger males and a newly arrived female showed up to pull Gene from the bed.

Tyler stepped out of the way. "Oh, hey—please be careful. He's hurt. We both are…"

"Looks like you boys been beat up pretty good," the taller one said.

Tyler finally took Floyd's hand. "Sorry. I'm Tyler." He then addressed the other. "We were captured by the drug cartel and taken to Seattle." *The cartel!* he suddenly realized. *They're here! I need to get word to Phil!* His face showed the sudden surge of urgency.

"What is it?" Floyd asked.

"The cartel!" Tyler explained. "They're here!"

The taller one started to interject. "Drug dealers ain't nothing new."

"Quiet, Henry!" He looked at Tyler. "Please forgive my brother. He's been kicked by one too many horses. Please continue."

Tyler didn't know why, but he found Floyd's voice soothing… reassuring. "These aren't the local dealers. The Mexican cartel has taken over Seattle." He expected to see shocked looks, but both men just patiently waited for him to finish, their only emotion being one of calmness. Tyler continued. "We were tortured." He watched Floyd's family put Gene on a backboard and carry him off. "We were lucky and escaped. But—they're here. They're planning some sort of attack. I need to get to Bartlett and report what I know!"

"Easy does it, Tyler," Floyd said. "You should probably warm up and get some rest, first."

The old man turned and started to lead Tyler up a path toward a double-wide manufactured home. It was older but in decent shape. It looked as if it had some repairs made to it as a result of earthquake damage.

As they passed the trailer, Tyler could see the truck bed was actually not attached to a truck at all. It was a converted trailer being towed by a horse, which the young man who had brought him a blanket was now detaching from the trailer. Tyler followed Floyd into his home, trailed by Henry. He stepped inside and felt the warmth of a fireplace. *Oh, man! Does that feel good!*

"Have a seat, Tyler," Henry said as Floyd turned up a hallway. "Keep that blanket tight. I don't want your dirty butt on my couch!" Henry started laughing loudly again.

Tyler plopped down and realized there was a danger of falling asleep again. *NO! You need to get going!*

Floyd returned with a child of maybe ten years old holding a bowl of soup. She gave it to Tyler.

"Oh, wow! Thank you so much!" Tyler said graciously. The girl left and Floyd and Henry sat down in easy chairs.

"I think we can scrounge up some clothes for you. I'm sending my grandson to go fetch one of our tribal medics. Your friend's grapefruits aren't looking too ripe," Floyd said matter-of-factly.

"They used a welding machine to do that," Tyler explained. *And I know I'm selfish, but I'm so glad it wasn't me,* he said to himself.

"And I'm betting you had all your teeth before this started," Henry said, this time not making any jokes.

Tyler nodded and looked quickly down at his soup, stirring it. "You're correct, I should stay and heal. But I can't. I would be in your debt for some clothes and a ride to Bartlett. And if you can look after Gene until I can get back."

"As you know, there is no hospital. Your friend will be my honored guest as he heals, unless we can get him some better care somehow," Floyd explained. "And we will help you get to the far side of the rez, on the way to Peterson. I'm sorry, but that's the best I can do."

"Yeah," Henry said with a smirk. "We don't go off the reservation anymore!"

19

Not All news is Good.

Tahoma's Hammer Plus 32 Days.

John felt the butterflies in his stomach as he watched his son swooping around, doing rollovers and sharp banking turns and dives. The weather had broken enough for him to come do his first flight in over five weeks. They needed it to not be raining. Water droplets on a wing could cause it to collapse. *If God doesn't give us some good weather when we need to use this thing, it was all for nothing,* John realized. He watched the square, parachute type wing over his son stayed filled with cells of air and reacted to his every command, applied through two pair of control cables and brakes and one electric throttle.

They had slid over the ten miles to a large mountain that had been frequented by paramotorists and their non-motorized cousins, parasailers, before the hammer fell. There were two security teams keeping watch and perimeter guard. Seeing a paramotor this long into the strange, new world was sure to bring some spectators. The idea of word about these tests getting to the cartel was foremost in John's mind. The group had been hard-pressed to convince him to let them come out this time. *Things better work, that's all I have to say about it...*

John was watching as Alex and Dexter busied themselves in prepping the craft. They had made a tow line out of a double strand of 550-paracord and had attached it to a hula hoop that Tucker could try to hook with his arm as he did a low-elevation fly-by. Typically when he flew just a few feet off the ground he tried to maintain a good portion of his power, which maxed out at over forty-five miles per hour. Flying low was the most fun and most challenging aspect of the sport—pilots needed time and space to climb if they came up on a tree or powerlines unexpectedly. Tucker was keeping his momentum at about twenty-five mph, which was enough to keep from stalling and landing.

To provide a small, shock-absorbing factor, the paracord line had been tied with a few alpine butterfly-loops and the cord had been run back and forth through them a few times. It had been secured with a large volume of wraps, similar to a noose. The intent was for the paracord tow line to grow in length as Tucker's initial grab had pulled on it, absorbing the sudden shock and slowly transferring the energy to the glider.

The glider had everything except the actual explosive, which was going to be in the form of a construction grade mixture of TXT and RDX. It was waterproof and stable, but also required the use of another explosive to set it off. The electrically-fire blasting cap wouldn't do it by itself. A common component in the construction and mining industry—ASA—was the small explosive triggered by the squib that would then explode the main charge. The small team had simulated the warhead by adding eight one-pound cornhole bags to the craft.

Tucker swooped down and pulled into a level flight barely four feet above the open sloping field. He lined up on Alex, who was holding the hoop out, ready to run aside before their glider caught him. About five hundred meters down the field, just before the next tree-line, Marshall had set up a weighted cardboard box covered in foil. He had traversed most of the way back towards the main group and was pointing a combat rifle with a civilian version of an IR laser pointer at the target. He and his target were off-line with Tucker's flight path by at least forty-five degrees.

Tucker used his right hand—his non-throttle side—to reach out and grab the hula hoop. He cocked his arm to hold it tight knowing the weight of the glider would try dragging his shoulder back. He hit the throttle to begin an ascent as quickly as possible. Trying to get as much of his speed back as possible before the clunky, fifty-pound anchor behind him caused him to crash.

The paracord shock absorber began to grow and stretch as the wraps around it tightened around the pulley system they'd made out of knots started to tighten. The lumbering craft rolled on its two wheels, slowly at first, and gaining speed quickly. The extra wide and thick wing had such good loft, that the craft picked up speed quickly and began to float just ten feet down the field. It quickly gained altitude, following Tucker like an eagle chasing a baby seagull. Tucker could see the long paracord towline was at least three times longer than the forty or so feet in altitude he and the glider had, so he banked slowly left and kept climbing to loop back around.

"T-bird!" John said into the radio, knowing Tucker would be able to hear him in his headset and helmet. "That wasn't the plan!"

"The glider needs more altitude," John heard back. "I also think I need to cut this hula hoop from the line and hold onto it. This whole cord thing is going to fall like a rock before the glider can get to where it's going!"

John knew there was nothing he could do—it was all in Tucker's control. He scanned the perimeter, once again checking for threats.

Tucker finished his loop. He and the glider trailing him were at least two-hundred feet above ground level. As he said he would, about the time he passed the group he cut the hula hoop free and let it fall. The glider, which had been seeking the IR beam from Marshall's rifle the whole time was now free to do what it wanted—no longer under the command of Tucker's powered wing. It made a couple of small adjustments as the four sensors did exactly as predicted, turning the craft towards Marshall. It flew right over him, dragging the paracord from its nose, and appeared to be headed for the foil covered box, but it landed about forty meters shy of getting to it.

John waited for the glider team to go check their craft and watched his son swoop low once more, pulling on his brakes as he came in for a smooth landing. He stopped his short landing trot and turned to grab his lines so he could control the descent of his wing.

"Looked like it was guiding itself that way," John said as he walked up to his son.

"It's the paracord. I'm certain of it," Tucker responded. "That whole shock absorber idea worked, but it uses way too much cord. And it made it hard to pull that thing. I was fighting drag because it was trying to turn the whole time. And since we're discussing holes in the plan," he said as most of the rest of the team was pulling in closer, "who's going to sneak in there and use the laser pointer?"

John had been dreading this question. *Man up. This is your son you're talking about.* "I am."

"Dad! No. You can't sneak in anywhere. Your back hurts just walking around the neighborhood."

"I won't be walking, son. You're not the only paramotor pilot here."

Tahoma's Hammer Plus 33 Days.

. . .

"How CAN you be sure this plan will work?" Stu asked Nick, his nervousness oozing out of his words.

"I can't, Doc. Nothing's guaranteed," Nick admitted. "Except that this guy won't stop until you're dead, and this is the one time we'll know exactly where he is."

Ten hours earlier, Nick had positively identified a sniper's roost on the back deck of the house above the Schwartz's. While tempting to take the 923-meter shot, the winds were too unpredictable. *I will not waste this opportunity on an ego-booster,* he thought. He studied the propped-up cover on the deck for quite some time, finally seeing a set of legs scoot backwards through the sliding glass door and disappear into the house. *Gotcha!*

Having already scanned and mapped every visible inch of the neighborhood, he and Josh packed up and beat feet back to his boat. They'd finally made it back to their hideout. It was pre-dawn and they were briefing Stu and Jeff on their findings.

"But how can you be sure he'll squirt up that trail?" Stu protested. They were all staring at Josh's hand-drawn map of the kill-zone, complete with yardages between structures. "And how do you even know how long these distances are?"

"The spotting scope has a range-finder and can mark off degrees of movement in the level-plane," he explained. "After that it's just a matter of doing some circular trigonometry with a calculator using the point we were planted as the center." *Most people never truly know just how much training we get,* Nick reminded himself.

"Alright, professor," Stu said with a tinge of sarcasm. "I'm still the worm on the hook, here!" He got up from around the coffee table and started pacing. "Hopefully you can understand that."

"Got it," Nick said seriously. "Would you rather die later? Slowly and painfully? 'Cause I can stop helping…."

Stu stopped in front of the picture window and looked east at Discovery Bay. He let out a big sigh. "Sorry. I've already learned, once…the hard way…to trust my partners." He turned back around and tried to muster a little humility. "So how does this play out?"

Nick looked at Josh. "You're the back seat."

"What? No! You're the sniper! Why wouldn't you—"

"The angle," Nick cut him off. "We'll be shooting up through the deck. It'll be a lucky shot, at best, that gets him from there. Make that first one count, but after that, pour on the fire. Make him run for dear life!"

"How are you so sure he'll run?" Jeff asked earnestly.

"He's an opportunist. I've studied this guy for years. He grew up rough. Running when you're outnumbered is Lesson 101 in the school of street survival. I'd be surprised it if takes him longer than a minute to squirt out of that house. Which leads to the next point." He looked back at Josh. "The second you need to change mags, both cars need to burn rubber up to the next street. That's how we'll push him up the hill."

"What if he doesn't go?" Josh asked, concerned about the possibility that they'd lose him.

"If he bolts down the hill or the street, I'll just take his head off his shoulders."

"What about vehicles?" Stu asked.

"In that big fancy garage right through that door over there." He looked at Stu. "Ever spun the tires on a Charger before?"

"Natalie!" Earl yelled from a few hundred meters back on the trail. He and Larry had taken flight for the rest of the night and well into the next day, only stopping to rest when they were sure they weren't being hounded by any stragglers from the ski lodge. They had made good time but lost some of it when they investigated the incident near the stuck vehicles. Earl had considered getting a good fire going to thaw the ground enough for a burial. *Nope,* Earl concluded. *A big fire would attract them if they're following us.* Ultimately, Earl's 'leave no man behind' mentality forced him to make another improvised stretcher. They wrapped Jack up in a mylar blanket and began to drag him home. *Ranger up.* It irked Earl that they had now abandoned three perfectly good vehicles, knowing they may never see them again. *But that's a small price for saving my sister...*

He and Larry trudged on, with Earl doing the dragging the majority of the time. Conner and Natalie's injuries were keeping their progress slow. Earl estimated they were maybe one more full day away from reaching North Bend when he spotted them up ahead. "I don't feel like getting shot, do you?" he asked Larry.

"Not particularly," the old hunter replied. The two began to yell and wave their rifles, eventually getting their counterparts' attention.

Natalie came running back up the trail. Earl could see hope on her face all the way up. He dropped the poles and tried to cut her off and hold her. When she was but a few feet from him, she finally realized it was Jack on the makeshift stretcher, not her daughter. She let out a scream that rivaled the wounded cougar's when the realization that Earl had failed to find Katherine fully hit her.

20

"Perhaps because I'll never be one, humans are interesting to me."
—Jeff Lindsay, <u>Darkly Dreaming Dexter</u>

Tahoma's Hammer Plus 33 Days.

The lower wood guardrail of the deck Sticky was laying on exploded into a hundred pieces of wooden shrapnel, as splinters showered the cover he had laying over his head and part of his rifle. But it wasn't just the one shot from that first, sudden muzzle flash. It happened again, this time coming up through the deck about two inches to his left.

"Balls!" he screamed out loud.

Crawling backward as fast and low as he could. His legs cleared the threshold of the open sliding glass floor. He was a good four feet away from the rifle before he realized that in his zeal for preserving life and limb, he'd failed to grab the stock and drag it back with him.

The area all around it—and indeed the rifle itself—was being peppered with copper-jacketed lead.

Screw that! he thought, as he shook the temptation to fetch the hunting rifle.

He had no idea who was in the two vehicles, but he knew they knew right where he was, and he had to change that—fast! He pushed up off the floor and started to run for the front door when it suddenly occurred to him he was being stalked. *What if they're already out front? Hell!*

Sticky ran down the hall toward the home's bedroom area. He didn't even care about finding any of his things—escape was his only instinct. He pulled back the closed custom blinds on a bedroom window that looked out the far side of the house. Seeing nothing but lawn and shrubbery, he ripped the blinds off the window, throwing them out of the way entirely, and slid the window open. He didn't even kick off the screen, choosing to punch and push his way through it. He leaned his body on the window's sill and squirmed the four or so feet to the ground, using his arms to break his fall into a roll.

In a split second, he pushed himself against the home's wall, trying to become one with it as he scanned in all directions hastily. *How'd they know I was there?! Who are they? Is it the Army boy who's been after me?*

Sticky low-crawled to the front corner of the house. *Dammit!* He'd forgotten how much lawn this property had. Most of the homes here were spread out from each other a bit and had what used to be custom landscaping and manicured lawns. He knew he had to move. He'd heard that when ambushed, the best option was to just keep moving. He started to slowly creep, stooping as best as he could, toward the street. He could hear tires squealing as at least one of the vehicles was tearing up the hill on a main road, looking for this street to continue its hunt. Sticky saw what appeared to be a community trail in the woods just across from the property he was on. *There!* He started to sprint.

Just as he made it to the trail's head, he heard the red Challenger round the nearest curve, followed by the gold Expedition a mere two seconds later. He kept sprinting up the trail, gaining altitude as he did. He heard the vehicles stop and idle at the house he'd just abandoned, but he didn't stop. *Dammit!* he screamed in his head for the hundredth time in the last two minutes. He could see the hill flatten out just a bit farther up, with a distinctive cedar and its roots on the right side of the trail. *I'll stop for a breather behind that tree!*

He got to the top and stepped behind the tree, turning. He slowly leaned back out just enough to look down the trail. *I don't think they're following me!* He sat there trying to catch his breath, looking just to be sure for another minute. He turned just in time to see the shape of a man in green. There was a rifle butt coming straight at his head. Wham! The light went out.

STICKY'S HEAD THROBBED. The pulsating pain in his forehead was almost unbearable. He jolted with a start as he came to, and it took a few seconds for him to orient himself. A man in camouflage stood not four feet away. Sticky squinted his eyes, but he couldn't make out specifics. His head hurt too much.

"What the—?" Sticky screamed through the headache. "You got no idea how bad you've screwed up, man!" Nick said nothing, and the pounding headache was blurring Sticky's vision, but he squinted until he figured it out. "It *is* you…! I knew it! How's yer sister?"

Nick remained silent for another moment or two before speaking. "I thought about just ending it for you," he said. "But it didn't seem right, somehow…"

He walked closer to Sticky, a combat-style fixed-blade knife in his hand. Nick was thumping it softly against his right thigh, slowly…rhythmically… He squatted directly in front of Sticky, who was tied to the big cedar, hands bound and in his own lap. Sticky's feet had been bound together and tied to a tree farther up the trail to keep them outstretched. He flicked Sticky's boot with the big knife, causing a nervous shudder to jolt through the wounded predator's body.

"You better back off!" Sticky squealed. "You better let me go, Army boy! If you know what's good for you!"

Nick said nothing, but he stood and moved to Sticky's left, checking on the status of an IV bag hanging off the big cedar's trunk by a wrap of wax-coated bank-line. Sticky hadn't even noticed it yet. The IV was dripping into a line that was attached to his left arm. When he realized there was an IV in his arm, the anger suddenly became confusion with a tint of fear laced in.

"Listen! We can deal! I got connect—"

"Listen to you, Christopher," Nick said calmly. "You just went through like three stages of grief in the last thirty seconds. You know this is it, and there's not a single thing you can do about it."

Sticky started to plead. "C'mon! I'm sure we can come to an understanding!" He was craning his neck each time Nick walked around, checking the ropes and IV. That's when he noticed three other men off to the side, just staring at him. "Hey! Listen!" he screamed at them. "I got no beef with you! Just help me out! I got connections!"

Dr. Stuart Schwartz walked over to a shaking Sticky Wood and bent down to get near his face. "I only wish you could've heard how they screamed like little girls as they bled to death, you lowly piece-of-crap," he said sternly but calmly. With that, he walked back down the trail, not wanting to waste anymore of his life on the Risen Dead Motorcycle Club. Jeff followed after him.

Nick looked at Josh, who showed no emotion other than providing over-watch for his fellow combat vet. Nick squatted in front of Sticky. He nodded in the direction Stu had walked off. "The doc, there, is the one who came up with this. Though he thought it'd be fitting to just poke you in an artery…not exactly what is about to happen... See…you're getting it so much easier than you gave any of your victims—including my sister." He looked off in thought for a second, collecting the words to finish the deed. "Aren't you curious what's in the IV, Christopher?"

"It's not too late, man," Sticky pled. "We can both walk awa—"

"Aspirin and Coumadin," Nick said, as if Sticky hadn't even been speaking. "Anti-coagulants we found. Common in older people's homes," he explained, almost lecturing Sticky. "In normal life, we would've used Heparin. But…" Nick picked up a cut-up t-shirt on the ground and stuffed it into Sticky's mouth, having to hold his sweaty head from shaking as he did. Sticky was writhing harshly. Josh came over with a roll of duct tape and put several wraps around Sticky's head while Nick controlled the animal. After the gag had been successfully installed, Josh stood back up and retook his overwatch position ten feet away.

Nick began to slice Sticky's pant legs up the front. Sticky was still writhing as best as his bindings would allow, terror in his eyes as Nick cut the man's shirt off. "Ever hear of death by a thousand cuts, Christopher?" Nick asked as he used the big, sharp knife to create a hard, deep incision up Sticky's left thigh.

"MMMRRRRMMMPPHHHHH!" Sticky screamed through the rag with intense fear.

"Sorry, Chris…" Nick said as he added several crosscuts to the same thigh with lighter pressure. Blood was quickly covering the man's leg. "Couldn't quite make that out."

Nick continued the process on Sticky's legs, stomach, chest, and arms. Sticky's screams started to die down behind the gag. Nick thought he could see the skin getting pale behind all the blood.

Sticky's breathing became more labored as his body began to ramp up the other vital signs in an attempt to make up for the dropping blood pressure. The human body could only leak so much and for so long before it had no choice but to shunt blood from limbs to vital organs. But the blood thinners were winning, keeping the vital clotting-function from happening in the several dozen cuts and slices. Nick had wanted to leave nothing to chance, slicing heavily into fat and muscle layers.

In his last moments, Christopher "Sticky" Wood's eyes displayed the same fear he'd become addicted to seeing in his own victims. Once Sticky's eyes closed and head drooped for what appeared to be the final time, Nick cut the bindings on the wrists, allowing him easier access to the man's arteries near the inside of his biceps. He gave both of those a good puncture with his knife, just to eliminate the chance of some sort of miracle healing.

With no words spoken, Nick and Josh headed back down the trail, listening to the sickening gurgle of a wounded, dying monster. Nick wasn't sure that ending this psychopath would bring him peace, but it did bring him closure, and on that day—it was enough.

Tahoma's Hammer Plus 36 Days.

Natalie was sitting next to the sleeping Conner, looking him over. His fever and infection had finally broken, thanks to the antibiotics Earl had vacuum sealed a few years earlier. He had purchased some pet medications without a prescription, taking care to purchase them from a reputable dealer, as he knew the filler materials would be much riskier from some of the cheaper, foreign websites.

There was a retired doctor who lived in North Bend. He had come down and performed an emergency surgery on Conner's shoulder. He removed pieces of clavicle that were never going to heal in place and excised some dead tissue. The wound had been open a long time, so he installed a drain that Natalie kept clean. He mentioned that Conner's shoulder would probably form in what was known as a malunion—not life threatening, but his shoulder would droop for the rest of his life.

She dabbed the sweat from his forehead with a damp washcloth. Conner had been staying on a cot in the same room as all four teenagers. In the two days since they'd been home and resting, Earl had noticed his sister had understandably been hawking over her sons. She had been prone to bouts of crying, nearly approaching hysteria when she tried to sleep. The rare times she would actually fall asleep, she would wake up screaming Katherine's name.

Earl waited quietly for her to finish what she was doing. He could tell she was stalling. "Nat," he finally said. "There's something I have to ask you."

She looked up, knowing full well what he wanted. She placed the washcloth back in its bowl and approached Earl with moist eyes. "Let's go outside," she suggested.

As they walked through the cabin, she found her sons pressure canning apples with their Aunt Tori and cousins. They passed through, grabbing their raincoats and walking out onto the covered porch to watch the river.

I do love the sound of that roaring water, Earl thought, dreading the question he had to ask. *Peaceful.* "Look, I know you're under a lot of stress," he started.

"Mom and Dad…" Natalie said, cutting him off with a statement more than a question. She started to cry, which was very easy to do.

Earl just nodded, already knowing. He looked out at the roaring river, running hard with rain and snowfall. He pulled his rain hood down as he'd just gotten very warm. "How?" he asked, looking back at her.

Natalie broke down, and her big brother came over and held her. She started bawling in the big man's chest. She finally composed herself a little. "Mom died on the day. A big pile up out on the highway. She—she—"

"It's alright," Earl said. "Whatever it is…it's alright, Nat." The hardened man had tears welling up despite finally confirming his suspicion that his mother was dead. "When the boys showed up, they couldn't talk about it. I guess…I guess I knew already." He let the river's noise take over for a couple of short minutes. "And Dad?"

"He wasn't doing good, Bubby." Natalie started crying again, though with a little less sorrow. "He wanted to stay. I tried to…"

Earl pulled on her shoulders softly so they were looking at each other again. "Let me guess—he was being hard-headed…"

Natalie busted up laughing at the inside joke, as it was the known, family blemish that Earl and their father both shared the same stubborn determination. He pulled his sister back in for a hug. "I'm sorry I wasn't there to help," he said, staring at the rushing, mountain river once more.

"Hey, Earl," John Cronin said from Earl's front door. "Glad to see you guys made it back. How's Conner doing?"

"Let me grab my coat," Earl said. "I need to go move a bit anyhow." Within a couple of minutes, the two men were strolling west along Earl's side of the North Fork. "Conner will heal, but he's gonna be laid up awhile. He took an AK round through the shoulder. Lucky, really…Stupid lucky."

"Man," John said slowly. "I heard you got your sister back. I hope she finds some healing…"

"We'll see," Earl admitted. "I went to go find her daughter, but…" He clammed up, not really wanting to get angry again.

"I was a cop, Earl," John said. "You don't have to tell me what kind of sick people roam the world." *There's only one reason someone would've taken your niece. I wish you could've found 'em,* John thought. Even cops knew there was a time justice just needed to be served.

Earl scanned the low mountain to his south, thinking once again about security. "Yeah, I sure coulda used some snowshoes. But, hey!" he suddenly remembered. "If you hadn't given me those firecrackers, Larry and I wouldn't have made it back."

"No kiddin'?" John said.

"Serious as a heart attack," Earl said flatly. "Word to the wise. If any of you need to head east, be ready for warlords. I took out a couple, but…well…nature hates a vacuum, as they say."

"Uh, yeah—that's kind of what I needed to talk to you about."

John was trying to play it cool. "And we could really use Conner, too, dad gummit…"

Earl stopped, forcing John to stop and face him. "What's going on, John?"

"Something you're much better trained to handle than I am. One of the other highly organized groups is trying to gather anyone with training for a big meeting tomorrow. It's about this cartel thing."

Earl nodded and started walking again. He was trying to make it back to John's side of the bridge—he knew there'd be coffee in that little guard shack. "Kinda what I figured it was about."

"We heard on the radio that they had a fancy drone attack. Pretty much wiped out what was left of law and order in Seattle. Place is turning into a real zoo."

"More than it already was?" Earl quipped. "Didn't think that was possible."

The two leaders passed the south side gate and made their way north along the bridge. John stopped so as to not make Earl walk even farther back to his own cabin.

"Don't stop now!" Earl ordered. "We're almost to the coffee!"

John busted up laughing. A few minutes later they were in the north side guards' break shack, staring at some papers. "Here's the nitty-gritty. Phalanx is but one part of a network. We've been building ourselves for years. There are groups like ours all over the tri-county area. My only regret is that we never networked with the militias in West Sound or the Southwest corner of the state."

Neither man brought up that the coastal region had been completely wiped out by the tsunami.

"How are you all laying out the battle plans without the cartel learning about it?" Earl asked.

"Digital HF," John said. "Or more specifically, a completely random set of digital HF frequencies that we picked years ago using a random number generator app." Earl made a snoring sound effect, which caused John to chuckle. "To put it simply," John continued, "we plugged in several types of digital equipment and multiple bands to use them on, along with a number of times per day. Four years ago, someone built a program to pick primary through tertiary modes and frequencies for every day, at randomly assigned times, four times per day, for the next twenty years."

"To put it simply," Earl mocked. "What's wrong with plain old encryption?" he wondered aloud.

John chuckled. "Ha! You career Army guys have the funniest senses of humor! As if we can get that!"

"Oh. Alright. So—years ago, you guys made a brainy commo plan. Now what?"

"There's a big meet tomorrow. I want you to be over here at 0745. We and a few others will be listening in at our HAM shack. If there's a plan to go fight these guys, my feeling is that we'll be linking up with the south end units somewhere near Renton."

Earl let out a big exasperated sigh. "Man, am I getting sick and tired of war! I just wish this ordeal was over!" It was a lot to process after the week he'd just had. He stood up, feeling his pockets for a can of chew he hadn't had in weeks. "Dang it!"

"So…that's a yes, then?" John said with a twinge of humor.

21

Plans.

TAHOMA'S HAMMER PLUS 37 DAYS.

"I THINK I can muster about twenty," Earl said the next morning. It went without saying that most of the volunteers weren't the spring chickens of any modern army. "We'll put the guards down to just the front gate and a roving patrol. Everyone on the road knows to be armed and extra-vigilant while we're away. This includes a few older teens, like my own daughter," Earl told John seriously.

"Same as us, Sarge," John replied. "We all got skin in this game."

John couldn't believe he was also looking at Conner. He'd insisted on coming, feeling a bit better. It took Earl impressing upon Natalie that all they were doing was going for a simple walk before she'd let him go.

"Shouldn't you still be in the sack?" John asked him. "You look like the one-armed man that killed Dr. Kimble's wife!" He was referring to the empty sleeve that resulted from Conner keeping his wounded, left arm slung to his body under his coat.

The joke went over both Conner and Earl's head. Larry gave it a quick chuckle. "You must be an ol' turd like me, John. I don't think those boys remember that show!"

Earl had also brought Larry with him, knowing the man's experience as a long-range game hunter might translate into a good sniping role.

The four men strolled east on the northside road to a point where it split into a Y. They took the left fork and walked about four homes and properties up, stopping at a small chicken and goat farm that had been built on a small flat on the hillside. Earl could see three different antennas mounted to the house and outbuildings. Some were just a pole, and some had little rods sticking out at the bottom.

John caught him staring as they headed up the short, gravel driveway. "Look up," he suggested.

Several wire antennas crisscrossed the property in different locations, running different cardinal directions. Earl even caught a big satellite dish in the back, pointed southerly toward the sky. He could hear the deep whine of a generator running behind the home.

"When does this guy have time for goats and chickens?" Earl sniped with a chuckle.

"His wife does all that!" John laughed. They made it to the front door, and John gave two quick knocks as he opened it to let himself in. "Barb?" he called out.

As he pushed himself through the door, Barbara Oakley was walking up. "They're all already in there," she said.

Small introductions and greetings were exchanged in the entry as John slowly led his guests up the hall and into what used to be the home's master bedroom. "Your guys' radio shack is in this dude's master bedroom?"

"Uh-huh," John replied. "It seems a bit weird, but they're older, kids live elsewhere and all that. They just use a smaller room for themselves."

As they entered, Earl just about crapped himself. A large oak dining table with two leaves extending its length was surrounded by a dozen, tightly packed chairs, some wood and some folding. The far wall had a workbench that ran the entire length of it. The bench and the shelving above it were covered in radios, meters, oscilloscopes, wires, and power supplies—electronic gizmos of all types. Not one, but two computers were powered up, each with two screens showing spreadsheets and technical data.

"Is that a map?" Earl asked jealously. He was looking at a map of east King County with their little river fork on the right and the Renton area on the left. He could see small electronic dots placed on the map by a computer program.

"Yep," John whispered. "Those are patriot unit locations. They're using APRS to transmit where they're at to us in real time."

Three or four small conversations were going on simultaneously, creating a small buzz. Maps and photos were on every available piece of wall. Conner leaned in and mumbled, "I always figured Darth Vader's sex dungeon looked somethin' like this."

Larry chuckled and Earl shot his buddy a stern look. *I guess you're feeling better, huh?* he transmitted to Conner without words.

"Gents," Marshall said aloud, breaking into everyone's talking. "Why don't you all get seated."

Everyone scooted toward the table. People were shedding coats, as that many heaters in a room warmed it quickly. Earl figured the gear was probably cranking out heat, too. There was a general buzz coming from that side, as several pieces had their small, internal fans working. A different radio operator with a headset on was turning knobs and clacking on a keyboard, trying to pick up the signal for the chat.

As everyone settled in, Marshall said, "While Tina gets us into the meeting, why don't you introduce the guests," he suggested to John.

John took a few minutes to introduce the men and what they'd just learned on their trip, not wanting to waste a chance to once again remind everyone of the reality of what the world beyond their valley had become.

They were interrupted when the woman at the bench leaned over to Marshall and said, "We're ready." She flipped a switch and suddenly radio chatter could be heard coming out of four speakers around the room in crystal-clear digital. *Surround sound,* Earl thought, laughing to himself. *We're using cheap Baofengs that China could probably kill with the flip of a switch, and they have surround sound...*

Earl heard several electronic voices calling in. "...Issaquah East, checking in." Then a new voice, "Issaquah West, checking in." The process repeated itself. Maple Valley, Mirrormont, on and on.... *Obviously alphabetized,* Earl thought. The speakers went dead as Tina keyed into a microphone, "North Bend, checking in."

John leaned close to Earl and whispered, "And this is just around here—our sector. The section leaders met earlier and are now disseminating information down. Later today we'll be relaying our statuses back up—committed numbers, whether or not we're low on ammo and food, known obstacles we have to travel around or avoid, stuff like that."

Earl, Conner, and Larry sat quietly for thirty minutes, listening to the initial battle plans being presented. *Sounds like they have retired infantry coordinating this. Maybe we won't all die in Seattle, after all.* Hope, which was a tree that could either grow or wither in the pit of one's stomach, had planted itself in Earl's gut that morning—though still just a sliver.

After the radio had grown silent again, Marshall passed the floor to John. "Thoughts, security lead?"

"Well, the special project we've been working on is ready to go. But you need to make sure they know—" he emphasized, stabbing a pointer finger at the radio beyond Tina— "that it won't work if there's any rain." He turned to his guest. "Earl and Conner are Army combat vets. I think they'd be able to provide some thoughts on what we heard."

Though not prepared to speak, the experienced NCO in Earl had been cast into this role many times. He stood up. "It's not rocket science. Lake Washington is a giant topographical obstacle that we all have to get around. In conventional warfare, you don't attack an entrenched enemy with anything less than three times their estimated strength. Your leaders estimated the cartel is at ten thousand. Which sounds like a SWAG to me."

A few murmurs broke out amongst the others. "A what?" one of them asked.

"A scientific wild-ass guess," Marshall explained, cutting Earl off.

"Exactly," Earl said. "That's supposed to be the invaders and the local gangs they absorbed."

"And broke out of the Monroe prison," John added, looking up for a moment before staring at the table again.

"That, too…" Earl said. "The bottom line is that we all have to link up with the South Sounders and move north. Everyone else needs to link-up up there and move south," he said, pointing at the north end of the map. "While it's good to hit them from two sides, it's also going to make commanding and controlling our operations more difficult. How will we resupply? How will we treat our wounded? Have our planners been working on all that?" He looked at John next to him.

"They have, though…admittedly without actual hospital care. We know we're going to have some Civil War type casualty rates." More murmurs. "We can always use more volunteers with medical training."

Natalie, Earl thought sadly. *Hasn't my poor sister been through enough?* "My honest assessment, folks, is that this cartel just may win. Maybe we can scrounge up the numbers to beat them. But they're much more battle hardened than we are. They have artillery, armed drones, even a helicopter. We have snowplows mounted to pickup trucks. We have no wildcard factors, unless we can get a break in this rain and use our aerial attack." He thought he was done and started to sit, but then suddenly shot back up. "And…they know exactly what two routes we'll be coming up and down to get to them."

"Two routes…" Marshall mumbled a little too loudly, deep in thought.

"Huh?" a couple of the others asked.

"What if we could attack them from a third direction?" he asked, looking at Earl and Conner.

JEFF WAS RIDING on the front of Nick's boat, calling for obstacles that may still be clogging what used to be the pristine waters of Hood Canal. Stu was digging through an under-seat storage compartment looking for a spotlight.

A thought had occurred to Josh. "We're going to be coming up on the submarine base very quickly."

"So?" Nick asked.

"So, an entire regiment of Marines showed up there by ship and helicopter like two or three weeks back. You know, to start extracting important things—as in *national security*."

Nick figured out what Josh was hinting at. "You think they'd stop us?"

"Wouldn't you?" Josh countered.

"Good point," Nick admitted. "What do you propose? Find somewhere here to land?"

"That depends," Josh replied. "Have you made up your mind what you want to do?"

Several days earlier, the four men put an end to Sticky Wood and then put Doctor Stuart Schwartz's parents to rest. They gave Stu a day to grieve and recover before making their way to Nick's boat, where they abandoned the vehicles. That was the first time

Josh asked Nick if he was heading to his nearby bootie call's ranch. Nick gave the trio a ride back to the house that they'd holed up in. He'd been tempted to just give them the boat and start hoofing south, but he knew he'd have to pass by the checkpoint he abandoned. Deep inside, he knew that wasn't an issue. The real issue was purpose. For the first time in his life—he had none.

The men made a fire to sit around while they answered some of Nick's questions about the gun range. *What's this posse thing? How many of you are there? You guys actually fought the law and won? And you get to kill meth dealers?* The more he learned, the more he felt like it was a calling.

Nick was an atheist, not prone to serendipitous feelings of fate and kismet. *Still…there's just something tugging me to stay with these guys…* Knowing he had enough gas to boat them around to Slaughter Peninsula, he bought himself a little more time. The men knocked back a few drinks with booze they found in the house—careful not to get too tipsy to defend themselves, but also enjoying watching Jeff get his first buzz—almost like things were normal, again, for an evening.

They'd finally made the slow journey around. Despite a medium rain while being out on the boat, the fact that they weren't walking was like winning the lottery to Stu and his swollen ankle. He was still wearing the boots he'd bartered for almost a month earlier, having failed to find adequate replacements in either house.

"Well?" Josh said, shaking Nick out of his reflective thought.

"I'm thinking if I go with you guys, I'll never see this boat again."

"Most likely," Josh agreed.

"But…I need to trade off ammo or gear for gas…an idea I don't like. So…maybe I'll come check this gig out with you. You say there's a place I can hang the hammock?"

All three men were trying to hide their smiles that Nick was joining them. "Big wood Common we just built, complete with rock fireplaces. You'll be fine with those high-dollar hammock quilts of yours!"

"Rather than park here," Stu suggested as Nick had started east for the shore, "I'd suggest you go back up to the broken bridge where people like us are bartering for trips across. You might just get a good deal for this boat."

"Shoot, Doc, that's actually a really, good idea," Nick said as he turned his boat north again.

TAHOMA'S HAMMER Plus 38 Days.

PHIL WALKED BACK into the EOC in Bartlett at about 1430 hours, a full half-hour before the meeting he'd called for with the other Posse units from Slaughter Peninsula. Charlie had relayed to the National Guard Major, Adam Matsumoto, that they would be converging there that afternoon. Phil didn't want to be the last to show up. He was asked to wait in the building's lobby based on his own recognizance—he had earned the right to be granted entry to the facility, though not the credentials to wander freely.

One of the remaining deputies came and grabbed Phil. "Charlie said to take you into the meeting room off the main EOC," Matty Wildman said.

"Hey, Matt," Phil said with a handshake. "Lead the way."

Forty seconds later he learned where most of the diesel generated electricity travelled. He saw fifteen people, a mixture of civilians, police and fire officers, and National Guard personnel staffing various stations, some with computers, some without. He scanned the room. *They all look as tired as I feel,* Phil thought. Everyone's attire was worn and showed signs of being worn way too much—coffee stains abounded, though the ring-around-the-collar was harder to see on the camo uniforms. He could see a communication room with a couple of radio operators during his quick scan.

Deputy Wildman led Phil into the conference room.

I wonder where the 'witch' wound up? Phil thought, curious if he should dare ask what had happened to Sandy McAllister. *Oh, heck... why not?* "G'afternoon, Sheriff," Phil said. "Thanks for letting us meet here today."

"My pleasure, Mr. Walker," Sheriff Raymond replied. "Charlie says you have a new security protocol for the community patrols?"

"That's a big part of it, yes. I need to get some new metal tags and code words distributed to the other civilian groups. The patches were fast, but as soon as our people were nabbed, they became a liability." Phil looked around at the messy conference room. "I figured it would be a good chance for us and you all to shore up our working relationship."

"Ahhh," said the sheriff. "Don't let me interfere. I need to go check on some things, but I'll be back before you guys finish. Promise." The sheriff began to depart.

"Say, Sheriff," Phil stopped him. "Before you go…" He trailed off, searching for the words.

The sheriff finally figured it out. "You're wondering what happened to her…" he guessed with the slightest of grins.

"Somethin' like that," Phil admitted.

"House arrest, Phil. You don't have to worry about her. We all make committee decisions." He turned to leave and said over his shoulder as he did, "And we have an odd-number for tie-breaking…"

Phil could see Charlie crossing the EOC toward him with several other posse leaders in tow, some from each end of the county, as well as his old lawyer Gary Stonefence from the next county over. After the room filled up and greetings were over, Phil sent a box around the room.

"Everyone take one of the tags and a flashlight. You'll need any type of portable UV light with your patrol teams for this to work."

He spent a pair of minutes explaining the new tags and the reasoning behind them.

"So, you're saying there's glow in the dark paint under this spray paint?" one of the women asked.

"Uh, yes—that's a key part of this. As long as the tags don't get compromised like the patches did, it'll be the failsafe way to know if the tag is legit. There's a clear coat between the two layers. You can scratch this spray paint off and the code word will stay intact. Of course...if the team you're questioning for authenticity is, indeed, nefarious, you'd better be ready to fight when they figure out what you're checking for."

"What's it say?" Gary the lawyer asked.

"Huh?" Phil said.

"The secret word."

"Oh—Spiritus Americae," he answered.

Gary chuckled, the lawyer knowing immediately it was Latin for American Spirit. "Alright...why Latin?" he inquired, still laughing.

"Easy enough to know what it means, but if it's in English... then it's forged...right?" A few heads nodded.

The meeting continued with updates for several more minutes when a messenger came in and fetched Charlie. Phil could see through the conference room's window as Charlie went to the radio room. The newer north end and south end units were explaining their recruitment and training issues when Charlie returned.

"I've sent a runner to go find the sheriff," he said. "There's something brewing that everyone needs to know about."

The room buzzed for several minutes while they waited. Sheriff Raymond, Adam Matsumoto, and Bartlett Police Chief Brandi Farrly showed up and squeezed in. Charlie reviewed the message forms he was reading quickly and looked up, addressing everyone as he scanned the room.

"I'm sure those of you whose groups have the right radio capabilities will be getting this from your own HAMs when you get back."

Charlie looks concerned, Phil thought. *Gravely worried...*

"There's an American militia network on the east side of the sound amassing in multiple locations. They plan on attacking the cartel tonight." The room stayed deadly quiet for two seconds and then exploded in noise.

"What?" several people all asked excitedly. Commentary started up and opinions started to fly.

The one thing that didn't die in the volcano was people's ability to spew their opinion, Phil thought, somewhat perturbed.

Charlie was using his hands to try and get everyone quiet, which they eventually did. "Listen!" he said respectfully but sternly. "This is happening. What it means for us is unclear. Understand? These are our countrymen, standing up to back the police and Guardsmen who've been slaughtered like cattle over there! Not so different than what you all are doing!"

The room grew quiet when Charlie mentioned that.

"Listen, folks," the sheriff chimed in, "You all need to think about what your plan of action will be when this cartel shows up with larger numbers. I mean—they already came over here and sent a message when they killed Phil's folks." Several heads turned toward Phil when they were reminded of that.

"What about the military?" someone shouted out. "What are they doing about it?"

"Our military liaisons are extremely sympathetic to what's happening, but they say their hands are tied," the sheriff explained.

The small room erupted once again. Phil wandered over to Charlie while all of the opinions and emotions filled the airwaves. "Are they asking for help, brother?" Phil inquired.

"Actually, yeah..." Charlie acknowledged. "But how? How would we?"

Phil brought Charlie up to speed on hearing a report about a 'posse-style' unit of boats patrolling the Strait of Juan de Fuca. "Maybe it's not just them," he posited. "Maybe there're other boaters willing to help, too...

"A lot of maybes, Phil," Charlie countered. "It would take everyone here a couple of days to go back, get their groups organized, and get back. The cartel will obliterate this patriot army before we even step foot on a boat!"

"Don't underestimate a guerrilla counter insurgency," Phil advised as he pushed past Charlie and out of the room.

His closest friend followed him out. "Where you goin'?"

Phil stopped and turned back. "Get up to the range and have Jerry get ahold of that group of boats. I'm going to the shipyard."

"The shipyard!" Charlie exclaimed. "Good Lord, Phil—why? We have their liaison officer here!"

"My son gave his life for that place, Charles," Phil said in the most serious tone Charlie had ever heard. "I need to go find out what he bought with it…"

22

Milestones.

TAHOMA'S HAMMER PLUS 38 DAYS.

Josh, Stu, Jeff, and their new friend Nick turned left on Canal Vista Highway. "It's like three or four miles from here," he said loudly toward the rear of the spread out pack. Nick was leading his new pet llama, which had a ton of his gear stacked on it.

"Please tell me there'll be a good spot to pin up Brian and let him eat!" Nick hollered up the pack. "I really don't feel like building a corral tonight."

The four men had acquired their beast of burden in trade for Nick's boat. The family that had owned Brian had camped for two days, waiting for a trade worthy of their walking meat-supply. When they found out Nick's boat was sea-worthy, they felt they'd finally found something worth Brian's value.

"And who in the world—"

"—names a llama Brian?" all three of the other men cut Nick off in unison, mocking him.

After the laughter that lasted longer than it should due to boredom and exhaustion died down, Nick said, "I guess I have said that a few times, haven't I?"

"To answer your question," Jeff said, "Yes, there's already a place where we're keeping horses."

"There's some small grazing spots that haven't been eaten or gardened yet," Josh added. "But we'll need to go find hay to get your llama through winter. Should be easy enough. We've been logging that kind of info as part of our neighborhood patrols."

An hour of careful walking later and the foursome passed the northwest fighting position on the gun club's property. "Heeeyyyyyy!" they heard from behind some covered sandbags. It was Don Kwiatkowsky. "You guys are back!"

"Hey, Pappaw!" Jeff called out, giving his grandfather a hug as he came out of the hole.

Josh led the team up the older and less used alternate driveway, past the secondary gate, and into the north end of the club's main parking lot. People were flocking to the parking lot, having heard on the radio that the group was approaching. There was a loud and happy chatter that broke through the early evening rain.

Payton and Savannah trotted up the stairs from the rifle line. *She was probably tending to post-supper dishes in the Common,* Josh figured. He was trying to look happy to see her without revealing just how badly he wanted to hold the two of them.

The Walker ladies grabbed onto Josh, and Payton planted a long kiss on her man. "I have missed you!" she said excitedly. "But Babe —you *really* need to brush your teeth!" Savannah was laughing.

Stu was shaking a few hands and trying to politely make his way back to his little bedroom and office at the far end of the rifle line. Phil hobbled up to the top of the stairs on his crutches and blocked his way. "Stu," he greeted. His face was asking how the trip went. Phil knew Stu's presence meant not well.

"They're at peace, Phil," Stu said with a smile, knowing what the unspoken question was. "And I'm just glad to have people I can trust, at this point."

"You'll have a home here, Doc, for as long as we all need to stay here…" Phil stepped out of the way of the stairs. "Other than people battling colds and flu, there are no surprises down there. We've been patrolling again. Supplements and salt are at the top of the scrounge list, just like you ordered."

"Good to hear," Stu called out as he made his way down and to the right.

Phil pushed through the people as their excitement started to taper. He noticed a new face and a llama parked behind Josh. Jeff had escaped his parents' hugs and started to lead Nick and the llama down past the office.

"Who's your friend?" Phil asked Josh.

Payton looked around to see what her dad was talking about. She hadn't even noticed. Jeff, Nick, and Brian rounded the corner just before getting to the main gate and went east farther onto the property.

"He's the real deal," Josh told him. "There's a long and harrowing story that I'll be happy to tell down by the fireplace with a bowl of soup."

Payton grabbed him by the hand and started to lead him and Savannah down the steps.

"Army?" Phil asked Josh before he could escape.

"Light infantry," Josh informed him. "Sniper."

Two hours later, with a roaring fire in the stone fireplace on the west end of the Common, Nick Williams began to hang his hammock from two nearby logs. He'd just been regaled as the big hero in the story of life and death of a vicious psychopath that nobody listening had ever heard of before. All they knew was that their loved ones and precious doctor had returned—albeit with a sprained ankle and a little dehydration.

"I'm sure we can find a trailer with an unused bunk, Nick," Phil said as the crowd was breaking up. "It's kind of what we do."

"I'm good, Phil, but thanks."

Josh had just broken free from Payton and Savannah's grasp as they headed off to get ready for bed. "What's wrong?" he asked Phil. "You haven't said twenty words in the last two hours."

"I was waiting for you guys to get some rest, but…" Phil trailed off.

"What?" Nick asked. "The last time I saw that look I found out some buddies had died."

"There's something brewing in Seattle. A big fight." Phil looked at his Luminox watch. "Any minute, now."

Tahoma's Hammer Plus 39 Days.

"What do you mean they can't find them?!" Reynaldo screamed into his headset.

"They know they're out there, Jefe," Ramon said. "The gang leaders we absorbed for the Renton area saw at least two thousand mustering at the municipal airport last night. By the time our south end unit got down there and set up for an attack, they were gone."

"They didn't just disappear!" Reynaldo scolded. "There must be tracks, or something. Find them!" He ripped the headset off and scanned to the person he was looking for at the far end of the big command vehicle. "What about the north front, Lupe? Did our inept inductees lose them, too?"

"No, Jefe! They're coming down the same highway we did—at least most of them—number 522."

"What do you mean most of them?" Rey screamed.

"There's so many of them that they're taking up every north-south arterial between the lake and Highway number 5," the man said, referring to the I-5 corridor. "They're avoiding anything with collapsed overpasses, just like we did.

Rey tried to compose himself a bit. "Get the reaction force moving that way," he said to a different man, who fled the rig to relay the order. Rey looked at his watch. *0330. Damn!* "Can you get the Alpha Team on the radio?" he asked hopefully.

"I can try, Jefe, but the protocol is for them to check in at midnight. I'm sure their radios are off to keep the batteries charged."

"You're sure…" Rey repeated. "You're sure?!" he screamed. "Why don't you get your butt in gear and try!"

"Si, Jefe!" the man said and began trying to raise the operators over on Slaughter Peninsula.

"Jefe!" another operator called for Rey in the chaotic rig. "South sector has some information for you."

Rey snapped the headset out of the man's hands and put it on. "Reynaldo!" he barked to make sure whoever it was knew exactly who they were speaking with.

"We've found them, but we can't keep up with them."

"What the hell does that mean?" screamed Rey. "Kill those bastards!"

"We're stuck to the streets, Jefe," the poor soul tried to explain. "They're using bull dozers and big off-road trucks to travel up the high-voltage lines! Big, American-style obnoxious trucks!" the man repeated.

"Wait a minute!" Rey looked at one of his equipment operators. "Zoom in the map!" he ordered, pointing at the big screen monitor on the side of the vehicle's wall. "Down in Renton area!" He moved over and leaned close the screen, studying it. "There! Zoom back out just a bit…travel north and zoom out just a bit more…"

It hit Rey like a ton of bricks once he'd zoomed back out and looked at the map as a whole. Like a giant, green highway, there was a two-hundred-meter-wide level road that was kept drivable by the utility companies for the annual windstorms that knocked power out in the Seattle area. It headed northwest for miles, mostly paralleling the unusable I-5 corridor. There was light brush and the occasional tree that kept it from being drivable by normal cars.

In a panic, he screamed, "Move north! Find out where these powerlines cross the highway!" Rey was starting to get hoarse.

"Here, Jefe!" the man yelled, pointing at his screen. Rey was looking at a point in Seattle's southern industrial section, a scant two miles from downtown.

He took a deep breath. "Eduardo," he calmly ordered one of the men over. "Start programming some drones."

TYLER and his hand-me-down clothing hobbled several miles from the Suquamish Tribal Reservation, through the nearest town and to the broken highway—the only major one in Slaughter County. Most of the overpasses on it had collapsed, though over the weeks, various private citizens had driven their tractors out and carved passable roads through or around the debris. There was a decent amount of foot traffic heading both directions, with too much county and National Guard related vehicle traffic for any people of lower moral character to try setting up a toll. Those had mainly been limited to the confines of neighborhoods and smaller thoroughfares due to one fact—the vast majority of people travelling thirty-nine days after the hammer fell were armed and travelling in packs. Survival instincts had gone through a rapid dusting-off in recent weeks.

Tyler was keeping a close eye on any vehicle, both for avoiding trouble and to find possible help. *Seems like I haven't seen one cop or Guard vehicle yet. Are they even still a thing?*

In the early afternoon, he'd progressed to a point between Peterson and Sylvan to the south. He clued in on a very large mob of people moving north on the highway. There was a group of four travelling about a half-mile ahead of him. He saw no less than twenty people peel off the northbound mob and start crossing the large grass median that splits the two directions. They were running at a high rate of speed. Tyler heard gunfire. *Oh, Heelllll no!* he screamed in his head. He back pedaled three hundred meters to the one road that cut west in this section of highway. He knew he could take it over to a parallel road dotted with farms and ranches. That road ran along the perimeter of the submarine base.

Forty minutes later he was standing on that road heading south when he heard a rumble. It got louder by the minute, and he saw a United States Marine Corp vehicle rise over a small peak in the road. *What the…?*

The thing showed no signs of stopping, so he stepped into the tall grass on the east side of the road. He had a better vantage of what was happening and saw one vehicle after another crest the little peak. By the time the first had passed him, he could see ten with no sign of it slowing down. A Marine was sitting behind a machine gun, sticking out of the roof on that very first vehicle. Tyler saw the man look at him and start talking into a microphone that was part of his helmet as they passed by.

The fourth vehicle in the convoy was a Humvee that stopped directly in front of Tyler. The diesel engines and giant tires rumbling by were so loud that Tyler could hear nothing else, and he didn't need to—Halt was an easy word to read lips with. Like the larger trucks, the Humvees were carrying a mounted machine gun on top. Instinctively, Tyler put his hands above his shoulders. After thirty seconds, the junior officer riding shotgun in the rig stepped out and approached Tyler.

"Sorry, sir," the polite Marine said. "I need you to stay here until we've cleared this road!" he yelled over the noise.

Tyler finally saw a big semi crest the small rise, pulling a giant, low-boy flat trailer. On that trailer were wood crates of varying sizes covered by tarps and secured with many straps. The sole marking—and only on a few—was a single propeller shape. Tyler had no misunderstandings—the former Air Force officer knew only too well what that meant and what the Marines would do to keep it secure. He just nodded, still too hoarse to try and yell. The officer stood there with a polite but defensive posture for the four minutes it took the convoy, complete with military mobile crane trucks, to pass by.

"Very well, sir," the young officer said as he turned to head back to his vehicle.

"Wait," Tyler hollered after him. He was ignored as he saw the man open his Humvee's door. Tyler started to move toward the officer and yelled, "Wait!"

The top gunner swung his barrel toward Tyler and kept it pointed just above his head as he yelled, "Halt!" Tyler heard it loudly and clearly that time.

The officer reached into the cab and brought an MRE out. He closed the door and started walking to Tyler. "This is all I can give you," he said.

"No. I mean—thanks. But that's not what I need. I have an urgent message to get to the county EOC!"

"Not our mission, sir," the officer said. "Have a good day." He started heading back to the vehicle.

"I know the cartel is here on the peninsula!" Tyler yelled in desperation. "I know how many and how they're outfitted." The officer turned around. Tyler could see him squinting under his battle helmet, not wanting to have to deal with this headache. "It's a matter of national security!" Tyler finally said.

The officer deflated just a bit, and the top gunner actually rolled his eyes and dropped his head. "Look!" Tyler yelled. *They're still here! Have to keep trying!* "I was a Captain in the Air Force. I'm not screwing with you."

"Good day, sir" the 2nd Lieutenant concluded with some finality.

"They used an RPG to kill my friends and kidnap me, damn it!"

The Marine walked back over and studied Tyler's face. "Get in," he finally said.

Thirty minutes later, Tyler was sitting in a fairly secure shelter in the middle of Bogdon Submarine Base. It had been constructed by the Navy Sea-Bees as the regimental HQ for the Marines that had arrived to supplement the base's normal security forces. Tyler could still smell fresh paint. He was seated in a folding chair with thin padding, under the watchful eye of a Lance Corporal, though not one of the men who had picked him up.

Another Marine, this one wearing sergeant's stripes, came through a door behind a counter to talk to Tyler. "Sir? Can I get your name, please?"

"Tyler Wilson," he replied. "Look, I don't mean to be snide, but the information—"

"I'm taking you to see Sergeant Major Piercy, sir," he said. "As soon as I get back." The young man started to go around the counter.

"I take it he's your Battalion Senior NCO, Sergeant?"

"Regimental, sir." With that the young man disappeared.

About twenty minutes later—*Hurry up and wait is still a thing in the military, I see,* Tyler thought—the door opened, only it wasn't the young sergeant. An older, distinguished Marine stepped out and closed the door behind him. *Gray temples, and this man looks like he could fight the cartel himself.*

"Mr. Wilson? I'm sorry to keep you waiting. Sergeant Major Greg Piercy," he said shaking Tyler's hand. "Why don't you follow me?"

"Su-sure," Tyler said.

It had suddenly dawned on him that he and Gene were going to make it—that the nightmare might actually be over. *Teddy!* he thought to himself. *I'm going to see him again!* He followed the tall Marine back through the door and down a hallway.

Three doors down, Greg opened an office door and led Tyler into a nondescript room with two brand new desks. They were both covered with papers, though care had been taken to make sure none of them were face up before Tyler had been brought in.

Greg took the wheeled office chair from the one desk and

pushed it toward Tyler. "Have a seat," he said politely. He passed Tyler and opened the door. "Stone! Bring me two waters, double time!" he ordered. He reclosed the door and sat down in his own desk chair. "Sorry about the wait, Mr. Wilson—"

"Tyler. P-Please…call me Tyler…"

"Tyler…" Greg repeated with a subtle smile. "We had to make sure you were who you said you were."

"Please forgive me, Sergeant Major—"

"Greg," he interrupted.

Tyler chuckled. "Greg. But in my ten years in the Air Force, we never got anything done that quickly."

This time it was Greg's chance to laugh. "Well, we already had a full report on the incident you reported to our unit that picked you up. We had to consult it. So far, you have the details right. What else can you tell me?"

Ohhhh…I see what's going on here, Tyler realized. "Is this a test? Look, Greg—I'm not kidding! This cartel is real. They're powerful and they're—"

"Here?" Greg said, still being polite. "Are they multi-racial?"

"Yes!" Tyler exclaimed.

"Speak English with no accents?"

"Most of them. Look—"

"Subversive? Sneaky?"

Tyler exhaled. "Aaannddd you need to make sure I'm not one of them…"

"I need you to tell me something they wouldn't have learned through torture," Greg said. "Give me some detail they couldn't have known. Or at least wouldn't have thought to ask…"

Tyler thought for a minute. Just then there was a knock on the door. After being told to enter, a young Marine provided two bottles of water, along with a tray of hot chow—two plates of pork adobo. Greg excused the Marine and set some food and water in front of Tyler.

"I'm stuck, I guess. There's nothing they couldn't have gotten out of me and Gene." He looked away, thinking about what he and his new friend had endured. He started to tear up.

"Then how 'bout this?" Greg said. "Tell me something that will make the people at the range know you're you."

"Acapulco," Tyler said. "It's where Teddy wanted to go on our honeymoon. I insisted we go to Nassau."

Greg looked up into the corner of the room. "You guys get that?" he said to a camera.

"Roger that, Sergeant Major," Tyler heard a voice on a radio squawk from near Greg's belt.

"Hooollyyy crap!" he said as his jaw nearly landed in his adobo. "Is this even your office?"

"Oorah!" Greg announced. The two men laughed a bit and pulled little, plastic sporks from sleeves. "Look," Greg said. "After you wolf down that chow, you can tell me all the juicy details, and I'll make sure the right people get it ricky-tick. When you check out—and I'm sure you will—we're going to need to keep you here for a day or two."

"What?" Tyler said as he gagged on a noodle. "Why?"

"Can't tell you."

Tyler rolled his eyes. *But of course you can't.* "I should've known…"

"It'll make sense tomorrow. I promise," Greg said. "In the meantime, we'll give you a checkup and some fresh clothes."

"You shouldn't make promises you can't keep, Greg."

"I don't," came the even reply.

23

Key Events.

THE AMERICAN PATRIOTS APPROACHING FROM THE SOUTH HAD, indeed, foreseen an issue when they reached the I-5 corridor. The maps showed that the powerlines crossed the highway, but there was no overpass or underpass for their close to 1,800 members to cross and continue on. They'd made a strategic decision in planning the day before to divide the column into two formations and use Beacon Avenue and 15th Avenue to travel north. The columns would use their Cat dozers, which had been covered in welded steel plating, to push through any obstacles. This was going to be a one-way trip for the Caterpillar D-9s—the beast weighed fifty-four tons once the plating had been added and had been towed to the Renton Airport with Kenworths. Though topped off, they were going to burn through almost all of their fuel on the mad rush to get into downtown Seattle.

The biggest risk in the plan was going to be getting the columns over I-5. Three routes were planned. The column using 15th Avenue would divert up Columbian Way and enter the northbound lanes of I-5 for just a few hundred meters. The pair of Cats leading that column would push through the jersey barrier and the trucks would then cross over and exit at the nearby Forest Street exit. The units would then sub-divide and take 4th, 6th, and 8th Avenues north. The rail lines were clogged with train cars that had been tossed off their tracks and were not an option.

The other column would split into two. One half was going to use one of the few overpasses that had survived due to its short span —the Beacon Avenue overpass. The other half were going to move over to 23rd Avenue and push north past the Mount Baker Tunnels that I-90 dove into. They would push north and attempt to use whatever cartel route they could find over the interstate. It was going to be the element that tied the gap between the rest of the southern units and those approaching from the north. The groups from the Pierce County area were assigned this task, as they had the highest percentage of recent combat veterans. The Phalanx group had been assigned to this task as well, due to the special mission they would attempt if the weather broke. The vehicles had been filtering through all of the neighborhood streets, spreading out to minimize their risk and have a much larger front for the cartel to attack.

The various trucks and SUVs trailing the Cats had received only sporadic gunfire for the majority of the trip, to their pleased surprise. This changed for the Pierce element—call-sign Tarboo on the radio—as they approached Garfield High School in East Seattle. Earl Garren recognized the sounds of mortars instantly.

"Incoming!" he yelled to everyone riding in the back of the black Ford F-350. He looked back through the quad cab and saw terror and confusion. The Cat at the head of the column had been the first rig targeted. Four rounds overshot it and took out the two trucks and SUVs behind it. "Drive east!" Earl yelled at his driver.

"East!" the man objected.

"Do it!" Earl yelled. "Most of our trucks are to the west! We need to flank this school and get up there!" He pointed to the roof of the high school. "If they're not launching from there, that's at least where they're spotting from!" He yelled back past the three people in the back row and through the open window. "Make sure John's truck follows us!" he ordered.

As the Ford turned right to head east, the men and women riding in the bed waved the next truck back to follow. *We need to keep together!*

As the truck started to speed east on Alder Street, Earl saw the football field opening up on their left. "Stop!" he yelled. The driver hit the brakes and Earl pointed to the left. "Push us up against the building!" Both his and John's truck did as expected. "Dismount!" he ordered everyone in truck one. The sounds of fresh explosions could be heard falling on more elements to their west.

As the infantry started to hop out of the two pickups, Earl ran back to John, Tucker, and several Phalanx in truck two. "Anyone directly tied to the aerial weapon stay put and pull security around these trucks!" he ordered. *Dang it, I wish Conner were here!*

His buddy had reluctantly agreed to play security for Tarboo's medical squad, which had brought Earl a great sense of relief. *Protect my sister with your life,* he ordered his friend, though he knew he didn't have to.

Earl pulled a small, telescoping inspection mirror from his plate carrier. The militia soldiers were pushing themselves into the bushes along the school building's south side. Earl ran from John's truck and over to them. "Nine of ya! Congratulations! You're still alive! Keep hugging these bushes while I—"

Just then another SUV from Tarboo element sped east on Alder, trying to escape the 81mm shooting gallery that 23rd Street had become. It sped right past the two stopped trucks.

"Nooooo!" Earl yelled, too late. As the SUV cleared the building, automatic machine gun fire with a red tracer round every fifth bullet, began ripping the truck to pieces. It crashed into a house to its right side and stopped. The rounds were making a snapping noise as they cracked through the air, destroying the truck and everyone in it. "Damn it!" Earl screamed.

He ran to the corner of the building and used the small telescoping mirror to look down and see where the fire was coming from. Behind the school's rear entrance, about one hundred meters north, was a crudely constructed sandbag bunker with an M-2 barrel still smoking. He ran back to the scared team. "Lesson two in combat! Do not go past blind corners! Ever!"

"Wh-what's lesson one?" a young lady from Spanaway asked.

"They're learning it right now! Push through an ambush!" Earl said. He started scanning up the brick wall over the rookies' heads. "Make a pyramid!" he ordered.

Two of the men figured out what Earl was looking at and got onto their hands and knees. Two more followed.

"Maybe you should be on the bottom!" the same young lady suggested, eyeballing Earl's size.

He was shoving the next guys on top of the first row. "I'm going in first!"

Earl unslung his rifle. As soon as two more men were sitting on top of the first row, he started climbing. He felt men's back muscles tighten as he stepped on them. "Sorry, dudes!" he told the second row as all two hundred and ten pounds of him stood up on their backs.

He shattered the window with his rifle's butt, showering everyone with glass. He re-slung the rifle and pulled out a multitool, cutting through the remaining security wire. *Doesn't have to be pretty in combat*, he thought. He pushed his body through his starter hole and wiggled through, falling onto a chair-desk in a clatter. He found his knees and squatted on them, raising the rifle in the dark building. *Nothing...so far...*

Earl stood and reached back through the window, pulling the two girls and one man who were climbing up the pyramid inside with him. "What about us?" the middle row soldiers asked.

"Do you have a grenade?"

"Yeah!"

"Then get in here and take out that machine gun!" he spun around while lowering his night vision. "On me! Keep it tight!"

Earl cleared the first corner and scanned both directions. *Main hallway, over there!* he thought. He led the three youngsters to the corner of their smaller cross-hall and stopped.

"There's probably a guard or two covering the stairs going up to the upper floors. Let me do the shooting, since none of you have suppressors!" Without waiting for a reply, he sliced the corner until it was clear and started walking up the hall with controlled steps to keep the muzzle from bouncing.

Pop! Pop! Tink-tink-tink… Once the first scumbag fell, Earl knew that their element of surprise had been blown.

"Just the man I was hoping to get a message to," Sergeant Major Greg Piercy said to Phil on the secure radio that the Submarine Base Liaison had provided to the Slaughter County EOC. "What're the chances that you'd be there?"

"Funny, Sarge, I was thinking the same thing," Phil quipped. "I just got done visiting the Navy a bit ago. I have info you may want, as well."

"I believe one of your missing souls wandered into my base looking for help…more or less."

Phil couldn't believe his ears. "Repeat your last?" he requested.

"You heard right," Greg assured him. He spent a few minutes relaying everything he'd learned to Phil and Charlie. "Look, fellas, there's some stuff I have to tell you, and it won't make much sense to you how I know. You're just going to have to trust me."

"We're all ears," Phil replied. "And I have a feeling I have some stuff you may want to hear as well. No—you need to hear, so that a bunch of good people sailing down the Sound don't get shot. You first."

"Using what your man told us, we were able to pull up some video from...an asset. We went back to the moment your boys escaped from a boat. Using said asset, we were able to track a cartel unit's movements—all the way to a house less than one mile from your gun range."

Greg thought he heard a pin drop through the radio. After ten seconds, he heard Phil say, "Well, that's just a bit unsettling."

"There's more," Greg said with a serious tone. "There's a total of four vehicles there."

Phil went quiet for so long that Greg finally asked, "You copy? We still connected?"

"We're here," Phil said. "Just wondering for how long, that's all..."

EARL'S RAG-TAG team arrived at the main first floor intersection in the old school. "Gimme a smoke!" he ordered, looking back at the girl behind him. He pulled the pin and let the smoke-cannister cook for three seconds before tossing it up the stairwell. "Last man—cover this stairwell! Remember, two more coming up behind you in a second. Don't shoot them!"

Once again, he cautiously rounded a corner and started up the stairs, which were filling with a thick, magenta smoke that reeked of potassium chlorate. Earl's night vision didn't help, whereas a FLIR device would have allowed him to see a human heat signature. He knew that when he broke through the hall above, though, that his NOD would once again be effective in the dark building.

Earl could hear the two women in their twenties, keeping right on his heels and hugging the wall. *At least they haven't frozen up yet*, he thought. He cautiously cleared both directions around the corner and saw that the stairs in the old, brick school went up to a third floor in the center and north end of the building. *Couldn't see that from our insertion point...*

There was little of the smoke from the cannister one-and-a-half flights below to contend with when he neared the corner of the stair entrance onto the third floor. The enamel brick corner near his head exploded as the roar of an AK round ricocheted down the hall from around the corner. Earl's face contorted with focus. *Your mistake, dead man. Shoulda waited to see me...* He got onto his knees on the stairs and shoved his rifle, hands, and top-third of his head out onto the hallway's floor, stuffing them in a position to quickly acquire two targets running into a doorway. He filled it with 5.56 mm bullets and heard at least one of them cry out in anguish as they slammed the door shut.

The experienced Ranger pulled himself back up to the cover and concealment of the open stairwell wall, performing a magazine change and stuffing the partial one into a pouch hanging from the left kidney area of his plate carrier.

"What's your names?" he whispered.

"J-Jessica," said the one of Hispanic descent. "Sh-she's Renee!"

Earl recognized them as two of the Phalanx members from his river. "Stay here until I call you up," he quietly ordered. "But cover me! Fourth door down, left side!"

With that, he rounded the corner, muzzle end of his rifle first. Earl sped walked with as much muzzle control as he could and got to the wall of lockers on the far side of the hall, the same side his target door was on. He continued to proceed as cautiously as speed would allow when that door opened.

Jessica opened fire on a hand with a grenade, and both of them retracted into the room. "Watch out!" she screamed at Earl, who had sped up and gotten into a gap of the lockers where a classroom door was.

Ka-Boom! The hall echoed as the wood and glass door exploded into small missiles, covering the hallway in smoke and shards. *Now!* Earl said to himself. He ran up to that corner and rounded it, firing into the room as he acquired the two almost-dead cartel members.

Keeping his rifle and posture on the room, he slowly took two steps backwards into the smoky hall. "Move!" he ordered Jessica and Renee as he scanned the now-broken shelving in the small janitorial closet. *Great!* he thought angrily, seeing the old school vertical ladder leading to an opening in the school's roof. He kept his rifle trained at the ceiling opening as he stepped over bodies and moved closer to it. *If whoever is up there heard the grenade, all they need to do is drop one right now!*

"We need to get up there—fast!" he hissed at Jessica as she entered the janitor's closet. "If they're watching the access, we're going to get shot! So don't waste time!"

Earl let the muzzle fall to his legs as the rifle's sling kept the weapon to his body. Simultaneously he was pulling his pistol out of its holster on his right hip and holding it skyward. Raindrops clouded his NODS, so he flipped them up and started using his left hand and feet to scoot up the ladder. The door hinged to the south.

As Earl's head got near the opening, he could hear the mortar team launching from that side of the access cover. *Thank you, God,* he thought as he propelled himself onto the roof, straight out, hoping that the open metal covering was hiding his movement. He spun around on his butt, holding his pistol out to the south to cover the girl's movement up the fatal chokepoint.

"Keep low!" he hissed to Jessica as he saw her camo boonie hat crest through the access. Earl transitioned to a knee. Using his left hand to pull his rifle up, he re-holstered his pistol without looking. He scooted back a couple of feet to make some room. Soon both girls were crammed in the tiny space between him and the hole.

"Shoot anyone up here! I'll go left, Jessica you go right. Renee, you stay behind this hatchway and shoot over the top of the door!"

He didn't give the girls time to think or ask questions. Earl zipped around the doorway and saw four cartel members manning a mortar station twenty meters to the south. Three were operating the weapon and one was leaning against the roof's parapet with a set of binoculars and a radio.

Pop! Pop! Pop! Earl pumped three rounds into the one who was reaching into the mortar box first. He could hear Jessica opening fire, too. In a matter of five seconds, all four cartel were dead.

"Clear the roof! Keep covered! We need to make sure there aren't others!" Earl ordered, not wanting the girls to get tunnel vision after their surprise victory.

As they proceeded, the old veteran's mindset on women in combat had shifted. *Proud of those kids,* he told himself. *If we actually live through the night, you need to remember to tell them that.*

24

Critical Junctures.

Tahoma's Hammer Plus 39 Days.

Much had happened in the ten days since Jennifer's Navy had been formed. The alliance of boat operators, with the help of a locally based gun store and holster manufacturer, had defended international shipping efforts from Shotgun's pirates one week earlier. That first victory hadn't been pretty, costing one boat and three lives—but the pirates had been successfully repelled for the first time. In the days since, her Navy had grown by eleven more boats.

Word of the new defensive force was spread by that first relief ship, a Japanese flagged cargo carrier. The South Korean ship that followed thirty-eight hours later was the first vessel in almost three weeks to dare a direct entry, versus the narrow strait around

Vancouver Island's east side. They anchored off Port Townsend, Washington, for six hours to donate fuel to the protection force.

After that first fight, local welders and boatwrights helped Jennifer's Navy install better mounts for donated armament. Jennifer had solicited local HAM radio operators and folded them into the network, eager to avoid the Marine bands she knew the pirates used. She had received word that there was an outfit in Puget Sound soliciting their help. After having a conversation with their leader, she decided it was probably a legitimate request.

Her HAMs filled her in on the fact that Seattle was, indeed, in the beginning stages of an all-out fight. She called for a meeting of the vessel operators in the early afternoon, back at her father's firepit.

Though reluctant to leave their families, the charter boaters agreed to follow Jennifer on her mission. She had reminded them all that, like Mrs. Sults' father in the 1930's, they were at a point in their lives where they had to make a decision based not on what was safest in the moment, but one that would reserve their families' right for existence in the future. Like the spread of radicalized socialists of the 1930's Germany—*after all*, she said, *that's what the Z in Nazi stood for*—the cartel would eventually enslave the people who came to rely on them for everything.

Jennifer's HAM operators had received weather reports from their peers across the nation, and those reports validated what their own radars were saying—the storm system was starting to thin. "We'll probably actually see the moon tonight," she told her Navy. "It should be a smooth ride all the way to the battle."

SEVERAL MEDICAL VOLUNTEERS had established their primary triage center in a parking garage near Seattle's Swedish Medical Center. The Tarboo element had secured the several blocks between Broadway and the structure by mid-afternoon. Fighting had decreased, though firefights could be heard in all directions. Tarboo was waiting until dusk to begin a new push into downtown. The north was still fighting, though they'd taken heavy losses via a series of explosive drone attacks. The south element was fairly stable, having made it to the big sports arenas.

Conner was with four other men, patrolling the perimeter of the structure, though from inside the outer walls.

Natalie was changing the dressings on the belly gunshot wound of a woman who desperately needed a surgery she wouldn't get when she sensed Conner staring behind her. "You okay?" she asked looking back at him.

He had plopped down next to a load bearing column, quickly draining a disposable water bottle. "This garage is a fairly safe bet from anything they can throw at us. The exploding drones aren't so well programmed as to find the gaps between the half-walls and the next floor, I think."

"That's not what I asked," she said. "Are you doing alright?" She could see that he was pale.

"I've been worse," he said, growing a bit quiet.

"What's wrong, Con-Man?" she said, using her brother's nickname for him. "I can tell something's bothering you."

"It's hard to tell exactly where all the firefights are," he admitted. "Lots of noise bouncing around off concrete buildings. I'm pretty certain there's still skirmishes east of us. Just be ready to bug out if we give you guys the order."

"Ha!" Natalie said. "Where can we go that's any safer?" she asked skeptically. "Besides—I'm not leaving any of these wounded behind."

Conner finished draining his bottle and stood up, not wanting to argue. He gave a whoop to one of the other guards and pointed to himself and the area above him, indicating he was going to the roof.

Natalie stood up to check on the next wounded militia member. "Be straight with me, miss," she heard the woman she'd been tending say. "Am I going to be okay?"

Natalie was an experienced triage nurse and knew the truth. "You bet," she lied, smiling. "We have a few people trying to go set up a surgery site in Swedish." Which was true, but Natalie knew a belly and intestinal surgery would only result in an agonizing and painful death from infection a few weeks down the road. She also knew the cardinal rule of patient care—*never say anything to destroy a person's hope*.

JOHN LOOKED around at the forty men and women—ten four-person teams that were a critical piece of their aerial attack. They learned that the weather would be clear enough for Tucker and him to fly their paramotors. They planned on getting airborne at 0300.

The members—all from Tarboo element—had been hand-picked by Earl and John, based on their observations during the preceding eighteen hours of urban warfare. They had amassed under a grove of trees, taking care to stay out of the open sight of any drones. Like a gnat, they could be heard but hard to spot. They listened to the symphony of firefights from every direction while they caught naps and had supper.

John was getting ready to brief everyone on their roles and take questions. He knew Earl wasn't a big fan of a plan this intricate with such ill-equipped and barely-trained people—but they both realized they needed a big surprise or two if they were going to drive this cartel out before they all died.

"Everyone start gathering on me," John called out to the tired patriots. They were hunkered down on the campus of Seattle University.

"Fall in!" Earl ordered the troops. He could tell which one's were combat vets by the way they responded. The group formed themselves a semi-circle around John and Earl. Tucker and the rest of the team that had built the two laser-guided bombs were two blocks away, guarding the two trucks and all of the supporting gear—the paramotors, the wings, and the precious delivery vehicles.

John held up one of the infrared strobes. "These are the most important things in our lives tonight. They represent your mission, and they're literally a life and death matter to me and my son!" He wanted to gauge everyone's seriousness. "I'm going to let SFC Garren brief you on your mission. We can't tell you the why—if one of you gets nabbed by the cartel, they'll torture you to spill the beans."

"We're going to operate as ten four-person teams. Each team has to deliver two of these strobes onto 8th Avenue, or within one block of it in either direction." Hands started to shoot up. "Lemme finish! Each team will be assigned two blocks. We'll show you which ones on the map. Know your target buildings, as well as those of the other teams. These IR beacons represent that you have cleared that block of all enemy. Got it?"

He and John heard, "Yeah, we got it," and a few other mumbled replies.

"What?"

"Yes!" several yelled. "Got it!" came from a few others.

"Good," Earl said a little more calmly. "This will make or break our initial strike effort at the cartel's command and control infrastructure," he explained. "It is imperative," he said, emphasizing the word, "that everyone get their strobes up and running."

John took over. "We're outnumbered, especially when you factor in the American gangs that are the bulk of the cartel's numbers. But…if we can get in and cut the snake's head off, they'll start to fall apart. My guess is that we can help end this thing, just by making them disappear into the woodwork when they see us attack their core."

After fielding a few more questions, the men broke out a map and showed the teams their sectors. Earl's team consisted of Larry, Jessica, and Renee, who refused to operate with anyone else.

"Do we really have to go all the way to the north end of this thing?" Renee asked.

"If you want to run with me, you do," Earl said with a small grin. "You're tougher than you realize, young lady."

"Won't they just see us all marching up 8th Avenue and figure out what we're up to?" Jessica asked.

"Which is why we broke into small elements," Earl explained. "Staggered departures, everyone taking a different route to get to their designated blocks."

"When we leaving?" Larry asked. "This old man don't run for nothin'," he joked.

Earl looked at his watch. *Gets dark around 1700,* he thought to himself. "Half-hour," he answered. "Everyone fill up your water bladders and bottles, grab extra mags, extra smoke canisters, some snack bars…" He started to walk over to talk to John and turned back to his team. "Oh—and extra batteries for the strobes." *We can't give Murphy anything to grab onto for this Charlie Foxtrot…*

25

Rope-a-Dope.

T‍ahoma's Hammer Plus 39 Days.

It was long past dusk and evening soup for the range residents. The look on Phil's face was as concerned and serious as he could make it. "We need to bug out. We need to do it as quietly in the dark as we can. And we need to go now."

"What?" Alice Huddleston, the club's president, exclaimed, drawing a chorus of shooshes from everyone else in the office that wasn't much quieter.

"It's my firm belief that we're being surveilled by the cartel, and I have a serious hunch they're preparing to attack," Phil went on. "And there's the fight in Seattle that finally kicked off in the wee hours this morning." This announcement made Josh shift his weight and look around the room a little bit.

"What's that got to do with us?" Don asked. "And just where are we supposed to bug out to? This *is* the bug out location!"

Phil looked around to make sure all club officers were listening. "This is exactly why Eli and his crew have been extending the eastern trail! For just such an emergency!" He was tired and losing patience, but he also remembered that impatience had led him to make a humiliating set of decisions when he almost lost his life to the local gang.

"Listen, everyone. We have a plan," he said, casting a glance towards Josh, Eli, and Lonnie. "We can't afford to debate this. I need you to trust me. I can't say how in a way that will make sense to you, but we have actionable intel that the cartel is here. If we bug out now, quietly down the eastern trail and to the Blackberry Hills neighborhood a couple of miles east of here, we'll be alright. Like it or not, this is a trust Phil decision that I'm asking you to make. I'm grabbing Payton and Savannah and leaving in twenty minutes, whether you all do or not."

Don looked at Eli and then Josh, studying their faces. They were his daughter's family, and he knew he could trust their judgement. "Okay, Phil…" he said slowly. "I trust you." With that the old man stood up.

"Thanks, Don. When we're down the trail, a lot more will make sense."

Joe stood up, then Alice. Soon everyone was standing. "How do we do this?" Joe asked.

"Quietly," Phil emphasized. "Start with your own families and tent-mates, then as quickly as you can, tell the next tent or camper over. Grab and go! You need to emphasize the danger. Grab and go! We assemble and leave from the field in a half-hour. Got it?"

With that, the remaining officers, trustees, and security experts at the West Sound Sportsman's Club began to activate a hasty bugout. Even after being attacked—first by the local meth-heads and then by the National Guard—the thought of bugging out had always seemed impossible to them. They had not planned for or practiced it.

"Phil!" Josh hissed before he got too far away once outside the office. Phil turned to listen. Josh spent a minute explaining an idea he had, to which Phil agreed. Josh hopped in the Gator and took off for some materials he would need to enact the idea of planting stuffed clothes in all three west side fighting positions to make them look like they had people in them.

Most everyone busied themselves with spreading the word and stuffing their backpacks with as much food as they could carry. Some of the more devout preppers still had their assembled bug out bags. They were going around and reminding people to keep their lanterns and flashlights turned off.

Phil passed Big Tony, who said, "Just heard, brotha. Let me know what you need."

Phil stopped and his face showed he was lost in thought. "You up to a trip?"

"Whatever you need."

"I can't guarantee your safety, Tony. Only your family's."

Tony slowed down his words for emphasis. "Whatever…you need, Phil…"

Phil patted the big man on the shoulder. "Then make sure you grab your rifle and pack." He thought about the irony of that—Phil had given his big friend Crane's rifle after he'd saved his own life with it in East Bartlett just a couple of weeks earlier.

Moments later, Phil reached the trailer he'd converted into a living space for his girls. While Payton had resisted the urge to argue when she sensed the urgency in her father's voice, Savannah wasn't quite so ready to participate.

"Grannnnndpaaaaaa!!!" she cried with a tired whininess. She'd already fallen asleep for the night. Phil was patiently trying to stand her up from her cot.

"I'm sorry, Peaches. This is an emergency. We've got to go." He looked at Payton.

"It's okay, Dad, I got her," Payton told him calmly.

"Half-hour, Olive," Phil reminded.

"I got it, Dad! We'll be up there! Go bother someone else," she said, shooing him back out of the converted cargo trailer.

It wound up being closer to forty-five minutes, but Phil could live with that. *Not bad, all things considered,* he thought. *God bless these people. Lord knows we've been through enough.* He noticed that people were amassing at the eastern edge of the field, but nobody was leading the way. *Where's Josh?*

Phil had dressed in his full Posse kit, so he flipped his night-vision device down to more easily scan the close to two-hundred-person crowd. He could see Josh, Nick, and the last of the western perimeter guards walking across the field, the last to arrive. *And... Jerry?* He found Jerry within about twenty feet, who gave him a thumbs up, which told Phil he had packed and secured the Command Post as best he could.

Phil started pushing his way east. As he passed the last few people before the trail's head, he could finally feel the buzz that everyone understood the sense of urgency. "Follow me," he whispered.

So began the procession in mostly single file. No light, other than red-filtered flashlights or welcomed but uncharacteristic moonlight. Very little talking. Some of the younger kids had to be continually silenced by their parents or siblings, but the toddlers were mostly still asleep, carried by tired family members.

The going was slow with Phil shining his filtered light on tripping hazards every once in a while. *These guys did a good job making this trail wide enough to get an off-road rig up,* Phil thought. *Good thing the moon is out. Can't believe the clear night.* Fortunately for the club members, it was mostly a downhill journey. About a half mile down the trail, they finally hit the old forest-service road. The pace picked up as the group made an east-northeast trek into a neighborhood not too far from the central town of Sylvan. Knowing they were almost to his arranged rally-point, Phil used his light to scoot back up to the front of the pack. He halted them near the head of the forest service road, where it started off a major service run that ran north to south. The neighborhood was just past the powerlines.

The farther from the gun range the pack got, the more vocal some of them were starting to get about the unexplained evacuation.

"Single file, everyone!" Phil said in a semi-normal tone. "We're almost there. You all will have food and shelter in an hour, just bear with me."

He started east again, toward the neighborhood, hearing a few people repeat his words to those who missed them. They re-found the road for the twenty meters that it cut through the greenbelt on the other side of the now-dead power lines. Through the greenbelt of firs and cedars, the group emerged into a cul-de-sac. Several earthquake-damaged homes looked eerily vacant...and several United States Marine Corps vehicles were parked in the middle. The pack of gun club residents had been allowed to pass right through a perimeter of Marines back at the powerlines, never seeing them. Phil, Josh, and a few others were the only ones who knew they were there.

Phil walked right up to the waiting hand of Sergeant Major Greg Piercy and shook it. The Senior NCO was standing next to a command Humvee with several antennas. All of the other Humvees had belt-fed M-2 machine guns— "Ma Deuces"—mounted to the top. One had an Mk-19 belt-fed grenade launcher. There were also several MTVRs—cargo and utility trucks—of varying types.

"Phil!" Greg said. "Good to finally meet ya!"

"The honor's mine, Greg," Phil said, grinning. "Gunny!" he exclaimed as he released the Sergeant Major's hand and shook Gunnery Sergeant Twogood's hand. "I'm sorry it had to be like this, but I'd be lying if I said I wasn't glad to see you and your men."

"We get it, Phil," Greg Piercy said. "But this cartel thing is getting out of hand. Is the plan still the same on your end?"

Phil scanned the crowded cul-de-sac with his NOD. "Assuming

the National Guard has shown up…" He started to recognize some of them to the east, by their different vehicles and uniforms. They were out on the road that the cul-de-sac was attached to.

"They are," Gunny Twogood confirmed.

"Alright," Phil said, scanning between the two. "We had a rapid bug out, so the majority of these folks don't know what's happening. I need a few minutes."

Phil started to gather his flock so he could bring them up to speed. "Folks!" he called out a few times. Even though most were maintaining a whisper, there was an excited collective buzz that was hard to cut through. Once he finally held the group's attention he continued, "Most of you are getting on these Marines' transport trucks and heading to safety at the submarine base."

There was a collective gasp as people were pleasantly surprised to hear that. Phil saw Payton and Savannah towing Josh up to the front of the pack.

"What do you mean most of us?" she asked point blank. Payton knew when her father was holding back, and she had a feeling he was going back to attack the cartel at the range.

Her face told Phil he was in trouble, even in the moonlight, so he ignored her. "Everyone! This is the Gunny Sergeant. You all need to listen to him. I need all guards and patrol to fall-in on me. We're going to a different set of trucks."

"No!" Payton yelled at her father, turning to glare at Josh. "You just got back!" she cried to the man she was in love with.

Josh couldn't bring himself to say anything as he pushed past the ladies in his life. Savannah started to cry. "Where are they going, Mama?"

Phil was trying to stay on task—*Lonnie, Eli, Nick, Tony*. He was checking off names in his head as he scanned. *Jeff, Stu—Stu?* "Nooooo—no. You're not goin', Doc," Phil said with authority.

"Wherever all the gunfighters are going, Phil," Stu said, stating the obvious, "you're going to need a doctor."

"You're probably right, Stu, but you ain't going. Josh and the others worked too hard to bring you back. You're staying with the group." Phil kept looking past Stu, counting off people in his head.

"It's not up to you, Phil!" Stu argued. "If there's bad people that need fighting…" He was at a loss for how to finish. After ten more seconds of silence from Phil, Stu finally resolved, "I have a duty to be there, just like the rest of you!"

Phil admired the little doctor's tenacity, but it wasn't the moment he wanted to hear it. "Actually, Dr. Schwartz, it *is* up to me. This is a military action. I'm the CO of this little unit. And I say you're not going!" He looked at the refugee group of range residents boarding trucks. "They need you, too, Doc." He pointed right at Payton, who had been twenty feet away and hanging onto every word. "She's having a kid in a few months. We can't afford to have you killed!"

Payton had enough and rushed to the assembled Posse. "Where are you going?" she pled with her father, who was trying not to let emotion impact his pre-departure tasks. Payton let the tears flow, and she looked at Josh. She grabbed onto him, arms around his neck. "Would one of you please talk to me?" she begged.

Stu backed down from Phil once he saw Payton. He gave him an almost fatherly look. "Alright, Phil," Stu said quietly. "You win. I'll let it go." Stu shook Phil's hand, turned, and headed for the trucks.

Payton let go of Josh and turned back to her father. "You're going back to ambush the cartel, aren't you?" she scolded.

Phil finally stopped ignoring his daughter. "Something like that, Olive," he said softly. He opened his arms for a hug, which she slid into.

"It's just land and buildings, Daddy!" she pled. "Please don't go!" she screamed as she sobbed. "First Mom! Then Crane!" She glared at Josh again. "Now you, too?!"

"It's more than that, honey," he consoled as he pulled back to look her in the eye. "And you know it. Things will only get worse if we don't stop it now."

She grabbed onto her father again. "Promise me you'll come back." Phil stayed quiet, but he seized the moment, slipping a sealed envelope he'd been holding into the water bottle pouch on her backpack. "Promise me!" she demanded.

Phil slowly pushed his daughter off and nodded at a Marine who was waiting to gently guide her toward a truck. "Ma'am," the marine said.

She began to follow the young Marine but stopped in her tracks so firmly that Savannah's clasp on her mother's hand slipped out as she kept walking. Payton turned back to her father and Josh. She began to bawl.

"Everything will be okay, Mama," Savannah said in the voice of an angel. She didn't grasp that many of the others weren't also headed toward the Humvees.

Ignoring her daughter, Payton cried out, "I love you both!" She then turned, sobbing loudly as she hurried to the waiting Marine and vehicle, with Savannah tagging along.

Phil watched his daughter and granddaughter turn to look back through the thinning cul-de-sac as they walked to a filling truck. Gunny Sergeant Twogood had just finished giving his Marines their orders. They were busy mounting up into their Humvees, ready to head in the direction that the bug-out had just come from.

"About three-point-five kliks up the service road, you'll find our trail, Gunny. Another 700 meters to the property. Good luck." The Gunny silently nodded to Phil to acknowledge the information.

Phil and the Posse left the cul-de-sac and boarded the National Guard's trucks. He could sense the sadness and foreboding as everyone stared at the Marine vehicles, which were whisking their families and loved ones north and out of the abandoned neighborhood. Phil finally knew what it meant to feel the full weight of command, wondering as he looked at the forty or so men and women, which ones would be living their last night.

. . .

Tahoma's Hammer Plus 40 Days.

The moonlit night's cold, November air was quiet, save for the small DC motors that pushed four propellers at a high rate of speed. The red and green lights on the device had black electrician's tape over them. There was no camera—the drone flew at four hundred feet above ground level to a very specific spot and lowered itself. It set down between the corner of the log structure and the rifle-line's awning. One second after it stopped its descent, the little drone's computer sent an electrical signal to a long delay electrical relay, which in turn zapped one kilogram—about 2.2 pounds—of C-4 plastic explosive. The explosion sent logs flying well over one-hundred feet in the air, propelled by a fireball and shockwave that broke the glass out of every small building and trailer on the property and the homes to the properties south of the West Sound Sportsmen's Club.

The cartel soldier's timing was nearly perfect, as the vehicles that had been travelling south on the Canal Vista Highway rolled right over the center of the roundabout with Salal Road. Vehicles two through four came to a screeching halt fifteen seconds after the fireball had turned the Common into a million toothpicks and sent stones from the two rock fireplaces flying hundreds of feet away. Men got out of the four vehicles and used rocket-propelled grenades to send high-explosive shells into the club's northwest and front-gate fighting positions. The lead vehicle had travelled down and sent an RPG round into the southwestern fighting position.

The four fire teams then entered the gun club's property from the three insertion points. One of the teams then sent two more RPG rounds into the office, turning it into shrapnel. The three gun-safes—each weighing over a thousand pounds when factoring in the contents— went flying onto where the rifle line roof had existed only a minute earlier, crashing onto the concrete pad below.

The fire-teams began a methodic search and destroy mission, each one assigned a variety of trailers and tents to kill the occupants in. They systematically rounded the ends of berms, heading into the action bays and firing full bursts from their M-4s into the various tents and camping trailers. They dropped hand grenades through busted trailer windows and immediately moved on to the next area to clear. As they meandered through the action bays to the north of the rifle line, firing blindly, it started to dawn on the cartel's most elite special operations forces that they were attacking...*nothing*.

"Yankee, check in," the team leader ordered on his tactical radio. "Have you seen anyone?"

"Negative, Six," the team's leader said.

"X-Ray?"

And so it went, the squad leader of each fire-team concurring—*we haven't seen a soul...*

"Fall-in on me," the leader ordered. He was standing on the cross-range road, east of the burning log structure, staring at the fire. As all fifteen of the remaining operators began to migrate toward him, he thought his ears were playing tricks on him. Whoompf...whoompf... then a slight pause. Then another pair of the ominous noise. Whoomph...whoompf...

At the top of his lungs, the leader of the group, a Nicaraguan who had over thirty years of true combat experience, yelled, "Incom—"

Ka-Boom-Boom-Boom-Boom! Four mortars landed within fifteen meters of the clustering group, sending almost half of them to Hell before their body parts rained down on the burning logs. Dud-duh-duh-duh-duh-duh-duh-duh-duh-duh! Four M-2 belt-fed 50-caliber machine guns opened up on the pile of men. The remaining cartel soldiers were scrambling to find cover behind the burning logs, their ears and heads ringing. Two of the Humvees were hiding in the woods at the top of the cliff above the range's 250-meter line. One was at the berm by action bay eleven and the south road. The last was at the far end of the cross-range road, just a stone's throw from where the Slaughter Peninsula Posse had been born.

The fury of the United States Marine Corps was fast, furious, and effective. The north and south Humvees began to slowly approach the destroyed cartel unit, under the protection of dismounted infantry who were using cover to rapidly approach on foot as they sought out and shot the cartel infantry.

Out on Canal Vista Highway, two more Humvees appeared. One of them used its Mk-19 belt-fed grenade launcher to destroy all four of the stolen vehicles the cartel had arrived in. As much as Sergeant Major Greg Piercy wanted to search the rigs for usable intelligence, he just wasn't going to chance the lives of his men. *Besides,* he reminded himself as he looked up at the sky, *we already know what they're up to.*

Greg's Command Rig received an all clear from the Platoon Leader. His driver took the rig past the smoldering sandbags by what used to be the range's front gate and took the little road down to the rifle line road, where he stopped. Greg's Marines were already well into performing their secondary search of the property.

"Any problems, Lieutenant?" he asked 1st Louie Jamal Johnson.

"No, Sergeant Major," Jamal said as he approached the Regiment's top NCO. "We'll have our assessment ready to transmit in five mikes," he said, using the military lingo for *minutes.*

"Very good, sir," Greg said.

Gunny Twogood walked up as Greg was getting ready to start a secure comm with his bosses via a battle tablet. "Feel good to get out of the office for a change, old timer?"

"Oorah," the older leader said. "The old man wants to know ASAP that we had no casualties. Estimated enemy KIA?"

"Sixteen," Dale Twogood said.

"Roger," Greg said. After a couple more minutes, he was face-to-face with none other than Colonel Isaiah Franklin. "Mornin', sir."

"Sergeant Major," Colonel Franklin replied. "Give me some good news so I can hit the rack."

"Excellent news, sir," Greg informed him. "This threat to our base's southern flank has been dealt with. Zero casualties. Sixteen estimated enemy KIA. You'll have our full report in the system before you've had your mornin' joe, sir."

26

"Be content with what you are and wish not change; nor dread your last day, nor long for it."
—Marcus Aurelius

Tahoma's Hammer Plus 40 Days.

The monolithic ship sat like a giant, gray ghost. Any tidal movement in her mooring on the east side of her homeport pier just outside the shipyard was barely discernible. It was surprisingly clear for a Pacific Northwest November. Phil noticed that when their trucks were far enough in between the generators and tall floodlights casting long shadows on the navy base, he could just start to make out the stars. The base and accompanying shipyard were mostly very dark, at night only using the fuel needed to provide security lighting and time-sensitive work. The criticality of resources had forced the nuclear-powered titan to use her reactors in homeport.

She, too, was keeping her profile as low as possible for security reasons, though Phil could easily see red light emanating from the sole hangar bay door on the vessel's portside, rear corner.

The road along the quay wall ended at the head of the aircraft carrier's pier. There was one last gate to pass through, staffed by camouflaged sailors with rifles. Phil kept his eyes on the 70,000 tons of Freedom as he felt his truck in the convoy turn right and continue toward the far end of the pier. *The USS Halsey,* Phil thought solemnly, once more thinking of his beloved son, Crane. *Please be worth my son's life, whatever your mission is…* Phil closed his eyes to talk to his son and ask God for wisdom in what was ahead, if even for only a few seconds. The brakes squealed as the truck clunked to a stop.

Phil reset his below-knee prosthetic back into a hard-suction onto his stump and climbed out of the cab, allowing the Guard soldier to go to the back and start guiding Posse members out of the enclosed bed. The pier was a commotion of vehicles, both military and civilian. Phil could tell some sort of gathering spot was in the middle of it at the far south end, past a long row of dumpsters and forklifts. He started hobbling toward the crowd. *A lot of sailors up and about for 0300,* he thought, seeing that there were quite a few small huddles of sailors on the ship's lowered aircraft elevator, observing the militaristic hubbub assembling on their pier.

As he passed the last forklift, he stopped to turn back and look, double-checking that his convoy's troops were following. Most had their kits donned, a hodge-podge of plate carriers, chest mounted rifle magazine pouches, gun belts and backpacks. Many were working in pairs to carry ammo crates. A few were pulling or pushing small carts filled with water and medical supplies. *Is this really happening?* Phil was both proud and worried—not so much for his own safety, but for that of the others. He had an idea of what to expect when they *hit the beach,* but he didn't know how most of these men and women—*kids, a lot of them,* he corrected himself—would react to incoming mortars and bullets. *But we were all kids,* he reminded himself of his own military service. Militaries throughout history had always preferred kids—*they're long on adrenaline for combat and short on the courage needed to question bad orders.* He turned back to walk towards the canopy where he recognized several people.

"Mornin', Sheriff," Phil greeted Sheriff Ward Raymond. "Shouldn't you be staying back to guard the county?"

"Shouldn't you?" the Sheriff quipped back.

Phil just stared at him for a second or three. "Fair enough," he concluded. "Charlie...Major Matsumoto," he said, acknowledging them as he walked over for handshakes. "What's the plan?" He could see a number of National Guard members to the south, standing at ease but in formation. He nodded toward them. "I take it that's all you can spare without opening up the EOC to marauders?" he asked Adam.

"Let's just say 'yes' and leave it at that," the Major replied. He was ashamed to admit just how badly depleted his unit had become. If it weren't for the stored food, he was sure there would be no National Guard at this point.

A small group of naval officers approached from the direction of the USS Halsey's brow, or gangway, on the southeast side of the pier. Phil could tell it was the Shipyard Commander and a few other higher-level officers. He had just met her for the first time about fourteen hours earlier. *Smart...and fair*, he assessed. They walked up to the canopy and a couple of them grabbed some coffee out of the urns that were on a table. Phil saw the coffee pot and realized it had been a couple of weeks since he'd had any. *Ohhhh, maaann—I wish I hadn't seen that...* "Good mornin', Captain," he said to Captain Marie Darnell, as she approached their little huddle. Major Matsumoto offered a crisp salute, which Marie returned.

"Phil," she said, offering a handshake. "Once again, thank you for coming to see me. This little effort you and Major Matsumoto have thrown together is more important than you realize." She turned slightly toward the man next to her. "This is Captain Reese, the Commanding Officer of the base, and Captain Carpenter, the Halsey's CO. Technically we're on Captain Reese's pier."

"Captain," Phil said to Captain Reese, acknowledging him. "We appreciate the support. Have you heard from our little patriot navy?"

"Yes, Mr. Walker. They're all bobbing out there past the security fence. It's hard to see that until you get closer to the pier's end. When you're ready, Port Operations will open a section and they can start tying up to the three barges over on the west side of the pier. We've set some fuel tanks that have hand pumps to top off boats that need it."

"Much appreciated, sir," Phil told him. He looked at the other Unified Posse leaders and received a set of facial expressions and head-nods that said, "Let's get going."

"We're ready, Captain. Based on radio chatter, they needed us yesterday."

Captain Reese and the Lieutenant Commander following him used a set of hand-held radios as they stepped away from the group. The Sheriff, Major Matsumoto, Charlie, and Phil headed out to go start briefing the militia leaders, including Gary, Skinny Kenny, and some from the two ends of Slaughter Peninsula.

"Uh, Phil," Marie said quickly. "Just a quick word?" He stopped as the others kept going, looking back and forth at Marie and Captain Carpenter, the aircraft carrier's CO. "Captain Carpenter, here, wanted to meet you."

"Oh—sorry, sir, just a bit preoccupied," Phil said sticking his hand out.

The captain took it, but he didn't let Phil's hand go. "Richard, Phil," the accomplished man said. "I prefer 'Rich' when formality isn't necessary. Listen, I'm not in a position to say too much, but I just felt you should know that your son's sacrifice was not in vain."

Boom—instant tears filled Phil's eyes. He looked down and away as he didn't want to seem like a cry-baby. "Well, Rich," he said, trying to choke the words out, "I appreciate that." He really didn't at that moment, but he knew he probably would appreciate it one day.

"I mean it, Phil. We have orders. Things are happening to the world dynamic as we speak. If this community didn't rally after the volcano, to get my ship out of dry-dock..." He paused looking behind Phil at the several hundred community members, soldiers, and police officers who were mobilizing. "...Or tonight, to ensure we can even sail up Puget Sound safely...sooner than you think... we wouldn't be able to go do our jobs. You'll find that Team Halsey found some 'spare' munitions to donate to the effort. They're on the barge already." The old man smiled as he said, "Ah—the barge without the fuel bladder, that is!" His smile turned down to a fond smirk once more. "Thank you for your sacrifice, Phil." He finally released the grip on Phil's hand.

Phil was at a loss for words. He just looked at the two Captains for a moment, giving ever-so-slight of a smile, nodded, and walked off to his Posse.

JENNIFER LOOKED around as her family's vessel slipped through the breach in the big, floating security fence under the watchful eyes of two Federal Police Officers in a patrol boat. One of them was standing behind a mounted M-60, ready to install holes into anything that suddenly started acting like a threat. Though Jennifer never saw them, her craft was also being covered by machine gun nests on the pier and carrier's flight-deck, too. Her father guided the forty-foot Rampage through the waters, following the lead craft, a twenty-foot whale boat operated by the shipyard's personnel, toward the west side of the pier. *I think we've picked up some local vessels in our fleet,* she thought as she looked back and saw the size of her armada. She and Andy were ready to tie up to a barge at the Navy base in Bartlett and start loading troops.

"What's the plan, again?" her dad yelled from inside the cabin for the fourth time in three hours.

"We're tying up first and leaving last!" she yelled back with a tone that said, 'Quit asking!' "We'll probably need to let the smaller craft tie up outboard of us, just to keep the foot traffic moving."

She had been told there would be two or three large barges which were light enough that they were drafting about five or six feet from the waterline to their decks. *Too tall for some of these craft to let the militia members jump down from. Especially with gear, loading ammo...* Her plan had been to tie up the larger fishing vessels to those and then all smaller vessels would in-turn tie-up to their craft.

For over an hour, the plan slowly became reality, as vessels in the Patriot Navy began to fill with armed women and men, and supplies. Fishing boats and small cabin cruisers would take on six, eight, sometimes twenty people and then pull out of the way. A line had formed up on both sides of the security fence breach, as full vessels competed for a slot to pass through with empty ones.

Jennifer watched, as the middle-aged red-head and a handsome Native American deputy assigned boats to certain team members. The National Guard members and most of the other deputies and police officers were doing the same thing on the other barges. She could tell by the uniforms that some of the militia members were from the fire department. *Maybe the medics?* She wondered.

As the barge was finally emptying of people, the last thirty or so were boarding her Rampage. "Permission to come aboard?" Phil asked with slight amusement. The former Marine wondered if anyone would get it.

"Granted," Jennifer said. "I'm Jennifer. I'm guessing you may be the 'Phil' our radio operator told us to look for."

"That I am," Phil said. "These are Charlie, Nick, and Josh," he said pointing to his three comrades-in-arms. "We're some of the leadership for the Posse. Bear in mind, there are Posses and militias from at least two other counties here tonight, along with the soldiers. It can get a bit confusing."

"I get it, Phil," Jennifer said. "This redneck flotilla isn't exactly an organized unit itself," she joked. She turned to Andy and ordered a cast-off from the barge. As her father guided one of the last craft back out of the Navy base's security perimeter, she finally took a moment to gaze at the giant aircraft carrier. There were generators on the pier and the ship itself that allowed her to see it—and the gawking sailors. *Is that...is that a cell phone?* She couldn't believe her eyes. Sailors were on the end of the flight-deck, waving and saluting as they filmed the Patriot Navy. Jennifer immediately defaulted to her natural sarcasm in her thoughts. *You act like you've never seen a Howdy Doody, rag-tag flotilla sail off for war before...*

"You look like George Washington crossing the Delaware River!" Charlie cracked, laughing at Phil. The huge moon hung in the eastern sky like a beacon of hope.

Phil had been deep in thought and didn't realize he was standing as far forward on the fishing vessel's bow as he could. He had subconsciously put his half leg up on a cleat, using his hand to hold the ship's hull, which was a little shy of four feet high.

He had been watching the procession slowly make its way through the snake-shaped inlet, past the landslide on the south end of Russell island, and start plying toward Seattle. The vessels were slowly spreading out to make the wakes between them not churn up too much rocking action. Phil guessed they were doing about ten knots, so that they could travel as a pack.

He turned and looked at his closest friend. He pulled the fake foot off the cleat he was leaning on and took the two steps down the deck toward Charlie, careful not to step on Joe's legs in the process. Everyone was sitting for the ride over. He looked around. Some were carrying on quiet conversations, others looked like they were praying or trying to catch a quick catnap. *God bless anyone who can sleep right now.* He reached for his buddy, and the two friends embraced for a 'bro-hug.'

"Try to keep your head down, brother," Phil said worriedly.

"You're telling me?" Charlie joked with fake exasperation. "I'm one of like sixty brown or black dudes in this shin-dig, and most of us are in Army uniforms. You just make sure people know I'm not part of the cartel!"

"Don't worry, Charlie!" the two men heard Big Tony call out. He was sitting on the deck, just below the windows to the cabin. "I got your back!"

That made all three of them bust a gut laughing, releasing some stress in the process. Phil glanced at Tony and said, "I don't think I told you how glad I was you and your awesome family made it out to the range, Tony."

"Feelin's mutual, Phil. It's all good." With that Tony, closed his eyes and Phil started scanning faces. He saw Jerry creeping up the port side of the boat, trying to reach Phil past the feet and legs of napping or praying people.

"So, I was able to link up with the radio operators from the other Posses while we were staging," Jerry said.

"Oh?" Phil replied. "What'd ya get?" he said, spying the toy in Jerry's hand.

"I figure you'd be best to decide where to use this!" Jerry said with the excitement of a nerd who just received a new Star Wars toy. "Man, I wish I'd thought of this! It's a homemade FLIR periscope!"

"A what?" Phil knew that FLIR was an infrared scope, but he was confused—basically looking at a cellphone on a selfie-stick.

"One of the other HAMs put a bunch of these together! It's a phone with a FLIR camera plugged into the charging port. Only they were able to use a cable and camera stick to provide some separation between the two. See?" Jerry said. He raised the stick and camera about six-feet into the air over his full arm's-reach. Phil could see the heat-images of various bodies on the deck at the stern of the vessel. They were looking over the trawler's cabin.

"Holy schnikies!" Phil said. "That's pretty cool. Tell you what—hold onto it with your gear-bag. I'll find you when we need it." As Jerry made his way to the stern again, Phil started scanning faces once more. *Josh, Nick, Eli, Tony, Charlie…thank you, Lord, for these people. Please watch out for them.*

He looked back to the east, the 'Space Needle-less' skyline of Seattle slowly becoming more visible with the slightest hints of late-fall dawn. They were still far enough out that the sounds of waves lapping the hull and the diesel engine's rumble was all he heard. But the lights of gunfire flickering off of buildings in multiple spots was unmistakable. He could see the occasional muzzle flash and tracer rounds, which worked with the moon and the growing dawn to reveal the windowless skyscrapers and leaning hulks of ships that had partially submerged, pulled into the sound by their sunken piers.

The seed of anxiety planted itself in Phil's gut. He scanned south and north, seeing nothing less than fifty boats in the Patriot Navy carve the black water of Puget Sound. They bobbed up and down as they plied through the salty brine, carrying over five-hundred men and women who were headed to defend the thin-line between America and the Cartel.

27

The Battle for Seattle.

Tahoma's Hammer Plus 40 Days.

"How the hell are we going to move eighty-three wounded and deceased?" Natalie yelled at the guard. "And where would you advise we go?!"

"Look!" said Stan, the old Viet Nam vet. "There's about fifteen gang members marching down 16th Avenue! There's not enough of us to fight them!"

Janet, one of the other people helping bandage the wounded, ran over to the northeast corner of the parking structure. Her view was mostly obscured by the rubble of the next structure to the north, which had crumbled in the massive earthquake. She ducked when the sight of gang members, mostly decked out in black clothing with red undertones, came into view. They were running from car to car to cover their advance. She came running back over to the center of the facility at about the same time loud gunfire started echoing loudly throughout the concrete walls. "They're practically here! Grab a gun! It's too late!"

Where on Earth is Conner?! Natalie yelled in her head as she felt the heft of her .357 in the waist pack she'd been wearing on her hips. What she didn't know was that he and one other of the five-man contingent had begun to snipe at the encroaching enemy, drawing their fire to the top of the structure. Natalie ran to the tables they'd started piling the tactical gear from the wounded on and dug through it—*a shotgun! I know how to shoot one of these!*

Stan had rejoined the other two guards on the ground floor, shooting out of the structure at anything that moved. "They're going to try to flank us from the west!" he yelled. "I can feel it in my bones!"

One of the other two, who was about half of Stan's age, began sprinting, dodging the wounded and dead who were lying on the tarps in the middle of the garage. He made his way over to the western side. "He's right!" He started firing, trying to shoot back and forth at two different angles. Twenty seconds later, the young man took a bullet in the side of the head and crumpled to the floor.

Natalie was flipping tables up on edge, trying to place them in front of her wounded. *I have to try!* She then placed the gear behind the tables, hoping that it may provide some form of ballistic protection for the people she'd assumed charge over. The car-entrance to the ground floor was about fifty meters south and on the east side. Stan and his comrade moved over to it to begin covering any invaders that tried to penetrate it. Not ten feet from it, a hand reached over through the gap that made a breezeway at the top of the first floor and dropped a grenade in. *Clack-clack-clack* it said as it bounced on the concrete floor behind the two guards. KA-BOOM! Smoke and noise spread throughout the place, sending a shockwave that made people's ears ring.

"Conner!" Natalie yelled at the air, wondering if he'd already died on the roof. As the smoke cleared, she could tell that both of the remaining guards had been killed by the blast. She looked left and right. Janet was holding an AR-15 while their other teammate, a retired psychiatrist, was holding a smaller caliber Ruger pistol. All three of the team had taken up positions behind load bearing columns. The doctor cried out in agony as he was shot in the back. None of them had thought to keep an eye on the west side of the garage after the young guard had been killed a minute earlier. Janet spun and started shooting at the face that had shot the doctor. Natalie wasn't sure if Janet got the invader, but he had disappeared from view and stopped trying to shoot them. "Just keep watching the west!" Natalie ordered.

She peered back around her column at the vehicle entrance and saw three gang members start to enter. They had their rifles raised and were sweeping as they started to progress. One of them started firing into the side-leaning tables. "Noooo!" Natalie screamed, as she saw her wounded start to get shot again. She swung the shotgun down and blasted the closest man squarely in the chest. He let out a scream as he fell to his knees, clutching the eight holes that had just entered his body.

Both of the others began firing wildly in Natalie's direction and she retracted herself behind the column. She could hear nothing but both rifles barking. She looked over at Janet and saw her get shot in the side three times as one of the cartel-inducted gang bangers finally had the angle to see her. In her panic, Natalie couldn't remember how to pump the shotgun. Her hands trembled as she fidgeted with the zipper on the waist pack. Her motor skills had been completely lost in the cortisol-fueled fight-or-flight reactions that moment. *God, please protect my babies!* she thought as she started to claw at the bag, unable to feel the small metal zipper-tag.

POP! POP! POP! POP! POP! POP! POP! Natalie's' vision exploded in muzzle-flash as Conner came running off the parking garage's stairs on the north wall. He'd freed his wounded arm from its sling and was marching almost straight at Natalie's column, firing a few feet to her east. Natalie heard a strange voice cry out just a couple of feet on the other side of it. POP! POP! POP! POP! Conner kept shooting as he got to the column and then passed it, out of her sight. "Now! Now!" Conner screamed into the radio immediately putting his left hand back onto his rifle as he marched to the next column. He was pouring gunfire onto the entrance. A team of the Tarboo militia began to pour over the air-gap in the western wall of the garage, dropping in, rolling and taking cover behind the columns and few remaining cars in the facility. Within a minute, they'd killed any remaining members of the gang that had tried to invade the makeshift infirmary.

Natalie looked out at the militia members as they strolled through, checking to see if any of the enemy on the ground were still a threat. She walked out past her column and saw the man who was four feet from killing her, missing the space where his nose and eyes should've been, fresh red blood pouring onto the floor. She heard screaming coming from behind her shielding for the already-wounded. Natalie scanned around and found the wheeled cart they'd been keeping their supplies on. *Get back in the fight!* she yelled at herself in her head. She grabbed the cart and made a beeline for the psychiatrist who'd been shot in the back. She used her shears to cut the man's shirt off, exposing a wound in the region of his left lung. Slamming a piece of gauze on it, she wondered if they had anymore chest seals. Natalie took a quick glance up at Conner, just in time to see him take one knee...than another...before falling forward on the concrete.

JOHN HAD FORGOTTEN JUST how cold one could get cruising around a few thousand feet up. Tucker had advised him to layer up and tether everything—rifle, binoculars, even the gloves themselves, just in case he took them off for a task. Even with a base layer and several additional layers over it, though, the clear November night was cold. He had apprehensively taken off on his first paramotor flight in fifteen years a half-hour earlier from the soccer field at Seattle University Park. This had been his first night flight. Paramotorists weren't required to file flight-plans, but the law also required them to only fly during daylight hours, except for permitted events like air shows. *The laws on such things really don't apply anymore, do they?* he asked himself after he started his ascent.

His role and Tucker's were vastly different—he would be a high-altitude spotter. He could keep his motor turned off for several minutes at a time, drifting quietly a few thousand feet above the action below, providing a semi-stealthy aerial reconnaissance to the Patriots. The nearly full moon was both a blessing and a curse—there was no rain to endanger their flight ops, but they would be quite easily seen once someone had actually noticed them. For this reason, John was trying to stay to the west of the action, out of the moonlight to those on the ground. John pulled on his sleeve and scanned his watch.

"Peanut Butter, this is Chocolate Actual," John heard Earl call out on the pre-designated frequency. "All cups are in place."

John fussed with his glove to get his hand onto the transmit button near his earbud. "Roger and copy. Wait for further." He heard a double click for Earl's acknowledgment and fired up his motor, staying a few hundred feet higher than the highest skyscraper in the north end of Seattle. He didn't have to worry about the construction cranes—every one of them had fallen forty-one days earlier. John could see pockets of fighting. He had been calling in enemy positions to the militia units up until a few minutes earlier. John throttled up the re-warmed engine on his back and pulled on his handles to move farther south. *I want to make this run at a safe height before my boy risks his life.*

John flipped the night vision down on his helmet and immediately saw the twenty strobes echoing off the steel skeletons and concrete walls below. *We need to hurry—those cartel most assuredly see them, too, and are trying to figure out what they mean.* He caught direct sight of a strobe a couple of times, but at this height it was mostly just the reflections of their rhythmic blinking. Earl's team had just created a runway right up 8th Avenue, except for a couple of spots where they just couldn't root out all of the enemy cartel. John swung around back west to find his picket that was less in the moonlight to ground observers. That's when he noticed dozens of black dots in Elliot Bay, creating wakes as they approached Seattle. *What the....? Stay on task!* he scolded himself.

"Nougat, this is Peanut Butter! Creamy goodness. I say again, creamy goodness." He waited for the reply.

Finally, "Peanut Butter, Nougat copies. Creamy goodness is a go."

He's airborne, John realized. He went back to scanning the action on the waterfront, wondering if he had time to call any of it in before he had to go spot for his son. He decided he needed to fidget with his radio and report it when something on top of a building caught his eye. *Cartel!* He was sure of it. *Setting up mortars!* It was then that he realized the Patriot leaders had, indeed, made good on the idea that he had relayed up the chain. Marshall had suggested that they try to make contact with the West side Patriots. Phalanx had relayed the idea and never been given an update on what became of it. *Those must be ours!*

John did have a rifle with him, but he was a key piece of the attack—he was going to lase the target for the guided-bomb's tracking system. "Peanut butter, Nougat," he heard in his headset. "Melt in your mouth. I repeat, melt in your mouth." *No time,* John thought. "Copy," he replied, banking his paramotor to the northeast to reacquire the target he'd picked out near Seattle Center.

"Holy moly!" Tony screamed, eyes wide as flying saucers. "They never even made it to shore!"

Phil ran back thru the crowd of Posse members, who were

trying desperately to duck and be ready to jump off the boat with their gear. He pounded on the window of the boat's cabin rapidly. "Get us on that shore! Now!"

They had all just watched a mortar round take out the craft that was two boats to the right. It was the one that Sheriff Raymond had been on, Phil was fairly certain. More mortar rounds were splashing around the vessels. *I knew sailing straight for our insertion point was a bad idea!* Phil had tried convincing the vessel's crew that they needed to zig-zag randomly, but they weren't hearing it. They just wanted to drop off their raiding parties and get back out. The destination was the very shore that Tony had scrambled onto several weeks earlier when he went on a mission to rescue his girls.

Phil tried to see what building the mortar was coming from. Most of the buildings in this area were only a few stories tall. *Still, those mortars could be coming from several hundred meters away! We may not find them!* He felt the boat surge with power, as he and nearly everyone stumbled backwards when Jennifer's father bumped the throttle.

"I can't see nothin', Jenn!" he yelled out of the cabin. "Gonna need you to say 'when'!"

"Move!" Jennifer yelled as both she and Andy pushed their way through the crowd to get an eye on the rapidly approaching shore.

"Everyone brace yourselves!" Phil yelled out. "Hold onto your gear!"

Ka-Boom! A mortar hit the water just a few feet away from the vessel to their port side, which was also trying to speed to shore. They took several casualties and the boat had a giant hole in its side. It started flooding just as streams of machine gun fire from two different nests on buildings started raking the boats.

"Now! Now! Now!" Jennifer yelled, repeating herself to make sure her father heard. He slammed his throttle into reverse and cut his helm hard to port, causing the craft to lurch to starboard. Everyone felt the power cut out, and the forty-foot Rampage lived up to its name as it drifted up to the erosion control rocks and slapped them with a thud. "Off! Everyone off!" Jennifer was barking.

Andy jumped onto the nearest rock and ran a few feet south. One of the Posse threw him the stern line. He held it to keep the vessel from wandering off. Posse bodies began to pour off. As soon as he hit the rocks, Josh turned to Jennifer and yelled, "Throw me the line!"

She did as directed, and the vessel stabilized while about thirty other people began jumping off. Some of them hit the frigid water directly, a few others slipped on the rocks and slid in. People were trying to grab those who were slipping, while others trying to get off the boat were trying to hand over ammo and packs. *Chaos!* Phil realized. *Get control!* "Charlie!" he yelled for his friend who was already on shore. "Pick three people to guard the east and three to take the supplies from the ship!"

"Phil!" Jennifer called to him just as he was about to stick his whole, right leg over the boats side and feel for a rock. He looked at her. "What do we do?"

"Get out of range of those mortars!" he screamed. "But be ready to come back! We may need a ride somewhere!" He could see the girl looked terrified as he slipped off the boat, sinking up to his waist. Nick was ahead of him, and he reached down, giving Phil a hand and pulling him up. "Where's Tony?!" Phil yelled toward Charlie, who was directing people in their tasks.

"Right here, Phil!" Big Tony said from the eastern side of the pack. He was facing out towards Seattle.

Phil wobbled the thirty feet over to him and turned around, taking a knee and facing the boat. "Good," Phil said a little more calmly. "Hang tight!" He could see Andy had jumped back onto the boat, and Josh was just giving the bow a shove. Phil was scanning his team. "Jerry! Over here!" He kept scanning once he saw his comms guy duck-walking toward him. Phil was now extending his scan north and south, trying to see what teams were making it ashore. He observed people from the entire armada clamoring for cover behind rocks, as the cartel gun nests were finding their marks.

Nick had just shown up to Phil's spot and took a knee, too. "We need to get off the X, Phil," he suggested quite calmly. Phil looked at the sniper, who was a virtual calm in a storm of rage, battle rifle on his front and sniper rifle sticking straight into the air on his back.

During the staging period on the pier, the Posse had quickly divided itself into four teams of seven or eight people. Phil's fireteam would be calling the shots for all four teams. "Josh!" he called over to him, knowing Tony was part of that team. "Have Tony get us over those train tracks and past that park! Double time!"

"Roger-Wilco!" he heard Josh yell, "Alpha! Two four-man teams in diamond formation! Tony, you're on point! Don't worry, I'll be twenty feet behind you!" Tony led the small unit out, while Phil had assessed the rest of the shore landing. He could see much of Major Matsumoto's group had landed over the immediate several hundred meters to their north. The rest of the Slaughter Peninsula Posse was still scrambling to shore to the south. "Nick," Phil said without yelling since the sniper was still just a few feet away. "Scouts out! You guys find some high ground to the north! See if you can stop those machine guns!" Phil said pointing that way. He then pointed back to the south. "And see if you can find those mortars, too. Hurry!"

"Delta! Let's roll!" Nick yelled, channeling his inner Todd Beamer. His seven-man squad rolled out in the shadow of Alpha but veered north as soon as they crossed the train tracks.

"Lonnie! Have Bravo Team spread out in a line along these tracks to the south over the next one-hundred meters. It looks like the rest of the Posse is having a hard time getting those smaller boats near the shore. Give them some cover! Go!"

"Whadda we do if you guys take off on us, Phil?!" Lonnie asked nervously.

"Everyone stay on our freq. Just check in. Jerry!" Phil yelled.

"Yo!" his HAM called out, causing Phil to snap his head that direction.

"You tech-nerds worked out a comms plan, right?! We got a dedicated frequency?"

"Yes! Just remember—nothing's secure!"

Nothing's secure! Phil almost choked in sarcastic laughter in his head. *Understatement of the year, Jerry!* he thought. "Right! Great point, Jerr! Everyone! Fall in! Keep your heads down!" he started to stand to a crouch and turn and realized he'd made eye contact with Charlie, one of the few Slaughter County Sheriff Deputies on the invasion force, and the only one in Phil's Posse Unit. "Sorry, brother," Phil mumbled, knowing Charlie had watched a few of his brethren die in the explosion. Charlie just nodded.

Collectively, the four small squads under Phil's command were call-sign Peg-Leg. He had chosen the moniker Echo for his command squad to avoid any confusion with the real 'Charlie.' Phil turned and led his fireteam into the black under the occasional burst of mortars and machine gun fire. As the first hues of morning dawn started to paint the sky, the Slaughter Peninsula Posse had officially entered the Battle for Seattle.

28

Momentum.

TAHOMA'S HAMMER PLUS 40 DAYS.

IT'S JUST CANYONS, boy, John thought as he scanned the area south of downtown for his son's wing. *Lord, please help him!* Though not a religious man, he was a loving father and was as worried for his son as he'd ever been. John knew that mid-level flying through a city in daytime would be extremely hazardous at best. The winds could easily whip themselves around a building and deflate or slam a wing into another building. *But at night, in a city wrought with destruction?* There were already a variety of obstacles in the air before the devastation—flag poles or utility wires, trolley lines…But now people had begun to build clotheslines, antennas, watchtowers…

Tucker Cronin had actually been wearing the helmet with night optical device for about a half-hour before launch, trying to acclimate his depth perception to it. He didn't want to chance the risky nighttime launch off the soccer field with them, so he flipped them out of the way. After he'd attached his wing to his motor harness and made sure the brakes and steering straps were exactly how he wanted them, he pulled the wing and just the action of getting the leading edge a few feet in the air was enough. The sixteen-meter long sail's foils began filling with breeze, inflating them instantly. The wing jumped up and kited itself behind Tucker. He began to walk backwards and then turned himself, running to make sure that wing stayed just behind him a bit.

He applied full throttle and reached a point where he knew the wing had stabilized with forward momentum. That was his cue to pick his feet up. He double checked the throttle and put both hands on the steering cables, pulling the handles off their magnet mounts, but barely pulling on them. He could feel the wing's performance through those cables. He rose into the sky south of Seattle University and course corrected to do a wide arch to the east. His goal was to fly over the university and come back down on a southerly approach to the same soccer field, much like an F-18 landing on an aircraft carrier—and hook the hula hoop with his foot. His ground team had performed every possible preparation to the delivery device that they could. They had shortened the towline and constructed it out of a much thinner run of fishing line—three wraps of fifty-pound test. They didn't want to employ the shock-absorbing wrap in the line, for fear the friction of the line's extension would burn and break it. Instead, they used a medium sized spring-scale normally used to weigh fish up to twenty pounds. It was tethered to the hula hoop end and would fall away when Tucker separated the bomb.

The weapon pickup had gone about as smoothly as it could—other than running behind schedule, everything in the intricate plan was going okay.

Tucker had opted to hook the hoop with his foot, not wanting to have his hands impacted by the towline having to wrap itself around the protective cowling around his motor. After he hooked the hula hoop, he pulled his right foot up to his butt and used a bungee cord he'd attached to his belt to positively hook onto the ring. As he gained altitude and began an arch to the west, he could feel the ten-foot wide, Styrofoam and carbon fiber bomb buffeting the air behind him.

"Nougat, this is Chocolate Ten. Everything looks stable." The one report that Tucker, John, and Earl had been waiting on arrived in their earpieces. The unit farthest south in the flight-path operation had the authority to wave off if the glider was misbehaving.

This is it, son, John thought. He was so tempted to begin air controlling for him, but he knew the cartel was listening. Any extra radio traffic was just giving away information—everything had to be spoken in memorized phrases. John had to stay on his picket, ready to provide a last-minute laser for the glider. His only backup was Earl, who would have to scramble to the top of the shaky and leaning Amazon building to be able to lase the cartel's camp if something happened to John.

Tucker battled the buffeting winds, resisting the temptation to check out the beautiful sunrise that was just forming. He caught the first pair of blinking strobes in his NOD and started decreasing his throttle, trying to get down to about two hundred feet above 8th Avenue. He descended over an older Seattle neighborhood of apartment buildings and museums, crossing the broken I-5 highway and Washington State Convention Center with a slightly west-of-true-north heading. He pulled on his right steering cable with just a few ounces more of pressure than his left, banking around a circular, fifteen story building and shooting for the canyon gap. A block later he had to course correct the opposite, taking on a slight left turn in the process.

The winds hadn't been as bad as he was expecting. Tucker figured it was mainly due to so many of the buildings missing their glass—it was pouring through them naturally, versus being forced to go around and in between them.

He could see firefights happening below. The whole point behind this canyon run was that unlike his father, who had high-altitude that allowed him to shut off his motor—he had to keep power applied at near-full throttle to tow the dead weight behind him. Up in the sky, and he would've been heard and seen, and surely shot down before getting the precious cargo delivered. About mid-run, Tucker could see the strobes were on 7th avenue for just two blocks, before picking back up on 8th. He had to trust the ground team that they had secured that zone of enemy. He grabbed his brake cables and pulled down on the leading edge of his wing for just a moment, to change the angle it was attacking the air. He stowed those, pulling hard on the left steering strap to perform a wingover maneuver that allowed him to practically pivot in the air. He kept the throttle up, knowing that providing forward propulsion was the only way to keep the glider towing properly.

Tucker's wing and the homemade guided missile broke through the small gap between the U.S. District Court building and the tower to its north. He banked to the right and flew a block, reacquiring the next set of strobes to the northeast. He looked hard right quickly to see what had driven this dangerous maneuver. There was an intense firefight happening.

John Cronin caught first sight of his son and the cargo as Tucker had veered back over to 8th Avenue to resume his path to the Seattle Center. After one last, round skyscraper to pass, he was through the canyon and into the dangerous open. Tucker adjusted his cables and pressed the last ten percent of throttle he had to the max, beginning to climb.

John had been performing a loop to the west of the Seattle Center. When he estimated about a minute until his son's arrival, he cut his throttle and pulled slightly on his brakes, dumping air and altitude. He guided himself toward the gap near 8th Avenue. When Tucker broke through, John Cronin was only four blocks west and about four hundred feet higher, travelling mostly east. *One last adjustment,* John told himself. He pulled on his left cable and banked himself to aim toward the vehicle in the football field…*the one with all the antennas.* John pulled the rifle hanging from his neck up and placed the scope up to his eyes. He found the pressure pad that engage his aiming laser with his left thumb. His invisible laser glowed like a bright green rope in his NODs. He finally settled it on the important-looking truck…

Reynaldo Hernandez had grown tired of monitoring the battle behind a screen and radio operators. *Incompetent fools!* he screamed in his head. *When this is over, I'm going to burn you alive! Then drown you! Or, perhaps, invent a way to do it at the same time!* He ran out of the vehicle, snatching the battle rifle out of the hands of the nearest guard. His two personal guards had to run to catch up as he headed east. Three minutes later, a rapidly moving and angry Rey was breaking through the roof access of the south building of the Bill and Melinda Gates Foundation. He found one of the many machine gun bunkers he'd worked so hard to establish over the preceding days. "Can you see anything?!" he demanded angrily.

"Mostly just muzzle flashes, Jefe!" one of the two men replied. "Over toward the east!" he added, pointing past his sandbags and toward 8th Avenue. Most of the illumination was being provided by the moon, but as the dawn built in the eastern sky, the shadows were growing long. The difficult visibility was compounded by the muzzle flashes and grenade explosions in dozens of downtown locations, the reflections shining through the broken gaps where windows used to exist.

Rey was scanning with the outpost's binoculars and trying to keep an ear on radio traffic. He grabbed his handheld set and screamed, "I want an update on those IR beacons! Now!"

"Jefe, this is Unit 116! They're fighting ferociously to keep the street clear of us! It doesn't make sense!"

Rey replied with a loud word that would have gained him an

FCC fine, if the FCC had still had the ability to levy it. He dropped the radio to the roof. "Vamanos!" he yelled to his guards, getting ready to go back to his CP. In his anger, he had defaulted to his native tongue. Something caught his attention. "What is that?" He looked around.

"Que?" one of his guards questioned.

"The noise?! What's that noise?!" Having been in the insulated truck most of the night, his ears had not been rung by the gunfire too much. He started scanning around.

"Give me your night vision!" he demanded of the machine gun team.

"The batteries are dead, Jefe!"

After Rey repeated that FCC non-compliant word at the top of his lungs, he started looking south toward downtown. *There!* he thought. "Right there!" What is that?!" In an almost slow motion, cartoon-ish feel, Rey caught the motion of…something. "Is that a bird? No, a drone! They have a—"

The glider, though it had been spray-painted black, was just too big not to be noticed. It course corrected up and down with just a slight hint of left to right. It was headed northwest. Rey followed the trace of its path, right back to his…"Noooooooo!" Reynaldo Hernandez saw a giant toy, seemingly being radio-controlled by someone, fly directly for his Command Vehicle. "Shoot it down!" he screamed at anyone listening. As his machine gunners tried desperately to swing their barrel west and acquire the glider, Rey began looking around for the source of the noise. He saw a parachute steering away to the east, only noticeable when it crossed over something on fire. It was climbing and an engine could easily be seen pushing whoever it was to safety.

The gun-team had lost the descending craft below the threshold of the building before they could get a shot off. With fire in his eyes, Rey scanned around and found his radio near a sandbag. "Everyone get out of the—"

WHUH-BOOOOMMMM!

Both Cronin men had caught themselves a case of the giggles—and tunnel vision. The fact that his son had just pulled off what was perhaps the greatest paramotor stunt ever made the old man proud. John started his motor back up after he lowered the rifle slung around his neck. Tucker was supposed to go back and grab the back-up device, but John could see the young man bank north. He watched his son's wing and, it eventually turned west almost a half-mile north of the fiery center of the cartel's operation. John had had enough. "Nougat! Stay focused!"

The young man had been overcome with adrenaline upon seeing his heroic deeds pay off. All of his recent training had fallen to the wayside. "Did you see that, Dad?!" he screamed excitedly into the radio. "We beat 'em! They're going to fall apart at the seams, now!" The younger Cronin had become mesmerized by the initial, devastating explosion, which was now causing vehicles, fuel bladders, and ammunition supplies to catch on fire.

"Nougat!" John yelled in his dad voice. "Gain elevation, bank north, and vacate the area! Immediately!" John had resumed a northerly flight between the cartel and Elliot Bay, trying to regain the safety of altitude.

He heard machine gun fire erupt, as several locations around the cartel encampment started firing at his son. It would be a matter of moments before one of them was able to gain a bead on him. "Descend!" John yelled into the radio. "Forget altitude! They've seen you! You need to hit the treetops!"

Tucker started to execute an emergency drop by cutting throttle and pulling on the brakes. He had to be careful as to not do it so long that he collapsed his wing entirely. In the rescinding fires that had enveloped the football field cartel basecamp, John caught a motion rapidly ascending from the fountain area east of Climate Pledge Arena. "Dammmmiiiitttt!" he screamed out loud before keying the radio. "Nougat! Evacuate! You have incoming!"

Earl had been intensely listening to the exchange, trying to scan the area with binoculars. He had acquired Tucker and was trying to see where he would go down, should it come to that. The young paramotorist was wildly zigging and zagging to escape the machine gun fire. Suddenly, a quad copter drone came shooting out of nowhere. Though it could only match speed with the paramotor, it had cut him off with a sharp angle. Whoever had flown it shot it straight into Tucker's cords keeping him attached to the wings.

"Nooooo!" John yelled, as he watched his son's wing start to collapse. The youngster had pulled a series of evasive maneuvers that had put him dangerously close to the cartel's eastern perimeter. Time slowed down for John, as he suddenly became paralyzed with the realization he was going to watch his son die the same way he had to watch his friend die in his recurring nightmares. He made sure his throttle was as high as it could be and changed course. There was a natural point where experienced paramotor pilots knew they could glide and make a landing somewhere. John watched his son deploy his reserve chute as he fell. The device came out and inflated, slowing the descent as he lost sight of the boy somewhere a couple of blocks southwest of the Gates Foundation. He cut his engine and began his descent, hell-bent on getting to his son before the cartel did.

"I got him," Earl yelled to Larry, Renee, Jessica. "Let's go! Girls, follow me! Larry! Gain some altitude!" With that, Earl Garren and his two female warriors ran north as fast as they could scan for threats.

29

Ultimate.

T̴ahoma's Hammer Plus 40 Days.

"It was some sort of guided bomb!" Nick yelled to Buddy Chadwell, who was on the roof of the ten-story apartment building with him. They were west-southwest of the explosion, and the rest of his squad was pulling security at the base of the building to ensure they could make it off. He had continued to watch the action through his binoculars.

"Do you want me to start getting your fancy scope out of the case?" Buddy asked.

"No! This thing is unfolding too fast! We'll be moving in a couple of minutes!" the experienced veteran told him. "Hold up!" He was watching the action unfold. "There's a parasail!" he exclaimed. "The kind with a motor! They must've dropped it!" The multiple bursts of gunfire caught his alert eyes. "That dude's going to be in deep kimchee!"

"There's another one!" Buddy yelled, causing Nick to look high up and to his left.

He swung the binoculars. "He's turning toward the one being chased!" Nick started looking that way again. It took him several seconds to reacquire Tucker's deflated wing.

"The first one is falling! Wait! Some sort of reserve parachute!" It dawned on Nick quickly that the cartel would make that man pay dearly and slowly for what he'd done. "Get Phil on the horn! Tell him what's up. I know exactly where that guy fell! We're too far away here—let's get going!"

JOHN PULLED hard on the brakes as he drifted at almost thirty miles per hour barely four feet over the ruins and wreckage of Denny Way, stopping a mere fifty feet shy of the concrete wreckage that used to be the monorail. He estimated Tucker was two blocks north and two blocks east of where he was letting his wing slam to the ground. As he started to undo the leg straps on his motor harness, a bullet ricocheted off the ground next to him. He realized that someone from the south was shooting at him. He ran back toward his wing to get some slack in the lines, and then ran around an abandoned car to take cover. He squatted behind the wheel and axle and unclipped his wing, and then finished doffing the motor. *They must be a couple of blocks away still.* He bolted to the corner to his east and turned running north, out of sight of whoever had been approaching from downtown.

John kept his rifle up, trying to scan in all directions in the free-for-all shootout that Seattle had become. He climbed to the top of the monorail wreckage and scanned along the top of it, all the way to where the Space Needle had crushed it in its fall. *Clear as its gonna be!* He crawled over the debris and continued his journey, desperate to save his son. He cut up a long alley, using the ruins of a destroyed apartment building as cover as he ran north. He rounded another corner and saw Tucker's wing, lying in a heap in the old Best Western parking lot. John Cronin started sprinting for his son.

As he cleared the corner of the building to his north, crossing Taylor Street, a burst of fully automatic fire from a Humvee to the north hit the pavement two feet in front of the rapidly stopping senior Cronin. He scrambled backwards. He was once again covered by the building to his north but was in the wide open to any threats from his east. He could see Earl and his small team approaching from that direction.

"Dad!" his son called into the radio. "I-I'm hurt! I can hear them coming!"

"Nougat! This is Chocolate Actual!" John heard in his earpiece. "We're approaching from your east!"

The fog and confusion of battle was landing on John Cronin, who could think of only one thing—*I must rescue my son!*

▲

JOHN STREET, Earl thought, consulting the map after reading the street sign. *Now that's ironic.* "How we doin', ladies?!" Earl asked tensely. "Remember to speak up when in doubt!" They were covering his rear flank while he tried to figure out an approach to get to Tucker.

"Those cartel we cleared off 7th and 8th are east of us!" Jessica yelled. "It's a matter of time before they find us!"

"Have faith!" Earl commanded. "The rest of Tarboo is coming in to take that heat off of us! Right now—we got to save that kid!" He looked up, not liking the parking lot and trees before him. He only had a couple of blocks to go, but a belt-fed had an angle on him was chewing up pavement when he tried to poke an eye around the corner. *Effer must be right on the corner of the Gates Building,* he thought. *And it sounds like there's a second one to the west.*

"Okay, girls! Keep it locked down here! I'm going to try to clear this shooting gallery!" He no sooner than made it ten feet when fifty-caliber bullets started chipping up the asphalt in front of him. *Dammit to hell!* He screamed in his head as he made his way back behind his tree. *Definitely two of them!*

"Chocolate Sniper One, are you listening?" Earl keyed up on his radio. *Please be paying attention, Larry!*

"I'm hearin' ya," came the country drawl.

"Can you reach out and touch someone?! Need you to make a long-distance call, old timer!"

Larry had made his way to a ten-story building on the south side of Denny Way and 9th Avenue. Without replying, he calculated his yardage using the built-in scale on his hunting scope. He took a guess on the wind and started adjusting the clicks on the scope. Without so much as a word, the old hunter exhaled half a breath and let the shot fly. He hit the sandbags below and to the right of the machine gunners on top of the Gates Building. He ejected his casing and rechambered, never taking his eye out of the scope.

"Sorry, Chocolate actual. I got 'em to duck! Woulda been a hit on a bull elk, but no kill!"

"I WANT HIM ALIVE!" Rey screeched through his teeth. He and his men had just dismounted. A full block south of the Gates Foundation building, one of his captured Humvees, complete with a belt fed machine gun, came to a screeching halt in the intersection of Taylor Avenue and Thomas Street. They were maintaining a close eye on the corner of a building a few blocks south, keeping a would-be rescuer at bay. The gun-nest on the Gates Building was covering Rey and his ground-based capture-team one block further east as they methodically bound past each other. As badly as Rey wanted to run, he knew there were militia elements all over the city just to the south. *They undoubtedly fought-for and held a clear flying lane for this craft,* Rey realized with an intense rage. *An operation this man will regret for the rest of his pain-filled life!*

Rey heard the snap of fifty-caliber rounds whizzing over his head, hitting the ground where a different rescuer had tried to slip through. "The pilot must be a block up and on the right!" Rey yelled to his men. "The far end of this hotel!" His men were all using fully automatic M-4 rifles. "You! Stay here!" he ordered one of them while popping and throwing a smoke canister to conceal their approach. "You two! Get on that corner!" he commanded, pointing a finger. He was dispersing his pawns—seventeen, counting himself—amongst the chess board, a small insurance policy in case the couple of hapless rescuers got lucky.

"Dad!" Tucker was yelling from the ground in front of a concrete pillar that held up the awning to the hotel. "I'm sorry!"

"Tucker!" John yelled. He stepped out, once again, and was almost hit by both machine gun and automatic rifle fire. He ducked as he took pieces of concrete shrapnel to the face. One chunk cracked his safety glasses, which he stripped off and tossed aside. The former cop had never felt so helpless in his life. "Arrrgghhhh!" he screamed, wishing he could wake himself up from the nightmare. "Hang on, Tucker!"

John Cronin moved the barrel up as soon as his eyes and hands crossed the protective threshold of the building, on the far side of the parking lot to his north, shooting at the truck and machine gunner. He felt a round rip through his throat at the same moment two others tore through his legs. John hit the ground and clutched at his open esophagus.

"Dad!" the wounded Tucker screamed. Earl stare in disbelief

from less than two blocks to the east, unable to do anything but watch.

The shot had missed John's cervical spine, but it nicked the carotid artery as it destroyed his neck muscles. The former Seattle police officer died of hypovolemic shock, knowing his son was a hero, and wondering if they would soon meet in Heaven.

30

Violence of Action.

TAHOMA'S HAMMER PLUS 40 DAYS.

ALPHA, Delta, and Echo squads of the Peg-Leg Posse unit were quickly approaching the zone that the unknown parachutist had fallen into. "Delta One!" Phil yelled into the radio. "Can you get eyes on that closer belt-fed?!"

"I need thirty seconds, Actual!" he heard Nick Williams say back into his headset.

Phil's Echo squad was lining up behind the cover of the broken monorail tracks, waiting on Josh's Alpha squad to call that they were set.

"Alpha stacked at Point Zulu!" he heard Josh bark into the radio, indicating the corner of Taylor and Denny. He didn't want to give the street names on the air. "We can move north as soon as that thing is eliminated!"

Nick and Buddy were sprinting up a slightly angled piece of the former Space Needle's broken legs, a part that had held close to a hundred feet in length and was about thirty feet high where the north end had settled on a piece of the monorail tracks. He slid to a stop on his knees in the grit and gravel, holding his aim from a kneeling position. It was only one-block to the fifty-cal that was laying suppressing fire.

Ka-Boom! The machine gunner's head exploded east with the sudden insertion of a 7.62 mm projectile, ending the barrage of gunfire that had trickled to short bursts after John Cronin's demise. "Now, Peg-Leg!" Buddy yelled into the radio upon Nick's shot.

Phil's squad and part of Nick's all clambered over the broken monorail segments and began to bound east. Phil could see a presumably dead body at the far end of the block. They reached the vehicles just west of the downed man. Phil had Jerry pull out the homemade FLIR scope and scanned past the pilot in the hotel parking lot. "There! And there!" He began to pinpoint where the Cartel were hiding to his team, rendering their smoke less-effective.

Josh's crew had eyes on the same body. They were between two fairly tall buildings, sprinting to make up the longer distance than Echo squad. Josh saw the driver of the Humvee two blocks farther get out and suffer a similar fate as his gunner had a few seconds earlier. He and his squad favored the building on the right and slowed to a stop as they approached the corner. Phil's crew was stacked up on the left side of the same intersection. "Smokes!" Josh heard Phil yell into the radio. The entire Peg-Leg Posse had loaded up on the canisters provided by the USS Halsey. Four canisters quickly began to fill up their half of the parking area, intermingling with the thinning waft coming from the north.

As the yellow and purple plumes began to spew south and southwest of the hotel parking area, Josh did one last scan and saw the parachute fabric. He heard Phil begin to call out specific positions of approaching cartel that had been identified with the homemade FLIR scope. "Contact!" he yelled. "Moving! Alpha, push right! Multiple hostiles by those flipped over vehicles to the northeast!"

Phil and Echo did the same to the north, each of the squads laying suppressing fire over Tucker. They could occasionally make out enemy soldiers as the smoke thinned. Pop! Pop! No less than six rifles from the squads were barking at any given second. The sounds of gunfire ricocheted off the buildings, covering the music of the brass hitting the ground. Acrid gunpowder smoke added to the fog-of-war created by the cannisters. Phil and Charlie took up a spot to Tucker's left, keeping cover behind part of the driveway's covering-structure. Josh and Joe did the same thing on the right side, forming an arch with Phil and Charlie to protect the wounded pilot. A cartel member stepped out of the mixed smoke to within six feet of Joe, who sent two rounds through the man's face. "Reloading!" Joe called out, as he peeled off the line, immediately replaced by Vince. Glenn did the same thing with Charlie as he stepped off the line, crouch-running back to a dumpster for cover. Josh spied the one giving orders and shot him squarely in the plate carrier, sending him rolling under a pickup truck. Back on the Space Needle pile, Nick scanned for the machine gun on the Gates Building, but he was too close and low in elevation to get a shot.

"WHO ARE THOSE GUYS?!" Jessica screamed past all the gunfire.

"I dunno!" Earl screamed back, still trapped…still trying to get into the fight. "But I'm glad they're on our side!"

"Daaadddd!" Earl could hear Tucker yelling, emotion roiling from the young man who'd just seen his father ripped apart by a machine gun.

"Hang tight, Tucker!" Earl yelled. He was south of the Cartel advance, but the smoke from the canisters was obscuring most of the ground approach from the north. What it didn't do, however, was prevent that machine gun from pinning Earl's fireteam down to their corner. All they could do is watch as this well-trained band of strangers moved-in to shield Tucker Cronin from capture and a certain, painful death.

TONY KEPT his giant frame as low as he could as he ran up to Tucker, laying on the ground behind the two fireteams that were shielding him. "Can you move?!" the big man asked.

The distraught young man yelled, "I think my hips are broken! You need to cut my harness!"

"I gotcha!" Tony said. "Don't worry, big man!" Tony yelled. He used his knife to slice through the paramotor leg and shoulder straps. He reached down and picked Tucker up under his armpits, hefting him onto his shoulder. Tucker cried out in pain as the Mack-truck sized rescuer began to run south to the next block.

"Peg-Leg! Fall back!" Phil ordered. "Center peel!" As rhythmically as when they approached, the team began to cover and peel back. As some would run for a spot, they would plant themselves and provide covering fire as the remainder walked backwards, firing. As they ran out of ammo in their magazine, they would turn and run, reloading on the move, and pass their teammates. They would plant themselves and repeat the process. The next-to-last man would always hit the last-one on the shoulder so they knew they were the most exposed. Charlie grabbed the fallen John Cronin, the big linebacker grabbing the dead man in a fireman's carry, using the 'ranger roll' that he'd learned in one of Phil's tactical classes.

Throughout it all, Phil had noticed a small team pinned down to the east. They were obviously friendlies, having been taking fire from the north the whole time. Using hand signals, he told the approaching man and two women to stop. He mentioned that they were falling back to their rally point in the south. The big man a block east gave Phil the okay sign.

"Drive!" Rey yelled at his soldier, who had never seen his boss lose his cool so...volcanically... There were still a few trying to make their way back to the Humvees.

"What about—"

"Drive!" Rey yelled again, this time holding his pistol up to the temple of the young pawn. He threw the rig into gear and stabbed the accelerator pedal with a booted foot, sending the captured National Guard rig back to the north. "Head to the pier!" The soldier took the most direct route they'd discovered through the Queen Anne neighborhood and past the broken rail-lines to get to the command ship over by the grain elevator.

Rey sprinted up the pier, leaving a pair of guards behind a sandbag bunker in the parking area with confused faces. He made his way up the brow, forward and up five levels to the office behind the ship's bridge. He found a couple of the ship's compliment who had been in the radio room, monitoring the action.

"Jefe!" one of the exclaimed. "There was an explo—"

"Get hold of Oso Negro!" he yelled, referring to his Cartel's headquarters in Mexico. It was named after a fabled story of a wounded black bear that had slayed thirty men before they finally brought it down. "And send out the emergency evacuation order!"

PHIL TOOK a quick assessment of his Peg-Leg squads in the Slaughter Peninsula National Guard's secure staging area down the hill near the waterfront. They were in the Olympic Sculpture Park. Most of the Guard had taken up operations linking with the elements approaching from the south, clearing out the remaining cartel and gang units that had been cut-off from their headquarters. He noticed that four familiar faces were absent, including Eli, Josh's brother. The remaining Slaughter Peninsula Posse members were gulping water, eating protein bars, and topping off magazines. "To open, how are our fallen?" he asked, dreading the answer.

Lonnie spoke up. "We've lost Madison, Bobby, and Tyson," he said with a deep sadness in his angry voice.

Jeff had been obviously crying. "My dad was shot in the leg! He's lost a lot of blood! The medics from Bartlett are trying to operate on him!"

Phil was overcome with emotion, his eyes swelled with tears. He was taking a knee on his good leg, forearms on the other knee. He looked back up at his crew laying on the hillside around him. "It's okay, everyone. Take a moment to get it out. We'll be able to grieve properly when we've sent these bastards to Hell!"

Earl wandered up to Phil's team, and recognized it was a good time to be quiet. Phil cast a glance up and decided to stand. "Come on over," he said.

"We just wanted to come over and offer our appreciation for saving our man, back there," Earl said. "Name's Earl. The rest of my team is checking on him."

"You guys were a pretty small unit," Phil said, wondering.

"Just the tip of the spear. We had never planned on trying to rescue a downed pilot. Murphy..." he admitted, looking around at Phil's unit. "Anyhow, didn't mean to interrupt. Just sayin' thanks." He turned to leave.

"Make sure and tell that kid that we're all proud of him," Phil said. "What he did may be the thing that wins this for us. How's he doin'?" he asked, causing the tall Ranger to stop and turn.

"He'll recover. But his old man bought it trying to save him. That's who you guys scooped up in the retreat. That's something the kid'll have to learn to live with." He turned to leave again. "Someday..." he said as he wandered off.

Phil noticed that the Guard personnel in the area were starting to gear up. He looked at Jeff, who suddenly realized that hope wasn't quite dead. He scanned the remaining members of his team. "You should get that bandaged," he suggested to Glenn, who had been grazed in the retreat from their rescue operation. "Anyone else with scrapes and sprains, get them looked at. I'm going to go find out what our next mission is." *These Guardsmen are getting ready for something...*

Phil took a long pull off his hydration bladder hose. *Need to fill this thing,* he realized. *Drained it in less than three hours.* Charlie caught up to Phil as he was walking under a ten-by-twenty pop-up canopy being utilized as a hasty Command Post. Adam saw them both, and shut down the conversation he'd been in. "Hey, guys," he said with a look of dread on his face. "Charlie, I..."

"I saw," Charlie said. "Direct hit. Nobody could've survived that."

"Doesn't that make you the ranking Sheriff Officer?" Phil asked earnestly. Charlie didn't reply, he just gave Phil a look that said, 'not now'.

Phil picked it up from the tall deputy and turned back to Adam. "We're here to find out what's next..."

Adam held out an electronic tablet for Phil to take. "Good timing. We're getting ready to send everything we got straight up these train tracks."

"What am I looking at?" Phil asked semi-excitedly. "Is this... today? Now?! Where did you get this feed?!"

Adam pointed up. "Our Raven." He was referring to his unit's hand-launched reconnaissance drone. "And our friends pulling security at the submarine base have a Reaper sending us images, too."

"A Reaper?!" Phil damn near screamed. "Are they done playing this 'we can't get involved' game, yet?" Phil knew he wasn't giving them full credit for the operation they'd performed hours earlier. He was just venting that it had taken them so long to help.

"Phil," Charlie said trying to calm his friend down, who wasn't listening.

"Just have them send a missile up those guys' hind-quarters and finish them off!"

Adam just gave Charlie a look, who said, "Phil!"

Phil took a deep breath and then sighed it out. "Sorry," he muttered as he started looking at the tablet. "What am I looking at here?"

"A retreat," Adam said. "Twelve minutes ago, they started moving en masse toward that ship on that grain pier."

"What?!" Phil handed the tablet to Charlie as he stepped out into the mid-morning sunshine. He reset his frequency on his little radio and keyed it up. "Rampage! Rampage! You still got your ears on?!"

Twenty seconds later, he heard Jennifer get on the radio. "We're here, Peg-Leg!"

"We're going to meet you where you dropped us off in ten minutes! Copy?"

"Copy! Ten minutes!"

The other two had followed him out when they saw him key up his radio. Adam said, "Phil, what're you doing? We have a ground assault moving forward!"

"They'll shred you guys alive, Adam! They've had drones, mortars, and RPGs every step of the way! You really think they haven't pre-ranged some heavy weapons on those train tracks to cover their escape?"

He ran right past the water refill station and back to his team, who were starting to fall asleep. "Peg-Leg! Mount up! This one's gonna hurt!"

THE RAMPAGE PULLED up to the east side of the grain elevator's pier to offload the first group of Peg-Leg operators. Nick heard artillery and RPGs but realized those were impacting the rail cars to the south. *They're going after the ground assault,* he realized. Every soul on board was laying as low as they could on deck, using machinery and the side of the boat for cover, trying desperately to return the fire they were receiving.

On the quick, one-kilometer cruise after being picked up, Phil had ordered Lonnie and the remaining few members of Bravo to join Josh and Alpha on the boat's second insertion. "Now, Delta and Echo!" Phil hollered as he led the scramble off the fishing boat.

The big diesel engine didn't take too long to start backing up with the reverse thrust that Jennifer's father had applied. He slipped it into neutral to give the fifteen or so fighters time to scramble off the boat. A bullet impacted his port side cabin window, sending cracks throughout the safety glass. Then a second hole. The old captain reengaged the transmission and throttled the prop as high as it would go in reverse. The two squads of Posse members had barely taken foot on the pier, each of them scrambling for cover.

The elevated beltway above was held almost a hundred feet over the pier by a steel structure. There were four primary and one backup booms that could telescope out over a waiting ship and use giant hoses to start dumping grain from the conveyor. There were a few electrical panels, a couple of mooring bollards, and the legs to the structure—ballistic cover was difficult to find from the cartel's incoming rounds. Buddy Chadwell took a shot in the gut and fell to the ground, writhing in agony. Jeff pulled him over to a pile of mooring line and dragged him behind it, laying on Buddy to try to protect him. "Keep moving!" Phil ordered. "We need to make our way to that brow!"

Nick looked up at the grain elevator from the safety of the leg closest to the Seattle side and end of the pier. *I need to get up there! I bet they already have a shooter up there themselves!* The tower on the south end of the pier was a crisscross framework of load-bearing legs, and both horizontal and vertical diagonal bracing that gave the platform the strength it needed to carry tons of weight. There were five of these on the pier, with each being a spot that tethered one of the giant hoses. At the top, the conveyor connected them all on two levels—an enclosed room with the grain-hauling belt, and an open-air machinery space at the very top. Nick took the battle rifle off his front, needing the space to be able to climb the tower, leaving him with his sniper rifle and a pistol. He began to climb the framework, trying to get up to the conveyor deck before his whole team was killed.

By that time, the boat had made a speed run to the north end of the pier. Jennifer told her dad to keep it tight to the giant ship, keeping them out of easy sight of the various cartel riflemen on board. The battered little boat sped past the ship and turned hard to starboard where the pier angled over toward the shoreline with a different section. Before he hit a third, small pier extension that jutted north, Captain Smith once again parallel parked on the angled pier by jamming reverse throttle. "Everyone off!" Josh yelled, hopping onto the pier. They all took cover and began firing at the cartel who were still trying to board the pier from shore, effectively trapping those already near or on the ship between Alpha and the Delta-Echo squads to the south. While Lonnie and several others held off the advance from shore, Josh started trying to provide Phil and Charlie's advance some covering fire.

As Joe Santillan tried to run across the pier to take cover behind a different part of the conveyor tower, he took a shot directly in the head, dead before his body buckled at the knees and crumpled to a heap. "Joe!" Josh yelled, too late. He tightened his own cover up. "Echo, this is Alpha! I think there's someone sniping from the top!"

31

The Path of Most Resistance.

TAHOMA'S HAMMER PLUS 40 DAYS.

NICK LOST his traction on a beam as he tried to climb another layer. He held onto the cross brace for dear life as both feet grasped at the free space below him. He high-kneed his left leg and got that foot to grab back onto the horizontal piece. He was able to strengthen his grip after that, and hoist, yanking his right foot back up. *Whew! Don't look down!* He could see he was only five-feet from the conveyor deck, which meant the fall would've been deadly—even into the water.

The conveyor deck was enclosed with corrugated sheet metal to keep the wind and rain off of the grain, but it had a series of windows—*probably for ventilation,* Nick thought—and the actual doors in which the big hoses on jib-arms actually ran into the tower. Nick grabbed the lip of the vent window on the very end of the tower he was climbing and began to pull himself in. "Mira!" he heard a cartel soldier yell from the far end of the space.

Crap! Nick thought. He quickly scrambled back down the structure five feet as he heard the sheet metal being perforated by bullets above his head. *Sniper and a spotter! They're going to hear me above them if I take the upper deck!* With shaking arms and legs, already filled with lactic acid from the climb, Nick began to crawl under the structure below the conveyor, almost one hundred feet above the intense firefight directly below. *No good!* he yelled at himself. *You're a sitting duck, Williams! Think!* He scanned the conveyor system itself, recognizing that there was a crawl space where the pulleys and return loop of the belt existed. *Yes!*

"Nick! That sniper has a good angle on the north assault! They could sure use a hand!" Phil yelled into the radio. He could tell that the conveyor itself was keeping the enemy sniper from seeing his southern team, though once on the ship, he'd be able to pick them apart at will. His assault had advanced to within twelve feet of the gangway that led directly into the ship's loading hatch, a pair of doors on its vertical side, that literally showed the giant, red cross of a relief organization when they were closed. Phil looked around, seeing some of his people had been shot, and others were just pinned down. "Charlie!" he yelled. Phil was the farthest north along the south assault team's approach, and Charlie was right behind him, though on the Seattle side of the pier. "Covering fire! I'm running to that brow!"

After switching to a new magazine, Charlie leaned out and sent six, rhythmic shots about a second apart at the cartel soldier who'd been using a shrink-wrapped pallet of rice bags as cover. Phil leaned out from behind the tower leg and ran to the brow in a crouch. When he rounded the corner to it, he kept his rifle pointed straight up at the hatch at the far end.

Charlie yelled backwards, "Covering fire!" Jeff and Jerry both leaned out from their cover, as did Vince and Glenn, who had both taken gunshot wounds. Everyone was shooting down the pier, Charlie knew it would be a full miracle if one of his own didn't shoot him. He took a step out and paused for just a half-second, hoping his team would see him moving—then the former college linebacker sprinted for the brow opening at full speed.

"Thought you'd never show up!" Phil quipped as he shot a soldier trying to cross the opening at the top. "Stop for coffee?!"

"Would you move, already?!" Charlie yelled. The big deputy wasn't able to squat quite as low as Phil behind the brow's sidewalls.

Phil picked himself up a bit and started low walking up the gangway. He stopped at the top, feeling Charlie stop right on his back. Charlie gave him a hard squeeze on the right shoulder. Phil stepped into what was essentially a storeroom, swinging left to clear the corner, where he saw a cartel soldier trying to hold the blood in his side, rifle on the floor. "You're just a kid!" he yelled at the Hispanic boy of maybe sixteen years old, wide eyed and scared. Phil shot the soldier in the head as he moved in behind a pallet of beans and squatted. *There'll be time to pity this kid, later…*

Charlie had taken cover behind a different pallet on the forward side of the hatch they'd entered. Both men changed to fresh magazines in their rifles. "We need to hold this position!" Charlie said, excitedly.

"No!" countered Phil. "Feel that rumble in the deck?! The engines are on! She'll be leaving any minute! Two of us will be able to sneak through easier!"

"Stop, Phil!" Charlie argued. "Use your head for once! If this thing takes off and it's just the two of us…" Charlie drifted off.

It was a critical moment, not one for making snap judgments— but with no time to think. Phil had faced this scenario twice in his life, losing a leg in the process, and darn near losing his life to a local gang just a couple of weeks earlier. "Moving!" Phil said as he finished up his magazine change just a split second earlier than

Charlie. He moved toward the interior hatch and paused, letting Charlie catch up. "We need to get to the weather deck!" Phil said. "To cover the rest of the team trying to board! I'm guessing it's two decks up!" As a former Marine, Phil had practiced this exact exercise a few times in his youth. "We'll head aft, find us an inclined-ladder and cover each other going up!"

The men rounded the corners into the passageway, Phil leading aft with Charlie covering the forward direction behind them. "I see one!" Phil yelled. He was surprised that they had encountered so little resistance.

Eighty seconds later, as the two friends were stacked on a hatch that led to the ship's starboard side overlooking the pier, it became obvious. They could hear commotion as several soldiers were at the two extreme ends of the ship trying to cut through the giant mooring lines with axes. "They're going to make it, Charlie!" He scanned out to the train tracks beyond and saw the National Guard engaged in a severe fight with the enemy who never made it to the ship. "It's just us, bud!"

"Most of those guys have set their rifles down, Phil," Charlie said as he took a quick scan aft. "We can buy some time. We don't need to stop both ends from casting off!" Charlie realized "Just one!"

"I guess we could try to buy a little ti—"

"Heading aft!" Charlie said, cutting off Phil as he crossed through the hatch, trying to keep low and against the bulkhead.

"Son of a..." Phil muttered as he followed his friend out. They slowly progressed to the old cruise ship's stern, an open-air deck about eighty feet by eighty feet in size. It had cheap camping style chairs and some bolted tables, and not much for taking cover except for a few of the ship's fixtures themselves.

Charlie cleared the starboard outer passage and entered the open space. There were three different lines tethering the stern to the pier. The one closest to Phil and Charlie had already been severed. Charlie opened fire on the busy soldiers, sending all ten scrambling for weapons and cover as he plinked them off like a carnival duck game.

Phil scanned out and realized that they were angled away from the pier by dozens of feet. "Charlie! Look!" he said tapping his friend on the back where they were squatting behind a vent plenum that came out of the deck and bent over in a horseshoe shape. The remaining two lines on the stern were taut as the ship's propellors and rudders were sending power forward and port. Someone had prematurely started the escape.

"Kinda a bad time, Phil!" Charlie yelled back. He did a quick scan over his shoulder to see why his friend wasn't shooting and saw it. The grain elevator was nearby at their end but ran away sharply from the ship. A round ricocheted off the plenum, bringing both of them back into the moment.

"These last two lines are it!" Phil yelled. "We need to kill these guys and keep those lines from being cut!" As he spoke the words, he caught movement back aft. "Looks like they're going to try and get us from port." Phil swung his rifle and started shooting at the three who'd made it to the port aft corner, hitting one of them in the head.

"I'm thinking there's about seven left!" Charlie yelled. We need to spread out a bit!"

"I think you're right—"

Ping! Phil's words were cut off as around hit Charlie in the upper, right arm, and then ricocheted off his humerus into the vent plenum. Blood sprayed out of holes on both sides. "Aaahhhhh!" he screamed in pain.

Phil was already grabbing the tourniquet off of Charlies gun belt, pushing the hoop around his friend's hand, trying to keep them both low behind the plenum. "It's about to hurt like a mofo, brother," Phil said. "Trust me!" He started turning the windlass, and Charlie's face creased with wrinkled tension, the pain shooting up to his brain.

"Mother fu—"

"I think you may have been right, brother! We need to get out of here!" Phil said after securing the tourniquet's windlass. *Once again, I've ran right into the shit without thinking!* He stood just over the plenum and emptied his magazine on every location he knew they were hiding. He hauled his friend over to the side of the vessel. The Posse leader heaved the wounded Native American deputy over the side and into the water twenty feet below.

Phil felt a round hit his fake leg. He squatted and turned, reaching for his rifle but raised his hands instantly. Four cartel soldiers were approaching him from point blank range, rifles ready to shoot. Phil could see the last two mooring lines being severed as he raised his hands above his head. "Alto!" he heard someone yelling in Spanish.

"Soooo," Phil heard a smooth voice let out slowly. He turned his head to see a good-looking man in all-black tactical gear walking up to him, waving off his men to ensure they didn't shoot their captive. "Your little 'posse' sure seemed to turn the tables on my men, last night! My sources in your county's EOC—" Phil's face filled with rage. Rey Hernandez just laughed. "You fool…we're…*everywhere.*" He smirked at Phil and pulled the SPP patch still attached to the front of Phil's plate carrier off with a gentle tug, staring at it for a moment before he threw it off the ship. "You may've outsmarted us last night, but we'll be back. And with greater numbers…"

"Did you really think you'd succeed?" Phil asked incredulously. He let out a defiant snort. "Are you so arrogant that you thought we wouldn't fight back?"

"Do you want us to kill him and dump him, Jefe?" one of his lieutenants asked. Some of the men had resumed firing at the small boat harassing them.

"No! Stand him up! Remove his weapons!" Rey yelled as he was doing the same. "This one I will handle myself!"

32

"Desperation is sometimes as powerful an inspirer as genius."
—Benjamin Disraeli

Tahoma's Hammer Plus 40 Days.

Josh could see the ship parting off the pier and began to frantically wave for Jennifer's attention. The Rampage had moved off pier a bit and were firing at the soldiers who were firing back. "Get over here!" he yelled, not remembering in the heat of the fight what frequency her navy had been using. He saw her acknowledge and turn to issue orders to her dad in the cabin.

The craft pulled up to the eastern running section of pier with its port side, ready to drive out into the bay on Josh's command. "Everyone on!" he ordered. Men and women were dragging their wounded back with them and helping them get onto the craft.

That's when Josh saw Charlie get dropped into the water. He was about sixty feet from the grain pier. "Move it!" He was watching for Charlie to surface, which he did. But the big deputy was having a hard time treading water.

Josh turned and jumped into the craft, grabbing Jennifer by a shoulder. "Look there! See him?"

She scanned to see what Josh was pointing at. "I got him!" She pulled free from his grasp and went to relay the mission to her father.

Josh looked at the tired and bleeding bodies. "Everyone! Line up on starboard! Get low!" He looked at Tony. "Get aft and be ready to yank Charlie into the boat!"

Tony was confused by what that meant, but he went along with it. "O-okay, brothuh!"

The Rampage began to lurch forward and Captain Smith gave it one-third throttle as he turned port around the corner of the pier, motoring into the widening gap between the cartel ship and grain pier. "If you see a soldier, you shoot him!" Josh commanded the battered team.

Now! Nick yelled in his own head as he popped the small access cover open and stood up waist high in it. There were small covers that led down into the conveyor crawl space—one at each tower—for maintenance workers. He had taken off his sniper rifle to increase his maneuverability, choosing to clear the opening with his pistol. The space was dusty, as the two cartel men had been moving around in the grain, stirring it up. He kept his pistol red dot in focus as he swung, picking up the spotter who was four feet away and trying to draw his own pistol. Pop! Pop! Pop! Three shots in seven-tenths of a second. He pivoted toward the sniper. He hadn't time to swing the rifle off its bipod and try to get it on Nick. The sniper merely sent a foot toward him in a low roundhouse, kicking the pistol right out of his hand. It fell back into the space at Nick's feet.

Nick threw a knee up onto the deck, followed by the other leg's foot, and sprang, propelling himself at the cartel sniper, who was trying to draw his own pistol. He grabbed hold of the man's right wrist, trying to keep it under control while he grasped the back of his enemy's neck with his right hand. The two men both spread their feet out, trying to widen and lower their center-of-gravities in the life-and-death tussle. Nick tried to do a neck-whip on the man to throw him off balance and cause a forward stumble, but it didn't work. The man let go of his pistol and tried to round his hand out of Nick's grasp. As he did, both of them tripped on the belt of the conveyor and fell into the grain, sending more dust into the air.

The man scrambled for the top position. Nick was on his back and locked his legs around his adversary's waist, keeping him trapped near, trying once again to lock the man's right arm and keep it from reaching the pistol in his holster. The man desperately tried to start punching Nick with his left hand. He adjusted his neck and head, forcing the man to punch into his battle helmet and NODs.

The younger man telegraphed that he was about to throw a giant punch at Nick's nuts, so Nick released his leg trap, planting his boot soles on the man's hips and gave a huge kicking thrust, sending him flying backwards and onto his back on the grain conveyor. Nick immediately crunched his knees to his chest and kicked, thrusting his hands on the ground behind his shoulders and popped to an upright position. He ran over and dove onto the man, trying once again to gain control of the man's right arm, barely stopping the hand from getting to the pistol and holster on his right leg. Nick tried to straddle the man by sitting on his waist while also leaning forward, using his grip on the man's wrist to pull the arm up and away. The man sent another crashing left into the side of Nick's helmet. *I've had enough of this!* Nick thought, as he took the blow and threw the heel of his right hand straight up into the man's chin and jaw, stunning him. He reached back to his knife scabbard, yanking the blade out of the kydex holder and jammed it into the man's throat as fast and hard as he could. For the second time in a week, the long-range sniper's knife had claimed a victim.

He gave the knife a quarter-turn twist and then sliced out through the left side of the man's throat, sending blood spraying everywhere. Nick then plunged the blade down into the man's chest, causing a bone-crunching sound to join the dying gurgles. *No! Time! To lose!* Nick staggered back up to his feet and stumbled over to the little hatch, hopping into it. He retrieved his rifle and popped back up through the hatch, scrambling to get to the sniper's window. He stepped over the man's corpse and pulled the folded bipod legs down. He flipped the protective covers up on both ends of his scope.

Nick was breathing heavily from the intense hand-to-hand fight. He peered through the scope, which was waving wildly as his body reacted to being out of breath. He estimated the ship was about three hundred meters off the pier at the stern, the gap growing rapidly. He could see the Rampage down below, engaged in a firefight with the ship's crew on the aft end. He took a deep cleansing breath, blowing it all out and then repeated the process once more. He started picking off cartel members on the ship as quickly as he could. After the fourth one dropped dead from exploding-cranium syndrome, the rest all started driving themselves forward and off the stern. One even jumped into the water to evade the shooting-barrel he'd found himself in. All that was left were the two…*fighting?* Nick took a harder look. *Phil!* As the ship's angle changed, he could see Phil and a cartel member who seemed well-trained in a brawl very similar to the one he'd just endured. He lined up on the other man, but they were both moving fast. He tried to follow them in his scope, but their rapid fight movements, coupled with the movements of the ship and even the way his own breathing were affecting his ability to keep crosshairs on the action. Both Phil and the man he was fighting were moving wildly in nick's scope. The sniper couldn't take a shot.

PHIL WAS TRYING to keep both his real foot and the fake one under him. *This guy's younger and stronger! If he gets me on the ground—it's over!* He and Rey had been exchanging blows and grappling for control of the other one's hands. Phil wasn't sure how the man was going to use his bare hands to kill him, but he assumed it would be choking him to death once he'd tired out. *Not! Gonna! Happen!*

Phil used his half leg to send a knee into the man's gut as they kept their arms interlocked on each other. He connected with the man's core, below the plate carrier, but the man just tightened his toned abs and grunted through it. If anything, it added to his anger and resolve to kill Phil. He released his right hand from Phil's neck and sent a crashing blow into the redhead's face, sending him backwards and to the deck. Wasting no time, Rey ran over to Phil and tried to grab his throat. Phil counter-punched from the ground, trying to grab Rey's arms at the same time.

Rey felt something hit him hard and squarely in the ceramic ballistic plate on his back. It dazed him, but the plate did its job, destroying itself to stop the bullet. Reynaldo Hernandez had been shot in both plates that day, which only bolstered his fight with Phil as if he were on a just-cause mission. "A sniper?! This is between you and me!" he demanded. He grabbed Phil and dragged him backwards toward the centerline doors on the former cruise ship. He pulled Phil up in front of him, using him as a human shield.

"Unnngghh!" Phil grunted as the man tried to put him in a choke hold. He used everything he had to start clawing at the side of the ship. *Need to make it over there!* He knew his only hope was to escape into the cold water of Elliot Bay. He leaned forward, forcing Rey up onto Phil's back and started walking.

Sensing what was happening, Rey lowered his grasp around Phil's waist, trying to keep on the deck and out of the sniper's scope. Phil managed to make it to the four-foot tall side wall and grab on. "Unngghhh!" he grunted again, fighting for the chance to jump.

Rey was squatting, keeping his feet and gravity low behind Phil. He made one last reach with his right arm around Phil's waist, pulling his own head into Phil's back and letting go with his left. Like any soldier, Rey knew there was no such thing as a fair fight. He reached into the waistband behind his pants, finding his last-ditch gun, a single stack Glock 9mm.

33

Sacrifice.

Tahoma's Hammer Plus 40 Days.

"Dammit!" Nick yelled out, realizing that his shot went low, hitting the man who was winning the fight in the back plate. The pair of men had spun around and were now facing Nick as Phil clawed his way to the near side of the ship. *The range is getting farther with every second!* he scolded himself.

Nick took a deep breath and pulled the laser range finder out of the pouch on his belt. *Better to burn a few seconds and know!*

He lased it and realized the ship was now 587 meters away and growing. Nick made a couple of adjustments to his scope, centering the reticle for a 600-meter shot. He re-found the fight happening before him, seeing that the man and Phil were both low behind the bulkhead. "C'Mon, Phil!" Nick yelled to nobody in particular.

"Move!" He was ready to shoot the cartel man as soon as Phil cleared.

Nick could see Phil pulling himself up and over. *A head!* Nick realized. He took a deep breath and then started to blow it out... Suddenly the head disappeared, lowering itself behind Phil's legs and rump. Phil was pulling hard! Nick could see Phil's belt getting pulled backward by the foe's grasp! As the ship moved farther away, Nick was constantly having to move his scope with microscopic adjustments. Then it was too late.

As Phil started to break free of the grasp on his belt, a left hand popped up. Nick squeezed the trigger slowly, shooting at the hand. He saw the bullet impact the steel deck on the far side of the hand 600 meters away! *Clunk!* As Nick tried to cycle his bolt, it gave him the familiar bout of resistance it always did when its magazine was out of rounds. Nick could do nothing, as he watched the Glock silently discharge into Phil's left side five times. A long, horrible moment later, the sniper heard the worst gunshots of his life, as he watched Phil Walker tumble headfirst over the guardrail and into the cold, dark waters below.

PHIL BOBBED in the cold waters of Elliot Bay, knowing he'd been shot, but not knowing if he was light-headed from blood-loss or the chill of submersion. There were an unknown number of burning sensations passing through his chest. They felt like hot tunnels, bored by worms of fire, but much more intensely than the event that cost him half of a leg a few years earlier. He thought he could make-out Jennifer's boat gliding toward him. Though he could see several rifles flashing gunfire over his head just a few feet away, he couldn't hear them. *Strange...*

"Now!" Jennifer screamed toward her father, who cranked the stern hard to port and reversed the throttle on the big diesel engine. The fishing boat yawed hard to the starboard as it turned port, throwing those shooting rifles at the escaping ship to slam into the rail, some nearly going over into the drink themselves.

The boat continued to turn and slowly started to creep its stern toward Phil, where Josh was leaning over the transom just a bit too far, with Big Tony practically laying on Josh to keep him in the boat. "Phil!" Josh screamed, seeing his friend's face turning paler by the second. "Hang on, Phil! Stay with me!" Tears were streaming down his face.

"Cut it!" Jennifer yelled, turning to her father to give him the throat slashing sign when they were about ten feet away from the wounded leader. Her father left it just barely engaged in forward gear for a second, to slow the vessel's reverse course just a bit, before throwing the transmission completely into neutral.

Josh was ready. He shuffled a little to his right as the boat's backward arch still had a bit of curve to it. He plowed his hands into bloody, frigid salt-water and got first his right hand, and then his left, under Phil's armpits and yanked. He curled Phil a couple of feet up, and as he maxed out the pulling range of his arms, felt himself go practically weightless as a giant named Tony heaved both of them up and over the transom. Josh couldn't keep his feet as he landed backwards on the deck, and Phil came falling directly on top of him.

"Cut it off!" Charlie was yelling as he saw the blood continue to pump out from under the plate carrier. "Get those wounds exposed!" he was hollering. He was trying to get in and help, despite his own right arm being in the air and with extreme pain from the tourniquet.

Josh had been through this before, in Iraq. He was tuning out Charlie's yelling as white noise as he scrambled to his knees. He pulled his fixed blade knife out of its scabbard on his belt and began to saw through the shoulder straps on Phil's plate carrier.

"Find an aid kit!" Tony was yelling at Jennifer, who was frozen in place, watching Phil bleed out.

"I got one!" Josh said tensely as he pulled Phil's combat IFAK—his trauma kit meant to be used on himself—off the left side of the plate carrier. "Get that off!" he ordered Tony as he pointed to the wet and heavy chest rig.

As Tony complied, multiple bullet holes had allowed massive bleeding and salt-water to turn Phil's green shirt and chest into a big, wet mess. Josh was ripping open the IFAK, searching for Phil's largest trauma dressing. He tossed the remainder at Charlie, who was continuing to try to get in and help. "Find the chest seals!" he yelled.

"Guys…" Phil mumbled softly.

"I got 'em!" Charlie said as he saw Josh applying pressure to the holes closest to Phil's heart. They weren't even hearing Phil.

"Guys!" Phil coughed out with a new and unusual raspiness, as blood that was in his esophagus helped push the word out. A little of it splattered on his ghost-white face. He raised his hands up weakly. Charlie grabbed Phil's right hand with his own left as Josh was continuing to hold pressure on the chest exit-wounds

"There's just too many wounds!" Josh screeched in exasperation.

"Josh…" Phil said calmly, causing the young man to look into his eyes for the first time. "It's okay…."

"No!" Josh yelled. He looked back at Charlie, expecting some back-up.

Charlie just looked at Josh and shook his head no.

"It's okay," Phil repeated more softly. He continued to hold his left hand in the air, trying to get Josh to take it. "Charlie," he said, slowly turning his head toward his right.

"I'm here, brother" Charlie said, crying…not believing what was happening before his eyes. He held his right arm in the sky, but the immense pain in it was pushed to the back of his mind. He felt like it must be some bad nightmare, once again seeing Phil Walker bleed to death before his very eyes. Only this time there was nothing he could do. Hot tears were starting down Charlie's cheeks.

"You're the key, my friend…" Phil whispered.

"Phil. I…I"

Phil cut him off, knowing he had to get a couple of things said quickly.

"You're the key, Charlie. The Sheriff is key to keeping Liberty alive…" Phil's eyes were glassing over as he lost his train of thought.

"I-I got it, brother. I got it," was all Charlie could think to say through his tears.

Phil's mouth curled up just a bit at the corners. "Josh…" he said as he turned his head left. Even laying on the boat's deck, it looked wobbly and unsteady.

"I'm here, Phil," Josh said. He gave Phil's hand a squeeze to remind him, unsure if Phil was losing his vision as he bled out. He was trying and failing to choke back his tears and emotion.

"My girls…" Phil said, quietly.

"I got 'em, Phil. Don't worry! I'll protect them with my life!" Josh said through a wavering voice.

"My girls, Josh," Phil said, almost as if he hadn't really heard Josh's reply. "They'll save you, too…if you just give them a chance. They love you, you know…"

"I know, Phil!" Josh said as he used his other hand to wipe his eyes. "I love them, too. Don't worry!"

"They're yours, now, son. Their love can save you from the things you want to forget." Phil's voice was growing barely discernible. "Tell them I'm with the others…" Phil's smile eventually started to fade, and though his pupils remained the same size, they lost…*something*. As the life was leaving him, Phil weakly said through barely moving lips, "Caroline…Crane…" almost as if he were talking to them. The last of the energy in Phil's neck muscles relaxed —his head slowly turned the rest of the way left. On a beautiful and clear fall day, as the large cartel cruise ship continued to slip out of range of the Posse members still firing at it, Phillip Edward Walker died.

34

"In three words I can sum up everything I've learned about life: it goes on."
—Robert Frost

ONE NIGHT AFTER TAHOMA'S HAMMER

AT 35,800 FEET IN ELEVATION, Air Force One was currently almost three times higher than the storm system that was dumping tumultuous rain on Western Washington, and yet only half as high as the hammer had been when it peaked a few hours earlier. The top sixty percent of Mt. Rainier was conspicuously absent, an anomaly seen by very few people up to that point. The gray fist of the hammer had mostly dissolved overnight, evolving into a steady column of dirty steam. The jet-stream had taken the ash to the northeast, forcing the colonel flying the 747 to take a more southerly approach.

The flying bunker had departed the other Washington at 9 PM, when it had become apparent to Shannon Sahr, the President's Chief of staff, that her boss had better be seen over the Rainier Impact Zone as soon as possible. This was no ordinary natural disaster. Advisors could use words to inform the President that the left side of the country was without power, but Shannon knew that POTUS would need to see it with his own eyes to truly receive the message. About two decades earlier, another President had learned the hard way not to be seen as dismissive of a natural disaster to the media or the rest of the country. They had circled for a few hours, waiting for the sun to catch up so they could observe from the sky.

"It's obvious we're not going to see much from up here," President Jeremiah Allen said. "Tell them to find a place for us to land, JJ," the President told his primary assistant, Julia Jacobs.

"Sir," she said, getting out of the taupe, swiveling, custom recliner and making her way aft down the carpet of the portside aisle, where she disappeared around the corner of the meeting room.

"So far the thing that has impressed upon me the most is seeing most of everything west of the Rockies in the pitch black," Jeremiah told Shannon as he craned his head back to his viewing port. The pair and JJ were occupying three of a four-chair cluster on the portside in the Presidential Staff area aft of the living quarters in the craft's nose. "Impressive in a horrible way, of course," he clarified.

"Yes, that is definitely something we're going to start hearing from all the Governors about," Shannon agreed. "While you were resting, I had Terrell start pulling some data on how much the other western states rely on Washington for power. Which then led me to think about Amazon and Boeing...then Microsoft...and then Intel..." She could see the worry return to POTUS' face as she paused to scan her wristwatch. "I think you know where I'm going with this..."

"What time?" Jeremiah asked, implying he'd already figured on a full briefing when he woke up.

"About twelve minutes, sir," Shannon replied as her boss rose from the plush chair and start forward for his personal space in the craft's nose. "I'll make sure nobody knocks," she said, getting out of her own chair. She knew her boss and old friend well, and twelve minutes to piss, brush his teeth, and slam a coffee was all about any president ever got, even on a normal day. Both of them stopped and turned when they heard footsteps pounding on the carpet behind them. JJ was returning with an Air Force major in tow.

"Mr. President," she called the last ten feet, just to make sure he didn't escape to his berthing space. "I figured out pretty quickly into my conversation with Major Thompson here that he'd better come brief you personally. Major?" she said, looking at him to begin explaining the bad news.

"Sir, there's nowhere in the RIZ where we can land," he said using each letter individually.

"Well obviously not SeaTac or Boeing, Major," the President chuckled softly. "Just have them set us down in Portland or Vancouver." He started to turn.

"Sorry, sir. That won't be possible."

Jeremiah turned back. "What? Why not?" The thought that the quake had damaged every runway for hundreds of miles seemed too impossible to be reasonable.

"Well, sir, the –"

Jeremiah cut him off as he figured it out. "Okay, Major, I get it. Can we at least land at Fairchild or Spokane International?" he asked, expecting a yes.

The major started shaking his head, tipping off what was about to be another negative answer.

POTUS cut him off again. "What?!" He looked at the blank look on Shannon's face, then at JJ, who was trying to maintain her best game-face, but was clearly worried, too. "Good Lord, Major! What are you saying? Airliners can't even land in Spokane?"

"No, sir," the major confirmed. "At least—not until the FAA and the Army Corp of Engineers can get there and perform a mandatory inspection. Both SIA and Fairchild have reported some major cracks in the runways. The next closest airport with a runway long enough to handle Air Force One is Beale Air Force Base in Northern California.

"Well, rat balls!" exclaimed the President. He didn't just want to get on the ground for the photo op—he really did want to see things, smell the fear…let people know that the government would be there to help them.

"Thank you, Major," Shannon said, taking over. "That'll be all for now." Once the major had excused himself, she told Jeremiah, "Go, sir. Get a cup and meet us in the conference room in ten minutes. We'll brainstorm this as a team."

"Thanks, Shannon," he said with an ever-so-slight smile. "See you in a few," he said as his headed for his lavatory.

Shannon's motive to shoo away the President wasn't completely altruistic. She always liked to hear what the staff was about to tell him before they actually did. She hated surprises. She and JJ headed into the filling conference room, and she plopped herself down in the end chair in the far-end of the room's large, oak conference table. That was everyone's cue to take their places, which most of them did as they wrapped up their sidebar conversations.

"Who has anything that they feel needs head-of-the-line?" she asked her staff as she looked around at the dozen faces.

Half of them raised their hands, which caught Shannon off-guard. It was usually one or two when she asked that question. She pointed at the person closest to her left. "Sam, you got thirty seconds."

Sam Gilson, Shannon's Operations Director, took a quick breath before speaking. "I just came back from the Comms Center. I received a message from my counterpart on Secretary Locklear's staff." He was referring to the Secretary of Defense. "SecDef is requesting a video-call with him as soon as we can make it happen."

"Any idea what it's about?" Shannon pressed.

"Something about troop movements and navies starting to load up with supplies. An offer of 'assistance and relief efforts' he said."

"Already?!" Shannon exclaimed. "That didn't take long. Who? Russia? Or China?"

Sam's voice contained the concern that his face was trying to hide. "Both."

Tahoma's Hammer Plus 41 Days.

"...AND lastly, as you feel out your roles in your new promotions, I'd like to leave you with this thought," Captain Richard Carpenter told the more than two-hundred sailors in formation in the aircraft carrier USS Halsey's Hangar Bay Two. "Maybe it will bring you inspiration in this time of turmoil that the world hasn't known since the last World War. It's from an old Greek general named Thucydides. 'The secret to happiness is freedom. And the secret to freedom is courage.' God bless you all, Team Halsey. Now, let's get back to work and make ready for tomorrow's departure."

With that, the Commanding Officer, decked out in his dress blues, turned sharply and walked away from the podium with the Executive Officer in tow. The Command Master Chief called the promoted sailors—mostly junior enlisted, but a few new Chiefs and promoted officers, too—to attention. As the formation broke apart, Culinary Specialist 2nd Class Petty Officer TaiIsha Johnson walked up to Carmen Martinez. Both of them had big grins. "Ooooo, girl! You made 3rd Class and changed rates on the same day!" referring to Carmen's successful attempt to change to the Damage Controlman trade. "Congratulations!"

"Thanks!" Carmen said, giving her closest friend from her old job a hug. "Congrats to you, too! I bet you can't wait to get home to your family in San Diego!" The big ship was returning to homeport, its overhaul cut short by the massive events caused by the Cascadia Subduction Zone. Many of the sailors' spouses and children had opted to stay in their homeport city, a decision that was tough, but often impacted by a longer-vision for their career.

"I am! But this stuff goin' on with China an' Russia got me worried…You heard the scuttlebutt, right? That they got a real fightin' war goin' on, now?"

"Yeah, I heard," Carmen said, lost in thought as the two women made their way to one of the hatches out of the hangar bay.

"What 'bout you?" TaiIsha asked. "You got plans to get up to L.A. when we get back?"

"I dunno," Carmen admitted.

"But I bet you're as glad as I am to get out of this crappy town…" TaiIsha said, as she started descending the inclined ladder to the 2nd Deck.

Out of the whole stinking state, Carmen thought. Her mind turned to Dr. Stuart Schwartz, wondering if he were still alive. Her tempest-borne relationship with him was the one piece of Washington State—other than the brand-new promotion—that she would ever look back on fondly.

NAVY CAPTAIN MARIE DARNELL, Commanding Officer of the Washington State Naval Shipyard, was watching the operation closely. In the preceding weeks, her staff had carefully rebuilt a setting in a drydock, the one they normally used to recycle old submarines. They re-used the wood from a prior setting, something they'd never done before. *But these are unique times, fitting for this one-of-a-kind mission,* she thought.

The submarine USS El Paso had been severely damaged. Even in the absence of a historic-level natural disaster, the ship might've been scrapped instead of repaired. But the catastrophe had impacted the shipyard and accompanying navy base's ability to conduct even the most routine business. Many of the older buildings, vital shops and tooling for conducting repair and fabrication work, had simply crumbled to pieces. Two of the mobile cranes had fallen over, as had the giant one that was the hallmark item for the small city's skyline—*not that we actually use that one anymore*, Marie reminded herself. The El Paso had been buttoned up for some basic buoyancy as quickly as possible. Even the emergency clean-up of radioactive contamination had been put on hold, just to get the boat into a dry-dock with a functioning caisson.

With the sub's emergency move one dry-dock to the east came a new mission—*make it be able to dive, one time, to at least four hundred feet*, Marie had been ordered by her superiors. She had no idea why, but the fact that a team of Ordinance Experts from the submarine base had installed several secret munitions packages on the ship had given her a good idea. Marie wondered what would come next for her barely limping command as she watched the submarine's tow pendant being installed. *War is in the air*, she realized, *but who will fix the ships?*

"Bubby!" Natalie screamed, as her exhausted brother walked into his hunting cabin. She led a pack of family members, soon to be elbowed out of the way by Tori and Earl's kids. Everyone was competing for Earl's attention.

After a couple of minutes of being trapped at the front door, he finally dropped his gear and started wandering in. "Babe, I could really use some water…" he hinted at his wife. He scanned over to the living room and saw Conner laid up on the couch in front of the picturesque view of the river. "Man, you are really nursing, this thing, aren't ya?" he teased his buddy.

"Which one?" came the feeble reply. Earl saw Natalie walk back over and grab his friend's hand as she sat next to the couch.

"What?!" Earl exclaimed. "What happened?"

"I got shot—again—and you come in uninjured—again!" said his best bud.

Earl got close and looked at Natalie for an explanation. She looked at her brother, tears welling just a bit. "He saved my life!" *Again!* she added in her own head.

Earl noticed their connected hands and smiled. "I'm starting to think he's just trying to impress you, Nat."

Natalie burst with laughter as a couple of tears flowed out of her eyes. She looked back at Conner. "Maybe!" she said, showing a somewhat happy emotion for the first time since the disasters started seven weeks earlier.

"Through-and-through," Conner told his friend. "Right side, missed my liver, clipped the bottom of the lung. Doc from across the river dug-in and sewed it up. And now," he said with a grin, "I'm on some goooooood druuuugs!"

Earl gave Natalie a look. "Not just pain meds," she explained. "Your friends across the river donated some higher-grade antibiotics, as well."

Earl just nodded silently, thinking his buddy must have a guardian angel watching out for him. The group went quiet for a bit, and Conner broke the ice again. "Thinking about trekking east as soon as the pass starts to thaw. Should be good and healed by then…"

"Makes sense," Earl said, nodding. "Get to Montana…let your kids know you're still alive…"

"Yes, that," Conner said as he cast his eyes at Natalie when she wasn't looking at him. "And before I leave, we need to find out everything we can about this 'Max Volkov' person…" Conner said in a coldness that pushed through his pain meds. Natalie looked down at her lap sadly, once more reminded of her missing daughter. "I think maybe I've found my life's next mission…" Earl gave his usual nod, upset with himself for not being able to bring young Katherine home.

"What's the update on Seattle?" Tori asked, wrapping her arms around her husband's waist from behind, head poking around his side as she handed him a glass of water.

Earl took it from her and downed the whole thing. "The cartel ship escaped. Those not on it have disappeared in droves. Those that couldn't escape have been surrendering—mostly. A few are fighting it out, still. The mop up could take weeks. Not to mention winter is here, and everyone's starving. It's going to be a long time trying to get through next summer when we might be able to pick some crops...." Earl scanned around the room, looking at his family. "But I think we'll be fine."

Tahoma's hammer Plus 44 Days.

Interim Sheriff Charlie Reeves acquired one of the large, air-cell tents and the blowers necessary to keep it inflated from the National Guard. Well over half the range's residents had been using it as an emergency shelter for the prior two nights, ever since the Marines that whisked them to safety brought them back. The move to the submarine base had been part of an emergency pact to preserve life until the immediate threat was eliminated. Several wreaths had been constructed and hung from a wood frame on the far end of the one-hundred-foot-long tent. Everyone except for those on guard duty had crammed themselves in for a remembrance-of-life ceremony.

Tyler had been reunited with Teddy, and Gene, still decked out in donated pajamas and bathrobe, sat on his other side. Though not due to cancer, a tribal doctor recognized the need to conduct a life-saving inguinal orchiectomy on Gene, removing both severely damage testicles before they could cause a deadly infection. Despite having a difference of theological opinion, he and Tyler had bonded in a way that few would ever understand.

Charlie looked down at his flashcards, then at the crowd before him. He gave Payton, Savannah, and Josh—all sitting in the front, a warm smile. "God," he opened. "Yahweh...Jehovah...Mother

Earth...or Grand Father," he said, thinking of his own heritage. "Whatever you call Him, today is a time to remember those who gave up their lives...and ask Him to watch over them in their next world."

Charlie looked at the eight wreaths...then down at the ground. He tucked the flashcards into his pants pocket. "We all lost friends and family," he said. "You all—we family...all—have had to see so much suffering these last two months!" He started to tear up, still having a hard time believing his friend and mentor was gone. Many of the audience had, themselves, been wounded in the fight for freedom. "This...thing—this...pure evil. It isn't new." He started to pace a little bit. "This is history...repeating itself..."

The entire tent was quiet of people talking, so the hum of the fans outside keeping it inflated, powered by generators, overtook the room for a long pause. Charlie was trying to find the thing to make it all worth listening to. "My friend, Phil. Your friends and loved ones! They wouldn't want us to grieve like this. They'd want us to find a way to make things better. This greed that drives people, now —it isn't just cartel, or criminals, or drug addicts. It's us! It's humanity! I'm sorry, folks! I don't have the magic words that will make it right! All I know is that my friend Phil died loving something bigger than himself! What he loved...what he gave it all up for...was preserving our rights to Liberty...happiness...family..." he paused once more. "...and love. That's the thing that allows people to respect each other's differences. To share food with a neighbor in need. To recognize when we're hurting others out of selfishness! You all have started picking up the pieces...rebuilding the common area...feeding each other...that's Love!" Charlie started to cry a little more. He looked at Melinda, who walked up and guided him back to the empty chair by her and their kids.

Josh stood up and turned around. "I was looking at a calendar, yesterday. Found it in the rubble. I think it came from the office." He scanned the room, wondering if anyone else had figured out the importance of the day. "It's charred and water damaged, but I was able to flip it and read it…a bit…" There were a few puzzled looks. "You see, I started ticking marks off for each passing day on a tree out by Don's RV…Today is Thursday," he explained. He could tell a couple of people were nodding, knowing where he was going with it. "The last Thursday in November." The light bulb came on for most adults in the blow-up tent. "Today shouldn't be about mourning! It's a day of appreciation…of Thanksgiving…" Josh continued by listing the things that he was alive to appreciate, thanks to the sacrifices of the others. He eventually surrendered the floor. Over the course of the next hour, several others took their turn, saying the things on their heart as part of their healing process.

After the service, Tony began to shoo people out so that he could begin to set up tables and chairs that had somehow managed to survive the attack. The need to cook and serve another meal was always around the corner. Always. And as Fall slowly became Winter, food would continue to get tight. Tony knew hard times were coming. "Hey, Doc," he called out to Stu as he saw the short man mingling with the crowd headed for the big, blow-up tent's opening. "Gotta sec?"

Stu stopped and wandered back over to Tony, who had plopped himself into one of the rain-soaked, padded folding-chairs. It was dirty and smelled of smoke. He unfolded the next chair from the stack and sat facing Tony. "Everything alright, Tony?" he asked.

The normally jovial titan wore a tired and sad look, just like everyone. "All things considered, doctor," he said in his deep bass voice. "Hangin' in there. Look—the reason I wanted to talk is twofold. First off—thanks for comin' back. My wife…my daughters…heck, I think I can speak for everyone when I say we're glad you made it back."

"I'm the lucky one, Tony," Stu said humbly. "Buuuut…I got a feeling that's not all you wanted when you called me over…"

Tony shook his head in agreement. "That's right, doc. Food. I'm worried 'bout the food situation. We're gonna need some guidance on things like nutrition and intermittent fasting. My feeling is it'd be better to start getting people used to the idea before we run out of food, not as it's happening…"

Stu thought a minute, slowly cocking his head and shifting his eyes as he drifted into a deep thought. After a minute, he stood up and looked at Tony. "There's some books I'm going to need to pick up. We should talk to Josh and the club leaders about a mission to procure or trade for them." He started to turn and walk away, but then stopped and turned back. "Tomorrow, though. It can wait a day, I think…" He walked off, missing Tony's nod as he walked off lost in thought on this sudden worry.

Two hours later and across the gun club property, Josh, Payton, and Savannah took a stroll up the hill. "I wish Nick didn't feel like he had to leave," Payton said, sadly.

"I knew he wouldn't stay," Josh said. "He blames himself."

"That's…" Payton started to cry again…"just nonsense! Why do you men always have to beat yourselves up for stuff that happens in war!"

"That's a fair question, beautiful," Josh said grabbing her hand. "I don't think I can answer it…If you've been there, you already know. If you haven't…"

They got to the field and turned left toward the north end. They passed the still, orange Kubota that had recently dug the fresh graves for their fallen loved ones, still parked in the mud. They stopped and looked at Phil's grave marker, a wooden cross placed carefully next to his beloved dog Dakota. "Maybe one day we can have Crane moved up here," Payton said, turning to Josh with hope in her eyes.

Josh's hand tightened on both girls' hands, Payton on his right, Savannah on his left. Then he released his grip and pulled both of them closer to him around their shoulders. He recalled the very last word Phil had spoken. "Yes," Josh agreed. "I think he'd have liked that."

. . .

Tahoma's Hammer Plus 13 Years.

"Phil!" Josh yelled.

"Over here, Dad!" the strawberry-blonde twelve-year-old said. Phillip Edward Bryant was sitting on the concrete bench of the Tahoma-Rainier National Observatory, trying to stay out of the way. There were hundreds of people from all around Western States of America wandering about on the solemn, October day, marking thirteen years since the Cascadia Subduction Zone had sent the former USA and the world onto a new course of history.

Josh wandered over to his son. "Sorry, son. I haven't been trying to ignore you. Just lots of people to catch up with. Some of them I haven't seen since…" he thought back to that beautiful November Day in Seattle. In some ways it felt like yesterday, and in others it felt like a past life.

Phil could always tell when his dad was getting sucked into one of his bouts with PTSD. "Dad," he asked pointing to the burnt-out Chinese tanks out in the mudflat between the observatory and the cratered volcano. "Were those from the Cartel war?"

Josh shook the fog and looked. "Oh—no…the one that followed…the big one."

"Geez, Dad—how many wars have you been in?" the young man asked, trying to be clever but sensing it was a mistake.

Josh just cupped his boy's head. "Too many," he replied with a smile as he turned it into a chance to shake the kid's hair messy.

"Dad!" Phil exclaimed. He'd worked quite a bit to get it just right. A Bryant Man just never knew when he might meet a lady…

"Did you go see the rock, yet?" Josh asked. "Or the wall with your uncle's and grandpa's names?" The observatory was centered around an eighty-ton boulder that had flown the several miles northwest and landed in what used to be a runway at Joint Base Lewis-McChord.

"Not yet," Phil answered. "Too many people for my liking. I will when it thins out."

"You're more like your grandpa than you realize, son," Josh told him. "Which is why your mother and I decided to give you this." He pulled a worn, stained envelope out of his coat pocket and handed it to him. "We were going to wait until your coming birthday, but…somehow…today just felt right."

"What is it?" Phil asked inquisitively. He looked at the sealed letter-carrier. *To my unborn grandchild* was hand-written on it.

"It's your namesake, son," Josh said. He patted the boy's reddish-blonde hair once more and turned to go find Payton, Savannah, and their youngest son, Crane. Young Phil opened the envelope, carefully pulling out eight handwritten pages.

"Dear, Grandchild," it began. "My name is Phillip Edward Walker. If you're reading this, it likely means I had to give my life to make sure you could have yours. And even though we've never met, I love you more than words could ever say."

EPILOGUE

Blades of Grass.

Tahoma's Hammer Plus 41 Days.

"And you're sure this is them," President Jeremiah Allen asked the two men he'd been primarily talking to in the emergency meeting. He looked back and forth at his Secretary of Defense and Leading General of the Joint Chiefs, scanning their faces.

"This is solid, Mr. President," Army General Judah Montgomery said with extreme confidence. "We had a Reaper following it from the moment it left Seattle until our AWAC from Tinker could make it on station. The ship has been under direct observation the entire time, sir."

"The timing is key, Kell," President Allen told Defense Secretary Kelly Fitzgerald. He looked at his watch. "This isn't just political theater," he reminded them. "Doing this live will send a serious message to both China and Russia. One they can't ignore." He scanned his advisors once more, fully aware that the other twenty-three people in the White House Situation Room were deathly quiet.

"Mr. President, General Montgomery has my every confidence," Kelly said, himself a retired Admiral. "If you give us the go, we can make this happen in time for your broadcast."

President Allen looked down at the cold cup of tea staring up at him from the table, feeling the weight of the world shift under and around him. He had a stern and angry resolve on his face when he looked back up. "Go."

USS Bunker Hill, CG-52
   North Pacific, 0630 Local

"Mornin', Captain," Lieutenant Jax Warner said to Captain Patricia Cooper. The Officer of the Deck, or OOD, was in charge of the bridge until properly relieved. Jax knew that Captain Cooper would sit in her chair on the starboard side of the bridge for ten minutes before leaving again.

"Lieutenant," Patty said with her normal chipper tone. "Going to be an interesting day."

"That it is, ma'am." The OOD went about giving the captain the normal report—weather, known contacts on, under, and over the ocean, status of fuel and various systems. About three minutes into the routine conversation, a messenger from the ship's radio room entered the bridge and approached the captain, standing somewhat impatiently.

"Yes, Seaman?" Patty asked.

"Ma'am, CIC has flash traffic for you. Marked urgent," the young lady said, as she handed the captain a printed message form.

Captain Cooper slowly sat up in her stool, scooting her butt back to get more upright. She leaned over to get more light from the bridge-wing window, not wanting to turn on the small reading lamp.

The ship rolled gently to the port and starboard one full cycle, plying through the rough near-winter Pacific waters, as she read and re-read the message.

"Sound General Quarters, Mr. Warner," she said calmly. "Make your heading one-seven-zero. All ahead flank." She handed the lieutenant the slip to read after he'd made her orders come alive.

As the ship's claxon started ringing, sending sailors scrambling to their battle stations, she felt the 567-foot long ship turn sharply to starboard while rolling hard to port as it made a high-speed turn to the south. They'd just been ordered off what was—until that moment—the Navy's highest-priority mission to help escort the aircraft carrier USS Halsey out of Puget Sound.

She picked up the phone next to her and rung the Combat Information Center. "Find me that target," she ordered.

White House Oval Office
1800 Local

Every major media outlet in the world was showing the Seal of the President of the United States, waiting for the White House Media Center to finally start the feed of President Jeremiah Allen's face. At one-minute past 6:00 PM, United States East Coast time, he looked up and spoke three familiar words, followed by a message not ever quite spoken before.

"My Fellow Americans…" he began. "I come to you tonight with a grave message, vital to our nation's, and really—the world's—well-being.

"Thanks to the wonders of modern technology, I'll be able to show you diplomacy in action. You see, there are actors who have been trying to weaken and destroy our nation. Actors in bad faith... actors without morals...or any purpose other than one of greed, hatred, and pushing suffering onto others."

As he spoke, a feed popped up over the president's shoulder. It was gray and hard to see at first. It appeared to be the deck of a ship and waves. Suddenly the feed expanded out, letting the viewers see the entire front-end of a US navy Ticonderoga class cruiser in the foreground of the screen and some sort of merchant vessel in the background, perhaps six miles ahead of and to the port side of the Navy ship. Though nobody knew it from looking, the feed was being transmitted from the camera of a MQ-8 Fire Scout helicopter drone. The *USS Bunker Hill* was carrying one of the twenty-four-foot-long surveillance tools as part of its ship's equipment. The operators had programmed it to match the ship's speed perfectly, sending an image of both ships from an elevation of three-hundred feet.

President Allen continued. "And what I mean by actors, are snakes!" He started to get a little heated. "Snakes who have been striking fear into the hearts of Americans in almost every city west of the Mississippi! These snakes are directly responsible for the deaths of thousands, probably dozens of thousands, of Americans over the last several weeks. The ship you see is an American Navy ship, tracking the snakes of the Mendoza Cartel, as they try to slither—" he screamed that word— "back to Mexico! Don't be fooled by the red cross on the side! That's what snakes do—they pretend to be harmless as they bite!"

He paused briefly. "Captain? Are you there?"

Suddenly, the world heard the friendly but firm voice of Captain Patricia Cooper broadcast over their televisions as she acknowledged her presence. The president disappeared off the screen, allowing people to see both ships in high-resolution digital.

"Fire when ready," the president ordered in front of over a billion people.

"Aye-aye, sir," she said calmly.

As the world watched, the sounds of several voices calling out or repeating orders in the *USS Bunker Hill's* CIC could be heard, followed a few seconds later by the giant barrel of the five-inch diameter gun-mount on the front of the ship swinging to the southeast and pointing directly at the vessel downrange.

"TAO, verify target designated uniform-zero-one…"

Multiple sailors in the loop verified that the ship they were about to fire upon was, indeed, the correct vessel. Range, bearing, and an order for ten seventy-six pound five-inch shells with most of the fuses set for direct contact could be heard.

BOOM! Then two and a half seconds later…BOOM! The cycle repeated itself over and over again, the huge powder casings clattering to the deck in front of the gun mount. Nobody could hear it, of course, nor could they hear the first-round impact the fleeing cartel ship at roughly the time the seventh shell was firing…but they could certainly see it.

"What do they think they're doing?" Rey laughed defiantly, looking through the binoculars.

He could see the 'haze gray' naval vessel quite clearly and could sort of make out the small helicopter beyond it. They had noticed it shadowing them almost an hour earlier, merely keeping pace and attempting no other combat action.

"I dare them to try and board us," he said to nobody in particular.

He was standing on the starboard wing of the old cruise ship's bridge in the forward end of the fake humanitarian relief ship. When he saw the bright orange fire billow from the ship's cannon, he thought his eyes must be deceiving him. A few seconds later there was a second one…then a third…

Reynaldo Hernandez put the binoculars down and just smirked, wondering how many seconds he had left to contemplate that old, dusty orphanage he grew up in. *Wouldn't Father Morales crap himself if he could see me now....?*

The first two shells were actually fused with proximity settings, designed to airburst over the vessel, ripping open the ship's hull and exposing any fuel or ammunition compartments. Shell number one airburst over the ship's bow, sending metal fragments flying in every direction as the high explosive broke the shell part. Incoming round number two burst directly over the ship's bridge, taking out Rey and everyone in it. Over the next several seconds, every part of the ship was ripped to shreds in fiery explosions, flooding the non-combatant vessel and causing it to sink in less than three minutes as the world watched. Rey didn't live long enough to realize the irony—President Jeremiah Allen had shown him the way to both burn and drown someone at the same time.

THE SCREEN slowly faded back to President Allen's face, red with rage. "Let this be a lesson to all aggressors and agitators who are lobbying for their chance to strike at the United States while we're wounded! At this moment, throughout every major American western city aside from Seattle, the US Armed Forces are engaging in Operation Venom Spear, re-instilling law and order by actively engaging and eliminating the drug cartels! Whether it be the snakes of the Mexican cartels, the Bear of the Ural Mountains, or the Dragon by the Yellow Sea, be warned! Behind *every blade of grass* is an American who will kill your ass!"

President Jeremiah Allen stood at his desk in the Oval Office, ripped the wireless mic off his tie, throwing the battery pack on the desk and stormed out of shot. The Presidential Seal screen popped back up showing the words *End Transmission*.

— The End —

The Cascadia Fallen Universe continues with Venom Spear: Blades of Grass Book 1.

STAY INFORMED OF MY COMING BOOKS

Look, my author newsletter is **NOT** like most others. I don't dangle a free short story to entice you, because you can find <u>all my free ebooks</u> and other bonus scenes, etc. ON MY WEBSITE—**Free, and with NO obligation to get on a newsletter.** <u>But here's why you should consider it.</u>

I send out a Substack newsletter most Fridays called <u>**The Thriller Forge.**</u> This humor based, life-blog-style content is the Yin to the Yang of writing action thrillers. *It allows me to decompress; to place a lens on middle age in a way most of us can laugh at.* Sometimes I talk about writing and the book business, though it can just as easily be about my chickens, pets, travel, hobbies, or life. I brain dump thoughts and feelings in a positive way, which is desperately needed in this negative world. With the *obvious exception* of New Book Launch Day, **these purposefully avoid the "please buy my books" vibe.**

Lastly, I will include just a snippet of an update about my current progress and other relevant news <u>near the end of most issues.</u> And as a "book launch" approaches, I will also include links where you can find excerpts I've put up on my website. I hope you'll check it out!

Thanks for your consideration!

ALSO BY AUSTIN CHAMBERS

Cascadia Fallen Trilogy
Book 1 Tahoma's Hammer

Book 2 Order Divested

Book 3 Spiritus Americae

Box Set The Complete Trilogy

Blades of Grass Series
Book 1 Venom Spear

Book 2 Dragon Unleashed

Book 3 Blood Red Sky

Book 4 Patriot Shield

Box Set 1 Books 1 - 3

Book 5: Eye for an Eye

Book 6: Fractured States

Echoes of the Just Trilogy (From Aethon Books)
Seven Days 'til Mayhem: Echoes of the Just Book 1

Fourteen Days 'til Chaos: Echoes of the Just Book 2

Twenty-one Days 'til Anarchy: Echoes of the Just Book 3

ABOUT THE AUTHOR

"Austin" is actually Navy veteran and Dad-joke extraordinaire P.K. O'Dell. Originally from Austin, Texas, he worked most of a career in management at a naval shipyard. He and his wife tend to chickens and watch Combat Kitty slay squirrels near the Hood Canal in Kitsap County, Washington.

Made in United States
Troutdale, OR
11/10/2025

41623485R30215